MURDER MOST JUDGMENTAL

A DETECTIVE JAKE SWANSON

MURDER MYSTERY

M. J. HATCH

ISBN 978-1-4675-3902-9 (hardcover)

ISBN 978-1-4675-3903-6 (soft-cover)

ISBN 978-1-4675-3904-3 (e-book)

Library of Congress Control Number PCN

A Terra Fina Book/ printed by Lightning Source, a subsidiary of Ingram Press

All Terra Fina Books are available for order through Ingram Press Catalogues

CONTENTS

ACKNOWLEDGMENTS

When writing a book such as this, it is difficult to address all the people who have contributed their knowledge along the way, since so much of what I write is based on my experience as a lawyer. I have read countless police reports, coroners' autopsies, and crime lab analyses such that they all blend together. Also, I borrow personalities, conversations, and entire characters from people I know or have met during the decades I have worked as a criminal defense attorney.

Therefore, let me use this page to thank all of you who work in the criminal justice system and toil thankless at jobs that are vital to our society's safety. You all do your professions proud.

Most of all, let me thank Thomas Hill, my editor who despairs of ever teaching me punctuation and, of course, spell check, which helps me keep the manuscript clean. However, *fie* on Microsoft's grammar program. *You* make me crazy when I take literary license to write my characters' dialogue. Do you never quit trying to correct me?

Lastly, thank you to my patient and understanding husband/law partner who tries to live with me when I get temperamental about characters who speak to me and insist that I take time to write their stories. You, my dear, are the true unsung hero.

DEDICATIONS

To the siblings, Mary and R. J., who have done everything they can to see Jake come alive. My deepest gratitude.

PROLOGUE

The clock on the wall in the courtroom held steady at 4:32 p.m. Time seemed to stop as the litigants continued to drone on and on about the faults of their soon-to-be-ex-spouses and the inequities of their new lifestyles. Judge Mark Henning listened without reaction. He could feel the heat of the courtroom clerk's stare boring into the side of his face. But he refused to turn his hazel eyes to face the clerk, knowing he would be met with a glare capable of peeling the skin off his face, so intense was her rage.

Reflexively he ran his hand over the high and tight haircut, feeling the nakedness of his temples and back of his neck recently left bare by the military-style trim. All that was left of his once-too-thick brown hair was a slight bush of hair on the top of his head. Gone was the distinguished gray that usually framed his face.

It was Friday afternoon. Everyone wanted to go home. The bailiff was barely awake, the clerk tapped her pen on her desk in a not-too-quiet staccato, while Judge Henning sat waiting for the couple in front of him to run out of invectives.

Finally, at 4:35, the judge interrupted the couple and told them to sit. "Have you anything else you wish me to know that bears on the issue of support?" he asked them.

"I just want you to know that I work hard and this leaves me with no money for me," the husband answered.

Judge Henning looked at the man, but said nothing. There was nothing to say. The California courts long ago decided to make the question of support a dispassionate, computer-generated algorithm to determine the distribution of funds, guaranteed to leave both parties in worse financial shape than before they decided to terminate their marriage. The judge knew that whatever numbers he plugged into the computer, neither side would be left with enough money on which to live comfortably. But it was his job as an Orange County Superior Court judge to make these rulings. It was his job to be the person who put asunder what God had joined together.

God, he hated his job.

"I now deem the matter submitted," Judge Henning said as his fingers flew over his keyboard. He hit the print button and made his ruling while reading from the printed page.

As expected, neither side was happy. The husband gasped, and the wife cried. The only moment of unity came when the two warring parties pushed back from counsel tables, muttering vituperation under their breath, as the bailiff escorted them from the courtroom, then locked the doors.

"That's a wrap?" the bailiff asked as he came back into the courtroom, jingling his keys.

"About fricking time," the clerk muttered as she slammed her computer keyboard back into its place under her desktop. Grabbing her purse, she pushed her chair back from her desk and made no secret of the fact she was late leaving.

"Have a good weekend," the judge said to the retreating back of his clerk. She responded by lifting her middle finger and waved it over her shoulder as she hurried out the door.

The bailiff just laughed and the judge shook his head.

"Attitude," the bailiff said as he hefted his gym bag over his shoulder. "You want me to walk you out, Boss?"

"No, not tonight, Chris," the judge said. "I have work to do on some files. I still need to make final rulings on the cases I have under submission."

"Don't stay too late."

Judge Henning didn't bother to answer; he just pushed back from his bench, unsnapping his robe as he left the courtroom for his chambers.

Mark Henning, Superior Court judge for the State of California, County of Orange, was assigned to the Lamureaux Center Family Law and Juvenile Court. He hated his assignment. He hated his chambers. He hated his courtroom, which he thought was way too small. Most days he was left feeling like he was gasping for air and longed for his previous position in the community as a well-respected criminal defense lawyer.

But that was the rub. It was his very prominence as a former defense lawyer that kept him out of the rough-and-tumble world of the criminal courts. He often chewed on the fact that the Office of the District Attorney would not stomach a defense lawyer sitting as a judge. They routinely removed him from cases on which he had superior experience and knowledge because of their fear he might make a ruling against them.

"Stupid shits," he grumbled as he slammed into his tiny chambers. Again he fumed at the prosecutors' closed-minded attitude. Didn't they realize he had heard all of the lies, all of the excuses, all of the stupidity from his former clients when he still sat the counsel table? Didn't they realize he could smell a rat-faced excuse faster than any of those newbie deputies? Just because he could also smell a lying cop, he was sentenced to spend the rest of his tenure on the bench hearing divorce and custody cases.

Kicking at the pile of files on the floor next to his desk, he threw his robe on the leather loveseat under the window and sat down to the task at hand. He needed to make final rulings on two cases specially assigned to him by the presiding judge. It would never cross his mind to leave them for another judge to try to follow the complexities of the cases assigned to him. At least his fellow bench officers had come to appreciate his tenacity and legal skills. They knew he would stay with a difficult matter and coax a fair decision from either the litigants, or from the law. Either way, Mark Henning sought justice and tried to uphold his oath to protect the laws of his state.

Several hours later, the judge looked up from his computer screen. The clock had magically moved up to almost seven p.m. He was late, again. His wife would be pissed or worried or both. Quickly he hit the "save" button on each of the rulings, then closed down his computer.

Someone else will need to send these on their way, he thought, as he wrote a note for his clerk telling her that the rulings were finished.

Mark needed to get home to his wife. Ever since her diagnosis with breast cancer, Nancy Henning has not been as patient as she once was. She wanted more of his time than she ever needed before, and jealously guarded her time with him. In fact, he was surprised she had not called to see when he was coming home. He decided he would call her after he jumped on the 5 Freeway.

Mark had no sooner transitioned from the 22 Freeway to the 5 when his phone rang.

"Hey," Mark said as he answered his phone.

"Hey, yourself," Nancy said. "Where are you? It's late. I have steaks ready for you."

"What, no pitcher of martinis chilling?"

Mark strained to hear the chuckle in his wife's voice. They both knew he couldn't drink that night. He would barely have enough time to eat before he had to leave. As expected, Nancy's snort sounded only slightly peeved, but that was followed by a short inhale. He quickly explained that he was on his way home and should be there within twenty minutes or so, depending on the traffic, which was surprisingly light for a Friday night.

Henning could hear his wife expel the breath she had been hold-ing. She seemed to do that a lot lately, holding her breath, as if waiting for something bad to happen. But of course it had. The worst had hap-pened. She had cancer and he had to leave her at her most critical time.

Inhaling a breath of his own, Mark spoke quietly into the phone. "Hey, sexy lady, I love you."

"Love you, too."

Damn! Mark thought as he disconnected the call. His other life was encroaching on his marriage again. Once again his position with the Naval Reserve was turning his life inside out. Two weeks ago he re-ceived the news he was being activated and sent overseas, but not to the Middle East. No, he was being sent to the Far East. Worse yet, he was being sent in a capacity that would prevent him from having con-tact with Nancy, her doctors, or anyone in the States.

How could the military take so much from me? he agonized. He'd al-ready given more than thirty-two years of his life to them. Yet, at age fifty-eight, he was still eighteen months from retirement age. Worse yet, as a senior officer, he belonged to the Navy. Retirement was at the discretion of the Secretary of the Navy. To date, the Department of the Navy had refused his retirement papers.

The more Mark thought about his crummy life and the fear for his wife's health, the faster he drove. The Porsche Carrera leaped forward as he jammed his foot onto the accelerator, leaving the crowded 55 Freeway onto the 74 South. He flew down the uncrowded highway to the MacArthur off-ramp, and slammed a hard right onto the boulevard. Cutting around and through traffic he drove like the fighter pilot he once had been. This time the enemy he hunted was his own fears. He feared the unknown of the cancer invading his wife's body; feared the likelihood of being left to rot in the family law courts; and he feared the fact he had been activated to hunt for something that could destroy the world as he knew it.

The dark cloud pervading his mind did not lift as he turned left onto Harbor View Drive from MacArthur and wound his way up to the top of Sea Lane. Mark swooped up the steep driveway to his house perched high above the street. It was a quiet home in a quiet neighborhood. Most houses had at least a peek-a-boo view of the Pacific Ocean, and others had a full-on view. When he pulled into his driveway he did not stop to admire the view of the setting sun off the Newport Beach coastline. Normally the view from his driveway was enough to lift his spirits, but tonight his mind was only on scooping his wife up into his arms and holding her tightly.

As he angled the gear shift knob down into first, he hit the button opening the garage door. So occupied was the judge's mind with the fear of loss and the need for his wife, he missed the sound of footsteps coming up behind him that quickly closed the distance between the two of them.

A gun rose and fired, but only a soft, explosive "poof" came from the barrel. Two bullets struck the back of Mark Henning's head. He was dead before he hit the ground.

Nancy Henning heard the garage door open, left her kitchen to meet her husband at the door. Love and longing to be near the man she had loved for all of her adult life filled her heart as she rushed to the door. Throwing it open she stepped into the garage in time to see a figure crouching down next to the Porsche.

"Mark?" she called. "Mark, Honey, what's wrong? Did you drop something?"

It was too late for Nancy to realize the figure was not Mark.

It was too late when she saw the gun come up.

It was too late to run, too late to live.

The figure quickly closed the short distance between them; the gun leveled at Nancy's chest. Two fast shots and Mark Henning's beloved wife, Nancy, lay dead in the open garage doorway.

As silently as the figure came, it left.

CHAPTER ONE

Ah, life's good. There's nothing better than a late summer's night out on the Balboa Peninsula of the California Newport Beach coast, especially when there's a front row seat to the channel of water making up the Newport Bay.

Newport Beach is known for its large man-made bay, surgically enhanced women, rich old men and, to keep things interesting, a few predatory older women known as "cougars." It is the place where the extremely wealthy come to live and play. They build their mansions, one on top the other, park their million-dollar boats in the slips next to their waterfront palaces, and spend their days trying to outdo their neighbors in wealth, toys, and marriages. It is also the place where the wish-they-were-rich come to hang out—hoping some of the wealth will rub off onto them. Young girls come to find a rich husband; young men come looking for a wealthy widow or widower to take care of them. Wannabes come looking for the next victim to scam, until they are scammed themselves and slink back into the shadows.

However, Newport Beach, with all of its social idiosyncrasies, is still a beautiful place to be. And me? I was lucky enough to live in the midst of all of it.

Here it was, a Friday night in late August and I was staying home. But then, who wouldn't want to be home when you're surrounded by beautiful scenery and beautiful women, with a chilled martini in hand and a dog at your feet?

Yep, my life was good.

My name is Jake Swanson, and I am a senior detective with the Newport Beach Police Department. People wonder how a detective can afford to live in an apartment over a three-car garage on the Peninsula in Newport Beach, California. But then most cops don't have a friend as a landlord who was convicted of multiple counts of federal racketeering and drug running. Fortunately for me, he left me in charge of his house. In exchange for making sure the house fronting the water was rented, I got to live in the apartment rent-free.

Double fortunately for me, my other close friend, Sally Deming, is a woman who runs a discrete escort service and needs a place for some of her girls to live while they finish their various college degrees. How great is it that I have five women living in the four-bedroom house; they are five extraordinary women who are not only beautiful, but have brains and a desire to keep their lives filled with homey smells of great cooking and soft music. Oh yeah, they also think I'm funny and brave and cute. Not bad for a man with forty-two years of hard living, chasing women, waves, and the bad guys of Newport Beach.

Like I said, it was a Friday night, the sun was setting, and the fog decided not to appear that night. A soft offshore wind blew in from the eastern desert, brushing back the clouds and keeping them beyond the breakwater. The clear skies heated up the coast, making the weather perfect for the impromptu deck party.

I snuggled down even further into the wicker chair's soft cushions and let the New Age jazz music from the house wash over me. I held a perfectly chilled martini in my hand and listened to the chatter of the three women who were home that night. Of the five women, two had gone off to 'party' with clients, and I was left to watch over the others.

My dog Mandy lay at my feet. As I wiggled my bare toes in her fur, I again marveled at her shiny brown and white long-haired coat. It was soft to the touch, and the thick white ruff around her neck enhanced her beauty. She had her sharply pointed shepherd-dog nose tucked into her fluffy tail, and her eyes were closed in apparent contentment. Life was now good for her, too. She seemed to be over the grief of losing her young master several months earlier when he decided to commit suicide instead of facing prison for killing his mother and uncle. He had left Mandy in my care just before putting the gun to his head and taking his life, leaving me with his sorrow and gray matter splattered all over the front of my shirt. Just thinking about Michael Sandini's death took me to my dark place, a place where all my failures and fears waited to consume me.

Mandy, sensing my changing mood lifted her nose and gave my fingers a quick lick. It was enough to rouse me and bring me back to the pleasantness of the evening. I watched a late- arriving sailboat come through the channel. It was under power, its sails neatly stowed under the canvas wrapped around the boom. Laughter and the sound of a popping champagne cork came from the boat. I smiled. Life was good for someone else, too.

I raised the chilled glass to my lips. The sweet-tasting vodka felt velvet smooth on my lips and tongue. A slight hint of citrus came from the sliver of lemon we had harvested from the dwarf lemon tree grow-ing in a pot next to the back door. Ice chips floated on top of the vodka, making it look like the North Adriatic Sea in winter. I crinkled my nose at the still unfamiliar sweetish flavor of my drink. Recently I had dis-covered Grey Goose vodka from France. It was hard breaking up with my old Russian favorite, Stolichnaya, but the girls had introduced me to the "Goose" and I thought it was rude to insist on Stoli when they always poured the more expensive Grey Goose.

I was just starting to lull myself into a satisfied stupor when I heard my name being called.

"Hey, Jakey," called a sweet voice. "We need some help here. The coals aren't staying lit."

I opened my eyes and redirected them toward the house. Standing at a table-top hibachi were two of the younger girls, a willowy red-head named Raeline and her Latina counterpart, Teresa. They were students at the local junior college in Irvine and were twenty-one and twenty-two, respectively. They'd been playing with the lighter fluid and wood chips for almost a half-hour. Enough was enough.

"Okay, ladies," I said, struggling to my feet from the depths of the chair. "Let's just give it up and use the gas grill."

"Oh, Jakey," Raeline pouted. "I was ever so looking forward to smoked links tonight. I hate the way the gas makes the sausage all dry without the smoke from the chips."

I almost laughed out loud. I loved the Southern drawl Raeline brought to everything she said. Not only did she come with a slow drawl and leggy languid walk, she also came with a Georgia peach complexion of fair skin and blue eyes — perfection on two legs. Teresa was just as beautiful, with lush black hair and deep black eyes that constantly sparkled with her own private joke. The two of them kept me amused, though lascivious thoughts were usually kept mostly at bay given their tender ages. Sometimes when maudlin, I looked at them and believed the two of them were the age a daughter would have been had I ever stayed with one woman long enough to have children, thus giving rise to a latent paternal instinct. As I sauntered over to the hibachi and the two girls, a more determined voice floated out from the kitchen. "Enough, already. I'm starved. If I keep drinking without putting food in me, I'll fall down drunk."

I couldn't help myself. "Okay," I answered, as truly lascivious thoughts and desires crowded my good sense.

"Jesus, Jake," said a lanky blonde woman as she came out from the kitchen to the patio. In her hands she carried plates, flatware, and a bowl of what looked like potato salad. Snaking around her ankles was my gray tabby cat, Cisco. Anyway, I hoped it was potato salad because, if it was, it would be fantastic. The woman dressed in hip-resting jeans with a cutoff T-shirt, and setting my manhood to attention, was called "Scat," a graduate student at the local University of California, Irvine.

From the day she moved in I had teased her about her name and secretly schemed on how I would break down her defenses to get her into my bed. I couldn't help myself, with her beauty and intelligence, she was the kind of woman that every man who had a pulse would want. Unfortunately, my scheming had to remain secret since she also was an employee of my best friend, Sally Deming, and strictly off-limits.

Instead, I was left to tease her about her name, telling her that whoever gave her that name was not too far off from calling her dog doo. It always made her spitting mad. At thirty-four, a former teacher, and now studying for her Ph.D. in anthropology, she refused to give up the nickname. She said her grandmother, who had raised her, started calling her that because she was always telling her to "Scat! Get away from that!" I knew how her Granny felt.

Scat was curious, inquisitive, and beautiful beyond words in that homey way some women have that makes a man ache for them. But, more than that, she seemed to always be in my business, just like Cisco. She answered my phone if I left my portable anywhere she could get to it, and snooped my e-mails on my I-phone if I left it unattended. She always checked on me and seemed to know all my comings and goings. She and Cisco had teamed up to keep a constant surveillance on me. Yet, for some curious reason, I didn't mind.

"Jake," she said, putting the bowl on the table, "just get the grill started. I drink any more of your stupid Grey Goose martinis and I'll be on my ass."

"My Grey Goose?" I said, "it's not my Grey Goose. Anyway, let's talk about you being on your . . ."

She spun around and snapped at me with the kitchen towel she had draped over her arm. I laughed as I danced away from her, stuffing down my desire to grab her and molest her right there on the deck in front of everyone, including my dog, cat and the other girls. Instead, I sauntered over to the built-in grill attached to the outdoor kitchen, and prepared the grates for the sausages. The heat was just about right when my ever-present I-phone vibrated on my hip. Pulling it from its holster on my belt, I felt four pairs of eyes on me: three human and one canine. Only one pair of eyes was friendly.

"This is Swanson," I said, turning away from the women who gathered at my side.

"Detective, we have a double 187, and need you to respond."

I felt the skin on my forehead begin to scrunch; my breathing became more shallow and rapid. It was almost four months since there was a killing in my city. These two new killings gave us two more than we usually had in a year. I liked the fact that this enclave of rich and famous kept their killer instincts confined to the boardrooms and playing fields, not the streets. I liked the fact that as senior detective my workload was light. I could pawn off onto the newer detectives the car thefts, burglaries, and wife beatings. My detective skills were only needed occasionally. This left me plenty of time for other pursuits, important pursuits — like harassing the chief and keeping out of the way.

What I did not like was a call to a death scene on a Friday night. Worse yet, given that it was barely dark, and not far into the drinking shank of the evening, this killing wasn't likely to be a gang shooting or domestic violence. Those kinds of killings usually required someone to imbibe some sort of mind-altering substance, usually alcohol or methamphetamines. If it wasn't gang related, or domestic, I knew the killing would be problematic. This meant I would have to work to solve the case, maybe even work hard.

My forehead tightened some more. I forced myself to take a few deep breaths. Finally, I grabbed a napkin to write down the address. "Where?" I asked.

The voice at dispatch gave me an address on Sea Lane Drive near the Fashion Island Center. Instinctively, I lifted my eyes toward the hills rising up from the bay. From our patio on the Peninsula we could clearly see Fashion Island and the hills on which it rested. I squinted a little and thought I saw the flashing red and blue lights of a squad car.

"Crap!" I said. My worst fears were confirmed. The address was in one of our older areas; a more settled neighborhood of million-dollar homes, located high on the hill overlooking Newport Bay.

Actually most of the homes in Newport Beach were worth a million dollars or more, but this neighborhood dated back to the 1950s and 1960s. This was old Newport Beach money, with a great view. It was slightly east of the Fashion Island outdoor mall, just off MacArthur Boulevard. As the crow flies, it was less than three miles from the patio at my place to the driveway of the murder scene. Yet, I knew my journey to the crime scene would take me more than forty minutes on a Friday night.

I squinted again, my forehead even tighter, as I set aside my perfect martini.

"ETA?" dispatch asked, intruding into my dark thoughts.

"Uh, depends," I said. "It's Friday, you know?"

"Yes, detective," the dispassionate voice answered. "I just need it for the log."

I scrunched my forehead again. All the joy was gone. Being called out on a Friday night was the worst.

My apartment was located where Balboa Boulevard narrowed to two lanes, making the narrow streets difficult to navigate. On a Friday night it was next to impossible to traverse. The people using it were not there to travel quickly from one place to the next. The crowds were there to see and be seen. This meant traffic crawled at a pace more suited to a parade. It was a slow-moving train of cars showing off their freshly polished fenders, with interior lights on to show off their studied-casual occupants. The ritual was meant to allow those on the sidewalks to look inside; conversely, those inside the cars had enough time to examine the pedestrians. It was a long-practiced mating ritual dating back for longer than I could remember.

I rubbed my temple with my free hand.

"Detective Swanson," dispatch said, "I am getting a coded message saying you need to Code Three this."

"Shit," I answered, again forgetting our conversation was taped. I quickly tried to cover with, "Have you called out Sanchez?"

Melissa Sanchez was my new partner of four months. She lived in Santa Ana which could be an hour drive or more on a Friday night. She'd have a couple of freeways to traverse and traffic to slow her down. There was a good chance we would arrive at the same time, giving me some cover if any of the brass was present at the scene.

"My next call, sir."

"Well, get her rounded up, and I should be to the scene in twenty," I finally said, hoping the guess was not too far off.

I turned to face the women. Two of them were giving me the pouty-lipped thing. Scat just shrugged her shoulders and left to go back into the kitchen. Her leave taking left me feeling empty and angry, a feeling that crowded out the tension from the murder in my city.

"Gotta go, ladies," I said, shaking off the tension and anger. "Don't give Mandy too many sausages; otherwise, she's sleeping at your place, and she'll gas you instead of me."

It was enough to make the two younger women giggle. Hearing her name, Mandy came to my side, wagging her tail furiously between her legs. Seeing the hesitation in her eyes melted my heart.

"Hey, girl," I said, taking her soft muzzle in my hands. "I just gotta go to work. You stay here and watch the girls for me, okay?"

The dog looked over at the girls, then back at me.

Teresa took a sausage from the platter and held it out to the dog. "Lookee here, Mandy," she said. "As soon as it's done, I'll share with you, okay?"

With that, the dog left my side and wagged over to her new best friend.

I left the deck without another word, cutting through the house to the courtyard separating my garage apartment from the main house. I stepped into the garage hitting the trunk latch on my key ring. The trunk lid of my black Intrepid lifted, allowing me access to my gun lock box. I quickly retrieved my gun and shoulder holster. I shrugged into the holster and checked to make sure the clip of the gun was fully loaded. I also withdrew my trusty silk blazer from its place on the trunk floor.

I went around the front driver's side, and slid into the leather bucket seat. A quick push of the button on the visor and the garage door opened, allowing me to back out onto Balboa Boulevard. As I did, the headlights of the Intrepid held steady on the British racing green of the Porsche 914-6 parked in the other half of the garage. I smiled briefly at the sight, then put the Intrepid in gear.

As I feared, the Friday night traffic was exceptionally bad as I pulled out of the garage and onto the Boulevard. It was late summer and the school year was starting in less than a week for the local high school and elementary schools. The kids had to grab the last bit of summer, and the out-of-towners needed one last score before going back to their cubicles.

Everywhere I looked up and down the Boulevard I witnessed inline skaters, strolling couples, and cars backed up bumper to bumper.

I needed to get out there, fast, so I decided to skip the traffic by taking the Balboa Island Ferry, a small three-car ferry that travels between the Peninsula and Balboa Island. For whatever reason, Balboa's streets on a Friday are not usually as busy with vehicle traffic as the mainland, and the main street, Marine Avenue, would drop me right at the bottom of the hill at Jamboree. From there it was a quick hop up the hill to the Pacific Coast Highway and over to MacArthur.

Pulling onto Balboa Boulevard from my driveway, I hit my "whoop-whoop" on the siren, scattering pedestrians and a couple of cars. I knew I had to jump the line onto the ferry, so I swung wide onto Main Street, quickly dashing between two cars idling at the ramp. The kid at the loading ramp was the son of a guy with whom I had gone to high school. When the kid saw me, a broad smile crossed his face and he waved me into line for the waiting boat. We were rewarded with a few toots of horns and single-fingered salutes, but a shrug from the kid and wave back from me silenced the horns.

"Hey, Detective Swanson," he said, bending down into my open window. "Like, where you off to? Is it something cool, you know, like a murder or something?"

Instinctively I lifted my eyes to the hilltop overlooking the bay. The kid followed my gaze, and he too saw the flashing red and blue lights.

"Cool," was all he said as he slapped my window frame and waved me aboard.

The ferry bobbed its way slowly across the channel, taking at least five minutes to go about the distance of two football fields. But even with the slow progress, I knew I was cutting at least three miles and twenty minutes off my drive.

I was the first vehicle off the ferry and, once again, I hit the red light on top of the Intrepid. With the light burning brightly, traffic quickly and respectfully moved to the right… except for one BMW convertible containing a young couple more interested in making out than driving. The loud whoop of the siren startled them, almost making them drive into the parked cars on their right. They sped up and pulled to the right as I made a hard left onto Marine Avenue from Park.

I looked longingly at the Village Inn as made my turn. The Inn had the best steamed clams and chilled martinis anywhere on the local coast. Of course their ever-present heckler was standing one hundred feet and two inches past their door, carrying her sign and shouting incoherently about long ago slights she received from previous owners. She had been at it so long I think even she forgot what started her on the quixotic quest. Only the courts remembered she could no longer harass the new owners or their guests. The rest of us just laughed or averted our eyes.

The village was busy with couples strolling hand in hand. The atmosphere was not as frenetic as it was across the bay. Here the couples came to spend time with each other, not look for someone newer or better. Nonetheless, it was just busy enough and the street narrow enough that it took me several minutes to go the couple of blocks to the bridge.

Over the bridge the street opened up to four lanes as it turned into

Jamboree. I hit the accelerator hard up the hill and squealed a right turn onto Pacific Coast Highway. Less than a mile later I made a left turn onto MacArthur sliding through with the tail end of cars using the green arrow. I again got a couple of single-finger salutes as I slid over to the right lane and turned onto Harbor View Lane. Evidently, the drivers took exception to me taking the lane and cutting them off. I hit the "whoop-whoop" just to remind them of my importance and was rewarded with the same finger, again.

I slowed at the bottom of the steep hill, then stopped. The crime scene was clearly evident above, marked by the billowing yellow tape. My hands rested on the steering wheel of the Intrepid. The idling engine quieted my nerves as I sat contemplating what awaited me.

With a deep breath, I jammed my foot on the accelerator. The Intrepid leaped forward.

We were off. We had a murder to solve.

CHAPTER TWO

The Intrepid and I roared up the street, but slowed as I approached the numerous squad cars; their lights flashed red and blue, and their radios were turned up and crackling. It wasn't hard to guess the house. It already had yellow tape spread up and down the driveway and around several cars parked on the street. Neighbors were standing off to one side, watching while uniformed officers kept them from encroaching on the cordoned-off area.

A young officer came over to the Intrepid, bending down to greet me. "Hey, Detective Swanson," he said. "Isn't this cool? I get to work a scene with you."

I looked hard at the kid. He couldn't have been more than twenty-five, meaning he looked more like a high school student to me. Discreetly rolling my eyes toward his name badge, I tried to put a name with the face and voice. I knew I worked with him before, but the badge on his chest was just out of sight. I started to give the standard bullshit response, but he continued talking before I could answer him.

"Yeah, Detective, remember the day I brought in Mr. Lauderman?" he asked. "Remember how mad you were that he was handcuffed? Gosh, I'll never forget that. I was so scared you'd write me up for that, but you were so cool. Man, I'll never forget how cool you were."

Ah, I remembered him: Patrick Donahue, a new recruit with the force. A few months earlier I had needed someone to pick up one of our local attorneys for questioning about the death of his not-so-discreet squeeze. Of course dispatch had screwed it up and told the kid to handcuff the attorney, when all I really wanted was just a friendly conversation with him at the station. During the same incident, dispatch had sent other officers out to "detain for questioning" the attorney's new housemate who was crazy jealous. She was the one who should have been handcuffed, shackled, and face-masked. But, instead, with the "detain for questioning" tag, she had been left unfettered to fight the officers all the way back to the station, leaving them battered and bruised. Everyone got hurt on that one. The only good that came from that incident was seeing the crazy red-headed woman tasered and pepper-sprayed.

"Ah, it's Donahue, right?" I asked. "So what've we got?"

"Two dead, sir," the kid said, bowing his head slightly, as if doing a quick prayer. "But you need to check with Sergeant Novak for details; he doesn't want me talking without his say-so. And, of course, sir, you need to check in with him; he's keeping the list."

"Can I pull closer?" I asked, looking at the steep incline of the street and the house setting almost at the top of the street at the corner.

"Sure," Donahue said. "But leave room for the van, okay?" With that he slapped my open window with both hands, leveraging himself away from his squat.

Maneuvering around the parked cars and the cruisers left in the street, I inched my way up. I looked back over my shoulder to see the sunset had left the sky painted in vivid shades of deep pinks, reds, and purples. The ocean was deep blue and going to black. A well-lit party cruise was just beyond the jetty, churning a phosphorescent wake as it left the harbor.

Another beautiful night in paradise. Another dead body. Actually, in this case, two dead bodies. I gave an involuntary shudder and worried about my city and wondered what was happening to my people.

Sergeant Ryan Novak was standing on the apron of the driveway, clipboard in hand. He pointed at a place next to the curbside beside where he stood. Over his shoulder, I could see the steep driveway of the house belonging to the victims. Parked at the crest of the driveway's incline was a silver Porsche 911 Carrera, its driver's side door open, showing the tan leather interior. The car sat in front of an open garage door. The interior of the garage was lit by a row of fluorescent lights showing a neatly organized garage with a silver-blue Mercedes parked inside. I couldn't help but let my eyes travel to the fluttering blue body tarps, one at the open door of the Porsche, the other slightly inside of the open garage door. My stomach did a roll as it slid from its usual place down toward my feet, and my heart bounded upward to my throat. I momentarily let the sadness envelope me.

I parked the car and Sergeant Novak ambled over to greet me.

Sergeant Ryan Novak was about thirty-seven, making him five years my junior. He had joined the force the same year I had, but had gone directly from junior college to the Police Academy. I, on the other hand, had spent a few years testing my skills as a pickup artist and lay-about. While I was surfing the Pacific Coast, Novak had been studying criminal justice. He was hired because of his academics; I, on the other hand, was hired because my mother slept with the then chief and convinced him to "do something" with me. The "something" he chose was to hire me and put me to work. Novak and I had each progressed through the ranks, him because of hard work, and me, not so much.

He was a sergeant; I was the senior detective. Neither of us really wanted to do the other's job, but the built-in rivalry remained. He had stayed in shape despite being married to a wonderful woman who really knew how to cook and fed him well. He ran, lifted weights, and made sure his ruddy Irish-Czech complexion always had SPF 45 or higher on it. Ryan was balding slightly but, other than that, he looked great.

I, on the other hand — let's just say I had great genetics working for me. I'm six-foot, two inches tall in my flip-flops. I've never used sunscreen, even when spending all day on the waves surfing, and my hair was bleached white blond. I never ran, except when I had to; pretty much ate what I wanted; drank way too much; and lived a life with no structure whatsoever. Yet, I kept my waistline trim and my legs were muscular from swimming. Yep, in the overall roll call for genes, I had been first in line with my body and face benefiting from it.

Novak waited, standing at semi-attention until I had pulled myself from the car and was standing upright.

"Swanson," he said, nodding at me, then looking at his watch. He made a quick note on the clipboard, but made no attempt to put out his hand for a friendly shake.

"So, Novak," I said, deliberately slouching. "Still working swings I see. And on a Friday night, no less. Hmmm."

He slightly narrowed his eyes at me, but responded in a neutral tone. "My choice," he said.

"Hmm, okay," I answered.

Novak stepped a little closer and took a sniff of my breath. "Friday nights as usual for you, I see," he said.

"Yes in dee-dee-do," I answered, a small smile passing my lips. "Beach sunsets, martinis, and beautiful women." I don't think it was really a smirk, but then, it was Novak after all.

His eyes narrowed even farther. "How many drinks, Swanson?" he asked.

"Novak, don't start with me," I answered, my hackles beginning to rise. "You're not my drink monitor."

"Oh hell I am," Novak answered, moving close into my personal space. "I'm in charge of this scene, and I won't have a drunk officer on scene, Swanson."

"Hey, boys!" a voice said. "Stop the shit."

I broke off Novak's stare long enough to find the voice. It belonged to my partner, Melissa Sanchez. She was walking, half sliding down the steep driveway, her gorgeous dark brown hair blowing in the gentle ocean breeze. As usual, her makeup was at a minimum and she was dressed in slim-legged black jeans, low-heeled riding boots, a creamy white blouse, and a camel hair sport jacket. All of it showed off her superb figure and skin tones.

Sliding the last few feet down the driveway she quickly crossed the space from its apron to the street where Novak and I were standing. The pleasant fragrance of Plumeria surrounded her as she stepped between us.

"Sanchez," I said, "what are you doing here already?"

She also glinted her eyes at me in that cat-like thing women do when pissed, but she turned away from me and directed her comments to Novak.

"Swanson isn't drunk, Sergeant. It's early and we got to him in time," she said, taking my arm and steering me away from him. "Besides, even if he were drunk, which he isn't, we need him, and he's still better than anyone else. You know how the Lieutenant is about my partner."

Novak shrugged his shoulders and turned away from me, the conversation obviously over.

Melissa took me by the arm and started to drag me up the driveway. Under her breath she added, "You aren't, are you?"

"Aren't what?"

"Are you drunk, Swanson?"

I started to laugh, thinking of the perfect martini I had left on the outside bar after taking the call from dispatch. It had been the first of what I had hoped would be a long string of perfect martinis and a perfect Friday night at the beach. But no, I wasn't drunk. Hell, I wasn't even happy.

"Not yet. Why?" I asked, turning on my best smile for my partner.

"First off," she said, giving me that hair toss thing, "don't bother with the smile. It doesn't work with me, remember?"

"Oh, yeah, I forgot," I said, still smiling at her. "By the way, how did you beat me here? I thought the Friday traffic would kill your arrival time."

Oops, that was the wrong thing to say to her. She spun back on me and hissed through her teeth. I expected claws to emerge from her fingertips as she gripped my arm tighter, still pulling me up the driveway. "Oh, fuck you, Swanson," she hissed. "Don't tell me you forgot about your little assignment to me. I was doing paperwork, you dick. I was still at the station."

"Oh, yeah," I said, remembering that I had assigned the squad's junior detective to finish up the reports for the unit. Somehow I had forgotten that Melissa Sanchez was still the newest detective on the squad. Since she worked with me, and because she was so good at everything she did, I tended to forget that there were six other detectives between the beginning of her tenure in the squad and mine. Oops.

At the crest of the driveway, Melissa stopped next to the blue-sheeted form. She crouched down next to it and pulled back the plastic.

"Looks like the shooter dropped him as he was getting out of the car," she said as she pointed to the blood and gray matter splattered on the driver's window and front inside panel of the open door.

I said nothing as I looked at the lifeless body frozen in death. He had fallen forward onto the door of his car leaving him face down on the concrete driveway.

Melissa replaced the sheet over the body and walked me up to the open garage door. Another sheet was spread just inside the doorway. "The second victim is here," she said, not bothering to remove the sheeting. "I thought we'd wait for the Coroner to get here. I guess he's on his way."

I again just shrugged. I had nothing to say and I was clamping down hard on my imagination. Over the years I had found it was better to just let the evidence unfold and develop my theory from it rather than let my mind run wild with possible scenarios of why and how the deaths occurred. Yet, even as I tried to stop the churning of my mind, visions of black-clad intruders crept around the edges of my mind. It was an image I quickly banished with a shake of my head and shrug of my shoulder.

Melissa and I backed away from the garage doorway and turned away from the house. Night had completely fallen and the view from the top of the driveway was spectacular. The lights from the Fun Zone on Balboa Boulevard were twinkling, and the traffic from MacArthur Boulevard was starting to thin. Off to the distance on the southern horizon, a large white cruise ship was coming into view.

"So, how'd the call come in?" I asked.

"According to that kid, Donahue," Melissa said, gesturing with her chin toward the young officer standing at the yellow-taped perimeter, "the call came in as a security check."

"Oh?"

"Yeah," Melissa answered, taking a deep breath of ocean air. "Sorry," she said as she saw me watch her breathe. "Can't help it. The air here is so fresh. It tastes like salt instead of grit. I just want to take it in, especially a night like this."

"Yeah, pretty crappy getting killed on a night like this," I said, also taking a deep breath of my own. "But back to the call. Tell me what Donahue said so I don't have to walk back down the hill and ask."

A slight smile played on Detective Sanchez's full Latina lips, and her chocolate brown eyes danced. "Exercise might do you good, oh giver of extra paperwork," she said, a laugh beginning to bubble up from her chest.

"Shit, Sanchez," I said. "Things were slow, the work needed to be done."

"Hup one, hup two. Left, left, left," she said. "That's it soldier, start marching. Take that hill."

"Damn it, Sanchez, we're on a case now; no more stupid paperwork," I said. Inside I had to laugh. I knew she was already picking up my habits, both good and bad. It appeared that smarting off to a senior officer was one of the not-so-good ones.

"Well, okay then," she said. "It seems that a neighbor, make that a nosy neighbor, across the street and down, saw the garage door open and the lights on inside."

"So?"

"So, according to the neighbor, there are strict regulations about leaving a garage door open when the garage is unattended."

Oh, yeah, I remembered those days. When I was a kid, growing up in Newport Beach, one of the areas where I had lived with my mother and one of her three husbands—not my father—there had been a CC&R about garage doors. It seems that the neighbors don't want to see other people's junk.

"So, this neighbor sees the lights on and door open," I said. "How long before she called it in?"

"It was a he, and he waited about a half-hour. Then he climbed the hill and saw the open door to the Porsche. That's when he became alarmed and called 9-1-1."

In the background as Melissa was giving me this report I heard the crime scene SUV lumbering up the hill, followed closely by the unmarked coroner's van, both maneuvering to park across the driveway.

I was relieved to see the loud Hawaiian shirt and khaki cargo shorts belonging to Joshua Childs, the Orange County boy wonder, who bounded out of the van, black bag in hand, and climbed up the hill to greet us.

"Hey, Josh," I said, "good to see you. You catch this case?"

"Dude," he answered, shaking his head of moppish blonde surfer hair. "Not my night. Rotations have already started, and I should be at the hospital."

Joshua Childs was only twenty-one, but was already in his second year of medical school over at the local university. He had been working around and in the medical examiner's lab since he was sixteen and could run the lab with one hand tied behind his back. He was a genius who understood the human body as well as he understood the local wave break. Josh was also a world-class champion surfer and had been a junior champion at age twelve. But looking at him, one could only see a typical Southern California surfer-dude with perpetual tan, white blonde hair, and permanently crinkled eyes. Except, if you looked into his blue eyes, it was obvious they were piercing with their intelligence. It was very good he was assigned to the case.

"So, why are you here?" Melissa asked, then stopped as Joshua turned to look at her, his eyes freezing her in midstep.

"Dude, they called me," Josh said, shrugging again. "Said it was some judge or something. Said it was me or nothing."

"A judge?" I asked.

"Dude, you didn't know?"

I looked hard at Melissa who just shrugged. I whirled back around and stared hard at the Sergeant-on-Scene, Novak. He was briefing the two CSI technicians.

Josh followed my gaze and saw who was holding the clipboard. He turned back to me, shaking his head. "Dude, you just gotta let it go, man."

"Pffstt!" was all I could say.

Melissa looked at me, then at Novak, then over at Josh. She gave him that hunchy shoulder scrunch, chin thrust thing that means "tell me." But Josh just shrugged.

"Oh, hell," I said. "Hey, Novak, can you give us a minute? We need you over here."

Novak and one of the CSI techs climbed the hill to join us. I was slightly irritated that Novak's breathing was controlled and he didn't need to huff for air. The technician was not anyone I knew. She was young, pale, and not overly attractive, with mousy brown hair and eyes hidden behind glasses. Around her neck she had hung two sets of camera equipment, and in her hand she held a black bag similar to the one Josh used. She slipped backward as she approached, and Novak reached back to catch her hand.

"Yes?" he said as took his place next to the Porsche.

"So, you want to let us know what we're dealing with?" I asked.

"According to the neighbors, this house belongs to a judge," Novak said. He gestured to the other blue-sheeted body, saying, "and the judge was married. So I presume the woman inside the garage is his wife."

"Ah, shit," I said, knowing the case had just taken on a very bad profile.

"The judge's name is Mark Henning. He is a family law judge over at the Lamureaux Center. Presumably, the female vic is his wife, Nancy Henning. Per the neighbors, good folk."

I pulled back the sheet covering the man, while the CSI tech began to take photos of the body. First she used her standard still camera, a Cannon EOS digital. Then she angled around behind me and changed cameras, using a very small handheld camera that fit into the palm of her hand.

"Cool," Josh said as he made room for the tech next to the body. "One of those digital recorders?"

The girl blushed and nodded. "Yes, it's a Cannon HG 100 with a 40 gigabyte disk drive," she answered, shyly.

"Way cool," Josh said. "Here, get closer, okay? You're Amy, right? New to the Department, huh?"

"Yes, sir," the girl answered. "Amy Knight. And you're Josh?"

He just nodded and opened his black bag to withdraw the dagger-like liver thermometer. She moved closer, camera in hand, while Josh pulled up the deceased white shirt from his dress slacks and plunged the wickedly long prong into right side of the victim. He watched as the numbers began to flash on the digital readout.

"Ninety-seven point three degrees," he said as he jotted a note on his notepad.

"Hmm, maybe a little over an hour since death," I said.

"Yeah, given a degree of cooling for each hour beyond time of death," Josh said, "I would put his time of death at about — what, it's 8:20 now — 7:10-ish?"

"T.O.D. Nineteen, ten, then?" Novak asked.

"Sure, whatever, dude," Josh answered without looking up.

Amy continued filming while I reached over Josh and pulled the victim's wallet from his back pocket. It was a slender tri-fold containing his driver's license and a couple of credit cards. In the money fold I found three one-hundred-dollar bills, but nothing smaller. There were several photos in a plastic holder. One depicted a young woman with luscious auburn hair, green eyes and a wide smile holding two small children, both girls. The other was of the same woman taken more recently. The wide smile was intact as were the green eyes, but her head was swaddled in a vibrantly colored head scarf. In the plastic frame holding that photo was tucked a thin strip of paper with the red printing of a fortune cookie. It said, "Love is the good fortune that will always be with you."

My hand began to involuntarily shake as I held it. "Here, tech," I snapped, "bag it and tag it."

Amy Knight almost dropped her camera as she tried to reach for the wallet. However, close on her heels was her partner, Criminalist Jack Rankin. He reached over her, snatching the wallet from my hand.

"Touchy, are we tonight?" he asked. "I'm here tonight, Detective Swanson. Ms. Knight is only here to film. Try not to scare her away."

"Film?" I asked. "Why are we filming?"

Rankin shrugged his shoulders, turning to Novak. Novak in turn rolled his eyes at me and answered. "It's a judge, for Christ sakes, Jake. We need to make sure it's done right."

There was so much I wanted to say, but instead I kept it to myself. Josh was in full evaluation mode, and I needed to keep my attention on him.

"There's not really the beginning of slight rigor," Josh said, lifting the deceased's arm and watching it fall. "That is in keeping with the body core temp of 97 degrees. I would definitely say this victim has been dead just over an hour — maybe hour and a half." Then he lifted the victim's head and inspected it while Amy filmed. "Definitely a gunshot to the head. Given the damage, I would say it is either a high-caliber weapon or multiple gunshots. Can't tell till we do the post-mortem." Turning to look at the second criminalist, Josh said, "Rankin, bag his head just in case there's a bullet rattling around near the exit wound."

Josh carefully lowered the head back down onto the pavement. Rocking back on his heels, he turned back to Novak. "I hear there's a second victim?"

Without a word between us, Novak, Sanchez, Amy Knight, and I trooped over to the blue-sheet fluttering just inside the open garage door. Josh again squatted next to the blue sheet. He carefully lifted the sheet while Amy filmed the body first with her small digital recorder, then switched to the larger still camera and flash.

"You get all that, Amy?" Josh asked. "Can I move her now?"

"Yes, sir," Amy answered, backing away.

The victim under the blue sheet was a thin woman dressed in sleeveless sundress. She had very short auburn hair that was mixed with a hint of gray. Her eyes were closed, and there was a slight smile on her face. The shots that had taken her life had thrown her backward; she had landed on her back. In that strange, unchoreographed dance of the dead, she had landed with her arms crossed across her chest. It was a pose making her look even more vulnerable in death.

I can't say she was beautiful, but there was something special about her; even with a violent death she radiated peace. As Josh started to prepare to take her liver temperature, I moved away. Sadness again enveloped me.

I tried the backdoor leading from the garage to the house. It was unlocked and I stepped through into a wide open space. To my left was an area that looked like it had once been a bedroom, but was now semi-enclosed with a half-wall. Within its defined space was a feminine antique white desk, a vividly stripped and overstuffed love seat and chair, and floor-to-ceiling book cases. The room had a broad window opening out onto a landscaped patio and pool. Numerous household plants hung from the ceiling and were placed everywhere on the shelves. On my right was a door opening to a laundry room and half-bath. Beyond the semi-room was a large room making up what I have heard called a great room, and beyond that room was the kitchen. The great room was a huge expanse defined by a large glass window wall and an open beam ceiling running the length of the room. The doors of the window wall were open to the patio, creating a large indoor/outdoor room. I noticed the tile from the great room and kitchen matched the tile on the patio, creating the look of one continuous space.

The scene was restful, yet elegant, but most of all, peaceful.

Suddenly, Melissa pushed past me as I started to cross the room to the kitchen.

"Shit, Jake," she said, as she hurried to the kitchen. "Can't you smell that? Something's burning."

She ran to the oven and threw it open while turning knobs. The opened door of the oven allowed smoke to escape, setting off the smoke detectors. We were rewarded with the bleat, bleat, bleat of the detector.

"Oh, shit," Melissa said. "I don't have a clue how to disengage these things. Jake, help me! My dad always does it at home. Shit!"

I scurried around looking for the detectors. I found the one in the hallway, but it was hardwired to the house and simply removing it would not disengage it. The sound of the alarm felt loud enough to make our ears bleed.

Jack Rankin, then Josh, came tearing into the house. Rankin made a beeline for the front entryway, while Josh looked in the laundry room. Suddenly, there was silence. Rankin came back with a satisfied smile.

"I found the main board. Just needed to put it into safe mode," he said. "You'll probably get a call from security in a second."

He had no sooner said that when the telephone rang. By that time Novak had joined us.

"I'll get that," he said. "I'm senior officer on scene."

I would have protested, but I decided to let him have his moment of glory.

"Ahem, detectives," Rankin said, hovering next to us. "Are we forgetting protocols?"

In his hand he held gloves and booties. The booties were paper covers for our shoes, very similar to the kind worn by surgeons in the operating room. Our guys at the crime lab had been to a couple of seminars and had watched way too much *CSI* and now insisted all officers at the scene wear gloves and booties to keep the scene contamination to a minimum. I think they would have had us suit up into full surgical scrubs if they could have. But even the chief thought that was a little excessive.

"Nooo," I said, reaching into my pocket for my gloves. Unfortunately, my pocket was empty. Sheepishly, I took the offered pair of gloves, and slipped my feet into the protective paper booties.

"What?" Melissa asked, looking at the booties.

"Booties, for your feet," Rankin said, pointing to her boots. "You've already tracked in dirt from outside. God, I hope you haven't contaminated my scene."

Melissa rolled her eyes over to me. She already had on her gloves, but her boots were exposed.

"Put them on," I said. "We're being extra careful, remember?"

She shrugged and did what she was told. Rankin handed the gloves and booties to Amy, then left.

"Hey, Jake," Melissa said, "come here; look at this." Melissa was examining the oven and its burned contents. Set out on the counter next to the oven were two plates and a platter. On the platter were two beautiful rib eye steaks. One of the steaks, however, was half off the platter and had chew marks on it.

"Looks like they weren't expecting company," I said to Melissa.

"No, just a quiet dinner at home," Melissa said. "Two baked potatoes, now burned-out hockey pucks, and what looks like a homemade pie. Not sure what kind — too burned to tell."

"Missing cat, though," I said, pointing to the steak.

"Huh?"

"Look at the meat," I said, pointing to the steak. "It definitely has chew marks."

"Shit, Jake," Melissa said, bending to inspect the steak. "How do you know it's a cat?"

"My cat, Cisco, does the same type of thieving if I don't watch him," I answered.

"Oh, God," Melissa said. "This is way sad. Talk about life interrupted."

I couldn't think of an answer, so I moved away from the tableau and wandered out of the kitchen down the hallway. Beyond the great room area the hallway was draped in thick, long-looped carpet. It almost reminded me of the shag carpet of my youth. But this carpet was a pale blue, not puke-gold. On the walls were numerous framed photographs. Faces peered back, large smiles everywhere I looked. This was a family who enjoyed each other; it was clear from the staged photos, but also the more candid shots indicated love. I saw more evidence of affection from the number of photos with people with their arms around each other: husband and wife, sister and sister, parents and children, and probably grandchildren and grandparents. Love was everywhere. It was a gallery of a family who had grown up and moved out but remained close.

As I examined the pictures, I moved down the hallway opening doors as I went. On one side of the hallway there were two rooms. One was clearly a guest room with a queen bed and comfortable furniture. The other room's door was closed. I tried the handle, but the door was locked. I rattled the handle several times to make sure, but the door did not open. Leaving the locked door, I continued to the end of the hall where the space opened into a large master suite.

The room was spacious and comfortable. The furniture was large, but not overly masculine. One side of the room opened into a spacious bath and dressing area with two walk-in closets. Again the ceiling opened to exposed beams and cross pieces. A ceiling fan rotated slowly, slightly stirring the air of the room.

Everything was neat and clean. The house smelled fresh, no trace of cat litter... or the cat.

I stood for a moment, trying to feel the air. I was disturbed by the violence that had taken the lives of the people who lived in the room in which I was standing. It was too incongruent to what I could see in the house and its contents. This wasn't a life that called for violence. It wasn't a life that was disordered or reckless.

As I stood, lost in thought, Melissa came up behind me. She began opening and shutting drawers in the nightside tables next to the bed.

"Hey, partner," I said, roused from my thoughts. "What're you doing?"

"Looking for a phone book," Melissa said. "We gotta make some calls, right?"

She continued opening and closing drawers, shuffling through the drawer's contents. Finally she picked up the phone next to the bed, hit a few buttons on the handset, and pocketed the phone.

"What ya got?" I asked.

"This phone has a digital phonebook," she answered. "I think I'll take it back to the station and recover some of the numbers."

"Hmm, okay," I said. "Look, this feels dicey. There's something wrong about all this."

"You mean besides two people getting killed in one of the safest places in Southern California," Novak said, as he entered the master bedroom.

"Yeah, besides the obvious," I answered. "This house doesn't feel right for this kind of violence."

"Sheesh," Novak said, rolling his eyes at me.

I turned my back on him and watched as my partner continued her search. She opened the door to the first closet. From where I was standing, all I could see was women's clothing. It was neatly racked, and the shoes were neatly placed in pairs on tilted shelves. Plastic covers held what looked like sweaters that were stacked into cubicles. The air was lightly scented with from the cedar-lined walls in the closet.

"Nothing here," Melissa said, backing out and closing the door behind her.

Opening the closet on the other side of the short hallway, I heard Melissa expel a brief whistle through her teeth — a habit of hers whenever she came across something of great interest.

"Well, lookee here," she said.

Amy appeared from nowhere and followed me into the closet, filming as we entered. Hanging on a hook, separate from the rack of men's clothing, was a khaki uniform. Well-polished shoes set beneath it, and a hat and gloves were placed on an ottoman in the center of the room. A small duffle bag was placed next to the shoes.

"A uniform?" I asked. "Wasn't our guy a judge?"

"Yeah, so?" answered Melissa. "Look at this get-up. I bet our guy was a reservist. Navy, from the looks of the uniform."

"You know that by just looking at it?" I asked.

Melissa just rolled her eyes at me, then crossed over to the ottoman, picking up the hat.

"Holy, moly," she said. "This guy's got scrambled eggs on his cover!"

"What are you talking about?" I asked.

"Look, look at his cover, it has scrambled eggs on it." Melissa said, handing me the hat.

"I'm sorry, but this is a hat, and all I see are squiggles and a funny looking bird," I said, handing the hat back to her.

"Hat is a cover," she said, in her overly patient voice, the one she uses with me when she is convinced I am a moron. I hear the voice a lot. "Scrambled eggs are the squiggly things on the bill of the cover. The funny looking bird is an eagle."

"This guy is the equivalent of a full-bird colonel," she said.

As she said that, all the detective hairs on the back of my neck began to vibrate. I looked at the packed duffle bag, the polished shoes, the well-pressed uniform, and suddenly the house no longer felt so peaceful.

"Come on, guys," I said. "Amy, finish your shots and follow us out. Don't touch anything else."

Amy nodded and kept her palm-held camera going. Melissa also put the cover back on the ottoman and backed out of the closet.

"We need to notify the family and get permission to search," I said. "There's a locked door into a room, and now this uniform. This is beginning to feel a little hinky."

Novak, Melissa, Amy and I tiptoed back out of the room and down the hallway. Once in the great room I called Novak over to me.

"Look, Ryan," I said, "We need to close this house up tight—no more searching until we get permission or a warrant. This feels wrong, somehow."

Novak looked around, shuffled his feet a little, took a breath, then answered. "Yeah, I hate to agree with you," he said. "But the vic is a judge; now, with the uniform and stuff, like the locked door, I agree. We need more than just exigent circs here."

"Yeah," I said. "I don't think we can cover this with exigent circumstances of a hot pursuit. I don't think the perp ever came through the door from the garage."

"Yeah," Novak said, nodding. "I agree. The house isn't tossed, nothing is out of place. Doesn't look like whoever did this came this far in. Let's just close her down."

"I'll get started on a warrant," I said. "I'm on my way back to the station. You'll watch Rankin and that new kid — what's her name?"

"Yeah," Novak answered. "Her name's Amy, Amy Knight. Rankin will just do a cursory, and the kid, Amy's got it recorded already. I agree: we'll just shut her down. I'll post Donahue on it till you get back."

I thought a moment as the two of us walked back outside. It was already getting late. The sky was now completely dark and blended blackness into the deep blue of the ocean, obliterating the horizon. The moon had not yet come up, and the night was dark.

"Who's on tonight?" I asked.

"Greene," Novak said.

"Hammi?"

"Yeah, Sergeant Greene."

"Okay, good," I said. Sergeant Hammi Greene was a good as they come. He was good with his people and careful with evidence. He could be tough when required, but generally held tight to his good nature. He'd keep my scene intact.

"You'll hand it off to him when he comes on?" I asked.

Novak stared hard at me a minute, then smiled. "You mean I might get to go home on time for a change, even with a murder and all?"

"You've kept the log, and done your best, right?" I asked. "You got people canvassing, right?"

"Yep," he answered, pointing down the hill to two uniformed officers working their way through the few stragglers left standing on the street.

"Photos of the crowd?" I asked.

"Yep. Had Donahue doing it periodically through the evening."

"Seems like you've done everything you can," I said. "Nothing left Greene can't handle when he comes on with his crew."

We shook hands, and I slid down the driveway to the Intrepid. Close on my heels was my partner, Melissa Sanchez. In her hand were the phone and a couple of framed photographs.

"Back to the station?" she asked.

"Yeah, back to the station."

As I put the key in the ignition of the Intrepid, I felt my blood begin to rush a little harder through my veins. The adrenalin kick finally hit. I was on a case, and it felt good. Smiling, I patted the steering wheel of the Intrepid and took a deep breath. I fought back the anger, steadied my resolve, and put the car in gear. I eased out of the logjam of police units and set my sights on the station.

I needed a search warrant, and I needed it now.

CHAPTER THREE

The drive back to the station was quick. Melissa and I arrived at the station's back parking lot at almost the same time, pulling our cars into spaces next to each other. I couldn't help but smirk at her department-issued, unmarked vehicle, which was a white, mid-two-thousand Dodge Stratus. It was a little four-banger, with cloth seats, no radio except the police scanner, and had the required computer taking up the entire front passenger seat. The vehicle was saved for the newest detectives on the squad as kind of a "look at me; I'm new" initiation type thing.

She saw the smile playing on my lips and gave me her glinty-eyed stare. "Don't even start, Swanson," she said. "At least I'm not having to use my own car now."

"You get the card, too?" I asked.

"Of course," she said, referring to the department-issued gas credit card all detectives were issued. "So, do I get a thanks for that?"

"Pfsst" was all she said by way of an answer.

We both swung through the back door of the station and hurried down to the detective's bullpen area. The work space was a large room cut into individual pods by Herman-Miller soundproof panels, from which hung overhead bins and bookcases, with each area having a standard six-drawer desk, a computer station, a large lateral file cabinet and a single guest chair. The spaces were contained enough to give the illusion of privacy, but because the panels were only five feet high, most of us could stand up and see over the panels to converse. Overall, it was a pleasant enough place to work. I was lucky enough to have the pod furthest away from the door opening into the hall which was right across from the lieutenant's office. More importantly, my desk area placed me closest to the front door, which gave me maximum privacy and a discrete way to vanish when necessary. Melissa, being the newest detective in the squad, had the area fronting the back hallway, giving the lieutenant a clear view of her desk from his doorway. I suspected it was the reason why her desktop area was always clear of clutter.

Melissa and I took the few items we collected from the scene to her area. They included the personal phone book, several framed photos, and the phone handset from the master bedroom bedside stand. We spread them out on the tabletop covering her lateral file and I began the evidence log while Melissa began scrolling through the phone's contacts. From the handset we were able to find numerous names and phone numbers, most within Southern California, and one number from the 757 area code that neither Melissa nor I recognized.

When Melissa had finished her list, we tried to compare the names with the ones in the personal phone book we had found in the kitchen drawer. The phone book gave us addresses, but left us clueless about family. I finally turned to the several framed pictures I had snagged from the photo gallery in the hall of the house.

"Mystery solved," I said, handing Melissa the family photo I had removed from its frame. "From the names written on the back of this picture, it would appear the Henningses had two daughters and two grandchildren."

"Yeah," Melissa said, picking up the sheet of paper on which she had written names and phone numbers. "The older daughter in the photo appears to be Cindy in the 805 area code. The other daughter seems to be Lauren from the 757 area."

She picked up the phone book and flipped through the pages until she found a Lauren Hill in Virginia Beach, Virginia, and Cindy McDermott in Santa Barbara, California.

"So, we know where they are," Melissa said. "You want to make the call?"

Hell no, I didn't want to "make the calls." Notifying a family of a loved one's untimely death was the worst job a detective could have. I'd rather paw through dismembered body parts than call an unsuspecting family member to tell them someone had died. But, given the dicey situation of the locked room in the victim's house; the fact that the deceased was a judge; and the fact he was possibly active in the military; permission to search the parent's house was critical to the case.

"Oh, shit, just give me the phone," I said.

I dialed the number to the house in Santa Barbara. I knew it was getting late, but the call was critical. I took a deep breath while the phone rang. Three rings later it was answered.

"Hello?" said a calm, but tired, male voice.

In the background I could hear the sound of a woman speaking to what sounded like a small child. I couldn't make out what was being said, but to me it sounded like she was calming the child.

I shook myself again to clear my head. "Hello, may I speak with Cindy McDermott?" I said.

"I'm sorry, sir," the man said, "but it is late, and my wife is busy with the children right now. It is past their bedtime and she is trying to get them to sleep."

"Are you Mr. McDermott?" I asked.

"Yes. May I ask who is calling?"

"Sir," I said in my steadiest detective voice. "I am Detective Jake Swanson of the Newport Beach Police Department. If Mrs. McDermott is not available, may I speak with you?"

There was a hesitation on the other side of the line. A long pause followed. Finally, "Yes, Detective, you may. Is this about my in-laws?"

"Yes, sir," I answered.

"Has something happened to them?" he asked.

Before I could answer, the phone was obviously taken away from him and a woman's nearly hysterical voice came on the line. "What..,

what... what has happened to my mother? Is she dead? Where is my father? Why isn't he calling me?"

I was momentarily taken aback. I wondered why the daughter would immediately believe her mother was dead and her father missing. I made a quick note on the notepad I had next to me.

"Is this Cindy McDermott?" I asked, avoiding her questions for the moment. "I need to speak to you about Nancy Henning and Mark Henning. Are they your parents?"

"Yes, yes, of course they're my parents. Who is this?" she said, the fear in her voice beginning to tinge with anger. "What is this about? Are you going to tell me, or are you just playing games?"

In the background I heard a child start to cry, its wails clearly coming through the phone lines.

"Charles, would you take the children back upstairs," she snapped. "I have to take care of this. It's Mom and Dad."

I started again, "This is Detective Jake Swanson of the Newport Beach Police Department. I am sorry, but I have bad news. It would appear that your parents were the victims of a possible homicide this evening. I need your help . . ."

A loud wail followed by a few gulping sobs came back at me through the receiver. I heard the phone tumble to the floor. More sobs and a few muffled words came back through the phone. Finally, the steadier voice of Charles McDermott spoke.

"Detective," he said. "What has happened to my in-laws?"

"Mr. McDermott," I said, "It would appear that Judge Henning and Mrs. Henning have been the victims of a possible homicide, but I really don't want to discuss the details over the phone. I would appreciate it if you or your wife could come to Newport Beach and we can discuss it more thoroughly, here, at the station."

"Surely you don't think my wife had anything to do with whatever happened to Nancy and Mark, do you?" he asked. His voice had taken on a strange tone. It was abrupt and authoritative.

"Sir, I can't speculate about that," I answered. "But, I would like permission to search the home."

"I would have thought that you would have already searched the house to look for clues," he said.

"Yes, sir, we normally would have done so," I said, "but there was a locked door to one of the rooms and a uniform hanging in the closet. I thought it better to contact the family for permission to search."

"Listen, Detective," McDermott said, his voice becoming very annoyingly controlled. "I am an attorney. My specialty is real estate, not criminal law. I am, however, now very concerned and wish to consult with another member of my firm. This said, at this time I cannot allow you to search the premises."

"Mr. McDermott," I said, trying to keep my voice neutral as I pinged on the fact that the annoying voice came from the self-congratulatory voice civil lawyers always used on lesser mortals. My attempt to swallow my own desire to get snotty failed miserably as I answered. "You know I will just get a warrant and search without your permission."

There was a pause. The silence was the kind that precedes the battle just before engagement by two bulls, no matter what the species. We each snorted and figuratively pawed the earth.

"Then, Detective," he said, the battle began, "I suggest you do just that. Otherwise, stay out of my in-laws' house, or answer to me and my wife. I can assure you, the results will not be pleasant."

The condescending voice and the threat raised my blood pressure. I took a few long, hopefully silent breaths, and then answered. "It will be posted on the door when you arrive. I do assume you and your wife will be coming to Newport Beach?"

"My wife and I will meet you at the house at two p.m.," he said. "I have an early morning appointment that I cannot cancel. I will, of course, accompany my wife to meet with you. And, I presume you will not enter that house without us present, warrant in hand."

I wanted to slam the phone down in its cradle, but took another slow breath, and answered, "Thank you, sir. My condolences to your wife."

Melissa had been swiveling back and forth in her chair listening to my side of the conversation. When I hung up the phone as carefully as my angered hand would let me, she smiled her Cheshire cat grin.

"Well, that went well," she said.

"Dick!" I mumbled under my breath. I was now picking up my partner's bad habits. Using her favorite expression was becoming a bad habit, but one I didn't care if I broke.

"So, we need a search warrant?" Melissa asked.

"Looks that way," I said.

"And, is the wife calling her sister?" Melissa asked, still swinging the chair back and forth.

"What?"

"Is Cindy McDermott calling her other sister in Virginia Beach?"

"Shit, I don't know," I said, exasperated, but not sure at whom I should focus the emotion, myself or Charles McDermott. "We never got that far."

"Virginia Beach," Melissa said, looking at her watch, "is what, three hours ahead of us? It's almost nine now. Seems a little late to call."

"Oh, hell," I said. "Just when would you like to hear your father and mother were killed? Is there really a good time?"

Melissa didn't answer. She just reached for the phone and started dialing. The phone must have rung numerous times, but someone picked up on the other end of the line.

Melissa sat up straight in her chair, then began to speak. "Hello, I hate to disturb you this time of night. May I speak with Lauren Hill, please?" Melissa waited a heartbeat, but then quickly interrupted, and said, "No, no, this is not the Navy, ma'am. Wait, wait . . ."

Melissa pointed at me, and I picked up the same line on the phone on the desk next to hers. I heard a soft sleep-slurred voice, struggling to make sense of our words.

"Who is this again?" the voice asked.

"Is this Ms. Lauren Hill?" Melissa again asked.

"Mrs. Hill, I am Mrs. Hill," the soft voice answered, beginning to gather strength.

"Mrs. Hill," Melissa said, "I am Detective Melissa Sanchez of the Newport Beach Police Department. Have you spoken with your sister, Cindy this evening?"

"Why, has something happened to her?" Lauren asked.

"No, no, that's not it," Melissa quickly answered. "I need to speak to you about your parents, Nancy and Mark Henning. They are your parents, correct? And they live in Newport Beach?"

"Yes, they are, but why are you calling me so late?" Lauren answered.

There was a long pause. I could almost hear the women communicating with each other without saying a word. They both took a deep breath at the same time, and let it out as a sigh.

A soft mewing cry came across the miles as Lauren began to cry softly into the phone. Melissa continued with her message.

"I am sorry, but there has been an incident at the house. Your parents did not make it. I am so sorry," Melissa said in that sing-song voice she uses when consoling someone. I swear I heard her reach across the phone line and give the young woman a hug. "Do you have anyone close you can call? Is there anyone I can call to come be with you?"

The soft crying continued, but I could hear the struggle to control her voice as Lauren answered. "No, my husband in stationed in the Gulf. It would be difficult to reach him if his ship is out of range."

"Navy?" Melissa asked.

"Yes, he's a lieutenant," Lauren answered.

"Mrs. Hill . . . ," Melissa started to say.

"Lauren. Please call me Lauren. I'll be on the next plane. I'll try to be there by morning."

"Can I give you my cell phone number to have you call me when you arrive?" Melissa asked.

The two women exchanged cell phone numbers and disconnected the call.

"Well, Sanchez," I said, "while you were being all sweet and supportive, did you think to get permission to search?"

"Shit!" was her only answer.

"Just get Clara, the chief's secretary, on the phone," I said as I re-cradled the phone and stalked over to my own desk to turn on my computer.

"Can't," she yelled at my retreating back.

"Why not?" I yelled back as I slammed open my keyboard drawer and hard squiggled the mouse awake.

"She's out on maternity leave. You want me to call the temp?"

"Whatever," I answered and made a note to myself that I needed to stop sounding so much like a teenager.

I began the standard Probable Cause Declaration to support the request for the warrant. I described the house where the deaths of the judge and his wife occurred and the need to search the closed and locked room. I also asked permission to search his chambers at the courthouse and to search any of his vehicles. It was the standard stuff, with a lot of cutting and pasting from other warrants I had done in the past.

About thirty minutes later, as I was finishing up, I heard the back-door to the station swing wide open then slam shut. Loud voices came through into the bullpen, and the area quickly filled with people dressed in formal evening wear. The chief was the first person through the door into the bullpen. He was dressed in a tuxedo, but his face said anything but "festive."

"Swanson!" he said, his handsome face contorting in anger. "Why wasn't I notified immediately of Judge Henning's death?"

I had no answer for the question. I hadn't even thought to call him. This murder was an investigative issue. With Sergeant Novak on the scene, I had not thought to call out the brass. Usually the responding patrol sergeant made that decision. Admittedly, I had been surprised the lieutenant was not called out but, once again, that was not my decision.

While I stood silent, the chief continued to rage. "This is a judge, Swanson," he said, crossing the distance to my cubicle. "A sitting judge, Swanson. Killed in our jurisdiction, Swanson. I should have been called!"

The distance between the two of us had closed to less than three feet. The only thing standing between us was the five-foot-high Her-man-Miller panel. Given the chief's six-foot height and my six-two, we were standing virtually nose to nose.

So many thoughts swirled around in my head. I knew the chief, a graduate of Stanford and recently of the F.B.I., hated me. He was an uptight control freak and I was his direct opposite. I knew I would get things done — in my own way and in my own time. It was like waiting for the perfect wave: things would come together when the time was right. Unfortunately, the chief wanted and needed immediate gratification. Even knowing our differences, I still settled on the wrong response.

"Well, looks like you're here, now," I said, turning away from him.

I could feel the heat. I know his blood pressure went through the roof; I could hear him gasping for breath. "Swanson," he said, lowering his voice to a dangerous growl, "I am only here because the Lieutenant's temporary secretary called him about a search warrant to ask what she should do to handle it."

"Oh?" was all I said, still not looking at him. "Well, I have it right here; all finished up, sir."

I ripped the paperwork out of my desktop printer and waved it at the chief. As I did that, I realized the bullpen had filled with too many people. Standing off to one side was Dr. Dick Burge, the county's chief medical examiner and head of the pathology department at the local university. He was also dressed in a tuxedo and his wife of many years was standing next to him. Burge had a grin on his face and his wife looked pissed.

Next to him was Lieutenant Max Graber, also in formal dinner wear with his lovely wife holding his hand. Both had identical noncommittal expressions on their faces. Scattered around the room were other members of the Newport Beach Police Department's brass and a couple of high-ranking sheriff's deputies. Behind all of them stood the presiding judge of the Orange County courts. He was standing off to one side; on his arm was Ronnie, one of the girls from the house. She put a finger to her lips to signify the universal "shhh."

Looking at all the brass in their formal evening wear made me aware of my lowly status as a detective. I was slightly surprised at my reaction. I felt left out. They had been to a party, and I hadn't been invited. It hit a weird spot in my psyche, almost an ache. I had always been invited to all the parties. Why not to this one?

"So, you've been out partying, I see," I said, turning to face to the chief.

"Mayor's Ball," he said, the words slipping from his lips before he could hold them back.

"Explains the brown ring around your nose," I answered, my words slipping from my lips before I could hold them back.

Before any more words could be exchanged, Lieutenant Graber crossed the room to stand next to us. His six-foot, six-inch body hulked over both of us. Using his body like the professional football front lineman he had once been, he came between the chief and me.

"Chief," he said, putting his back to me, facing the chief. "Dispatch had been told about the Ball. You weren't called out because of the radio silence regarding the identity of the victims. We're here now; let's get Swanson's report, so we all can get to work on this."

With the wall of flesh standing between the chief and me, we both backed down and de-escalated the confrontation.

When the lieutenant felt some of the tension leave the bodies he was standing between, he turned back to me. "Can you give us a quick report of what has gone on so far?"

"The call came in as a safety check on an open garage door," I said, reciting the facts I had already committed to memory. "Patrol responded, found the first victim, and called in the Sergeant. Sergeant Novak responded and ordered a perimeter set at the foot of the driveway. He also found the second victim and called in the homicide unit, putting in a personal request for the senior detective, who was me. I requested dispatch to notify my partner, Sanchez. Novak then had dispatch notify the Coroner's lab and the crime scene criminalist, who digitally recorded all of our movement at the scene. Upon examination by Coroner's technician, Josh Childs, it was determined that both victims suffered fatal gunshot wounds, and had been dead approximately one hour to one hour and fifteen minutes prior to discovery. The judge was found dead next to the open door of his car; his wife was found slightly inside of the open garage door. Sergeant Novak then had members of his patrol unit start canvassing the neighbors while he kept the log of responding personnel. I agreed that the bodies could be removed from the scene. They were sent to the morgue for preparation for autopsy. CSI, my partner, the Coroner's technician, and I agreed to close down the scene and house until a warrant was obtained. Sergeant Novak closed the site and posted guards. The family was notified. They are expected to arrive tomorrow in the afternoon. No permission has been obtained to search, hence the request for a warrant."

"Good, Swanson," Lieutenant Graber said, still standing between the chief and me. "Anything you need?"

"Besides a signature on the warrant?" I asked.

"Why do you need a warrant?" the Chief asked. "Isn't the house a crime scene? Shouldn't you have access because of that?"

I tried not to stare a hole through the lieutenant's body, because I was sure my eyes were leveling the Death Star laser at the chief. I was hoping he'd just explode and leave me in peace.

Instead, I continued with my answer. "The oldest daughter's husband is a lawyer. He refused permission to enter the locked rooms or to disturb anything in the house." I said.

"Has the press been called?" the chief asked.

From the back of the pack, the presiding judge came forward. "No, no," he said. "I don't want word out that a sitting judge in our county has been shot. It'd give too many crazies ideas."

"I have to agree," I said. "I think we need more time before we get the crazies from the press involved."

The request for a news blackout caused an agonizing pause for the chief. He lived for the press. There was nothing he enjoyed more than a well-attended press conference with him standing in front of a bank of microphones, TV reporters filming him, and print reporters earnestly taking down his every word.

I could see his eyes shift to one side as he considered the pros and cons of the judge's request. The lieutenant was the deciding vote.

"Swanson," he asked, "was there something else that was causing you to want the blackout?"

"You mean besides the locked door to a room in the house and a well-pressed Navy uniform in the closet, along with what appears to be a packed duffle bag?" I asked.

"Oh," was all the three standing closest to me said.

There was an awkward pause, some shuffling of feet, and then the presiding judge stepped forward. "I'll sign the warrant," he said.

"I'll want to search his chambers, too," I said. "And go through his files."

The judge leveled a look at me, and stared hard for a second or two. I could see him evaluating the ramifications of a dead judge and a murderer related to the judge's workload. He nodded his assent, then signed the warrant.

Handing it back to me, he said, "You swear that the facts contained in the Declaration of Probable Cause are true to the best of your knowledge and recollection, Detective?"

"I do."

"Okay," he said, "I'll set up the search of the courtroom and chambers, for what time tomorrow? Tomorrow is good, right?"

"Tomorrow is fine," I said. "About ten o'clock or so?"

"Fine," he said, starting to loosen his bow tie. "I'll meet you at the courthouse at ten tomorrow. I'll have the staff available to you for help with the files and cases Henning was working on."

The presiding judge turned to the chief, made his good-byes, and left. He gently guided Ronnie with his hand in the small of her back. She placed her hand gently on his waist, and said something to him that made him smile. I heard the back door slam as they left the building.

"Well, then," I heard a voice boom, "I guess I have work to do. I will meet you at the house, dear. Don't wait up."

I looked over to see Dick Burge give a quick kiss on the cheek to his wife. She shoulder- rolled herself away from him and stalked out the back door. As always, I knew he was eager to get out of any time he had to spend with his wife. Their marriage was well past comfortable and had descended into barely tolerable.

The party in the bullpen began to break up. The various players began to make their good-byes and drifted out the back door. One or two of the sheriffs I recognized stayed behind with the chief and the lieutenant. They stepped into the hallway, away from Melissa and me. Burge angled himself so he was half in and half out of the bullpen room, slouching on the door frame so as to appear as if he wasn't listening.

I could hear the voices in the hallway, but was unable to make out what they were saying. Burge continued to slouch against the door frame, his eyes giving away nothing. As the voices began to drift down the hallway to the chief's office, Burge levered himself away from the wall and ambled all the way into Melissa's pod.

"Shit," he said. "I hope your chief doesn't give in to those limelight-hogging sheriffs."

"Ah, Burge," I said, laughing. "Too many answers to that statement."

"Dim widdies," he said.

I laughed out loud at the slouching medical examiner. He was still pissed that the prior sheriff had managed to take over the coroner's office and bring it under the control of the elected sheriff instead of the medical examiner. However, since the sheriff's removal on federal corruption charges, the coroner's office was still separated from the medical examiner, which caused all sorts of mischief for the other police agencies needing the services and opinions of the coroner. The County Board of Supervisors had yet to vote on restoring funding to again bring the coroner and medical examiner's office back under one reporting umbrella, while again making it independent from the sheriff's department.

"You still holding grudges?" I asked.

"Fucking dim wit," Burge said. "He just couldn't stand anyone having control. Afraid we'd see just how incompetent he really was."

"Well, you did, didn't you?" I said.

"Couldn't help it; I was subpoenaed," he answered.

The two of us looked at each other and started to laugh. It had been ugly. Burge's testimony regarding conversations he had heard between the sheriff and the under-sheriff onboard a boat, while floating off the coast of Catalina Island, had been just one more brick in the wall. Well, that and the sheriff being crazy enough to bring his girlfriend to one of Burge's parties had set Mrs. Burge on a quest to oust the man.

Never underestimate the power of an official's wife to do mischief if she is offended.

Melissa said nothing as the two of us joked and laughed about the demise of the elected sheriff and his posse of posers. Finally, as the clock on the wall ticked later and later into the night, she cleared her throat.

Burge and I looked over at her, as she pouted her lips at us. The hint was clear. It was time to get on with the work at hand.

"Meet you at the lab?" Burge said.

"You going to do it tonight?" I asked.

"Might as well," Burge answered. "I need to give my wife time to get to bed and to sleep before I get home. Otherwise, I'll be up all night listening to her harp about her stunted social life."

"Okay, then, we'll meet you there," I said.

Melissa stood, shuffling her feet. I looked at her tired face, and almost took pity on it. However, part of being a good homicide detective is understanding how a person was killed. Sometimes understanding the "how" helped to find out the "why," which led to the "who."

"Saddle up, partner," I said to Sanchez. "We'll meet you at the lab. Drive your own car, and you can leave from there."

My partner said nothing as she hung her head, but gathered up her notebook, recorder, and small camera, then swung her shoulder bag over her arm and followed me out the door.

CHAPTER FOUR

Sanchez, Burge, and I ambled out the back door of the station, with Burge whistling a happy tune. His ruddy complexion was heightened by the alcohol he must have consumed at the Mayor's Ball prior to coming to the station, and his mood was merry. He didn't seem to mind that his wife had left in a huff, taking his car with her.

"Yo, Swanson," he said, "think I can bum a ride with that tasty new detective of yours?"

Melissa rolled her eyes at him, saying nothing as she slammed the back door to the station.

"You'd have to ride the back seat," I said. "She's got the Stratus."

"Oh, hell," he said, veering toward the Intrepid. "Guess I'll just hop over with you."

I looked over my shoulder in time to see my partner mouth a silent "thank you" as she slid in behind the wheel of the tiny subcompact. Laughing, I hit the locks on my car and allowed the slightly inebriated medical examiner to crawl into the leather bucket seat of the Intrepid.

I had expected a running commentary from Burge on the ride from the Newport Beach Police Station to the medical lab. But once he hit the front seat he fell silent, closing his eyes, and falling into a deep sleep while I traversed the two freeways over to the University of California–Irvine's Medical Center and Hospital. It was late and the freeways were wide open. It was the perfect night to open the sunroof of the over-deluxe car. My mood was light as I turned on the car stereo and listened to a soft jazz radio station. Even with the snoring doctor sitting next to me I felt a smug satisfaction. I was the senior detective of a good department, and was now on the hunt for a killer. It was what I did best, and what I loved most.

Twenty minutes later I rolled into the parking lot next to the hospital. It was located next to the Lamureaux Family Law and Justice Center, the Juvenile Hall, and the Lacy Detention Center, with all of them surrounded by the Santa Ana Freeway to the north; the 57 Freeway to the east; and the Garden Grove Freeway to the south. I found it very ironic that Judge Hemming was brought back to a place so close to where he served as a judge.

As I roused the sleeping doctor, he snapped wide awake, snorting and grinning as he regained consciousness.

"We're here, already, my good man?" he asked, slapping his face a few times, then grinning at me. "God, it's good to be back in the saddle again."

"You were never out of the saddle," I said.

"Yeah, maybe not. But it sure felt like it," he said.

Although the newly appointed sheriff had yet to give full coroner's reporting authority back to the medical examiner, it was no longer likely that the lab would be moved from its current location at the university to the new Justice Center's science building. During the time Burge had lost his power and title, making him subservient to the elected sheriff, it had not been a good time for the examiner. The several months of what he called "captivity" had left him and his staff severely scarred. They had lost funding and, more importantly, prestige. In Orange County, California, the loss of prestige carried a heavy social stigma. It was that stigma that chaffed Burge's soul.

Melissa and I found parking spots close to the back door used by Burge. But as we huddled around the security pad for the door, Burge fumbled in his pants pockets.

"Damn!" he said, coming up empty for his wallet. "My wife made me leave the wallet in the car. Said my ass was lumpy enough without a wallet back there too." He slapped his butt, then leered at my partner. "So, what do you think, dearie? Too lumpy for you?"

Melissa did the eye glint thing at the good doctor, which was enough to make him laugh and veer off to the left, taking us in through the front entrance of the hospital. Melissa and I flashed our badges at the front desk security, one of us on either side of Burge, as we quickly passed through to the elevators. As in most hospitals, the morgue and pathology laboratories were located in the basement of the hospital. Death was not acceptable in the upper floors, and those who enjoyed discovering the causes of death were never wanted where hope and healing were supposed to take place. We took the employee's elevator down to the basement, then skirted around the pathology lab and down into the actual morgue. Lights were on in the autopsy theater, and we could see Josh working at the tables with another person. The two appeared to be examining the bodies they had removed from the black body bags. Each victim was laid out on a stainless steel table and fully clothed.

Josh had changed out of his loud Hawaiian shirt and was now dressed in scrubs. His assistant was also dressed in blue scrubs, but even in the shapeless blue wear, her figure was pert and sassy. Her dark hair was pulled back into a clip of some sort, and her face was devoid of makeup, yet her green eyes were piercing with their intelligence as she watched Josh work. He was bent over Mrs. Henning and examining her with a black light and magnifying glass. The assistant stood at his elbow, listening intently as he spoke. They were so engrossed in what they were doing, neither one heard our noisy entrance.

"Okay, see, here," Josh was saying as he bent closer to the body. "There is only the entry spot on her dress. We are looking for evidence of soot or gunpowder residue on the exterior of her clothing. Its presence and pattern of distribution will tell us how close the shooter was when they delivered the presumably lethal shots. If the shooter was close, say within ten feet of the victim when the shots were delivered, there should be some evidence of gunpowder residue. The closer the shooter is, then the more residue we would expect to find, and the tighter the pattern would be."

As he was speaking he handed the light to his assistant, and gave her the magnifying glass. "Do you see anything?" he asked.

The assistant bent close with the light. She also sniffed the dress. "I neither see nor smell residue," she said as she straightened up and handed the glass back to Josh.

"Smell?" he asked.

"Yes," she said, turning to face him. "I worked in a lab down home where my dad was the part-time medical examiner. He swore that you could smell the gunpowder if the shooter was close when the shooting took place."

"Hmm," Josh said, staring off into space. "I guess you're right. It's just a natural test to check for the presence of the acids. Cool."

The two stood, looking admiringly at each other, the dead body lying next to them. I could feel the sexual tension building.

"Hey, ya'll," Burge said, as he barged into the theater, breaking the spell between the two technicians. "Josh, you tainting one of my intern doctors?"

A deep flush colored the tan face of the young medical student. He turned away from the beaming doctor and coughed. Being the smart detective I am, I smiled, knowing we had just caught the boy wonder exhibiting some natural reactions to the beautiful young woman standing next to him.

"Doctor Young," Burge said, "are you down here to study with me, or to study my medical technician?"

To her credit, the young doctor did not flinch or even blush; she just stared hard at Burge and shrugged her shoulders. "Do you want to start the autopsy now, Doctor Burge?" she said.

"Oh, hell," he answered. "It's either that or go home to my wife."

"Well, sir, I guess you wouldn't want that, now would you," the pert little intern answered.

"Shit, Swanson," Burge said, turning to me. "She's only been with me about two weeks and already she's impertinent."

I started laughing, and caught my partner rolling her eyes, then fasten a stare on the female doctor. The two women did that funny female stare they do when they're communicating without words, and then they smiled in unison.

The medical examiner left the room, presumably to change out of his tuxedo. After he left, Josh sidled up to me, worry etched on his face. "Jake," he said. "Do you think she likes me?"

"Who?" I asked, momentarily taken aback by the junior high school question from the boy genius.

"You know," he said in a whisper. "Doctor Young?"

I took the boy by the arm and steered him away from the two women who were chatting amicably by then, and bent close to answer, lowering my voice. "Do you know her first name yet?" I asked.

"Of course," Josh said. "It's Tammy."

"Well, then, maybe you should try using her first name," I said.

The young man looked hard at me, trying to decipher my meaning. But his eyes remained vacant of any understanding.

"Shit, Josh," I said, "if you only use 'Doctor Young' when you speak to her, she'll never know you're interested."

"But, hey, Dude," he said, "You know, she's like, you know, an intern, and I'm only a medical student."

"Oh, hell," I said, acknowledging his reluctance, but not really understanding it. When it came to women, I rarely let position or status stand in my way. "Look, just ask her to have coffee with you. You could ask her to go across the street for Starbucks or, better yet, see if she likes doughnuts. Take her over to Krispy Kreme for coffee and a doughnut. If she says 'yes,' then use her name. Call her 'Tammy,' not 'Doctor Young.'"

Josh stared hard at me, but our conversation was broken by the re-emergence of Dick Burge.

"So, okay, ya'll," he said in his expansive voice, "let's get to it."

Josh hooked him up with the portable microphone and Burge leaned into the switch, starting the recorder. He set the time and date of the autopsy, then began his examination of Judge Mark Henning.

"Our first victim is a fifty-eight-year-old, Caucasian male. He presents having been removed from the transporting body bag, but fully clothed. He is wearing a white, long-sleeved dress-shirt, yellow- and blue-flecked silk tie, and gray dress slacks, dark gray socks, and what looks to be Italian leather loafers. There is some blood and what appears to be brain matter on the front of the shirt. There is a single exit wound from the left eye socket, with no other obvious signs of trauma on the front of the body."

Burge leaned into the switch again, disabling the voice-activated microphone. "A little more casual than from the days he was a top-notch criminal defense lawyer. Back then he only wore custom suits and handmade shirts from Hong Kong. Wouldn't have been caught dead in an off-the-rack pair of slacks and shirt," Burge said. "Hee, hee, little autopsy humor there, hee, hee, hee. 'Caught dead.'"

Josh and I had the sense to laugh, but the two women looked at the medical examiner like he had lost his mind. Seeing the looks on their faces, Burge turned back to the table, lifting Henning's head from the table, turning it slightly to expose the collar of the shirt. He flicked on the switch again and began to speak. "There is only a slight amount of blood on the collar of the shirt, but a minimal probe with my fingers indicates two entry wounds at the base of the skull. It indicates an almost immediate heart stoppage and flow of blood. Death was instantaneous. We will examine the shirt more closely for gunshot residue and blowback." With the examination of the first clothed victim finished, he turned his attention to the female victim on the other table.

"His wife?" he asked.

"Yes," Josh said. "This is Nancy Henning, Judge Henning's wife. I believe her CDL puts her age at fifty-four."

The medical examiner bent close to the female victim, examining her chest. He pulled at the front of the dress she was wearing and what at first appeared to be a single bullet hole, but it separated into to two distinctive holes. Blood soaked the front of the yellow dress she was wearing, and there were a few drops on the skirt. Her feet were bare, but with the tan lines of sandals.

Quickly Burge went through his protocols for Nancy Henning's clothed body. The only off-line comment he made was to his intern, Tammy Young. "As you can see," he said, "there was an extensive amount of bleed out of the chest wound. My guess is that either she fell forward upon death, or her death was not instantaneous. We won't know that till we open her up and see the extent of her internal wounds."

"Sorry, doc," I said, bending closer, "but we found her on her back, arms crossed."

"Hmm," Burge said. "It could just be pooling then. We'll check during the internals."

Turning back to Josh, he said, "Prepare the bodies for examination. You know the drill. I need some coffee before we start the open cavity examinations."

Josh nodded his assent, and he and Dr. Young began preparing the bodies. They would carefully photograph the bodies fully clothed, and then carefully cut the clothing from the bodies of the victims. The clothing would then be placed in paper bags and sealed with an evidence tag. It would be my responsibility to keep track of the evidence and check it into the crime lab for the forensic micro processing, not that I expected that there would be much relevant trace evidence on the bodies. My impression was that the killer had come in quickly and left just as quickly, not lingering over the bodies long enough to transfer evidence or having physical contact with either victim.

I followed the doctor into his office while my partner remained in the theater to watch the collection of clothing. I wanted to believe it was Melissa's way of being a good detective and preserving the chain of evidence but, actually, I knew she just did not want to spend time with Burge.

He started a small pot of coffee and we chatted amicably while we waited for it to brew."So, Jake," Burge said, handing me a cup of steaming coffee. "I haven't seen you since the two blondes came through here. Whatever happened with that?"

"Got lucky," I answered. "Got the bastards that killed the girl. Turned it over to the Feds, though. They've got it now. Seems like they are going for the max on it, maybe even death."

"Oh?" he answered. "You think they'll need me? I've never done the federal court thing. Heard the judges are dicks."

"You'll hear from the U. S. Attorney before then. They all go by way of grand jury indictments," I answered.

"Hmm, haven't heard anything yet," he said, sipping on his cup. "And the other? Was it Lauderman? I heard it was Lauderman. Good man. Would've hated for it to be him."

"No, the killer died," I answered, reluctant to talk about that last case. Sorrow still hung over me on how that one had ended. Too many people had been hurt by the death of Tawny Brighton. Good people — people who had not deserved to be hurt by her death.

Seeing my change of mood, the doctor changed topics. "Speaking of federal court," he said, slyly, "did you see the good Sheriff's perp-walk into court?"

"Sorry I missed it," I answered. "I must have actually been working that day."

"Naw, Swanson," he said, "you never work. Well, not hard, anyway. You were probably off taking in some waves or some chick somewhere. God, if I only didn't have the misses."

I looked at the man sitting in front of me. He was in his early sixties and had been married to the same woman for more than thirty years, probably complaining for most of them. Yet between the two of them, they had a good life by Newport Beach standards. Misses Burge had come with a ready-made source of income from her grandparents. Her trust fund had allowed her husband to follow his passion and stay in pathology instead of working in a more lucrative field. However, Burge himself had worked his way up the ladder at the university hospital and was making a good living as the chief of pathology and chief medical examiner. The money from his wife's trust fund and his income allowed them to have a forty-two-foot Grand Banks Trawler that they kept at the Balboa Yacht Basin, and they could afford a nice home in the Corona del Mar area of Newport Beach. No matter what his protestations, Dr. Dick Burge had a good life, and his wife was a major part of it.

"Yeah, right, Burge," I said, "Then what? You'd get in shape, surf, date women half your age, die in bed with your socks on?"

"Hee, hee, hee, Jake," he answered. "Yep, that's exactly what I'd do!"

Our conversation was thankfully cut short when Melissa appeared at his office door. "We're ready for you now, sir," she said.

"Ready for what, my sweet?" he leered back.

Her only answer was a snort and a dismissive shrug of my partner's shoulders as she turned and stalked away from us.

"You know, Burge," I said, "someday she's going to hurt you bad. She's got quite the temper."

"I can only pray," he sighed. "I can only pray."

We went back to the autopsy theater where the two bodies had been prepped and were waiting for us. Each was now unclothed and fully washed of all debris and blood. A special catch basin at the end of each table caught the blood and debris as it was gently sprayed from each victim. The examiner needed a clean body to do a better examination. Josh would empty the catch basin later and look for any pertinent debris.An unbidden sadness enveloped me as I approached the sheet covered bodies. Once again my city had been marred by unnatural death. I had come to hate disorder of any kind. After so many years of reckless abandonment, my life had become all about searching for order and answers. Deliberately calculated death was the highest form of disorder, as far as I was concerned. The only way I could restore order was to find the killer or killers and bring them to justice.

The enormity of the task momentarily overwhelmed me again. I swayed as I fought to catch my breath. Melissa, ever vigilant, caught my unease and lifted her eyebrow at me in her silent question. I shook my head in the negative at her concern. Her answer was a shrug of her shoulders. It made me afraid there would be discussion about it later, and I knew I didn't want to talk about it.

This time as Burge approached the table he donned a paper-like, back-opening robe over his scrubs. He had placed a cap on his almost bald skull and was wearing paper slippers over his shoes. Josh helped him snap on sterile gloves and the protective plastic shield to cover his face, then he reattached the doctor's microphone. Fully dressed in operating garb, the doctor's eyes became steely with resolve, replacing the former leers.

He approached the judge first, scanning his body from head to toe. Then he ran his hands lightly over Mark Henning's body, stopping long enough to examine several scars. The most obvious scar was located on the lower right abdomen where the appendix would be located. Clearly it had been removed on some prior occasion. The other two scars caused the doctor to pause. He stepped back, looking at their placement relative to the victim's body, then stepped back for a closer look.

The first scar was a small crescent located just above where the right arm seats into the shoulder area. The second scar was lower down on the right side of the chest, and was also the same crescent shape.

"Hmm," was all he said.

With Josh's help, Burge lifted and rotated the skull. He pushed two fingers into the base of Mark Henning's skull. He then gently placed the head back onto the table. With a heavy sigh he leaned into the switch for the microphone and began to speak.

"We are presented with a well-developed, well-nourished, Caucasian male, appearing younger than the stated age of fifty-eight. He is five feet, eleven inches in height, with a body weight of one hundred and sixty pounds. The body is exceedingly well-toned and has well-developed musculature, especially through the chest, arms, and legs. It would appear that the victim is a highly trained athlete, atypical for the sedentary stated profession of judge. His hair is cut short, brown going to gray. His eyes are hazel and he has a fair complexion with light tanning on the face, hands, and legs from below the shorts line to the ankles.

"The head is normally formed and shows two gunshot wounds to the base of the skull. This presents with a stellate defect measuring 0.6 centimeters with slit-like extensions surrounding the overlapping wounds. By palpating the wound, it appears that the shot came from below, missing the protective shield of the skull and pierced the medulla oblongata. If so, the death would have been instantaneous. There is a high amount of stippling around the wounds with large amounts of soot forced into the entry wound. It would appear there is an exit wound through the left eye socket. This is evidenced by the outward extension of the orbital anterior cavity and absence of iris, cornea, or lens of the left eye. There is an additional minor abrasion to the face, apparently from when the victim fell from the fatal wound. Other than the described wounds, there are no other injuries." Burge pressed against the switch to the microphone, pushing away from the table. "Doctor Young," he said, turning to his intern. "Can you prepare the body for the internal examination?"

"Yes, sir," she said, stepping up to the table. She took a scalpel and made the typical "Y" incision on the chest. As she prepared to open it up, Burge stepped back to the table.

"Wait, Doctor Young," he said. "At this point, the detectives don't need to wait around while we go through the entire procedure. Let me just do the skull, which appears to be the pertinent part of the exam."

"Very well, Doctor," she said as she moved back from the table.

I looked over at my partner. The last time she had witnessed the opening of the skull she had heaved an entire day's worth of coffee and breakfast into the waste can. I stole a look to see how she was handling the thought of hearing the skull pop.

She saw me looking and shook her shoulders, squaring them into attention. But as Dick Burge made the incision around the hairline and peeled back the victim's face in preparation of sawing open the skull, I saw her begin to back slowly away from the table. By the time the saw had cut through the skull and Burge was using the reverse clamps to lift the top of the skull, Melissa was out the door and standing in the hall.

"Oh, hell," he said as he exposed the brain. "Josh, give me my light and magnifier."

With the light fastened to his head, Burge bent in closer to examine the brain. "Oh, hell, Jake, look at this," he said.

Four heads bent in close to look at whatever it was that was distressing the examiner. Josh, the intern, and I were joined by Melissa as we looked closely at what was left of Judge Mark Henning's brain. It had literally been shredded to pulp. The damage was extensive. Burge gently removed the brain from the skull and placed it in the stainless-steel pan that Josh handed to him. We watched as Burge extracted several pieces of slivered metal from what was left of the brain matter. I handed him glycine evidence envelopes and he placed the metal fragments into them. I quickly marked and initialed them as evidence. He removed what looked to be a fragment of a bullet, and I also booked that into evidence.

With the brain removed from the skull pan, we could all see the two distinctive holes which pierced the base of the skull. The holes were tightly placed, with barely a centimeter separating them. Burge once again put his fingers through the holes, speaking as he did so.

"As I said before, from the external examination, it appeared that there were two shots. We now can see that indeed that is true. And, as also suspected, the shots were placed to damage the medulla oblongata." He straightened up and turned to Josh, saying, "Josh, can you tell us why death would have been instantaneous?"

"Yes, sir," Josh answered without hesitation. "The medulla oblongata is the brain stem which then becomes the spinal cord. It is the only part of the brain that is the same in all vertebrates, from reptiles to birds to mammals and humans. It is the part of the brain that is responsible for heartbeat, breathing, and all involuntary functions of the body, including reflexes, coughing, vomiting, sneezing, swallowing, and respiratory functions, as well as digestion. With a wound to this part of the brain, the heart would immediately stop beating and breathing would immediately cease."

"Basic anatomy and physiology," Burge said. "But absolutely correct."

I watched the two women. Melissa's eyes widened, but the intern's expression never changed. I was left to wonder if Doctor Tammy Young was bored by Josh, or just found the basic lesson boring. "Okay," he said, turning to Nancy Henning's body. "Let's get the pertinent part of this done."

He lifted the sheet covering Nancy Henning's body and began the external examination. Again speaking into the microphone, he recorded his external findings.

"We are presented with a slightly undernourished female appearing to be her stated age of fifty-four. The victim is five feet, four inches tall, and weighs 112 pounds. She has dyed auburn hair, going gray at the roots. Her eyes are blue, and there is no apparent facial scarring. There is scarring under both breasts, with what appears to be reconstructive surgery. Slight palpitation of the breast area indicates implants. However, due to the extensive amount of tissue repair, it appears to be reconstructive rather than cosmetic."

Burge again switched off his recorder, turning to the intern. "Why is it important for us to know whether she had reconstructive surgery versus cosmetic, Doctor?" he asked.

The intern's eyes widened. When no answer was forthcoming, the pathologist turned to his long-time technician. "Josh?" he asked.

"It could make a difference as to cause of death," Josh answered. "In some instances the defense in a murder case may wish to know if the victim was near death and wanted to end their own life, especially if they were end-of-life."

"Okay, Doctor Young," Burge said as he again bent over the body. "I want you to look closely at this victim's breast area. Admittedly, there is scarring, but it is minimal considering it appears that both breasts have been reconstructed. Also, look at the symmetrical placement of the implants, they are not too large, and look balanced for the body. As you can also see, the right nipple has also been reconstructed. It appears that the left nipple is intact. All of this indicates to me that this is reconstructive surgery of some sort. I would also guess that it is the work of Dr. Reichner from over in the city of Orange. He is the best reconstructionist around. Always does great work. I understand he was an engineer before becoming a doctor."

"So, why do you think she had the surgery?" Melissa asked.

"Don't know, pretty lady," Burge answered. "Let's open her up and find out."

Quickly the pathologist opened the chest cavity. He pointed out the shattered ribs just over the heart. As expected, the heart had been shredded, just like the brain of her husband. She also had been subjected to two closely spaced, well-placed gunshot wounds. As the medical examiner gently removed her heart, it was clear the heart had been decimated by whatever ammunition the shooter had used. Not only was the heart destroyed and almost unrecognizable, but the lungs were also ripped to ribbons.

"Oh, God," Burge said as he removed the damaged lungs. "Oh, God, oh God, oh God."

"What, Doctor?" Melissa asked.

"Oh, shit," he answered. "It was definitely reconstructive surgery for breast cancer. Look at her lungs. By separating the visceral membrane from the pleural membrane, you can see these hard, yellow, cyst-like growths. It appears that the lungs are filled with them, as is the pleural cavity. Whatever she had on her breasts metastasized to her lungs."

"Cancer?" Melissa asked.

All three medical personnel nodded their heads in unison. Josh stepped over to the body of Nancy Henning and removed her liver. It too was covered the ugly yellow growths, as were her kidneys.

Solemnly the medical examiner recited their findings into his microphone. His voice was devoid of all emotion. Lastly, as he began to inspect the spinal column, he again gasped.

"Shit, shit, shit," he said. "Finish her up, Josh. I'm done. Cause of death gunshot wound to the chest. Immediately fatal." With that he stalked from the autopsy theater.

Josh stepped over to the victim and peered inside. "Oh," he said, stepping back to let the intern see into the cavity.

Doctor Tammy Young took a deep breath, then also stepped away.

"What, Josh?" Melissa asked.

Shaking his head, Josh answered, "it spread to her spine. The cancer metastasized to her bones. She was dying, Melissa."

Melissa gasped. "Oh, my god," she said. "How long?"

"Did she have left?" Josh asked.

Melissa nodded.

Josh just shrugged his shoulders. "Maybe a week, maybe a month," he said. "Every day of her life would have been extremely painful."

"The tox-screen will probably come high for opiates," Tammy added. "In the end-stages like this, when it gets to the bone and lungs like this, it's just question of whether the tumor grows into a blood vessel and she bleeds to death internally, or she expires from an accidental overdose of drugs. Sometimes the pain just wears them down and they give up."

I said nothing during this exchange. Instead I watched as Josh fingered the heart of Nancy Henning. He suddenly stopped his palpitations and held up his hand. Grasped between his fingers was a large fragment of a bullet. It looked like it was large enough for the guys over at the lab to determine caliber and make. I snagged it and booked it into evidence.

He palpitated the heart some more and came up with a second fragment, as well as the same metal shavings found in Mark Henning's brain. I took possession of all of it, marking each of them into separate glycine baggies. I had all that I needed. I didn't want to wait while they finished the last of the protocols, which required them to extract and weigh all of the major organs. It was a time-consuming and tedious part of the autopsy. There was no reason for me to stay until the end. I motioned for my partner to follow me outside.

She nodded her good-byes to Josh and Tammy, who were quickly lost in their task of taking apart the final remains of the judge and his wife.

Outside in the hall we could hear the voice of Burge coming from his office. I held my finger to my lips to silence Melissa as we crept up the hallway.

"Hey, honey," we heard him say in a gentle un-Burge like voice. "Sorry for waking you. Yeah, I know, I know, I can be a real asshole. No, no, I can sleep here tonight, that's not why I called."

There was silence on his end of the phone call, then he continued with something that amazed me. "No, baby, I love you," he said. "I just want you to know that."

Again, silence. Then, "It's late, don't get up. Okay, then, if you insist. I'll see you shortly. Be safe. I love you, honey. Just be safe. Keep the doors locked while you drive."

There was a pause, then he chuckled. "Yeah, yeah, I know you're capable. I just don't want anything to happen to you. Bye, yourself."

Melissa turned to me in wonderment. "I didn't know he had kids," she said.

"He doesn't," I answered.

"Oh?"

All I could do was shrug. My suspicions finally confirmed. The old doctor really did love his wife of thirty years.

Outside of the hospital, Melissa and I checked our watches. It was past one o'clock in the morning. I looked at my partner and could see the light smudges beneath her eyes had taken on a deep purple hue. Her shoulders slumped and exhaustion colored her every movement. In her hand she held the paper bags with the clothing that had been taken from the victims. I had the glycine baggies in my pocket. All of it had to be booked into the evidence locker with instructions for it to be sent to the lab for processing.

I finally took pity on my overworked partner. "Here," I said, extending my hand to her. "Give me the clothing; I'll take it with me to the lab. I'm senior detective on the case; I might as well keep the chain of custody of it."

A grateful smile parted Melissa's lips, showing her plentiful and straight, white teeth. "Thanks, Jake" she said, handing me the bags. "I can leave from here, then?"

"Yeah, go home," I said. "Station is my direction, not yours."

She hesitated a minute, then turned to come back to me. "Hey," she said, "about tomorrow at the courthouse?"

"Yeah?" I said.

"Well, we're supposed to meet them at ten o'clock, right?"

"Ten, ten-thirty, why?"

"My brother has a soccer tournament then," she said, pausing, digging her toe in the concrete sidewalk.

"And?"

"Well, you know, he's been so hard to reach lately," Melissa said, not making eye contact. She paused again, still not looking at me. I looked closely at her, but she avoided my stare. Finally, it dawned on me what she was trying to ask.

"You need to go to that tournament. You need to go for your brother," I said. "I can do the courthouse meeting tomorrow. No sweat. You're just off doing canvassing, or something."

A deep sigh escaped from her chest. I realized she had been holding her breath. We both knew the next forty-eight hours were supposedly critical in finding the killer, but her taking some time to see her troubled brother's soccer game was definitely important. It wasn't going to impact the investigation all that much to have just me go to the courthouse. I had no qualms about her request, and admired her desire to keep on top of her family issues. More importantly, as a detective I knew that sometimes an investigation took its own sweet time to develop. I didn't need either my partner or myself falling down dead from exhaustion. My creed was to let things develop as they will. No need to push until there's a clear direction to go.

I spoke again to her, "Just go, Melissa. Family sometimes has got to come first. I'll cover for you. Just stay in touch, got it?"

This time she smiled. "So," she said, "can I meet up with you when the daughter gets in?"

"Yeah, meet me at the station after the game," I said.

With that, we said our good-byes, each heading home to catch a few hours of sleep before hitting it hard the next day.

CHAPTER FIVE

I wish I could say it was my eagerness to solve the new set of murders that awoke me the next morning, but it wasn't. Instead, it was the team efforts of Cisco and Mandy that got me up and going.

Cisco started head-butting me, purring incessantly in my ear, with his whiskers tickling my face. When I turned away from him, Mandy came to that side of the bed and snuffled softly, but insistently.

"Go away, both of you!"

Neither one moved.

"Leave me alone. Go bug the girls. They love you more than I do."

I opened one eye, staring into the soft brown eyes of my dog. She gently wagged her tail, then smiled, her tongue lolling out the side of her mouth. I couldn't resist.

"Fine, I'm up!"

Quickly I went through the morning routine of feeding the two animals, then opening the front door of my apartment to let them out. Cisco bolted down the flagstone stairs, but Mandy stayed to wiggle around my legs, while rolling her eyes to her leash hanging on a hook next to the door.

"Don't have time today, girl," I said. "Got to get to the courthouse for a search."

Mandy lowered her head, but kept wagging her tail. Finally, I took the leash from the hook, folded it over on itself several times and placed it in her mouth.

"Here, ask one of the girls," I said.

The dog took the leash and wagged her way down the stairs, disappearing from sight. I felt a slight shudder of guilt, but shook it off quickly, knowing I had work to do, and it was already eight-forty-five. The ten o'clock meeting was looming.

Exactly thirty-five minutes later I was out the door, coffee travel mug in hand.

In an ironic shift of fate, it was the reverse of the trip I had made earlier in the morning, since University Hospital was next door to the courthouse and the judge's chambers. Traffic was light that Saturday morning as I traversed the city streets up through Costa Mesa and over to Santa Ana. I made the trip with some time to spare.

The door to the courthouse was locked, but I was met by a security officer who opened the door for me to enter. He escorted me to the fourth floor to the judge's courtroom and chambers.

I was shocked at how small the courtroom was. In a very compact area it held only the judge's bench, an attached clerk's desk, a small area in the "well" for the court reporter, with the two counsel tables less than six feet from the judge's bench, and a small desk for the bailiff off to one side. A small arc of theater chairs in two rows spread on either side of the bar separating the gallery from the area in front of the bench. Missing from the setup was the usual area for a jury box. Obviously, the courtroom was designed for the business of tearing families apart, not for seeking justice from a jury.

The presiding judge met me at the doorway leading to the back hallway. He was dressed in pale green slacks and a short-sleeved knit golf shirt. He, too, was freshly shaved and showered, with his hair still slightly wet. Tiptoeing several feet behind him was a woman with tear streaks criss-crossing her face. She was in her late thirties or early forties, slender, about five feet, seven inches tall. Her pale brown hair was pulled back into a ponytail at the base of her neck, and she was dressed casually in jeans with a sweatshirt.

"This is Beverly Anderson, Judge Henning's clerk," the man said, pulling the clerk by her arm toward me. "She will be your liaison for this court. Also, she will compile any of Mark's cases that may be problematic. She'll can explain why they may, or may not, be relevant."

I nodded toward the clerk, who began to silently weep. Turning back to the presiding judge I asked, "Anything I should be careful of?"

"You mean publicity-wise?"

"No, my department isn't releasing any info right away. I thought we agreed," I said. "I mean that may be overly sensitive?"

Beverly swiped at her nose with a Kleenex and answered. "The judge left two of his most complex cases on his desk in his chambers.

He must have stayed late last night to work on them. One of them may be something you should look at, and I will go back through my notes to see if there are any others that could relate to his death. But, you know, any one of these family law cases could be involved."

"Oh?"

The presiding judge jumped in before the clerk could answer. "We gave Mark Henning some of our more difficult cases. As you know there is great wealth here in this county. Great power, too. When people are fighting over money, tempers can get roused, and sometimes because of that power, people forget that they are subject to the same laws as everyone else. They become used to—hmm, let's say—they become used to bending the law to their own purposes."

I nodded, well aware of the peculiarities of the extremely wealthy regarding law as something to be used in their favor, or ignored when it didn't suit them.

"You also are aware that none of this should be made public," he said.

"Hmm, any special reason?" I asked.

"Some of the parties are involved in business dealings that if they were made public could damage those businesses."

"Kinda like the McCourts in Los Angeles?" I asked, thinking of the owners of the Los Angeles team recently involved in a bitter divorce.

"Exactly. We don't want the tabloids combing through our files for fodder for their rags," he said with a snort.

"Gotcha."

"So we don't want this stuff leaked now that the judge is dead. It may give crazies ideas about how to handle their cases by threatening the judge. Worse yet, the attorneys might take this chance to start a rash of judge shopping. So the ugliness of publicity is only a partial concern," he said. "So keep it close, okay?"

"Got it."

"Now listen, Swanson," the judge said, becoming more earnest. "The death of a judge, any judge, is very unsettling to the bench as a whole. But to have a family law judge killed—well, that is something we just can't have, you understand?"

I didn't really, but I elected to say nothing.

"Family law is a terrible, terrible assignment," he said. "Judges do anything to keep from having to sit in this court. That's why we have so many commissioners. They're former family law attorneys who want the county retirement and benefits. So we hire them and keep them here. They know that going in."

"Okay, so why so unpopular?" I asked.

"It is the worst," he answered. "This courthouse is filled with es-sentially good people behaving very badly. They hate each other, hate the system, and hate losing to someone they dislike enough to shatter their financial security. As we say in the Courthouse, you know you've done a good job when everyone leaves here hating you equally."

"Knowing that, how's the security around these judges?" I asked.

"Exceptional," he answered. "We have a special branch of security funded by the State. They evaluate every threatening letter that comes to this court."

"Any I should know about?"

"My security analyst will be here shortly," the judge answered. "In the meantime, Beverly here will brief you on the judge's cases that he had under submission."

With that, the judge turned away from me and went through a door into a hallway behind the courtroom. I took it to mean we should follow him.

The three of us entered a very small room that held a desk, a small leather love seat, two chairs, a file cabinet, and numerous bookcases. There were several files stacked on the floor, and most of the space on the bookcases was not covered with law books, but rather with soft-backed reference books and notebooks from various conferences. There was an absence of any personal photographs of his wife, or their children or even the grandchildren. The small office was crowded and seemed to be not overly organized. It was not a comfortable space, and not reminiscent of judge's chambers I had frequented at the old courthouse in Santa Ana or the new courthouse in Newport Beach.

"Small?" I said.

"Everything here is small," the judge answered. "It was designed and built at a time when we needed the square footage for courtrooms, not egos."

I stood for a moment taking it all in. My impression was of a man not willing to put his personal touch on the area. It seemed devoid of any emotional energy other than overwork, completely different than his personal home that was filled with family and love.

Beverly, the clerk walked behind the judge's desk and heaved a file from off the bookcase beneath the windows, placing it facing the presiding judge and me. The case was several volumes thick and held together with large rubber bands.

"This file is probably the most problematic," she said.

"Oh?"

"Have you heard of the Cheneys?" she asked.

"The land-developer who did all those apartments and a mall in South County?" I answered.

"Yes, him," she said. "He has a daughter, Bridget Cheney McAllister. She married an L.A. cop. It's an ugly divorce with allegations of domestic violence and requested restraining orders."

"Requested... not issued?" I asked. "File's pretty thick for no orders."

"That's the point," the judge said, jumping into our conversation. "This case has already burned through over a hundred thousand dollars of billable attorney time. Old-man Cheney wants the soon-to-be-former son-in-law out of Bridget's life and no contact with the child."

"Pretty harsh, isn't?

"Old-man Cheney would see John McAllister dead if he wasn't a cop," the judge answered. "He always thought the kid was never reason enough for his daughter to have married the man in the first place. Worse yet, she did it without a pre-nupt."

"Ouch."

"How about the son-in-law?" I asked. "Is he a problem? Any real threats or anything?"

The judge turned to Beverly, "You answer, that, okay? You'd know better than me. Everything I got was thirdhand at the club. According to Old-man Cheney, the hoped-he-was-gone former son-in-law was a hothead and quick with cutting remarks. Cheney is convinced that behind closed doors McAllister was also quick with his fists. But, then, who knows. I sure don't, and Judge Henning was very tight-lipped about the case, knowing of my connection to the old man through the club." Looking at his watch he went on to say, "Speaking of the club, I have a tee time I can't miss. The other three of our foursome gets cranky if one of us misses, especially since it's Monarch we're playing today."

I would have been stunned at the cavalier way he handled the situation, but I also knew Monarch Golf Course was extremely expensive, and it was extremely hard to get a tee time. I probably would have chosen to play the gorgeous golf course over a dead body, too.

"Beverly," he said, as he stood up to leave. "You handle the rest. Remember, no files leave the Courthouse, got it?"

"Yes, sir," she said. "I know. I'll copy whatever the detective wants."

"All right, then, Swanson, I'll hear from you as soon as you get something?" he said, not really asking it as a question.

"Sure," I said. "I know the Chief will keep you appraised."

With the presiding judge gone, Beverly slumped into the chair behind the desk. She began to cry softly. I shuffled my feet a little, not knowing what to say.

Finally, she stopped, blew her nose, and looked at me. "I was very rude to Mark the night he died. The last thing he saw was me flipping him off."

"Okay, why?" I asked, thinking it was not typical behavior from a clerk to a judge, no matter how friendly, or hostile, the relationship.

"Man," she said, heat coloring her voice. "It was after four-thirty, and I had a date that night. I needed to leave and he was taking his time to finish a case. It just pissed me off that he knew I had to leave, yet he let those two people keep yammering on and on, about nothing."

"He do that often?"

Beverly sighed deeply, lowering her head. "Yes, all the time," she answered. "He thought the least we could do is listen to people who were having their lives destroyed. He was especially kind to parties representing themselves, you know, the pro-pers. Mark thought it was tough to go through the system when people couldn't afford an attorney. So he made sure to take extra time with them."

"This unusual?" I asked, thinking back on my own two divorces.

The first one I fought. I went to every court appearance and spent a shitload of money on an attorney. Still, I ended up with most of the bills and she got everything else, except a portion of my retirement. With the second divorce, my then-wife made more than I did, had more to lose than me, so I let her do the fighting. I stayed home and let the judge have his way with me. Again I ended up with all of the bills, but my pension intact. The only difference was I didn't have the bills for the lawyer.

"Very," she answered. "Well, then, why did he have a problem with the Cheney divorce?" I asked.

"Mark didn't think there had been any violence toward either Bridget or the child," she said. "I also think Bridget didn't really want the divorce, but rather Daddy did."

"So why the applications for the D.V. restraining orders?" I asked.

"Because Daddy wanted to destroy John McAllister," she answered matter-of-factly. "If the Domestic Violence Restraining Orders were issued, then John McAllister would lose his ability to carry a gun. If he couldn't carry a gun, he couldn't work the streets. If he couldn't work the streets, he was done as a cop."

I knew all of that. I had been witness to too many of my fellow cops being hit with restraining orders as an opening salvo in the divorce actions. Tough thing was, some of the guys deserved to have them issued, but many times they did not. Somewhere along the line women had learned through their grapevine that the best way to get livable temporary orders was to allege domestic violence. That accomplished two things: it got the husband out of the house, and it kept him from seeing the kids. Because child support was based on the time-share split, the less the husband saw his kids, the more money he had to pay in support. I believed that if the Legislature ever changed that ratio, the D.V. filings would go way down.

"So, okay, can I take this file to read?"

The clerk looked startled, then smiled. "Oh you, you tease," she said. "You heard the P. J.: none of the originals leave the Courthouse. But, I'll make copies."

I looked at the case sitting on the judge's desk. With all of the folders stacked on top of the other, it was almost 18 inches high.

"You going to do that now?" I asked.

"Sure," she answered. "We have a high-speed copier in the clerk's office. It will take me about an hour, but Mick is supposed to be here soon. He'll keep you entertained while I copy these."

I waited for the court security officer while Beverly Anderson left to go copy the large McAllister/Cheney file. I couldn't help but wonder why a person would want to spend their days listening to the travails and waste that comes from the breakup of a marriage. Nothing could be more soul depleting than watching people who once loved each other enough to promise to spend their lives together, turn on each other like a pack of jackals.

Spiraling deep into a depression, my revelry was broken by the sound of the courtroom doors swinging open then banging shut. I looked up to see a roundish, balding man dressed in khakis and a madras plaid, button-down, cotton shirt. He had a slight sheen of sweat dappling his face and his breath was slightly labored.

"Hey, Beverly, I'm here!" he said, apparently not noticing me sitting slightly off to the side of the doors. I squinted my eyes at the sound of the very familiar voice. Then it hit me: It was Mick Jeperson.

He retired from the local city of Irvine. He had retired early after stress almost caused him to eat his gun.

"Hey, yourself, white boy," I said. "Remember me, Jake Swanson, Newport P.D."

"Of, course, Jake Swanson," Mick answered, turning toward me, taking my outstretched hand and pumping my hand furiously. "It's been a while. How's your mother?"

Unexpected pain stabbed my gut. My mother wasn't necessarily my favorite person when she was alive, but with her passing, I realized how much I missed her.

I shrugged my shoulders at him, answering, "It has been a while. Mom died a few years ago; complications during surgery."

"Sorry to hear that, son," the retired cop said.

Trying desperately to change the subject, I asked about his new gig as security for the courthouse.

According to Mick it was an easy job he picked up after he retired because of injuries from a work-related accident. Mainly he read all the incoming mail personally addressed to the judges. It was his job to evaluate any possible threats aimed at them. If the threats appeared to be serious, he referred the letters and threats to the state police for follow-up.

"So, I understand you're supposed to brief me on any of the potential threats facing Mark Henning," I said.

"There's really not much, other than the usual stuff addressed to family law judges and their minions," Mick said. "I tried to pull together the stuff addressed to him after the P. J. called and said a detective would be coming in to look at the mail and stuff."

"Any of it credible?" I asked.

"Like I said, it is just the usual angry spouse shit," Mick answered. "There was one or two letters that I sent on to the State Police. But we didn't hear anything back on those."

Mick pulled a cotton handkerchief from his pocket and wiped his forehead. Heaving a large sigh, he settled himself into the chair in front of me and swung around to look at me.

"Jake," he said, sighing, "do you think we missed something? I mean, damn, Henning was one of the good guys around here. He didn't shirk work like too many of the rest of these bozos."

This started a long discourse by Mick about the various judges and commissioners assigned to the family law courts. He didn't have a high regard for most of them, with the exception of Mark Henning. He considered the deceased judge to be a prince among judges. In fact, the retired cop thought the judge should be in the criminal courts building, even though he was a former criminal defense lawyer.

Mick stopped his rambling about the pros and cons of the various judges with a startled look on his face. "Oh, my God, Jake," he said, "I just remembered a letter I thought was important enough to give to Henning and the D.A. investigators over at the Harbor Court in Newport Beach."

"Why's that?"

"Well, he's that Mark Henning, right?" Mick said. "He's that high-priced lawyer who defended a slew of CEOs during the bank melt-down and before that the electricity traders?"

"Yeah, I remember him from some of my cases. Bright guy, but pretty much out of the league of most of my mopes and thugs."

"Yeah, well a letter came addressed to him from behind bars. Turns out that the woman writing was his client for a time. She was convict-ed of murdering her husband. Case just got overturned on appeal, and she's out or getting out."

"You'd think she'd be happy?" I said, more as a question than statement.

"Yeah, well she blames Henning and Teddy Lawrence for the years she lost behind that conviction."

"You mean Teddy Lawrence, the supervising D.A.?" I asked think-ing of the hard-charging guy I had known for almost as long as I had been a cop.

"Yeah, him," Mick said, rubbing his chin, and taking another swipe with his handkerchief. "He evidently was the prosecutor on the case and she said she 'wanted to talk to him about making her whole' again."

"That just sounds like a lawsuit, not a threat," I answered.

"Yeah, except she included a drawing of a knife in the letter."

"Hmm, puts a little different spin on it," I said, almost laughing. "What she going to do, cut him with a paper?"

"Man, listen, I don't know," Mick said. "I showed it to Henning and he didn't seem too concerned, and I never heard back from the

D.A.'s office. So, I just don't know."

Just as Mick was finishing his statement, Beverly came back in carrying two brown expanding folders.

"Hi, Mick," she said, handing me the folders. "You have anything for the detective?"

"You know, not much other than the usual," Mick answered, sweat still glistening on his forehead.

The court clerk just shrugged and looked at her watch. I took the hint and said I would be in touch if anything came up. We exchanged cards and I excused myself, leaving the security guard and clerk to discuss the tragic death. I had people to meet and, with it almost noon, I needed to eat.

CHAPTER SIX

After leaving the Lamureaux Family Law Courts, I was headed back to the station when the call came in. It was my partner, Melissa Sanchez, looking for my ETA at the station. I winced thinking it would be impolite to stop and eat if she hadn't. But, then, my dislike at having a monitor, even if she was my partner, took over and I told her I was running late—late enough to grab a bite at my favorite taco stand on Bristol, in Santa Ana. It was on the way to the station, and the ladies at the taco stand knew I always needed extra meat and the spicy salsa. It gave them giggling fits as they marveled at my gringo ability to handle the extra spice.

Strolling into the station a little later than I had originally expected, I was met at the door by my very irate partner. She grabbed my sleeve and pulled me into the bullpen, hissing through her teeth.

"Damn it, Jake," she said, "the daughter is here, with her husband, Jake. The lawyer husband, Jake."

"Ooo, three 'Jakes' in one sentence, Sanchez. What's the matter, the lawyer got you scared, Sanchez?"

My partner rolled her eyes at me and tossed her long dark brown hair. Her 'hrrump' was loud and long as I sauntered past her to my desk to pick up my notes.

"Did the warrant come in?" I asked.

Melissa pulled it out from the file folder she was holding, and snapped it at me, doing the pouty-lip thing. I read it carefully before I lifted my eyes to look at her.

"Looks good," I said. "Shall we meet the lovely couple?"

Cindy and Charles McDermott were in the larger, more formal conference room across from the chief's office. Because of the glass wall fronting the hallway, I was able to take a moment to study the two of them before entering.

Cindy, the older daughter of Mark and Nancy Henning, was in a chair facing me. With her head down, her bob-cut thick brown hair with reddish undertones was shielding her face. Her hands were folded in her lap grasping something that was hidden by the table. I couldn't judge her height, but her husband was large, as well as tall. He paced the conference room with his back to me. But, even without seeing his face, I could read consternation in his step. He had his hands in his pocket, presumably jiggling his keys, and he exaggerated each step as he walked. On his return trip back toward me, he saw me, but stared right through me. As I entered, I saw him take a deep breath, as he reached out to take my hand. Melissa was a few steps behind me and missed the extra pressure he exerted in the grip.

"You are Detective Swanson, I assume?" he said, before I could introduce myself.

I knew the type. He was the kind that was going to take control and would fight me for it if I resisted. I decided the best course of action was to just let him run the show. The bodies would still be cold, and his wife's grief would not be abated by our silly games. Yes, just let him take control if it would give him some comfort.

"Yes," I answered as I extricated my hand from his grip. "This is my partner, Detective Sanchez."

Melissa only nodded and moved to the side of the table where the grieving daughter sat.

"This is my wife, Cindy McDermott, the daughter of the deceased," he said, gesturing to the woman sitting at the table.

Cindy heaved a sob at her husband's word choice and lifted her hands from beneath the table. As expected, a Kleenex was clutched tightly in her fingers.

Melissa bent down to surround the woman's shoulders in a hug, and spoke softly to her.

Consternation etched into Charles McDermott's face even more strongly. "As you see, my wife is upset. Have you heard from her sister?"

"As a matter of fact, she's due into John Wayne Airport about now," I answered. "I have sent a uniform over to pick her up and bring her here."

The man heaved a sigh, and turned to his wife. "I guess that squelches any chance of me taking the car home. You know we have that dinner tonight and, while I expect the others will understand if you remain here, I really need to get back to Santa Barbara."

The grieving wife clenched the tissue even tighter and grimaced at her husband. "Mother's car will be in the garage," she said. "Lauren and I can use it. I hate Daddy's car, but Mom's should be okay."

I was momentarily taken aback. It was unusual for a surviving kin to assume a murder victim's car would be available for them to use. I needed to take control back from Charles. The Mercedes parked in the garage was part of the crime scene and couldn't be moved until we got the okay from the crime scene guys.

"Sorry, Mr. McDermott, but I can't release the car that was in the garage, yet. We need to keep the scene intact."

The glare was instantaneous. "You do have the warrant, correct?" he said, making the point with his voice and body language that he was still the alpha dog in the room.

I pulled the signed warrant from my folder and handed him a copy without saying a word.

"But this is a copy," Charles said, looking at the warrant. "Where is the original?"

"I have to keep the original in my possession," I said, trying not to act smug. "But you are more than welcome to look at it."

"Oh, Charles, why do you have to be such a dick?" Cindy suddenly said, rising from her seat. "I am sure the detective has done everything right. You have, haven't you detective?"

"Of course," Melissa chimed in before I could answer. "Your father is a very important man in this county."

"My father, my father, my father!" the daughter stormed. "Doesn't anyone care about my mother? For everything my father was, my mother was the saint."

Both Melissa and I were momentarily stunned into silence.

Charles McDermott immediately crossed over to his wife and took her into his bear-like arms. "Of course we care about Nancy," he crooned. "I know that the detectives care deeply about your mother. She was a saint, and we all care."

I looked over at my partner to catch her eye. She shrugged at me, and a slight smile played at her lips.

The family tableau was broken by the arrival of a uniformed officer and a heavily pregnant young woman. He set her suitcase down just inside the conference room door and nodded to me.

"This is Lauren Hill, as requested," he said, as he bowed out of the room.

I would have liked to bow out myself. The tension in the room spiked up at least another ten degrees when the newly arrived sister air-kissed her brother-in-law as she crossed the room to fold her distraught sister into her arms.

"Cindy, Cindy, Cindy," she said, smoothing the other sister's hair. "I can't believe it. Mom and Dad are dead! How could they?"

At that, both sisters began the silent weepy thing that women of good breeding do when their grief overwhelms them. Their shoulders shook in wrenching sobs, but no sounds came from either of them. They clutched each other tightly, until Lauren finally staggered away and fell into a chair. She gasped a few times, pushing on her distended belly trying to catch her breath.

Melissa stood off to one side of the room watching, not saying a word. The husband clasped and unclasped his hands, finally settling on wringing them tightly in front of him. He shuffled his feet a few more times before saying anything.

He cleared his throat and turned to me, "Detective, the sisters are not suspects, are they?"

I shook my head in the negative.

"Well, if they're not suspects, do they need to have an attorney present?"

I stopped short of rolling my eyes and answered, "They are not suspects. Their alibis, if that is what you want to call it, are firmly established. What I need from them is a sense of who their parents were. If I know who their parents were, and who their friends and associates were, then I can get a better idea of where the investigation should go. Hopefully, it will take me to the killer or killers."

Cindy looked up at me, her eyes rimmed in red. "You keep using the past tense," she said. "It sounds so final."

Lauren took her sister's hand and answered for me. "It is final. They are gone. Just gone. . ."

I took a moment to look at the younger sister. She was probably about five feet, four inches tall. Before her pregnancy I was sure she had been very slim. She had burnished red/blonde hair caught up into a long ponytail. Her eyes were hazel, almost green in appearance, and freckles were splattered across her nose. She looked too young to be married, much less pregnant.

Again Charles McDermott shuffled his feet and cleared his throat. "Dear," he said, a little more gently that time. "Are you okay for me to leave you? I mean, we did leave the children with Juanita, and I hate to impose on her for any length of time."

"You mean you need to go to your stupid dinner meeting, don't you?" Cindy answered, not even bothering to glint her eyes at him.

"Well, yes, of course I do," he answered. "The detective said I wasn't needed here, so I thought if nothing else we could rent a car for you and your sister, and let me get back on the road." Turning back to me, he said, "I imagine the bodies won't be released for a funeral for a while, am I correct?"

I looked hard at the bull of a man standing in front of me. I knew he said he was a real estate lawyer, but did he not know what an insensitive clod he was? Even as careless I was with other's feelings, I knew a wife shouldn't be left alone after a parent's death. I did a mental shuffle in my head and decided not to add fuel to the domestic heat between the husband and wife.

"I don't image they will," I answered. "I will let you know in enough time for you to make arrangements for a funeral."

As I spoke those words, Cindy again broke down and began to cry. I thought for a moment she would turn on her husband again, but he silently withdrew from the room. I followed him out the door.

"Er, Detective," he said, his shoulder slumping. "Look, I know I seem insensitive not staying with my wife, but I have to be back in Santa Barbara. It is my livelihood. Is there anyone who can help her get a car?"

I gestured toward my partner with my chin. "I'll have Detective Sanchez help them out if I can't get the Mercedes released to them."

The man took my hand and pumped it a few times. This grasp was firm, but not tight. He nodded his head and left.

Back inside the conference room the three women sat speaking softly to each other. The two sisters each had their heads bowed, and Melissa was speaking to them. The all looked up when I entered.

"Charles gone?" Cindy asked.

"Yes, but he asked me to help with getting you a car," I answered. "I told him Detective Sanchez will help."

All three nodded in agreement, then sat silently looking at me. Meeting their eyes, I felt the weight of the responsibility of solving the parents' death come to rest firmly on my shoulders.

"Ladies, I really need to speak with you about your parents. I imagine you are hungry, and we can stop and get a bite to eat, or I can order in here at the station. What would you like to do?"

Lauren, without hesitation answered, "Please, Detective, can we go to the house. At least there I can put my feet up, and wash my face. It's been a long night."

Sanchez and I looked at each other. It was unusual for survivors to want to go back into a house that was a crime scene. In fact, in my years of experience I had never had such a request until long after cleaning crews had decontaminated the areas. Many times they never went back. I was momentarily stunned into inaction.

But, as usual in these kinds of dicey situations, my partner was quick on the uptake. "Ladies, normally we can't let you back into an area that is a designated crime scene until after it has been released by the technicians from the lab and the lead detective. I can call and see if the techs are finished, and I am sure my partner can figure out a way to get you back into the house, if that is what you really want to do."

"Lauren, are you crazy?" Cindy asked her sister. "Do you really want to go back to the house after everything that has happened there?"

Lauren heaved a sigh, and smiled a tired look in her direction. "Cindy, the worst has happened. Whether it's now or later, we have to go back. I am sure the Detective needs to go through the house, and wouldn't you rather be there when he does? Do you really want him going through Mom and Dad's things without us there?"

Cindy began that silent cry again, but finally looked at me, then Melissa, and shrugged her shoulders. "No, you're right, I guess. It makes more sense for us to go with them if they're really going to search the house. Maybe we can help them and explain whatever they find."

Of course! That was my way out. I would use the excuse that because there was a locked door, with presumably sensitive material behind the door, I needed the daughters' help explaining whatever we found. What better way to handle a search than with the two who knew the most about the victims?

"Makes sense to me," I said. "The really sensitive part of the scene appears to be the garage and the driveway—nothing else appeared to be disturbed—so it only makes sense for you to accompany us while we search. You know your parents the best of anyone."

I nodded toward my partner, who gathered up her file. I helped the pregnant sister to her feet and, without any more discussion, we all left the station together.

CHAPTER SEVEN

The streets were unusually clear of traffic. Given the balmy weather on that Saturday afternoon I would have expected more out-of-town beachgoers. Without the tragedy, the ride over to the house would have been pleasant. Lauren sat in the front seat with me in the Intrepid, stoic in her silence, though pushing on her swollen belly radiating discomfort, while Cindy sat in back, softly crying into a tissue. The ride was tense at best. Thank God it took less than five minutes. I was glad Melissa followed us to the house in the Stratus; three unhappy women in one car would have been more than I could stand.

When we arrived at the Henning home, wisps of yellow crime scene tape still fluttered in the sea breeze. A single uniformed officer waited in his patrol car at the base of the driveway. When we pulled up next to him, I introduced myself to him and to the women in my car. He jotted a few notes on a clipboard and waved us to park on the street. Although the crime scene technicians were through with their work, they did not want cars pulling up the driveway.

I pulled over to the side of the street, and Melissa did a quick U-turn to park on the other side. Looking at Lauren, I was afraid the slope of the driveway was too steep, but she took my arm to keep from sliding backward and march onward up to the house. Her step was steady as she fixed her eyes fixed on the front door. Cindy gave a slight gasp as she passed the deep red stain on the driveway. The Porsche was gone, and the garage door was closed, leaving the house to look peaceful.

Approaching the front door I had a moment of panic. I didn't have a key to the door, and I wasn't sure who would have thought to get one. But no sooner did I have that thought than Lauren pulled a set of keys from her purse. Without saying a word, she opened the door to her childhood home.

"Stop," Melissa said. "Your shoes—you need to remove your shoes."

"It's okay, Sanchez," I said. "The crime lab is gone. They have collected all the evidence they can, except from the locked rooms. If we find anything when we search those rooms, I will call them back out." Hearing her intake of breath I reconsidered and added, "But, maybe Melissa is right. If you don't mind, before you enter any of the locked room, we need you to put on the booties and gloves."

With a slight sniff, Melissa lifted her eyebrow at me as she snapped on her gloves. I sniffed back and pulled a pair of gloves from my jacket pocket.

"Do we really need those?" Cindy asked, turning away from the proffered gloves.

I paused a moment, looked over at my partner, then back at the overwrought and overly anxious woman standing in front of me. "Not really," I finally answered, deciding the fight wasn't worth the effort. "I guess, in the final analysis, you belong here. If you touch anything, your prints are expected. I doubt there is much here you haven't touched."

Melissa helped Lauren put the paper booties over her shoes, then guided her into the house. With a wan smile she headed for the large chair in the great room. Kicking off her shoes and the booties she sank gratefully into the chair. "Okay, Detective, now we can talk," she said.

"Your father had a fully pressed uniform in his closet," I said to no one in particular. "And there is a locked door to one of the rooms. Do either of you know about that?"

Cindy glared at me and shrugged her shoulders. Lauren sighed and answered. "Daddy is an officer in the Naval Reserves. He has to drill every month. This must have been his weekend to drill."

Cindy again sniffed and glared at the wall as she crossed the room and flung herself onto the overstuffed couch. "Yes, his precious Naval Reserves. His precious Navy. You'd have thought he'd outgrown it by now!"

Lauren shook her head at her sister and turned her attention back to me. "As you can see, my sister doesn't approve of my father's involvement with the Navy."

"Why's that?" Melissa asked, moving over to take a seat next to Cindy.

"Because Mother was dying!" Cindy flared.

"Cancer," I said. "She had cancer."

"Yes, she had cancer, and Daddy knew she was dying, yet he chose to leave her at this critical time!" Cindy said, starting to cry again. "Mommy, oh Mommy, why did you have to die? Why, why, why?"

Lauren started to struggle to her feet, but her apparent exhaustion and the depth of the chair held her firmly prisoner, leaving it to Melissa to soothe the crying woman.

"He didn't have a choice, Cindy," Lauren finally said. "You know that. Daddy had to go. He wasn't old enough to retire — once an officer, always an officer."

"You'd know all about that, wouldn't you?" Cindy cried. "Look at you. When are you due? A week, two weeks? Less? more? Yet where is your husband? He's gone, too, just like Daddy!"

"Tim doesn't have a choice. You know that. With all that's going on in the Mid-East, his ship was sent and he had to go."

I expected some sort of searing remark about Cindy's husband leaving her alone, yet Lauren made no reference to Charles's absence. Of the two women, the younger daughter was definitely the stronger.

Melissa, usually the more patient of the two of us, took a deep breath and stood up. Her posture told me she had no desire to be involved in more family disputes. She looked at me, and her message was clear: "Let's get this show on the road."

"So, ladies," I started, "do either of you have a key to the locked room down the hall?'

Both shook their heads in the negative. I started down the hallway to the locked door when the door open on its own and a tall, blonde man walked out carrying a rolled paper.

"What the hell?" I said, taking a step back. "Just who the hell are you, and who let you in?"

The man started to reach toward his back and before I could say or do anything, Melissa had her gun drawn and was shouting, "Don't move! Don't you move! Just keep your hands where I can see them!"

The man slowly brought his hand back around to the front of him as a wide grin split his face. "Well, ya'll, I guess the lady means business. Let me reach for my wallet, and I'll get my ID for you, okay?"

"Don't you move, mister," Melissa said again, her tone threatening. "My partner will come along back of you and get whatever you've got back there."

The man froze, but his smile never wavered. I moved quickly to his side, swearing under my breath that I had not thought to reach for my gun. I found his wallet in his back pocket and withdrew it. Flipping it open I found a badge and identification calling him out to be Andre Robinson, Naval Criminal Investigative Services."NCIS, huh? What kind of crap is this? What are you doing here? I thought you guys were just on TV," I said, taking another look at the badge before flipping it back to him.

He looked over at me and his grin got wider, as he turned his badge to look at it. "Hmm, maybe ya'll are right. Let me look at that badge again. I thought it was the real deal. Maybe I was mistaken in my believing it was real and all. I mean, it did come in the mail, and hmm, you know, I could be wrong, ya'll. Besides, I'm just here investigating to see if Navy personnel violated any protocols and to secure any Navy documents. You mean that there badge doesn't cover that?"

"Ha, ha," I said, not thinking his joke was funny, and his Texas draw irritating the shit out of me. "You still didn't answer my question on how you got in and who let you in."

"Evidently, ya'll haven't spoken to your chief recently," he answered. "Mark Henning is a dead naval officer and, until we're sure it's not related to his service, I guess we're involved."

I felt my blood pressure to go through the roof. Just like that idiot chief of ours to allow another agency to tap dance all over my stage and not bother to tell me until I bump into him. Damn, the chief.

"That still doesn't answer the question of how you got in here and how you got into the locked door," I said trying to save some face. "More importantly, what do you have in your hand?"

"I came in the sliding glass door from the patio that someone left open, and I opened the office door with a slight twist of my wrist," he answered.

Melissa bent to look at the door and whistled through her teeth. "Slight twist of your wrist, huh? That lock is broken!"

"Yeah," he said, turning to smile at her. "I guess they don't make locks like they used to, do they?" While we three investigative types were trying to throw our respective weight around, the two sisters entered the room behind the locked door. It was only when I heard Lauren's cry that I turned to follow her into the room.

"Oh, Daddy," Lauren cried, sinking to the floor sobbing.

Cindy crossed over to her and patted her on the back, then settled onto the floor with her.

The room was carpeted in thick beige carpet. Along one side of the room were custom bookshelves housing numerous books and notebooks. There was a large, executive oak desk in the middle of the room, and behind it was a credenza with a two drawer lateral file cabinet. A cork board hung on the wall with a faded spot about the size of the rolled sheet of paper the NCIS guy held in his hand.

"Okay," I said, trying to use my most authoritative voice, "whadda ya got in your hand?"

"This?" he said, extending his empty hand. "Why nothing, sir."

"Again, ha, ha!" I answered. "You can't remove evidence from the scene, or didn't the Chief tell you that?"

"Didn't ask," he answered.

While Cindy and Lauren sat transfixed watching us men argue, Melissa crossed over and grabbed the roll from the man's hand.

"Hey, you can't have that!" he shouted at her.

But by then she had flipped the roll open and exposed a map of the world. It looked yellowed with age, and had numerous holes in it, presumably from the pins that were stuck on the cork board.

"It's just a map," Melissa said.

"Yeah, it's just a map," Robinson said.

"No, it's not 'just a map,'" I said. "Otherwise, you wouldn't be skulking around here removing it from the scene. So, until someone else with higher authority than you tells me to give it back, it's mine now."

Lauren got up and came over to the map I was holding and pulled it around so she could look at it. She turned back to me and told me it was her father's strategic planning map. She had spent many hours in this office while her father placed pins in the map and educated her about strategic movement of troops and assets. Her husband also had one he used when plotting war exercises; but, without the pins, it was probably useless.

"So why's this clown want it?" I asked no one in particular. But when no clown answered, I decided to keep it.

The man named Andre Robinson slumped against the door jamb of the room, saying nothing as he watched us. I took a moment to look at him and wasn't sure I liked what I saw. He affected the attitude of someone who was way too confident in his exaggerated pose. He was dressed in pressed black slacks, a white-collared T-shirt, and black loafers. His hair was cut military short, and light blue eyes blazed back at me through his lowered lids. A slight smile played around his lips. I judged him to be about my height of six feet, two inches, and his build was definitely athletic. He gave me a lazy grin, and I slanted my eyes back at him as I felt him take my measure.

While we two men were staring down each other, Melissa had holstered her weapon and was beginning a systematic search of the office area. She started with the desk and jimmied the middle drawer open, and then found the latch to unlock the lower file drawer. As she started to withdraw files, Andre quickly crossed the room and put a hand out to stop her.

"You aren't authorized to take those," he said, covering her hand with his.

I heard a quick intake of breath from her as she withdrew her hand. Instead of the anticipated scowl, like she always gave me, a quizzical look crossed her face. Just as quickly, the look turned into a frown as she turned toward me.

I answered for her. "Of course we can take these," I said. "See this search warrant? It says I have the right to search and to recover all relevant evidence of a crime."

"These aren't 'relevant,'" Andre said, again covering Melissa's hand with his.

She instinctively withdrew her hand from the file drawer and turned to face me.

"We won't know if they're relevant until we look at them," I answered.

Again we two alpha dogs stared at each other, each trying to make the other back away. I felt a growl begin to form deep in my chest. He answered with a lifted eyebrow.

"Way too cool by half," I thought.

Lauren was the one who broke the stalemate. "I know my father was attached to a highly secret part of the Navy Intelligence unit. It hid under the name of Commander Naval Forces Far East. He was an expert in all things having to do with the Far East, including China, Japan, and Taiwan. If the drawer was locked, then whatever was in them had to be secret?"

The smirk on Andre's face widened into a smile. "Therefore, you are not qualified to look," he said.

Melissa finally spoke up. "I was attached to the military police when I served. I have security clearances," she said.

I turned around to look at her. Shocked! I never knew she served in the military! What the hell?"Okay, okay," I said. "Listen, we don't know how important this stuff is until someone reads it. We need to know who killed the judge and his wife. I suggest we box all these files up and take them to the station. I call the Chief and get the approval."

"I don't think so," Andre answered. "I'll call my superiors and settle this jurisdictional issue."

By that time both Lauren and Cindy were crying. Cindy turned on me and started to sob in my face. "Can't the two of you just stop? This bickering is not finding my mother's killer. This is crazy to think that anything in this room has anything to do with her death! Daddy wasn't that kind."

I wasn't sure what she meant by 'that kind,' but I let it go, and took Cindy by the arm and led her from the room. Lauren followed. I looked back over my shoulder at Melissa, who caught my eye and gave me a quick wink. I knew my partner well enough by then to know she'd find a way to handle the man and the files left in the room. I was safe to leave with the daughters.

Outside, in the great room, I motioned the two daughters to again take a seat on the couch. I took the chair.

"Ladies, I am sorry for all of this," I said. "I didn't know anything about this cross-jurisdictional issue. I didn't even know that it could be a problem. Can either of you fill me in on this?"

Cindy looked at Lauren. Lauren bowed her head a moment, looked back at her sister, then answered. "Okay, not that it should have anything to do with their death," she sighed, "but I heard Tim's end of a conversation with my dad just before Tim left to go to the Gulf. I guess Daddy was being reactivated."

Cindy gasped. "No, no, no! Daddy wouldn't have left Mom right now. Yes, he would have done his weekend, but he NEVER would really LEAVE Mom right now."

Lauren looked stricken, but nodded in the affirmative and took Cindy's hand. "I'm sorry, Sis but, yes, he was. I'm not sure why, but I think it had to do with something that was going on in Iran and with the unrest in the Middle East. You know, that 'Arab Spring', and the newest over-throw of the Egyptian government, and all those other unsettled governments, and all that stuff. That's why Tim was sent to the Gulf."

"Iran! Egypt! Daddy doesn't know anything about Iran, or even the Middle-East!" Cindy said.

"No, he doesn't, but I think I heard Tim say something about the 'damn Russians' and something about nuclear devices," Lauren said, shifting her eyes over to her mother's kitchen where we had found the domestic tableau the night before. All traces of the burned potatoes and steaks were gone. But, suddenly, I heard what sounded like the flap of a cat door swing open and shut, and a fluffy white cat scampered into the room.

"Tobias!" the girls cried in unison. "Tobias, what are you doing here?"

Cindy scooped up the cat and came to sit on the couch with the cat contentedly purring in her lap.

I turned back to Lauren. "Can you tell me anything else?"

Lauren just shrugged. "I just don't know. He was an expert on many things Far East. But the Russians?" she said, shrugging again. "The only thing I ever heard was when he and Timothy would rail against the existing government, and the possible fraud that put Putin back in power. They kept saying that their nuclear devices weren't properly accounted for after they signed the agreement to dismantle them. I think Tim and Daddy both agreed that someone in their military was making millions from selling off their weapons.

"I remembered hearing about that fear, but it seemed a little far-fetched that a sloppy, greedy Russian military would have anything to do with the death of a judge in Orange County, California. It was just too many worlds apart.

Cindy got up from the couch and took the cat over to the kitchen, where she opened a can of food for him, put it in a crystal bowl, and set him and the food on the counter. The cat eagerly chowed into the food. As the cat ate, she finally sighed and looked back at me.

"So you and everyone here thinks my mother's death is not important?" she asked. "You all think it was just a tag-along to Daddy's death?"

I just nodded.

"That was always the problem," Cindy said. "Daddy was always the center of our universe and Mom's. Everything we did was because of him. His military, his law practice, his judgeship. Everything always revolved around him."

Lauren struggled to her feet and came over to the kitchen. She put her arms around her older sister and laid her head on Cindy's shoulder, sighing. "Probably, Cin, probably. Mom was too good a person for anyone to want her dead. And, you know that Daddy loved her with all of his being. And, she loved him. Somehow it is almost poetic that they should die together."

Cindy let out another sob, and turned to again hold her sister in her arms as the two of them cried out their pain in silent sobs.

I left the two women and wandered back to the office to see if my partner had negotiated a peace with the NCIS officer. They had their heads together and were speaking softly to each other. I noticed that Melissa did the hair toss over her shoulder a couple of times. What was this? Was she flirting with the enemy?

"Well, you two didn't kill each other," I said as I entered the room.

For a moment Melissa looked guilty, but the look quickly passed.

"Here's what we think we'll do," she answered. "Andre is out of San Diego and, since our station is so close, we will box up the files, keep them locked in the old storage/conference room and decide who should review them and when. We both have agreed they are not safe here."

I looked over at Andre who just gave me a lazy smile. "Ya'll didn't do such a good job of keeping me outta here, did ya?"

"This is Newport Beach," I said. "Didn't expect someone to break in. Not a lot of burglaries up here in the Heights on a Saturday morning. Not when there is an officer parked out front."

The officer just shrugged and gave me another lazy smile. I wanted to reach out and strangle him.

"So, Jake," Melissa said, interrupting the staring contest, "do you want me to get the tech guys out here again and box this stuff? Andre and I can watch the guys and make sure nothing goes 'missing.' Okay?"

I heard something in her voice, but wasn't quite sure what to do with it. To my ear, her voice almost sounded girlish—very unlike my partner—and it left me a little unsettled. I just nodded my agreement. "I'll take the girls to a hotel," I said. "They don't need to be here."

Both of the other officers agreed and I withdrew to take the girls and their cat to a local suite hotel.

As I left I turned back around in time to see Agent Andre Robinson giving my partner a brief smile. Melissa tilted her head toward him as she placed the call to the crime scene techs.

Hmmm . . .

CHAPTER EIGHT

T he ladies and the cat were grateful for the nice suite of rooms I found for them at the local Embassy Suites hotel. The cat staying in the room was no problem, and the concierge was more than happy to arrange a car for the sisters.

I escorted the girls to their suite on the third floor. With them safely ensconced in their rooms, I was left to figure out what to do next on the case.

It was a Saturday afternoon, and I didn't like working Saturdays. Hell, I barely liked working at all, but this case was interesting. A dead judge who was a naval officer, who was also a spy! Hmm, didn't get much more interesting than that.

I suddenly remembered an old friend and drinking buddy of mine. He was rumored to be a retired spy, though he never admitted it, even when shit-faced drunk; though he did seem to know a lot about things happening in the Middle East. He kept a boat down in a marina on Pacific Coast Highway in a small community called Sunset Beach. I decided to take a drive down there to see if I could get him to talk to me.

I opened the sunroof and all the windows in the Intrepid, turned the FM radio up and let my trusty steed fly on up north on PCH. It was another glorious Southern California fall day. The air was still warm — in the mid-seventies — but there was also a smell of fall with a slight dampness in the air. I loved my beach, and I loved my town, but Sunset Beach was a place I knew I would live if I didn't have the perfect living arrangements on the Peninsula in Newport.

Sunset Beach had started out as a collection of shanty beach shacks and duplexes. It was considered to be the "wrong side of the tracks," because it was prone to flooding whenever a high tide and storm mixed with a full moon. Also, it also was sitting on the shore side of a weapons dump left over from the Korean conflict and World War II. The south side of town was formerly known as Tin Can Beach, and the backside was literally a swamp. The environmentalists nowadays called it a 'watershed' and 'waterfowl sanctuary.'

Unfortunately for the beach bums that first inhabited the town, a developer saw the swamp as another potential Balboa Island. He dug out the muck, making a series of islands with the dredged-out material, then piled the debris with mansions and high-priced condos, all having attached docks for the millionaires to park their yachts. With all of that going on in the inland side, the beach side became more popular. Eventually the shacks, shanties, and duplexes were replaced by vertical mansions. Millionaires now inhabited Sunset Beach, but many of them still wanted to be beach bums. Thus, the restaurants and bars still had a seedy ambience that attracted me.

My friend's boat was docked at a marina called Peter's Landing, and he hung out at the bar/restaurant located at the head of the dock. I expected he'd be sitting on his usual stool at the end of the bar watching the visitors make fools of themselves as they drank and sang karaoke.

I sauntered into the door fronting the street and found a bar rocking with well-inebriated karaoke singers. As expected, I saw his familiar baseball cap and a half-finished Coors Lite setting at the end of the U-shaped bar on the bar when I walked in. He was outside smoking a cigarette staring out at the boats.

"Enjoying the day?" I asked as I stuck out my hand to shake his.

"Ah, Jakey, my boy," he laughed. "I'm getting old. The young girls inside drinking and singing are young enough to be my granddaughters. I feel like a lecherous old fool staying and gawking."

Bill Dawson was my friend, and indeed he was getting old, but one would never know it from looking at him. I knew he was at least in his early to mid-sixties, but he still stood straight, had a bounce to his step, and other than sailor's lines around his tan face, he had no other signs of aging. I wasn't sure of his hair color anymore since he rarely went anywhere without his cap. So when I saw his balding head, I was a little surprised to see what little hair he had was pure white.

Bill put out his cigarette and shrugged off the wall where he had been standing. "Can I buy you a beer?" he asked.

I thought for a moment and decided that since it was Saturday, and I really had nothing else to do, I was technically off duty. A beer wouldn't hurt, I decided.

"Sure," I said. "But before we go inside, I would like to ask you some things."

"Not bar talk?" he asked.

"No, Bill," I answered. "This is stuff I know you know, but you have never said you know, but now I need to know it."

He laughed at me and remarked about all my 'knows' and agreed to sit with me outside. He quickly collected his beer and cap from the bar and ordered me a beer. We settled onto the stools at the outside bar and chugged our drinks in silence. When mine was half-gone and his was empty, I decided we could talk. I ordered Bill another beer from the passing waiter and turned to look at him.

"Yesterday a judge was killed there in Newport Beach," I said.

Bill just nodded.

I continued. "He was sitting in Family Law Court, which makes him an immediate target, but he also was a criminal defense lawyer."

"Probably some unhappy fool took him out," Bill said, taking a long draught on his new beer.

"Yeah, probably," I answered.

Bill lifted an eyebrow at me, his question unasked.

"Turns out, he was also a Navy reservist with a specialty in the Far East," I said.

Bill looked at me, then sighed. "Mark Henning was a good man."

"So you know him?" I asked.

"Why else would you be here?" Bill said, again swilling his beer.

"Ah," was all I said.

"Listen, Jakey," Bill said, suddenly serious. "There's not much I can say to you."

"Bill, there's a NCIS guy skulking around, and I don't think I like him."

"Yeah, they're hard to like," Bill agreed. "Arrogant sons-o'-bitches. Think they're gods or something."

"So, you know him, too?"

"Who?" Bill asked.

"Andre Robinson," I answered.

Bill just shrugged.

"Listen, Bill," I said. "This is serious. The killer took out the judge and his wife, Nancy. It looks like an execution, though that's not for publication. The shots were too close together and the bullets were some sort of exotic thing—completely fragment on impact."

"Hmm" was all Bill said.

"So, okay, there was a locked room and file cabinet in the judge's house. The NCIS guy was in the house without my knowing it. He said the Chief 'okayed' it but, even as much as I hate the Chief, I don't think he'd okay something like that without letting me know. If nothing else, the lieutenant would have a shit fit to have the investigation compromised without the lead detective knowing about it."

Again, all he said was "Hmm."

"And, I caught the son of a bitch trying to sneak out with a rolled-up map under his arm," I said.

"And you think I would know exactly, hmm, what?" Bill asked.

"Damn it, Bill," I said, "I know you were a spook or something like it. I can tell you aren't just a garage door salesman and contractor. I know you know this stuff. You gotta help me out before that NCIS guy shits all over my investigation. So, are you going to help me or what?"

Bill squinted his eyes behind his sunglasses and pulled his cap a little farther down on his head. He took a few more hits of his beer, then evidently made a decision. "Okay, Jakey, but not here."

He pushed back his stool, waved a twenty-dollar bill at the waiter, and gestured for me to come with him down the ramp. With a swipe of his key card we entered the security gate to the dock where his boat was berthed.

His boat was a thirty-two-foot Sea Ray with twin 250 Mercury Engines. It had a double berth in its narrow hull, and was built for speed. Bill started up the engines, letting them warm up while I untied the lines. A few minutes later we were pulling out of the berth and out into the channel. It wasn't until we were mid-channel that Bill finally began to speak.

"So, what exactly do you know that would send you here to talk to me?" he asked.

"I know that Mark Henning was attached to a semi-secret organization called Naval Forces Far East. He was also an expert in all things Far East. More importantly, though, he was a reservist, and he was being reactivated. About the same time, his son-in-law, who is also in the Navy, had his ship sent to the Gulf. The two of them talked just before the son-in-law shipped out. And, according to the daughter who overheard some of the conversation, it seemed the men were upset about the Russians. I also know that both men were concerned about the Russians not keeping track of their nukes. Somehow, I know it's all tied together."

"Hmm, Jake," Bill said, not taking his eyes off the channel ahead of him. "You know an awful lot for a land-hugging cop. What's the NCIS guy saying?"

"Nothing. That's the point," I said. "He's too cute by half and making me want to puke with that hickified Texas drawl, and all."

"You tell him about your suspicions that it was an ordained hit?"

I laughed at the implication that I too was hiding information. I didn't answer the question.

As we entered the exit channel from the bay, we passed by a munitions ship that was loading. The lane next to the ship was completely blocked by military seacraft, with their guns aimed at the channel and the boats passing by. Bill squeezed his craft through the narrowed channel, and we headed out to sea.

It wasn't until we were about a half-mile off shore that Bill finally cut the engines back to idle and he turned to talk to me as the boat drifted.

"The Russians have always been a problem for us," he said, scratching his sideburns. "Reagan thought he was doing the world a favor by tearing apart the Soviet Union, but all he did was destabilize that part of the world. The people in the Eastern European countries had always been under one form or another of oppression. Whether it was the czars or the dictators or the Communist Party, the people were always told what to do, what to think, and what to produce. They weren't familiar with 'free choice' as we know it. When the old organization fell, the people didn't know how to handle a capitalist society. Even their own leaders didn't know what to do or how to handle the changes."

"Sounds like what I remember," I said.

"So, you know that there was a vacuum created, right?" Bill asked.

"Yeah, and when a vacuum is created, usually my crooks find a way to fill it," I said.

"Right."

"So, what happened?"

"Well as you know, the Soviets were in the same war that we are now involved with, in a country that has not had a functioning government for a very long time," Bill said, disappearing below deck, only to re-emerge with two beers. "Beer?"

"Sure," I said. "So, you're talking about Afghanistan, right?"

"Again, right. The Soviets bled money and military lives into a war they could not win. In the end, it was the bleeding of money that did them in, not communism. The powerful communist government forgot one important thing. . ."

"What was that?" I asked.

"They forgot to pay their military. So the military fell back on a time-honored tradition: they 'liberated' some, if not most, of the nukes and sold them to the highest bidder. The only thing they did not sell was the technology on how to make 'em fly."

"So what does that have to do with an expert in the Far East?" I asked.

"The scientists live and work in the Far East," Bill answered.

"What?" I asked. "The Russians don't have their own scientists and stuff?"

"Sure, but we keep too close an eye on those guys," Bill answered, swigging his beer and pulling his cap further down on his head.

"So, okay, that may be the connection, but why the ships to the Gulf?" I asked, also taking a deep draught of my very cold beer.

"Jakey, I am disappointed with you. You didn't make the connection to the Gulf!"

I thought a moment, then answered. "Iran and the destabilized governments from the Arab Spring?"

Bill laughed, squinted into the sun, and then got serious. "Absolutely, Jake. Besides the destabilization of Egypt, Bahrain, Libya — and now Syria — the rest of the area is racing toward an overthrow of all that once was stable."

"But, Iran?" I asked. "Isn't Iran pretty much under the thumb of the Ayatollah? And I thought we just entered an agreement that prevented them from creating nuclear stuff for bombs."

Bill barked a harsh laugh, then answered. "Jake, don't you pay attention? The crazy president is out, an alleged moderate is in, but, for too many reasons, Iran is still extremely dangerous because the country is schizophrenic about its leadership. Even though the crazy president is out, the Ayatollah and Muslims are still hovering, wanting to destroy Israel. So, even though the country elected a moderate president, and even though the county as a whole is well educated and knows that craziness is not the way to a stable economy, the Ayatollah still has their religious heart. So, even though, in many respects, they are smarter about world affairs than most of the other countries in the Mid-East, they still can be dangerous. Besides, the agreement was to stop uranium enrichment. Nowhere does the agreement say anything about *importing* the stuff already enriched."

"Oh?"

"So, the government allows the inspectors into their nascent nuclear plants, and shows them how they have disabled all their centrifuges and, voilà, they pass the inspection, and the sanctions are lifted," Bill said, taking another long draught of his beer.

I looked at him and tried to figure out why what he said was relevant to my investigation. Finally, I gave in, and admitted I didn't understand.

"Look, Jake, the Russian generals still made the nuclear deal. The material comes into Iran, but it doesn't need to be 'processed' the same way as if the Iranians were trying to enrich the uranium themselves."

"Yeah, okay, but why?" I asked. "Why go for the stuff at all? And why should we care since the new government is moderate and possibly friendly to us?"

"Because nothing in that part of the world is stable. Look at Egypt," Bill said. "Their revolution was successful, but the people had no idea who or what should be next. Then, against all that the revolution fought for, they elected a dictatorial Muslim extremist who has grabbed power at every chance he got. Just look at what he did to the judiciary. Even with the military, which stayed neutral, he tried to assert power. So, guess where he got his cajones to make that power grab?"

"Russia and Iran?" I answered. "Yeah, but didn't he get the boot?"

"Yep," Bill said. "But, it didn't stop Russia from trying. And, if Russia or Iran can grab up Egypt, the whole Middle East becomes one rich pot of oil for the Russians."

"But Russia has its own oil," I said.

"True, but it is more arctic, like Canada — harder to extract and more expensive. But what if the Middle East gets nukes, and some crazy person lets them fly? What happens to the oil fields?"

"Saddam Hussein burning the fields all over again," I said.

Bill tipped his hat at me, but did not smile. "Yep, someone gets very rich, and very powerful. And, that someone is again heading Russia," he said, then continued. "Jake, I sometimes feel the entire northern-eastern section of the Europe — as well as the middle eastern section of Asia, and the top section of Africa — is populated by people who need dictators in order to function. Without an iron fist in their faces or a boot on their chests, their societies cannot, and do not, function. But, be that as it may, the populations have seen what they perceive to be freedom. But it is freedom in a vacuum. Something is going to rush in and fill the space occupied by the former dictators. With our reluctance as a country to go again and act as rebuilder and police, the area is going to fall to those who can move the fastest."

"Ah, my crooks, again. . ."

"You got it." Bill said. "The fastest way for crooks to take power is with force. What better way to force themselves into power than through *jihad*, nukes, and burning oil fields? We are in a dangerous time."

"But the scientists... you said the scientists are needed. What scientist is going to help a crazy bunch of jihadists?" I asked.

"Well, for one thing, China," Bill answered. "But, we've always known that. And now they are getting a little pissy about what is going on in the Mid-East, and they're screwed if they lose the oil fields. They can't afford to have the area destabilize too much."

"So, again, where will the scientists come from?" I again asked.

"Jakey, don't make me say it." Bill said, getting a little annoyed. "Think! You are the detective. What country has just had a major destabilizing issue with lots of spent uranium cells they need to get rid of?"

"Oh, shit, of course, Japan!" I said, thinking of the devastating earthquake, tsunami, and nuclear blowout. Their countryside was devastated and the nuclear program for energy generation decimated, first by the tsunami, then by politics.

"Look it, the nuclear generating program is a wasteland right now," Bill said. "There are a lot of scientists out of work, especially nuclear scientist. They're not going to let their families go hungry. That may be why Mark Henning was activated."

"He's an expert in Japan?" I finally asked.

Bill said nothing, which I took to be an affirmative. It left me with a lot to think about. More importantly, I needed to know what Judge Henning knew. Was he killed because he was a judge? Or was he killed because he knew too much about renegade scientists and Russian nuclear weapons?

Bill let me stew in my own thoughts as he put the boat into gear. As if to shake out the cloud of darkness our conversation had leveled over us, he opened up the twin Mercury engines for a fast, exhilarating ride back to the jetty outlet.

Back on shore from our little outing, Bill and I said our good-byes. But, before I left, Bill warned me to be careful. He told me that if my investigation took me too close to some of the powers that we spoke about, I too could be in danger.

I wish I could say I took his warning to heart, but I didn't.

CHAPTER NINE

It was late evening by the time I reached the house in Newport Beach. When I opened the garage door I found one of the girls had parked her car in my spot. Irritated that I had to play 'parking roulette,' I started my search for a place on the street to put the Intrepid. Luckily, I found a parking space just around the corner from the house.

My irritation quickly vanished when I entered the patio separating my apartment from the main house. I could smell wonderful scents coming from the somewhere deep inside the main building. Even though it was a Saturday night and usually the girls were gone on their dates, I found Scat and Raeline in the house. Between the two of them they were cooking up a Southern-fried feast.

We ate platters of Scat's heavenly crispy chicken, and fried dill pickles, creamy potato salad, and Raeline's biscuits with honey butter. For desert the two ladies conjured up an apple pie with a slab of white cheddar cheese. Overly stuffed and truly, physically contented, I excused myself to attack the file Beverly Anderson had given me earlier in the day.

The file was entitled *In re Marriage of John McAllister and Bridget Cheney McAllister,* and it was thick, heavy reading. It was the dissolution of marriage for Bridget Cheney McAllister and her husband John. What made it interesting was the fact that Bridget was the daughter of one of the county's wealthiest and most influential citizens, Jack Thomas Cheney.

In the file, most of the paperwork was filed by the Cheney's well-known attorney, Carmen Delgado. She was known to be a predatory shark among predators. She didn't extend the common professional courtesy of not eating other sharks; rather, she ravished them and spit out their bones. Worse yet, she was my second wife's attorney when our marriage fell apart. She was the one who made sure I got all the bills and my wife got the condo. But, then again, my wife made more than I did, and I guess it was only fair since I did cheat on her. But it was from those two women I learned never to marry again. I guess I just wasn't the marrying type.

After seeing my old nemesis's name on all the pleadings, I decided I needed a drink. I scrounged around for a bottle of my best friend, Stolichnaya Vodka. Grey Goose was for celebration and relaxing. Stoli was to soothe my aching soul. Yes, Stoli it was.

I took the file and inverted it so I would start with the oldest pleadings first. I thought that was probably the best way of finding out how the case got so complicated and maybe lead me to a killer. In my mind,

I still didn't want to believe that the judge had been executed by some foreign agent. That was just too Ludlum spy stuff for me. It was easier to believe that some wealthy, pissed-off father arranged to have his daughter's judge shot.

Yeah, right. Even that seemed far-fetched.

Reading the file, I found that the opening shot in the divorce was the request for domestic violence restraining orders. The petition alleged that John McAllister had threatened his wife with his service revolver and wanted her to have an abortion. McAllister denied the allegations, saying they were "completely false and made-up."

That pleading gave me pause. Whoever wrote that declaration for the Cheney girl knew what she—or maybe he, as in Old Man Cheney—knew that the conservative judges in Orange County would be outraged that a pretty young thing like Bridget Cheney McAllister was forced at gunpoint to contemplate an abortion. Anything to do with abortion was like waving a red flag in front of a bull. It was a very interesting opening salvo in the divorce wars. Of course the petition for the domestic violence orders was also followed up with a petition for dissolution and request for child support and spousal support.

What I found even more interesting was the fact that no domestic violence orders were issued. Shortly thereafter, the case was assigned to Mark Henning. Evidently, Cheney or his attorney did not like the commissioner not issuing temporary orders.

I realized that I was already assuming that Old Man Jack Patrick Cheney was behind the petitions and the dissolution request. I needed to put my prejudices in my back pocket and try reading the file as if I didn't know some of the parties.

The parties were sent out for mediation and, surprisingly, the mediator had said that maybe the parties would reconcile. It was her feeling that their issues could be worked out with counseling. Both parties were ordered into counseling.

Several months later, there was an Order to Show Cause hearing set by John McAllister to have a different counselor appointed by the court. He alleged that the current counselor the parties were using was influenced by his former, or soon-to-be-former, father-in-law.

Again, there were no orders, but there was an admonishment noted in the court minutes that counseling was confidential, and there was to be no interference by parties outside of the jurisdiction of the court. I wondered at that, and made a note.

The back and forth went on for two years. Every month or two the parties were back in front of the judge for something. Basically, it seemed that there was a war going on between the attorneys, as none of the supporting declarations sounded like the words of a cop or of a young wife. So, although I could see Cheney's fingerprints all over the case, I couldn't really find a reason for him to try to take out the judge. That was until the last pages of the court minutes.

According to the minutes, a petition was filed to have the judge removed for cause. The attorney's declaration stated that Mark Henning had consistently and repeatedly refused to rule on outstanding issues and was prejudiced against the petitioner, Bridget Cheney McAllister.

Also buried in the docket sheet of the divorce action was a note from the clerk that the file was to be sent to the presiding judge for a contempt of court hearing as well as the 170.1 petition to have the judge removed for cause. The complaining witness on the contempt matter was Judge Henning. The circumstances had to be extreme for a judge to set a full hearing on a contempt of court action where the defendant in the case was not a party to the underlying case. How had Henning made Old Man Cheney responsible to the court to explain his actions? Even worse, Judge Henning was to appear as a witness in the hearing to have him removed from the case for cause, meaning Cheney had proof he was prejudiced against Bridget. This was crazy, legal maneuvering. Whatever in the world happened so that Jack Cheney and the judge had mixed it up sufficiently to warrant a contempt of court action?

I leafed back through my files, but I couldn't find the supporting paperwork. Either Beverly Anderson had not copied it, or it was gone from the file. In either case, I needed to find out what was going on between those two men. Finding that paperwork became critical to the case, but who would have it?

It was closing in on eleven p.m., and I was getting sleepy. The lack of sleep from the night before, and the Stoli was working its magic. I was heading for the bed when I heard the telltale scratching at my door. I opened it to find Mandy, my wayward dog, sitting at the top of the stairs.

"The girls throw you out?" I asked opening the door wide enough for her to come in. Following closely on her heels was Cisco. "You, too? All right, you two, come in. If no one else will have you, I guess you can stay with me."

Mandy wagged herself into the bedroom, jumped up onto the bed, curling herself into a tight ball at the foot, and went to sleep. Cisco, though, begged for food. I opened a can of tuna, put a little in a saucer for him and watched him sniff at the expensive white meat tuna. He took a few bites, meowed again, and then sprang down from the counter. Then he, too, jumped up on my bed and curled up into a tight ball next to Mandy and went to sleep. Taking my cue from my animals, I curled up in my bed and went to sleep.

In the middle of the night, I awoke suddenly. I thought I heard something. Cisco did too. He jumped off the bed and ran to the bedroom door, slightly growling as he went. Mandy sat up straight on the bed and cocked her head to one side, listening. The three of us sat at attention, listening, not really sure if we had heard anything—and, if we had, what it was.

Mandy was the first to lie back down on the bed. Cisco went to the front door and sniffed it before coming back to bed. I reached for my gun, but had to curse myself for leaving it in the living room of my apartment, locked in the small gun safe under the sideboard. But with the animals off high alert, I too decided it was nothing and turned back to go to sleep.

Little did I know, below my window a shadow silently withdrew.

CHAPTER TEN

The next morning dawned bright and beautiful. I gave a quick call to the hotel to make sure the women I left there the night before were safe and secure. Lauren was evidently still on Virginia Beach time as she answered the phone on the first ring. She told me her sister was still sleeping, and that she was doing fine. The beds were comfortable, which was a blessing, and the front desk was helping her with directions to a market so she could buy food for her parents' cat, Tobias. I immediately thought of the opened can of tuna in my refrigerator, but decided it was too far to drive to the hotel to deliver it to Tobias. Instead, I added some mayonnaise to it and made myself a tuna sandwich for breakfast, which I ended up sharing with both the cat and the dog.

As the three of us were finishing our breakfast I decided to reach out to my partner to see what if any progress she and that Andre cretin had made on the judge's personal files. Two times I called her and both times the phone rolled over to voice mail. On the second try I just told her to call me.

Standing in my kitchen I could hear the wind chimes jangling outside my window, which told me there was on offshore breeze blowing, meaning the wind was blowing from the land to the sea, keeping the waves upright for a longer and better ride. With nothing much to do, I decided to take my short board over to the beach and catch a few waves.

I quickly changed into my board shorts, grabbed my wetsuit, and headed for the door. Being a smart dog, Mandy knew immediately where I was headed. With paroxysms of joy she began to twirl and leap in the air, barking and whining, telling me she wanted to go too. I handed her the leash, and she wagged alongside me down the stairs to the garage. I found my board, and the two of us headed across the street to check out the waves.

I was happy to see the shore break was excellent. The waves, though small, held perfect form for a decent ride. I zipped on my half wetsuit, and threw myself into the shore break, paddling out about 100 yards. As expected, the wind was holding the breaking waves in perfect form for a left-to-right ride. Before I knew it, a couple of hours had passed. It wasn't until I saw a very angry dark-haired woman storming toward me that I realized I had overstayed my time.

I took the next wave in and Melissa met me at the water's edge, Mandy wagging around her ankles, licking her hand.

"Damn it, Jake, I have been calling and texting you all morning!" Melissa seethed at me. "It's bad enough we just had a judge killed in our city, but now one of the D.A.'s has taken fire. What the heck are you doing out there playing all surfer boy?"

"What?" I asked. "What D.A.? Was he killed? Where did it happen?"

Melissa glared at me, and huffed a few times. She didn't say what I knew she was thinking: *If you were where you were supposed to be, you'd know all this.* Instead, she quickly filled me in on the details.

It was a drive-by shooting in the neighboring city of Irvine where the supervising prosecutor from the Harbor Court lived. The house had been hit, the front window shattered, but Teddy Lawrence had just gotten up from his chair when the bullets hit. Thank God his kids were already in bed, and his wife was in the kitchen. The police had responded immediately, but no spent casings were found.

"So why were we called?" I asked after she gave me her report.

"Some guy named Mick Jeperson has been trying to reach you. When he couldn't get you, he called the station who called me. He said he was sure the shooting had to do with a threatening letter our victim had received at the Courthouse," Melissa answered.

Of, course! I remembered Mick telling me that our victim had received a letter from an old client of his, but the judge had shrugged it off. Teddy Lawrence, the supervising district attorney at the Harbor Courthouse had been the prosecutor on the case, and he too had received a similar letter. Crap, maybe Mick was right; the two were probably connected.

I whistled up Mandy who was making friends with my partner

and ran back across the street to my apartment. Melissa followed me up the stairs and stationed herself on the couch, while I showered and changed. As I was drying off, I heard her rummaging around in the refrigerator, and soon she was standing at my bedroom door, sandwich in hand, evidently made from the leftover tuna.

'I didn't know you cooked," she said, taking another bite of the sandwich. "This is really good."

"You must be hungry," I answered, trying to act nonchalant as I was hopping around the bedroom on one foot trying to put on my slacks. "It's only tuna, mayonnaise, a little tarragon, and some dried onion flakes."

"Ooo, tarragon; fancy stuff for a bachelor," she said, as she slouched against the doorjamb of the bedroom door. I caught the twinkle in her eyes as she munched the sandwich and watched me finish dressing in my knit shirt, cotton slacks, and loafers.

I didn't bother to comment on her compliment, not wanting to tell her I learned to make the tuna spread from the ladies next door in the main house. From past conversations, I knew Melissa still wasn't sure she approved of them or their choice of profession. It was probably best just to let her think I was an exceptional chef.

Fifteen minutes later we were out the door. I handed Mandy off to the ladies downstairs, and scooted Cisco out the door. He pouted, twitching his tail and skin all the way down the stairs and into the house next door.

"So where we off too, Boss?" Melissa asked as she wiped her

mouth with a paper towel.

"I've got Mick's number here on his card. Let's meet him at the station and maybe he can bring in Lawrence."

"Lawrence?"

"Yeah, Teddy Lawrence, the D.A. whose house got shot up," I answered. "Follow me back to the station."

The two of us quickly traversed Balboa Avenue over to Pacific Coast Highway and up Jamboree to the station. Pulling into the station with us was Mick in his almost new Grand Cherokee. We got out and greeted each other, and I introduced him to Melissa.

"You get a hold of Teddy Lawrence?" I asked Mick.

"Yeah, but he's still with his own crew of investigators and some detectives from the Sheriff's Office," Mick answered as he gave my partner the once-over. A low whistle escaped from between his lips. Not that I blamed him. Melissa being Melissa was stunning in a natural beauty sort of way. Her long hair was worn loose around her shoulders; and her face, as usual, had minimal makeup. But it was her figure, dressed in black jeans, with her signature white or cream-colored blouse and low-heeled boots, that was enough to make most men stare.

Melissa, on the other hand, gave the balding, out-of-breath, former cop a mere nod of her head. It wasn't a brush-off; rather, she seemed to have no idea of the affect she had on men. At least she never paused long enough to note their admiration.

As we passed through the back door, Mick grabbed my sleeve and pulled me aside. "You lucky dog, Jake," he said in a stage whisper. "Is she your reward for being senior detective?"

I looked at Mick, then over at the retreating back of my partner. How could I ever explain to him that my partner, though incredibly competent, barely tolerated me? Most days she just ignored me, and on bad days her disdain dripped in an unrelenting stream. But, in Orange County, appearances were everything, I had my reputation as the ever-ready stud to think of, so I merely smiled at him and shrugged. I let him form his own conclusions.

Inside the station I was greeted by the fairly irate lieutenant, Max Graber. "Where have you two been?" he stormed at us, totally ignoring the other man with us.

Melissa took a step back, letting me handle the angry six foot, six inch former pro-football linebacker. I, on the other hand, tried not to let my surprise show. What was the lieutenant doing at the station on a Sunday?

"It's Sunday, Lieutenant. What are you doing here? Besides, Sanchez and I were just rounding up some witnesses," I answered, only half lying, as I pointed to Mick standing behind Melissa, who was trying to make herself invisible.

"Damn it, Swanson," Graber roared, which was unusual since he rarely raised his voice. "The Chief is head hunting and the head he wants is yours. If you want me to keep protecting you, you gotta keep me in the know of what's going on."

"Why's the Chief's tidy-whiteys all in a bunch," I asked.

The lieutenant leveled a glare at me that shriveled my manhood into a little tiny mushroom. I felt sweat break out and wondered if I had remembered to use my antiperspirant.

I tried again. "I'm truly sorry, Lieutenant. I was at an impasse in my thinking. We have a couple of ways of going on this case, and all seem possible, yet none seem probable."

The lieutenant leveled a stare at me, and flicked an invisible grain of sand off my shoulder. "Surfing?" he asked me, knowing me too well.

"Yes, sir," I answered, lowering my gaze.

"And?" he asked.

"And, I'm still not sure," I answered. "That's the reason I brought in Jeperson. He mentioned a letter the judge got from an old client and thought maybe it would lead somewhere. Then, with Teddy Lawrence's house getting shot up, it looks like it may be related. So, why in particular is the Chief in a dither?"

"Let's see," the lieutenant said, "besides a judge and his wife getting shot in our city, and besides a NCIS guy snooping around and threatening to bring the federal government into bug us, and besides a supervising D.A.'s house getting shot up in our county, and besides the Sheriff looking to hang a few new scalps on her belt before the next election, I don't see why the Chief would be upset. Do you?"

"You mean the Chief didn't invite the NCIS guy into the investigation?" I asked.

"Of course not," Graber answered, looking at me like I had lost my mind.

"But I was led to believe the Chief authorized his presence at the scene and made him part of the investigation?" I said, now truly puzzled.

"That's why we're in an uproar here," Graber said. "All of a sudden your partner and some guy showing a NCIS badge show up with boxes and he's telling me that no one is to open the boxes without a federal court order or permission from the Navy. He said it was all your idea."

I felt the slow burn that had been smoldering behind my eyes flame into a full-on conflagration. A red haze enveloped my eyesight, and I was sure steam was blowing out my ears.

"Where is the scum?" I raged. "I want that scum right now! Sanchez, where is he?"

By that time my partner had back stepped all the way out of the hallway and was hiding in her cubicle. I found her sitting in her chair, trying to be invisible.

"Give it up, Homes," I said to her. "Where is that guy?"

"I think he's staying at the same place you put the daughters," she answered. "I have his cell phone number if you want it."

"And if I call it, will he answer?" I asked.

Graber was watching the play-by-play between Sanchez and me. His eyes also began to slant a little. Finally, he said, "What exactly did he tell you, Swanson?"

"He said he had a dead naval officer and it belonged to NCIS, and that the Chief had authorized his involvement in the investigation."

"Hmm, funny, he said almost the same thing to me, but I had the sense to check with the Chief," Graber said. "The Chief denied meeting the guy, only saying that he knew the Navy was interested in our investigation, and that we were to inform them if it appeared the Henning murder was any way connected to his service."

As the two of us argued about why I hadn't called the chief to confirm and I mentioned that it seemed absolutely believable that the chief would authorize Robinson's involvement, the man in question walked through the back door of the station.

"You guys looking for me?" he asked.

We turned around to face the NCIS guy, who was smiling broadly at the two of us. When Graber tried his physical intimidation trick, Robinson did not move. He was not even swayed by the large mass of angry man standing in front of him. I was hoping for a physical showdown between the two men. But, then, Melissa stepped between them and sort of hip-bumped the shorter NCIS man out of the lieutenant's way.

"Andre," she said, "there seems to be some confusion about authorization for you to be here."

He just laughed. "Do you really think you could keep my department away from this?' he asked. "After all, it is a dead naval officer."

I felt myself go all squinty eyed again, as the red haze again began to envelope me. I felt the lieutenant's hand on my collar before I even knew I was advancing on the officer with clenched fists.

"We expect," Graber said, in a somewhat more reasonable voice, "that when there are jurisdictional issues, courtesy would dictate an honest exchange of information. I believe it was lacking in this case."

Andre Robinson took a step back, looked at the lieutenant, then just smiled. "Ya'll seem pretty ree-laxed up here. I was able to just tippy-toe right on into that crime scene; nobody even stopped me. Now ya'll asking for courtesy? Seems the next thing ya'll be asking for is to sit on my porch swing and drink sweet tea."

The lieutenant slanted his eyes, but said nothing. Melissa once again stepped into the breach. "So, what do we do now?"

"Son," Graber finally asked, his slow burn coming to a rolling boil. "Just who the hell are you, and where did you come from?"

"I told you," Robinson said, losing the accent. "I am with the Naval Criminal Investigative Services. I am attached to the JAG corps out of North Island, and I was sent here to make sure our national security was not breached."

"So you come here and lie to get in?" Graber asked.

"Once I saw how lax the scene was, I decided that I needed to intercede to secure important documents. I was in the process of doing that when detectives Sanchez and Swanson came into the house with the two daughters," Robinson said. Then, turning to me, he added somewhat derisively, "Seems that in my training I must have missed the lesson on bringing the victims' family members onto or into a crime scene. I guess I always assumed that if I did that, the scene could be compromised."

"The scene had already been swept by our CSI guys, and released," I answered.

"Yeah, right. And that's why you had a completely incompetent uniformed officer 'guarding' the scene by parking his marked patrol car down the hill of the driveway?" Andre asked, his smirk prominently displayed.

I wasn't sure why Sergeant Greene, the night patrol officer, had left a uniformed officer at the scene, but I wasn't going to let this intruder bad-mouth my department — that was my job!

"Listen, we always keep a uniformed officer on scene until we get the search warrant," I said. "And what I was doing with the daughters is really none of your business. As for me, I was serving the search warrant for the locked room. I was hoping the daughters might be able to explain what we found."

"Again, it seems pretty lax to me, since I came in an unlocked door," Andre again smirked.

I had my fists tightly clenched and was judging distance when Melissa again hip-bumped me away from the other man.

Lieutenant Graber, who had been listening to our exchange, was shaking his head. I couldn't read his expression, but was hoping he thought the guy was a mope and would throw him out of our station. But, Graber took a deep breath and motioned for all of us to follow him into the main conference room. Tagging along behind us was Mick Jeperson. We had all but forgotten him during the dust up between Graber, me, and Robinson.

Taking our seats, Robinson turned to Mick and asked, "Who are you, and why are you here?"

Mick made a quick introduction to the agent guy, telling him that it was his job to make sure a lapse in security from the courthouse didn't play a role in the deaths. For a moment, I thought Robinson guy was going to object, but when Graber slapped Mick on the back and invited him to stay, the agent shut his mouth and said nothing. Graber turned to me and asked me to fill him in on what we knew.

"So far, like I said earlier, we have numerous possible suspects, but only one seems probable. There's this crazy woman who was convicted of killing her husband, sent away for some years, then released when the Ninth District Court of Appeals didn't like the way our local courts handled the case."

Mick jumped in with her name: "Daylia Sherman."

"I have also gone through the McAllister/Cheney divorce case," I said. "There were some irregularities in the case, and I was planning on speaking with the Cheney attorney on Monday. Old Man Cheney's fingerprints are all over that file."

"Literally?" Robinson asked. "And who is Old Man Cheney?"

"No figuratively," I answered, surprised that anyone would take me literally. "Jack Thomas Cheney is richer than God and developed most of the apartments and shopping malls around here. He's used to getting his own way about everything. He either gets it because of political connections or he buys it, and he's even threatened some to 'kill' for it. Henning in his judicial position may have gotten on the wrong side of him. But, somehow I don't think it's probable Cheney had Henning killed."

"Okay," Robinson said. "Anything else?"

"Well, of course we have the secretive Navy reservist thing," I said. "He may have discovered some hinky stuff with Russian armaments and Japanese scientists."

I was watching Agent Robinson very carefully when I said that. Normally, I wouldn't have put that on the table until I had more information, but there was that crazy voice in my head telling me to "just do it." So, I did.

The reward was worth the risk. Some physical reactions are controlled by the part of the brain that is not subject to conscious control. Deep flushing in a light-haired blonde was one of those things that came without control or conscious regard. Andre Robinson flushed a deep red from the collar line of his shirt at his throat all the way up to his hairline. He knew he flushed, and he shuffled his feet trying to distract us, which only drew our attention more closely to him.

Sensing his distractions had not worked, he said, "How did you come to that conclusion Detective Swanson?"

"I read the papers," I said smugly.

His light blue eyes bored into me like a laser light beam. It was my turn to smile.

"So, Swanson," Graber said. "Those files in the other conference room, do you think they're relevant to your case?"

Because it was Graber asking, I was honest. "I don't know, sir," I said. "It's hard for me to believe a foreign hit man would come to this country to kill one of our own. It's scary, but really unbelievable. I really would like to focus my attention on other possible suspects before I pull the trigger on that theory."

Yeah, right. What I really was doing was trying to redirect Andre Robinson. I needed Blondie off my back. I saw his reaction, and I knew he thought I was not only dumber than dirt, but incompetent to boot. If I could throw him off, maybe I still could get to those files. I needed answers. So I smiled my most vacant imitation of a California blonde, and said, "I really think it is more likely it's the crazy woman with the threatening letters. After all, shots were fired at the D.A.'s office, too. I think I need to follow up on that."

Mick was bobbing his head like a bobble-head doll. Robinson looked around the table and made a quick assessment. He pushed his chair back from the table and said, "Well, it looks domestic to me. So, if you don't mind, I will take my leave."

Graber rose to his feet and extended his hand to the agent, saying, "Do you want us to keep you in the loop?"

Robinson looked over at me with a dismissive shrug, and said, "I am sure my superiors would appreciate that. If something more sinister than a crazy former client appears, would you let me know?"

"Of course, Officer," Graber said, taking the man's shoulder to escort him out the door.

If Andre Robinson had been paying more attention to my partner, he may not have taken his leave quite so quickly. Seared into her face were the conflicting emotions of longing and disdain—longing for Andre and, I am sure, disdain for her partner.

CHAPTER ELEVEN

Waiting until the lieutenant had safely escorted the NCIS officer from the conference room, my enraged partner turned her fury on me.

"You deliberately misled him!" she snarled.

I just shrugged, not really wanting to confirm or deny her accusation. But Mick was now hopping around like a bunny on crack.

"I knew it, I knew it! You really think it was that crazy Daylia Sherman, don't you?" he asked.

"Look it, Mick, I need to read the letters, and I need to speak with Teddy Lawrence about it," I said. "Who's following the shooting case in Irvine?"

"You know, Irvine P.D., and they have asked the Sheriff for help, and because it's a district attorney involved, they also have their own investigative department," Mick answered. "And, of course, I am also involved, just to make sure that if there is a connection to the judge's shooting. God, I hope it isn't. But, ah well, if it is, then I'll need to do a full report for future security training."

Mick stopped his erratic bunny-hopping around the conference room, and dropped into a swivel chair. Suddenly, he threw his head back against the chair. Sweat broke out on his balding head, and his face glistened with perspiration. He clutched his chest and moaned in pain.

"My pills, my pills are in my car," he moaned as his face got wetter and wetter. Melissa didn't wait for his pills. She grabbed the phone in the conference room and dialed 9-1-1 to report a heart attack. Within minutes Fire and Rescue were tramping through the station and into the conference room. Everyone's attention was focused on poor Mick Jeperson—all those except mine.

While everyone else's attention was focused on the keeping the court security officer alive, I took the chance to slip down the hall to the old conference room. That room and I were old friends. I had slept on that table too many nights not to know how to get into that room whenever I wanted. A few jiggles and a shove and I was in the room. I closed the door behind me and reached for the emergency flashlight stashed in the holder by the door. I didn't want anyone to know I was in there. What I needed to do was better done without an audience.

There were about ten banker's boxes stacked on the table. All had seals on them, but as far as I was concerned, I was the lead detective, and seals were to be broken. If ever questioned about the seal, I would just do my usual bumble act and swear I forgot to re-initial them when sealing them again. The trick would be to get the seals back on without disturbing the cardboard. That just required a little steam.

The coffee pot in the room was half full of sludge. It wasn't on, but I could reuse the leftover coffee to steam open the seals. The coffee was always so bad; no one would know the coffee had been re-run through the maker.

Two minutes later I had a steaming pot of tar. The pot gave off enough steam to loosen the glue on the seals, but not enough to damage the cardboard. I worked quickly and efficiently to loosen all the seals. It was only after all the seals were lifted and carefully left to dangle in place that I started my search.

From what Bill had told me during our trip on the boat, I had a fair idea of what I was looking for. Most of the boxes held reports from trips Henning had made in the past to places in Japan while on his yearly two-week tour. As I worked I realized there was some pattern to the reports in the boxes. The older reports were in the boxes closest to the door and they were on top of boxes holding newer reports.

"Ah, Andre, you clever devil," I thought. "You knew someone would search, and you suspected they wouldn't have a lot of time. So, you buried the good stuff. Melissa kept you from taking it, but you made sure it was buried."

Once I figured out his pattern, I delved into the boxes with the newer reports. There were satellite photos of rail lines and areas I had no idea of what I was seeing. They were identified with numbers, and appeared to be sorted by date. I was helpless to know what I was seeing.

Damn. I needed help. This was crazy. More importantly, I still didn't want to believe any country would try to kill a sitting judge in the United States.

Finally, with a helpless sigh, I closed the boxes and reaffixed the seals. My break-in was a bust.

Sneaking out would be harder than sneaking in, I decided. I waited by the door, listening to see if anyone was in the hallway before opening the door. I slowed my breathing, trying to use the superpowers of my dog and cat. But no matter how hard I tried to channel my animals, neither Mandy nor Cisco reached across the universe to help me hear or smell better.

Damn, again. I would just have to tough it out and lie if caught.

But I was lucky. I opened the door just as Melissa turned the corner into the bullpen area calling my name.

"Jake, darn it, where are you?" she called.

I slipped through the door and closed it silently, knowing that it would lock from the inside. I leaned against it like I was trying to open it and jiggled the door loudly. That's it, I thought, let her think I was my usual sneaky self and just wasn't able to succeed.

It worked. Melissa heard me jiggling the door and whirled around to confront me.

"Swanson!" she yelled. "What the heck are you doing? You know that room is off limits!"

I turned around to face her, giving her a sheepish grin. I even went so far and to do the toe stub thing. "Oh, damn, Sanchez," I said. "I was just trying the lock on the door. You know, while the cat's away, the mice will play."

She grabbed my arm and pulled me away from the door and marched me down to the detective's bullpen.

"So, what are we going to do now that Mick is on his way to the hospital?" she asked me as she threw herself into her chair.

"Did he bring his file with him?" I asked.

"Don't know," she said as she got up and headed back toward the conference room.

There it was, on the table where he left it before his brush with fate.

She flicked it with her finger toward me. "You open it," she said. "You don't care what's off limits. I still care about a career."

There was something in her voice that made me pause. I looked up to see a devilish gleam in her eye. Did she know about my break-in?

Naw. . .

I took the file and opened it without a second thought. Mick wanted us to have this information. He brought it to us. Therefore, it was mine to read.

The top most letter was addressed to "Scumbag Henning." Of course, that was the letter I wanted to read.

It said:

Dear Scumbag Henning:

I just want you to know that despite you abandoning me when I needed you most, I have won my freedom. Prison has taught me that old debts must be paid. I plan on repaying my 'debt' to you as soon as I get out.

See you soon,

Daylia Sherman

I reread the letter several times just to see if I could read a threat into the words. I just couldn't get her meaning. It was too ambiguous. I flipped it back my partner to see what she thought.

Melissa read it and said it was definitely a threat. It was her opinion that a forgiving person wouldn't start a letter "Dear Scumbag." She was also a little concerned about the "See you soon."

What I really needed to do was speak with Teddy Lawrence. I leafed through the file, and found a slip of paper with his number on it. Unfortunately, when I dialed it, it went to his voice mail at the office. I left a message and my phone number, asking him to please call me back.

By that time my partner was getting antsy. She kept looking at her watch and looking at me. Finally, I took the hint.

"You got plans?" I asked.

She blushed slightly and nodded in the affirmative.

"Then get out of here. If I need you, it'll just have to wait until tomorrow," I said. "I'm tired, too. My list is long of things to do tomorrow. When you first get in, I need you to collect all the reports from the canvassing officers. They should be done and reviewed by Novack, and ready for you by noon—no later. As much as I think Novak is a prick, he makes his guys toe the line."

Melissa just smiled, picked up her purse and left.

The storeroom/conference room beckoned me. But without knowing what I was looking at, it was useless to me. I decided the reward was not worth the risk.

Having made that decision, I was out the back door and cruising down the highway to what I hoped would be a great Sunday dinner.

Fortunately for me, the dinner was great, and as usual, the ladies in attendance were lovely. How lucky can one man be to have such intelligent, beautiful women cooking for him and waiting on him hand and foot?

Unfortunately for me, my evening was ruined by a call from patrol. Someone had tried to break into the Henning's house. . . again.

CHAPTER TWELVE

I was furious as I headed down Balboa Avenue to make my turn onto Pacific Coast Highway. *Damn it*, I thought. Couldn't I have just one evening alone with my martini and soft music out on the deck of the bay front house? Couldn't I just enjoy the fruits of my magical real estate management style and enjoy the young ladies that lived in the house?

Damn, damn, damn!

This time when I arrived, the house was lit up like a Christmas tree. There were lights on in each room of the house, and there were uniformed officers everywhere.

Oh, damn, I thought. *What now?*

When I approached the driveway, Sergeant Hammi Greene came out to greet me. His mouth was compressed into a grim frown.

"Hey, Jake," he said, extending his hand to greet me. "Shoot, I didn't know this was a crime scene until my officer called it into dispatch. When the call first came in, it must have gone to someone who didn't know about the shooting and murder here. My guy was all over the house and turned on all the lights when he came and found the front door open. You know, standard procedure is to clear a house."

"I know, Hammi," I said. What he said was true. If an officer got a call of a break-in, it was standard procedure for them to go through the house and make sure there weren't any of the mopes still in the house — or, worse, a victim. "Where was the tape? Didn't your guys see the tape?"

"Wasn't any," Hammi said. "I looked myself just to make sure their report was accurate. Not a shred of tape anywhere."

"That's strange," I said.

"Well, not as strange as this," Hammi said, handing me a piece of paper.

It was a single sheet of paper with block writing. All it said was:

TIT FOR TAT

"Tit for tat?" I said. "What the hell is that supposed to mean?"

"I thought you might know," Hammi said.

"Oh, well, book it under my log number for the murder," I said. "Anything else I should know?"

"Nope," Hammi said. "At first the officers thought the place had been tossed. But once they knew it was subject to a search by us, they changed their minds."

As I was sliding down the steep driveway a movement in the bushes caught my eye. Again I reached for my gun, and again it wasn't in my waist holster in the small of my back. I couldn't believe I left the house, *again*, without my service gun.

"Psst, Greene," I said, waving him over to me. "Over there. See, over there. There's something in those bushes."

"FREEZE!" we both yelled as we ran across the street. The bushes started to move, and I made a running tackle. In my arms I caught a disheveled woman who came up scratching and biting.

"Damn it, freeze!" I yelled.

By this time Hammi had run up to the two of us and had his gun pointed at her.

"FREEZE," he yelled.

"Fuck you both!" the woman said, as she sank her teeth into my arm taking a large chuck of it with her as she pulled away from me.

"Owww!" I yelled, letting her go to grab my bleeding arm.

The woman took off running down the street, and Hammi took out after her.

"FREEZE!" he yelled again. But she just kept running.

I heard footsteps behind me and looked up to see two patrol officers running down the street after the sergeant and the woman. In the darkness I couldn't see the chase, but I did hear its ending.

From the bottom of the hill I heard shrill cursing and deeper voiced commands. As I ran toward the group the distinctive odor of pepper spray wafted toward me in the night breeze.

When I finally ran up on the pile of bodies they were beginning to sort themselves out into officers and a screaming mad-dog woman. She was spitting and cursing the officers, but she was handcuffed. For me, that was enough.

"So, what're you doing here?" I asked her.

"Buzz off, sonny," she said.

"Tell me why you're here," I said again.

"Buzz off, I told you," she said.

"That's it," I said. "Take her to the station."

"You can't arrest me!" she said. "You don't have no probable cause to arrest me."

"Sounds like she knows the drill," I said. "Just get her out of here. But keep her at the station until I get back. I gotta go to Hoag to get a tetanus shot and have this bite looked at. I wonder if she has rabies."

"We can always cut her head off to check," one of the officers said. "I'll do the honors if you don't mind, sir. Look at what she did to my uniform!"

The knees of his uniform were worn thin with scrapes and the pocket of his shirt was torn. He looked like he'd been in a street brawl. But he was smiling.

Just like the young ones, I thought. The best part of their day is a good fight and hard arrest. Was I ever like that? Must have been, but I sure didn't remember liking it now.

Two hours later and numerous stitches, I was back at the station. Hammi handed me her sheet when I walked through the door. He'd run her prints and, come to find out, she had a record.

My, my.

"Well, Ms. Sherman," I said as I took a seat in front of her in the small interview room. Across from me sat an African American woman of indeterminate age. Her rap sheet put her at forty-seven years of age. Her hair was shot through with gray, and she was missing a few teeth — unfortunately not the front ones. Lines were etched into her face, and her skin, though dark, was flakey with white dead skin. Prison had not been kind to her. More importantly to me, however, was that her right hand was handcuffed to the ring on the table and the other hand was secured to her waist chain. Evidently, the boys at the station wanted to make sure there were no more wrestling matches that night.

"Don't know any 'Ms. Sherman,'" she said.

"Okay, Daylia," I said. "I am Detective Jake Swanson, and I want to talk to you about Mark Henning. But, before I do that, I want to read you your rights and make sure you understand them."

"Don't need no rights read to me," she said.

I pushed the button under the table to start the recording and proceed to read them to her anyway, but didn't ask her if she understood them. Her demeanor was enough for me.

"Daylia," I said, setting a copy of her letter in front of her. "Looks like you had a pen pal from prison. You want to explain?"

She turned her back on me and said nothing.

"Looks to me like maybe you had a grudge against Mark Henning. . ."

Still nothing.

"Well, okay, then," I said, "I guess I'll just leave you here till you want to talk."

She rolled her eyes at me and I left the room.

Coming around the corner from the interview room I ran headlong into Teddy Lawrence. He was dressed in jeans and a T-shirt, with his hair sticking out all over his head. It looked as if he had been interrupted from a Sunday evening nap.

"Swanson!" he yelled. "Is it true? Do you have her? Do you have Daylia Sherman here at the station?"

"Hey, Ted, just calm down a minute," I said. "You're a potential victim and you shouldn't be here."

"But I'm a prosecutor and she shot up my house!" he said, his voice rising in timbre.

"Yeah, and that's the reason you shouldn't be here. If she really was the one who shot up your house, I can't have you all up in her face and tainting her statements. You know that."

"Damn it, Swanson, she almost killed my wife," the man said, his voice beginning to quaver. "I have kids, damn it, Swanson—kids who live in the house! She could have killed them!"

"That's why you are going to come with me, have a cup of coffee, and tell me why you think she's the one who shot up your house." I led him away from the interview room and back to my desk in the bullpen.

The pot was empty, but a quick fill with water and a couple of scoops of French Roast, and the coffee was brewing. Soon the smell of fresh coffee filled the office. I waited next to the machine and caught two cups of it while it still brewed. The smell was intoxicating and I savored the idea of drinking freshly made coffee.

With the two filled mugs I went back to my desk to see Teddy Lawrence hunched over in his seat. His arms rested on his knees and he had his hands clasped, almost as if in prayer. I spent a few seconds studying the man the courthouse and defense lawyers called the "Holy Warrior." In his prime he had been a formidable trial lawyer, taking on the most difficult of cases and winning. He wasn't afraid of gang members, the press, or even other politicians. He represented the "People of the State of California" and he knew it was his divine calling.

But the man who sat at my desk-side appeared old beyond his years. I knew that Teddy Lawrence was not much older than me, making him in his mid- to late forties. Yet, his brown hair was shot through with gray, and deep lines etched his face. His hands shook as they lay in his lap, and there was a slight tremor in his body.

Ah, shit, I thought, *he has Parkinson's disease*. What a terrible fall for such a valiant warrior. I put my hand on his shoulder and gave it a squeeze as I put the coffee in front of him.

"So, Teddy, tell me everything," I said, knowing another agency was handling the case.

He took a deep draught of the coffee, put the mug back down and finally looked at me.

"Ah, Swanson, where do I start?"

"Let's try the beginning."

He took another sip of his coffee and began to talk. He told me of a case almost twelve years earlier when a woman was charged with killing her husband. The husband was cheating on her and she caught him red-handed. The two had gone to dinner and finished a bottle of wine between them. When they got home that night, she confronted him and he just laughed. He smacked her around a little for sport, then drank almost an entire bottle of brandy, and smacked his wife around a few more times before passing out.

Stupid, stupid man, according to Teddy.

Daylia waited until her cheating, beating husband went to sleep, got her sharpest knife out of the drawer then proceeded to slice and dice all of his manly parts into tiny little chunks. When she was done with that, and his screaming was getting on her nerves, she doused him with gasoline and lit a match. Bye, bye, husband; hello prison.

As far as Teddy was concerned, it was an open and shut case of premeditated murder, making it a first degree charge. But two things had gone wrong. The first was out of Teddy's control, and not something he had worried about given the law at that time. The arresting officers had kept her in their squad car and taunted her until she told them what she did. They hadn't actually asked her any questions, but rather just went on and on about cheating and beating until Daylia told them she was going to "cut 'em just like her husband and feed their manhood to her dog, just like she did to her husband." The officers had made sure the patrol car recorder was on during her statement. When the detective played that recorded statement for her, she confessed all over again.

It was only years later that the United States Supreme Court found that by holding Daylia in their squad car and taunting her until she made a statement, the officers had violated her Fifth Amendment rights. Not only was the first statement not admissible in court, but so was the later confession. Normally, that would not have been enough to set her free, but the second error, the one Teddy made, was enough to open the prison doors.

The defense for Daylia had tried to get the court to allow evidence of the husband's tendency to beat Daylia whenever he drank. Teddy had not thought it relevant to first degree murder because the husband was incapacitated by the alcohol and did not pose an immediate threat to Daylia in his unconscious state. Self-defense, Teddy had argued, was only appropriate if the defendant faced immediate danger, and they could only use as much force as necessary to escape the danger. So he had argued against an expert coming to testify about what was called "Battered Spouse Syndrome."

Later the courts decided that Battered Spouse Syndrome was a real defense, much like self-defense. The experts all agreed that when a spouse was repeatedly exposed to violence, the victim lives in a heightened state of fear, always believing she could be killed at any moment. Thus, the victim of the abuse waits until her abuser is asleep or incapacitated before striking a blow.

By the time the Ninth Circuit Court of Appeals heard Daylia's petition for Writ of Habeas Corpus, the law had changed so much that the cumulative effect of the errors in her case was enough. Daylia went free.

But all during her incarceration, Daylia believed she was innocent of murder. Thus, she blamed anyone who touched her case. Most of all, she blamed Teddy Lawrence.

As Teddy poured out his story, it still left me wondering about Daylia's connection to Mark Henning.

"Ah, Swanson," Teddy said in answer to my question. "She's as crazy as a loon! She blamed anyone and everyone who even touched her case. Mark Henning had the unfortunate luck to have Daylia's family come to see her about defending her. He met with her a few times, but the family just didn't have the money to pay him. He declined to take the case. She thought he should take it for free."

"Didn't she get a court-appointed lawyer?" I asked.

"Sure, but Daylia and the guy hated each other on sight," Teddy said. "Her public defender was black, and Daylia thought he was prejudiced against her because her husband was also black."

"But, so's she?" I said, not understanding.

Teddy just shook his head. "I told you she's crazy as a loon. She was somehow convinced that her lawyer had some kind of 'brotherhood' affinity for her husband. I never really understood her arguments, but then, I was out of the courtroom for most of them."

"Ah, the closed hearing, thing, right?" I said.

"Yeah, but she also made a point of yelling it enough times during the trial, I kinda got the drift," Teddy said.

"So, what makes you think she's a danger to you?" I asked, still somewhat puzzled.

Teddy settled back in the chair, rubbed his face a few times, then shoved his trembling hands back into his lap. He saw my eyes follow his movements and shrugged.

"Parkinson's?" I asked, concerned for my compatriot.

"Yeah," he said. "It's advancing quicker than anticipated. Doctors took me out of the courtroom. Too much stress, they said. That's why I'm now a 'stupidvisor.'"

I had to laugh at that. From what little I heard from the deputy prosecutors, Teddy was a god! They all loved and revered him.

"So why did Daylia become such a threat?" I asked.

Teddy sighed and then laughed. "She couldn't get her pound of flesh with money from the courts, so she decided to take it a different way."

"Huh?"

"She tried to sue Mark, myself, and the police, but the courts threw it out. She couldn't sue me because I have immunity. She couldn't sue Mark because she had to prove 'factual innocence' which, of course, she couldn't do. And for the police, the officers in question were long gone and the court would not hold the department responsible for the acts of the officers that were legal at the time they did them." Teddy said. "So, voilà, the suit was gone."

"Hence this other stuff," I said, putting it together.

"So it appears," Teddy agreed.

We sat for a while, saying nothing. Then Teddy suddenly looked up at me with a startled look on his face.

"Did your guys find the gun?" he asked.

"The gun?"

"Yeah, the gun she used to shoot up my house," Teddy said.

Now it was my turn to be consternated. I didn't know if the guys had even thought to look for a gun. I had left to go to the emergency room to get my arm stitched and get my shots. I had no idea what Hammi and the guys did.

"Teddy," I said, "you wait here and let me go check with the sergeant handling this matter. Our call came in as a straight break-in, no shots or anything. I doubt they even knew to look for a gun. I'll be right back."

I hurried over to the patrol side of the building to look for Hammi Greene. He was at his desk typing on his computer.

"Hey, Hammi," I said, "did your guys find a gun?"

"A gun?" Hammi asked.

My heart sank. Of course they wouldn't think to look for a gun. So I quickly told him why a gun was important. He immediately pushed back from his desk and spoke into his radio, rounding up his guys to go out and look for a gun.

I went back to Teddy and told him my guys were out scouring the area near her arrest to see if they could find a weapon. Taking the news better than I expected, the exhausted man shook my hand and took his leave.

With my arm throbbing in pain, I went back to my desk to write my report about Daylia's assault on me. I gave a silent prayer that my guys would find the gun, and that not only would it match Teddy's case, but that it was also the weapon that killed Mark and Nancy Henning.

But, again, my little voice and experience told me the Henning murder was too sophisticated for lunatic like Daylia. By the time I left the station to take my weary body home, I had yet to hear from Hammi Greene. The gun was still amongst the missing.

CHAPTER THIRTEEN

Monday morning came with me sleeping through the alarm. It was only Mandy's persistent snuffling in my ear, and Cisco walking up and down my side that finally roused me from my deep slumber. I had no idea what time I had finally hit the sheets, but my tired and aching forty-two-year-old body protested any thought of me getting up. If not for the animals wanting to be fed and let out, I would have stayed in bed till noon.

The morning routine of making coffee, feeding the dog, and letting Cisco out the door, gave me a chance to plan my day. I knew I had to meet with the 'Shark,' and I needed to go through some of Henning's old criminal files to see if any suspects jumped out at me.

I called the daughters at their hotel and both were up and willing to go with me back to the house to help me go through their father's old criminal files. We agreed to meet at ten. That barely left me enough time to try to set a meeting with Shark Delgado, the Cheney's family law pit bull.

I called Carmen Delgado's office but, of course, she was in court. Her overly solicitous secretary took my message and numbers, promising that she would have Ms. Delgado call me as soon as she was out of court.

Rather than go into the station, only to have to come back down to PCH to get over to the Henning house, I whistled up Mandy and took her for a short run. I don't know what it is about dogs, but they are a 'chick magnet,' but not just for young women. Women of all sizes and ages want to pet Mandy and ruffle her ears. Of course the dog loves it, but sometimes it seriously interferes with my run.

So it was that day. Too many women out with their running strollers wanted their toddlers to play with Mandy, and too many older women doing their power walks were eager to stop just a moment to talk to the dog. I gave up, went home, and took a quick shower.

Fifteen minutes later I was out the door, hunting the Intrepid, again, and not happy about losing my garage parking space. I needed to have a chat with the girls about whose garage it really was.

Needless to say, my mood was not the best by the time I reached the house. I was definitely verging on cranky. So when I arrived and saw the rental car parked at the top of the driveway, any good humor I had vanished.

The women were already inside the garage with Cindy pulling some boxes off shelves, while Lauren watched. Although the boxes had been covered, there was still residual dust. It was clear the boxes had been in their resting spot for many years, and left untouched. Not likely that they would produce anything worthwhile.

Cindy was the first to notice my arrival. "Hey, Detective Swanson," she said, "we decided to get started pulling some of the boxes of Daddy's old cases."

"Why these?" I asked, not feeling in a loquacious mood.

"Daddy destroyed his cases after ten years unless the sentence his client got was longer than that," Cindy answered. She didn't elaborate, probably expecting me to know what she meant.

"And?" I asked.

"And, these would be clients that would, more likely than not, be the most upset with Daddy because the sentences were the longest," Cindy said.

Lauren turned around and looked at me with sad eyes. "Do you really think that it is one of Daddy's clients that killed him and Mom?"

Her sadness and her pregnancy almost broke my heart. She seemed too vulnerable to be handling all of this without her husband. I suddenly felt very protective of her. I realized that if my first wife and I had stayed married longer than a few weeks, we may have had a child that would have been just about Lauren's age.

Without warning depression overwhelmed me. The emptiness of my life and its directionless spiral downward made me realize the years were speeding up, and I was losing ground. If I had a child Lauren's age, I would be closing in on being a grandfather. The conflicting emotions at that thought were enough to snap me out of my reverie.

Damn it! I had work to do.

Turning back to Lauren, I tried to answer her question the best I could. "I don't know, Lauren," I said. "We are still setting the course of the investigation. Your father and mother had such a varied background — some of it dangerous — with dangerous people who could want them dead. It's just too hard to tell. That's why we need these cases."

"But these are really old," Lauren said. "Would these people still have a grudge?"

I thought about what Lauren said. It made sense, in a way. How long could someone hold a grudge? But then, look at Daylia Sherman. She waited twelve years, and maybe she was our best and most viable suspect. But, since my gut still was not comfortable with that premise, I didn't share her arrest with the girls.

"You know, Lauren," I said, "maybe you're right. Does your father have any more recent files or places where he keeps his more recent correspondence?"

"Of course!" Cindy said. "I know exactly what you want! It's inside, in the office."

"The office that was locked?" I asked.

"Yes, of course," Cindy said, looking at me like I was a moron.

Somewhere in the last two days the women had changes positions. Cindy had stopped her weeping and had become strong, while Lauren had sunk into a quiet lassitude. She was barely moving and her voice was slow and tired.

Cindy bounded into the house through the open garage door. I helped Lauren to her feet and we followed her in.

The door to her father's office was closed, but Cindy quickly opened it and went to her father's file cabinet. She pushed her hip against one of the drawers a couple of times then gave it a hard bang. The drawer popped open.

"I thought your father kept this place completely locked down?" I said.

Both girls laughed at me, and Lauren explained. "Daddy liked to believe he kept us out of his office, but he didn't. We went in there all the time. We just didn't let him know, because it would have worried him. He kept his guns in here, and you know fathers: they're always paranoid about that stuff."

"But, the other night?" I said, letting the question hang.

"The other night we didn't know you, and we were upset," Cindy said.

"You mean I could have just had you two help with those files?" I asked, trying to figure out if I could get them back to the station to help me.

They just laughed at me, and did the secret pinky-swear with each other.

My original impression of the daughters was completely upended. I now could see the imp in both of them. They may have come across at one time as disciplined and rigid, but now I realized they, too, had a secret life. I also realized they may be my best source of help in unwinding the conundrum that was their father.

"This is Daddy's correspondence file," Cindy said, pulling a blue folder from the bottom of a steel two drawer file cabinet. This is the cabinet where Daddy kept just the odds and ends of his life. Not the important Navy stuff."

I already had the file flipped open and was going through it. But it was the very first letter in the file that caught my eye. Stapled to it was the envelope giving a return address at the Lompoc Federal Prison. It was from one of past his clients telling him he urgently needed to speak with him about recent developments that might assist the client in his Rule 35 appeal for a lower sentence.

"Do you know this client or anything about his case?" I asked the girls.

Lauren picked up the letter and read it. "Yes, Ado Ito was a CEO of a company that got on the wrong side of the Securities and Exchange Committee. He refused a plea offer, and Daddy went to trial. Daddy lost, but the judge still gave Ito less time than the U. S. Attorney wanted. In a way, it was a win, but the client never gave up. He always thought he should be out."

"And the Rule 35 thing?" I asked.

"Less time for information," Cindy answered.

"Oh," I said, then added, "Did your father ever talk to you about the info Ito wanted to give the government?"

"Actually," Lauren said, "I know he did have Ito sit with him and the Homeland Security guys, but I don't know if anything came of it."

"Do you know what it was about?" I asked.

Lauren just shrugged. "I'm not really sure," she said. "Daddy could be really tight-lipped about some stuff. Cindy, do you know?"

Cindy sat for a moment, and asked, "Lauren, wasn't that about the time you were bringing Tim home to meet the family? You know, before all that. . ." she said, pointing at Lauren's pregnant belly.

"Could be," Lauren said. "Didn't Daddy and Charles and Tim talk about something that night? Something about Russia and Japan?"

I felt as if I had been socked in the gut. There was that possible connection again. I just had to ask, "Was there any talk about Iran or the Middle East, too?"

"Always, talk about the Middle East," Cindy said. "Charles is obsessed by it and is always pumping Daddy for information on it."

"Would your father have kept any of his Navy intelligence here?" I asked.

"That's why he had the locked room and cabinets," Cindy said. "But it looks like it's all gone."

"Yes," I said. "Remember that man who walked out of the office? He made sure they got all of that stuff."

"You mean that NCIS officer," Lauren said with a sigh. "I'm not sure I liked him. He seemed to think he was too cute."

"Really?" I asked, liking the fact that someone else didn't like him either.

"Well, he should have let you know he was in the house," Lauren said. "It would only have seemed polite."

Cindy started to laugh and said, "Yes, I thought for sure your partner was going to shoot him. By the way, what did you find in Daddy's files?"

A myriad of answers floated through my head, but I decided on honesty. I liked the fact that the two were beginning to trust me, and I them. "Nothing," I said. "The boxes were brought back to the station, sealed, and I don't know what's really in them other than a bunch of satellite photos. I have no idea what they mean."

"Well, why haven't you gotten a better idea?" Cindy demanded.

"It's because the Naval Criminal Investigative Service and my department are still haggling over who should know what," I said. "And I can't interpret the files without someone who knows what everything means."

"Well, shoot," Cindy said, "Lauren can probably help you with that. She sat at Daddy's knee for years learning maps and how to read satellite photos."

I looked over at Lauren who sighed deeply. "I think Daddy thought I would go the Naval Academy," she said. "I know he was disappointed when I dropped out of college to marry Tim, but I love him, and well. . . there's the baby and all."

"Oh?" I said, finding it refreshing that some men still did the honorable thing and married the girls they got pregnant.

"My fault," Lauren said. "But Tim said he loved me and he married me. Daddy came around and Mom... well, Mom was just Mom, accepting of whatever happened around her."

"Do you think you could help me?" I asked.

"Help you with what?" Cindy asked.

"Do you think Lauren could help me with the maps and stuff?"

"I thought the boxes were sealed," Cindy said.

"Well. . ." I stammered, trying to decide if it was the time for a confession.

Both girls were staring intently at me.

"Umm, I kinda, maybe, you know, lifted the seals," I said. "If the NCIS guy knew that, he'd probably shoot me or have me fired." I added.

The girls looked at each other a laughed.

"I knew he was okay," Cindy said.

"You were right, as always," Lauren said.

Both girls looked and me and began another paroxysm of giggling.

Cindy came over and put her arm in mine, giving me a squeeze. "I know you think you're cute, and you probably are, but... I guess we can trust you. Just don't do that all surfer-blonde thing, okay?" she said.

I nodded my head, and tried to look sincere.

Both girls started giggling again, but Cindy added, "Of course we'll help."

"So what's the plan?" Lauren asked.

I quickly sketched out a plan to unite the girls with the boxes and help me figure out why Russia, Japan, and Iran kept popping up in the investigation. I also kept the letter from Dado Ito. The letter could be evidence, and Ito could be my best clue.

CHAPTER FOURTEEN

With our plan set, the daughters decided they wanted to go back to the hotel to get something to eat and for Lauren to take a nap. I put them back into their rented Buick, and slid down the driveway to the waiting Intrepid.

With a wave good-bye to the girls as they drove off, I put my Bluetooth in my ear and thought about trying to reach Carmen Delgado again.

Before I could dial her number, my cell phone rang. It was Carmen.

"Yum, Jake," she said. "I heard you called and wanted to talk to me. Have you finally decided to let me have dinner with you?"

"You mean have *me* for dinner, don't you mean?" I replied.

"Ah, Jake, are you still pissed about what happened all those years ago? I was young, eager. . ."

"And hungry, if I remember correctly, Carmen," I said, thinking sharks are always hungry. "Speaking of which, did you smell the blood in the water? You know Judge Henning is dead."

"Yes, I heard this morning," she said. "It's all over the Courthouse. I guess he was shot—he and his wife."

"So, you know why I want to talk to you," I said, more as a statement than question.

"McAllister/Cheney, of course," she answered. "But you know, Jake, there's that pesky little attorney/client privilege thing."

"So?" I asked.

"Hmm," she said.

I could almost feel the water swirling around her as she came in for the kill. My blood ran cold.

"Well, we could make it a 'social' thing," she said. "Just two friends chatting over dinner."

Ahhh, there it was. She took off the rest of my arm already chomped on by Daylia. I could feel my head getting light from the loss of blood. I tried to run through the other options, like subpoenas and depositions, but nothing registered as workable.

Oh, well, with my arm already gone, I might as well let her have the rest of my body, too.

"Carmen, I can't wait until dinner, but I'd be more than happy to have lunch with you," I said, hoping the end of my life would come quickly and without too much pain.

Her squeal of delight almost broke my eardrum. "Okay, Jake," she said. "I really think the treat should be on me. I belong to that new supper club and they're doing lunch service now. I'll make the reservations. Martini-thirty for you?" she asked.

"Yeah, twelve-thirty is fine," I said.

What Shark Delgado didn't know was that my best friend, Sally Deming, owned the place. Maybe I could get Sally's staff to protect me. *Worth a shot,* I thought, as I dialed Sally's number.

Sally picked up the phone after the first ring. "Hello, Jake. How's my favorite detective," she asked, her voice somewhere between flirty and soothing.

"Sally, I need a huge favor," I said, picturing the beautiful woman who was my friend. I wanted to close my eyes and picture her sitting next to me, holding my hand. At somewhere near or at fifty years of age, Sally was undoubtedly the most beautiful woman I had ever known. Though a few laugh lines radiated out from her intense blue eyes, her face was otherwise untouched by either time or surgeons. She kept her hair the perfect Newport Beach blonde, with it usually coiffed in a tight French twist—though I liked it best when she let it hang free, or had it pulled back into a ponytail. She worked hard at keeping just enough curves to make a man hungry. And her best feature was her voice. It had a way of making a man feel powerful. But, I quickly shook myself out of my reverie and returned my attention to the highway.

"Ah, Jakey, you only call when you need a favor," she burbled with laughter into the phone.

"You heard about Mark Henning's death, I presume," I asked, knowing full well she would know as much, or more than me, long before I did. Sally ran a discrete escort service and it was one of her girls with the presiding judge the night of the murder.

"He was a good, good man," she said. "One of the few men in this town who truly loved his wife and was devoted to her. So what's the favor?"

"Carmen Delgado is taking me to lunch at your club," I said.

"Ah, the Cheney pit-bull," Sally said.

"No, the Shark," I said. "But, you're right: I am meeting with her because of her connection to Cheney. But I need protection. I am afraid she'll order the sea food platter and eat me in her confusion."

"Ah, Jakey, still willing to prostitute yourself for your cases," Sally said, the laugh only slightly less cheerful.

"It was a trap," I said, my feelings hurt by her statement and definitely feeling a pout coming on. "I needed the info, and she said she'd only give it to me in a 'social setting.'"

Her laughter was like bells or wind chimes tinkling in the wind.

"Okay, Jake," she laughed. "I will see to it Carmen is put in Miss Vicki's station and you'll be safe."

With my physical safety assured, I pulled the Intrepid into the Starbucks on PCH to review the McAllister/Cheney file. I ordered a venti latte with extra foam, thinking I would need the extra caffeine to keep me on my toes. Spending any time with Carmen would be exhausting. I had to stay alert, not only for the information I hoped to get, but also for my personal safety.

With latte in hand, I sat at one of the overstuffed chairs and opened the *In re McAllister/Cheney* file. I was most specifically interested in the contempt of court action and the motion to have Henning removed for cause. I once again quickly reviewed some the filings and their supporting declarations. But, even rereading them with fresh eyes, I couldn't get a strong sense that it was a case worth killing over. There was harsh language over both Bridget's and her father's signatures, but I knew it was Carmen's writing, not theirs, having been victimized by some of the same language myself. Yet, somehow, Beverly, Henning's court clerk, had thought the case was important enough, or dangerous enough that it warranted my attention.

With the dreaded appointment looming, I closed my file, and again said a quick prayer to my guardian angels. Sometimes I wasn't sure I still had one, convinced they had left me as 'hopeless' many years earlier. But, just in case they were still around and interested, I still went through the motions.

The drive to the club took less than five minutes. Well caffeinated and hyped with dread, I pulled into the club parking lot, a few minutes before the appointed time expecting a valet. But none appeared to be working the noon crowd, which was just as well. The Intrepid didn't make much of a statement other than possibly "gigolo looking for a new score" — or maybe "poor boyfriend."

Stop, it, Jake, I thought, giving myself a mental slap. *You're a cop working a case. Stop with the fear. Carmen only chewed you up and spit you out once. Just because she's never given up her taste for Jake-meat is no reason to go all weak in the knees.*

A couple more mental slaps, and then I shrugged into my linen jacket. I was ready to face the dreaded Shark.

The club was on the second floor, overlooking Newport Bay. The room was designed to be discrete and elegant while still giving all the diners a view of the water and yachts. The banquettes were covered in deep burgundy leather, and the carpet was done is shades of teal blue, sea green, and rose. I knew those were Sally's favorite colors, and it gave me comfort knowing that secret. It somehow made me feel that Sally was close by and would keep me safe.

At that thought I laughed at myself. I was getting way too dramatic. I was a grown man, and Carmen Delgado was just a woman. I had been "handling" women all my life—even dangerous, killer women.

Pfftt! Let the games begin, I thought as I gave my name to the hostess.

Carmen was already seated when I made my entrance. She rose to her feet when I approached and gave me her cheek to kiss. Two air kisses later, I waited for her to take her seat.

"Oh, Jake," she said, "I was so disappointed. I was hoping to get the special room, but I understand it's booked. Boo hoo."

"Ah, Carmen, remember, this is just a lunch between two friends," I said, taking a closer look at her.

Actually, Sally had done the attorney a favor by not seating her in the octagonal room with the glass walls. Carmen's face would not have done well in the harsh sunlight. She was aging, and no amount of Botox would hide the damage done to her face and skin from the long hours of demanding work and stress.

Carmen Delgado was a second-generation Mexican. Her family came to work the fields and stayed. She had benefited from what were then excellent California schools, and had gone to the University of California at Berkley for undergraduate studies, and the same university's Boalt Hall for her law degree. Her parents had given her two things: her drive to succeed and their coloring and body build.

Unlike so many of the women who inhabited the Newport Coast, Carmen was not tall and lithe. Rather, she was of average height, and had the swarthy skin tones and coloring of her parents. But, instead of leaving her hair dark and playing to her natural coloring, Carmen had dyed her hair blonde, which left it brassy and dry. Presumably, she had work done on her face, but it still had toughness in color and texture. Even without the wrinkles, her skin looked worn. She hid her figure in well-designed clothing that usually hid her barrel chest and lack of hips, which went straight into long, thin, shapeless legs. She usually hid her legs by wearing pants suits that were flattering to her body style. With the money she made from fleecing opposing spouses and even her own clients, she could afford the best.

That day was no different. She was dressed in a monotone silver gray suit and camisole top. Her jacket, which was casually thrown over the back of the seat, was the same silver gray, but with a multi-colored silk lining. Her jewelry was also silver with multicolored stone insets. Overall, her outfit and style were stunning.

Unfortunately for me, the most disturbing part of her was her nails. They were unnaturally long and she kept them colored blood-red, reminding me of a shark's teeth just after it had eaten. And one couldn't help but notice those nails as she had a tendency to tap them furiously whenever she did not like what a judge was ruling or what someone was saying to her. Overall, she scared the holy shit out of me.

As soon as I took my seat, Miss Vicki appeared with a tray holding a glass of red wine and a martini shaker with a chilled glass. She set the wine in front of Carmen, shook the martini shaker a few times, and poured vodka into the chilled glass for me. I started to protest that I was on duty, but Carmen already had her glass lifted for a toast. Afraid of insulting her, and never turning away from a toast, I too lifted my glass.

"Here's to 'martini-thirty' and to friends," Carmen said, her deep brown eyes dancing.

"Ah, okay… to friends," I said, taking a sip of what turned out to be Grey Goose vodka.

We sipped our drinks, chit-chatting a little about nothing. After we ordered, I was ready to talk about the Cheneys.

"You know, Carmen," I started, "the presiding judge over at the Family Law Courthouse wanted me to look at the McAllister/Cheney file." I knew it was a fib, but it was a small fib. Actually, he had told Beverly Anderson to give me the most problematic files and she had given that file to me.

"Hmm, really, Jake," she said, staring hard into my eyes. "Did he give it to you or did Henning's clerk?"

Damn, I thought. But I decided not to give in too quickly. "Yes,

Carmen," I said, staring back at her, not blinking. "I met with him at the Courthouse on Saturday. He knew about the shooting Friday night and met me at the Courthouse."

"Hmm, I thought he was playing golf on Saturday," she said.

"He was. Monarch, I believe," I said, glad I had paid attention to that little kernel of knowledge. "He had to leave to make his tee time, so, I guess you're right, in a way. Beverly did give me the copy of the file, but it was the judge who blessed it."

"Well, Jake, you might as well know, Ms. Beverly Anderson doesn't like me very much," Carmen said.

"Was it because of that 170.1 motion you filed to have her judge removed for cause?" I asked innocently.

"Oh, you know about that," Carmen said. "I thought the pleadings in that were under seal."

Well, I thought, *that mystery was solved*. I would need to get the presiding judge to unseal the pleadings and give them to me. It was evidence, as far as I could see. More importantly, I didn't want Carmen to know I didn't have them, so I fudged. "This is a murder investigation, Carmen. Nothing remains secret," I said.

"Hmm," she said, tapping her nails on the rim of her glass. "So why do you think those pleadings are relevant?" she asked.

"I see Old Man Cheney's fingerprints all over that file, especially those pleadings," I said.

"Look, my client believed, and still believes, that Mark Henning was favoring John McAllister over Bridget," Carmen flared. "Henning had no right to bring Cheney in as a party to a family law action. The law is clear on that! The court has no jurisdiction over a non-party, and yet, that's exactly what Henning was doing when he ordered Cheney to not have any contact with his daughter until after six months of therapy and the report back from the evaluator!"

Ahh, I thought, *so that's what he did.* "Well, how did Old Man Cheney feel about that?" I asked.

"How would you feel, Jake?" she asked, tapping furiously on the rim of her glass with her blood-red nails. "Just how would you feel being ordered not to have any contact with your own daughter, your grown daughter, at that! And, his grandchild! His only grandchild! My, God, Jake, it was inhuman!"

"I would imagine it made him angry?" I asked.

"Well, he ignored the order, of course," Carmen said, taking another long drink of her wine. "It wasn't a valid order, anyway. The contempt charges were spurious and ridiculous."

"Wow," I said, "that must have taken some balls to just ignore a court order like that."

Carmen drained her glass and motioned for another wine. Before her glass hit the table, Miss Vicki appeared with another glass of red wine. At the same time a man appeared with a large tray of food. As feared, Carmen had ordered the sea food appetizer platter. All talking stopped for a few minutes while we ate.

"You know, Jake," Carmen said after a while, "Cheney is a very powerful man. He's used to getting his own way, and Bridget is his only child. He dotes on her. When she married McAllister, the man was devastated."

"Why's that, Carmen?" I asked.

"He did everything with her," Carmen said. "I've been around the Cheney organization for quite a while. I watched that child grow from a happy ten-year-old to a sullen teenager, making her father keep her on an even tighter leash. Well, that and of course, the fact that she is due to inherit her father's estate, which will make her incredibly wealthy. With her father's hovering and control, I could tell that she wanted out from under her father's thumb. When she met John McAllister at one of those charity Fun Runs for the various police and fire agencies, I think she saw a way out. I know John was immediately smitten with her."

"Speaking of John McAllister, do you think he killed Henning?" I asked.

"As much as it would thrill my client for me to say, 'Yes, I think John killed Henning,' I just can't," Carmen said. She swirled her wine in her glass, took another long drink, and then added, "John is a good guy. His only fault was he married over his head, and he had the balls to stand up to his father-in-law. Other than that, he's a decent, hard-working, good-looking man who adores his wife."

"So why'd you do it?" I asked.

"Do what, Jake?" Carmen asked, burying her face in her wine glass.

"Why did you file all those domestic violence restrainer orders and all that other stuff?" I asked, getting a little heated.

Carmen looked away from me, her stare on a faraway point some-where out in the bay. She took a deep breath and sighed. "It's my job, Jake," she said, finally. "Aren't there times you are forced to do things that turn your stomach because you have to get a job done? Aren't there times you wish you could just walk away?"

I sat dead still, not answering. I had the deep fear I was looking into the soul of the Shark, and it scared me to know she might actually have one.

The woman finally shrugged her shoulders and turned to look at me as she answered. "Look at me, Jake," she said. "I know what is said about me behind my back. I know I'm not from the blue-bloods around here. I'm not tall, not thin, not beautiful. All I have are my brains and my determination to work hard. That's what makes me who I am. I know I'm called the 'Shark' and other less flattering things. I know all this. Yet, I do my job and I do it well for my clients. I do it because it is my JOB!"

Miss Vicki appeared out of nowhere to check on our table. She looked at the woman who was close to tears and then at me. Her stare asked me if all was okay. I nodded at her and gave the universal sign for another round of drinks by swirling my forefinger in a circle. She nodded and withdrew.

By that time Carmen had snatched a tissue from somewhere and was dabbing at her eyes. She looked at me, gave me a half-smile, and started again. "Jake, I am a money whore. I admit it. I swore I would never be poor like my parents. They killed themselves working the fields. My dad died when he was only fifty, for Christ's sake. My mother is so crippled with arthritis she can hardly walk. My brothers are working just as hard and are getting just as crippled. I promised myself that would not be my life. So, instead, I crippled my soul."

Reflexively, I reached out and patted her shoulder. Again she smiled at me, then continued speaking. "Cheney was furious when Bridget married McAllister. As you may know, they ran off to somewhere up the coast to get married on the beach. Cheney wasn't even there. Never even got to walk his daughter down the aisle. It broke his heart. He swore revenge. He paid me enough money to pay off all my school loans, buy medical insurance for my mother, and a down payment on my house. So, yes, I did it. I set out to destroy a marriage because of money."

"But, the divorce never went through?" I said as more of question.

"No, Jake, it didn't," Carmen said, her voice getting a little firmer. "As much of a money whore as I am, I could also do other things to keep it from happening. But, if you ever repeat this... I will KILL you."

I couldn't help but laugh. The attorney sitting next to me started to laugh, too. She knew the joke and the craziness of her threat. I couldn't tell anyone what happened today because, well, because this meeting never took place. Yet, I still found myself wanting to get a little salt and throw it over my left shoulder.

I shuddered a little, then asked, "So, you agreed to send them to mediators and counselors and court advisors to drag out the proceedings?"

"You read the file," she said.

"Of course, and I saw all the minutes of the proceedings," I said.

Miss Vicki appeared with our drinks, her left eyebrow slightly raised at our laughter. I gave her a short nod to let her know we were fine. She left the drinks and withdrew.

"You trying to get me drunk, Jake?" Carmen asked.

"No, just a little alcohol to make the hurt go away," I answered.

"Yes, I've been making the hurt go away a lot lately," Carmen said, as she downed half the glass of wine. "I really believe that John McAllister loves Bridget and their daughter. I also know that Bridget wants to be back with him. And, I also truly believe that Mark Henning was going to dismiss the entire action at the next hearing. I set the matter to take status. . ."

"Status? I asked.

"You know," Carmen said, her words slightly slurring. "The questions about whether the party filing for the divorce really wanted it and if irreconcilable differences had occurred, that stuff."

I thought a moment, then it hit me. "So you think Bridget may have said she didn't want the divorce?"

"Absolutely!" Carmen said, taking another swallow.

I mulled that over for a few minutes, and then asked the most obvious question. "Did you suggest to Henning to make the order keeping Cheney away from his daughter?"

The attorney played with her wine glass, swirling it around and putting it down on the table, leaving a blood-red ring on the pink tablecloth.

"I could never, ever, ever do that, Jake," she said. "My ethics are such that I couldn't make the suggestion. But, when John told the judge that Bridget seemed to do much better when not under the influence of her father, I, of course, demurred and said nothing. Henning knew I agreed. He was a smart man and a very perceptive judge. He made that order on his own."

"So, we're all the way back to whether Cheney was sufficiently incensed to do something stupid," I said.

"No, we still had the motion to recuse the judge for cause," she said.

"And Bridget had you file that motion?" I asked.

Carmen just snorted at that. "Not likely. She liked Henning."

"Oh? Yet you filed it anyway?" I asked, then flinched.

Carmen saw my flinch and smiled. "We've already gone over that, Jake. Besides, there was no harm to Bridget for me filing that motion. It never would have been granted anyway. There was no 'cause' except in Old Man Cheney's mind."

"Did he know that?"

Carmen just shrugged her shoulders and didn't answer. She played with her drink, and I stared hard into my still full martini glass. I ran a few scenarios around in my mind, but finally let the subject drop while we finished our meal. True to her word, the Shark picked up the tab. And true to my nature, I let her.

But, as we said our good-byes, I said something completely out of character for me. I said, "Carmen, you don't practice criminal law, do you?"

"Of course not, Jake," she said.

"Hmm, it's a good thing," I said.

This made her laugh out loud. Then she added, "Why, you afraid of me?"

"You already know the answer to that," I said. "But, you might suggest to your client he may want to get one on retainer," I said. "You'll be a hero if you do."

Carmen looked hard at me. She nodded as she also picked up my meaning.

"Damn you, Swanson," the attorney said. "You are a gentleman, aren't you?"

"Oh, hell no," I said. "Just make sure you put this lunch on your expense account."

"No worries about that, Jake," she said. "I just can't let him know it was you. Remember, this meeting never took place. It was just a casual lunch between 'friends.'"

I helped her into her jacket, and she turned in to face me, giving me a brief kiss on the lips. She laughed as I instinctively put my fingers to my face, checking to see if my lips were still attached to my face, or if she had left the devil's burn mark on them. Worse yet, there was a pesky stirring in a place I had begun to think of as dead. Damn.

"They're still there, Jake," she said. "But it doesn't mean I still don't want to eat you up!"

I shook my head, and gave the woman a hug. It was the kind of hug a man gives a woman when he doesn't know what else to do.

She slipped her arm through mine as we rode the elevator down to the parking lot. I gave her another hug after I opened the door of her Mercedes. One more brief kiss and she laughed as she started her car.

I watched her pull away, and quietude settled on my shoulders. Cheney was now on my radar, and McAllister was off. I still had a lot of work to do. I whistled up Intrepid as I twirled its keys on my finger. Intrepid and I were on the hunt for a killer.

CHAPTER FIFTEEN

I felt only a slight buzz from the three-martini lunch. Actually, it was really a martini and a half for me. I had sinned and left two half-filled glasses of Grey Goose sitting on the table. But the sin was worth it. I had gotten what I went for. I wasn't ruling out Cheney, though I was sure he wouldn't have done the act himself. Nonetheless, with my brain slightly clouded, there was no way I was going to try to take him on until I was totally focused.

That left me part of an afternoon to get back to the station to see about making an appointment to see Ado Ito up in Lompoc prison. It had been a while since I had tried to breach the defenses of a federal detention center, and I knew the rules were sometimes very strict about seeing a sentenced prisoner, even for law enforcement. I needed some help with that one, and the best person to help me was the lieutenant's secretary.

At the station, my partner was working away at a folding table she had put up next to her desk. She was collating the various reports from witness statements gathered by the uniformed officers the night of the Henning shooting.

"Well, homey," I said to her as I pulled up a stray desk chair to sit across from her. "Anything interesting?"

"Don't call me 'homey,'" was all she said as she continued working.

"Whoa, why the attitude?" I said to her.

"Swanson, you're a pain the butt to have as a partner," she said. "I never know where you are. I never know what you're doing. And, most of all, I know you never follow the rules."

I swiveled a few times in the chair wondering if it was her way of getting me to confess to breaching the seals on the boxes. If it was, she was getting really good at this detective misdirection thing. I decided not to take the bait.

"Well, you knew that when you met me, remember?" I said in my most sincere voice. "I distinctly remember you telling Lieutenant Graber that you didn't like me and what I stood for, remember?"

"Pfffssst!" was all she said.

"So why the grumps now?" I asked.

"Well, for your information, Patrol found a loaded gun near the bushes where Sergeant Greene said you first saw Daylia Sherman."

"That's good, isn't it?" I asked.

"Yes, for the Sheriff's Department and Irvine P.D.," she said, still grumping at me.

"Okay, Little Beaver," I said, "don't drag this out any more than you have. I take it the ballistics matched the Lawrence shooting, but not ours?"

"Little Beaver? Where in the heck did that come from?" my partner asked, trying to suppress a smile.

"You won't let me call you 'Homes,' and if I remember correctly, 'Cuz' is also out, so it's now Little Beaver," I answered solemnly.

"Okay, great, Swanson," she said. "I guess 'Sanchez' or "Melissa' or even 'Detective' is too much for you?"

"Ah, my Little Beaver, you are too special to me to call you by names others call you," I said.

By that time she was in full-on laughter. "Okay, okay, I'll stop with the PMS-ing," she said.

"Whoa, whoa, no female stuff in the bullpen," I said. "We guys can talk about it, but you can't say it."

"Right," Melissa said, turning back to her desk. "You were right, as always. The bullets and ballistics didn't match the gun we found."

"Yeah, I didn't think ole' Daylia did it." I said. "The Henning job was too professional. Whoever shot our vics was good at their job and knew how to use a weapon. Besides, the bullets were some sort of exotic stuff, right?"

"Yeah, not the Wal-mart boxed stuff we usually find," she answered.

"Maybe that's where we should look, then?" I asked. "You know anybody you can shake down for info?"

My partner just smiled and didn't answer the question. Instead, she started on a new track. "So, does that leave us with that cop with the bad divorce?" Melissa asked.

"Naw," I said. "I got it straight from the horse's mouth — or should I say *Shark*'s mouth — that judge Henning was the best friend that cop ever had. Henning woulda probably thrown the case out if Cheney hadn't filed the motion to have him removed for prejudice."

"And Cheney?" she asked.

"Maybe," I said. "Not personally, but he would have had it done."

"You want his financials?" she asked.

"I'm pretty sure we don't have enough for subpoenas yet," I said. "He's too powerful for us to take him head-on, at least not quite yet. Let me see if I can stir the pot some and see what we get."

"You going to talk to him?"

"Maybe tomorrow, or the next day," I said. "He's got to be feeling kinda relieved that Henning is dead, especially since there was that contempt action pending. That will go away now. He might say something at the club or golf course. Sometimes the powerful get complacent when they think the heat is off."

"Okey, doke," she said. "You probably know these people better than me. I know my crooks and gang-bangers. With them, you got to come at them hard and fast... and lie your butt off."

"Our people here aren't much different," I said. "We all lie, but they're usually smart enough to let a high-priced lawyer do it for them. Can't come at them unless we really know what we're doing. Even then, hmm, still hard."

"Is that why you surf?" she asked out of nowhere.

"What?" I asked, surprised at the question.

"Is that why you surf?" Melissa asked, looking hard at me. "You seem to always have time on your board when you're neck deep in caca. What does it do? Clear your head?"

I looked hard at my partner. She wasn't wearing any particular expression other than curiosity. But the question was interesting. Surfing did clear my head. I was going against the element of water, stronger and more powerful than me. Yet, I won as many times as I lost. Picking the powerful wave and riding it into submission somehow cleaned me and made me feel alive.

I shrugged and smiled. "You're right, Little Beaver," I said. "With all this caca-shit we have on a daily basis, I guess it does cleanse me."

We both laughed, and it appeared that peace was restored between us.

I left her to her work and wandered off to find Jenny, Graber's secretary.

She was in her cubicle typing away at her computer, earbuds in, rocking back and forth to the music blaring through the tiny wires. I had to stand in front of her for what seemed like forever before she looked up.

"Hey, Jake," she said. "What can I do you for?"

"I need some help, and Clara's out," I said.

"So, I'm your second choice?" she said, removing one of the earbuds, music blaring from the piece dangling on her chest.

"Noooo," I answered. "You'd never be my second choice. You know that."

"Hmph, okay, whata ya need?" she said, removing the second earbud.

"I need to see an already sentenced prisoner up at Lompoc. How do I get in to see him?"

She turned around and reached for a small three-ring notebook on her bookshelf. She leafed through it and finally found a page she read to herself before scribbling a phone number and a name on a sheet of paper. "Here, Jake," she said, handing me the paper. "This is the number to the secretary to the deputy warden. Her name is Ann, and she'll help you. Normally, you have to go through security clearance and wait a few weeks. But tell Ann you're on the hunt for a killer and she'll help you get in."

"How long will it take?" I asked.

"Call her tonight. Fax her what she needs. She'll have you in tomorrow, if you want." Jenny said, putting her earbuds back in her ears and turned back to her computer.

I wandered back to my desk and pulled out the letter from Ado Ito. His prison number was on the attached envelope as well as his cell location and cell number. I hoped I had everything I needed.

A few minutes later I had Ann on the phone and quickly explained what I needed and why. She listened intently then asked for a few things from me. I promised her I would call her back when I was ready to fax the requested material.

In less than a half-hour I called Ann back to let her know the material was coming. I also explained to her the need for secrecy, as I was afraid the prisoner had information that could affect our national security.

I was so intent on what I was doing, I didn't notice Melissa standing behind me until after I hung up the phone.

"Hey, Little Beaver," I said. "What's shaking? You want to take a road trip with me to federal prison?"

I couldn't read her face. Maybe I should have tried harder. But when she turned on her heel, I didn't see any need to follow. It was a HUGE mistake.

CHAPTER SIXTEEN

With my appointment set at the Lompoc federal prison, I needed to prepare for the meeting with Ado Ito. I knew enough lawyers and spent enough time drinking with some of them to know that a *Rule 35* was the federal equivalent of a "Get out of Jail Free" Card. If a defendant under federal indictment gave information to the government that led to another series of arrests, then that defendant was rewarded with time off his sentence. As far as I was concerned, it rewarded the basest nature of criminals and rewarded them for turning on their friends, families, and coconspirators.

Yes, I guess that coconspirators in crime needed to be taken out of society, but the whole idea of snitching left me feeling that it was too much like the old dictatorships where information on neighbors was rewarded. Quite frankly, I hated the whole idea. However, something was going on with Ado Ito and Henning that may lead to something interesting. Something the NCIS guy didn't want me to know. That was enough for me. I needed Ito's criminal file, and I needed it right away.

As I ruminated about the implications of what Ito might have tried to give to the government, I knew it was even more important that I get back into the sealed files and develop a working knowledge of what the maps and satellite photos. I needed to know what they meant and whether it had any bearing on my investigation. Everything in my being told me that as scary as it was to think a local judge could have been killed by a foreign entity, it was not a lead I could dismiss.

More importantly, from my years as a detective I knew that corporate CEOs were a conceited bunch, prone to use their superior knowledge to intimidate what they perceived to be lesser mortals. If I were going to get anywhere with Ito, I needed to know the criminal file, and I needed to know the military implications of the satellite maps. Maybe if I knew the background, I could keep Ito from blowing smoke in that place where sun didn't shine.

Since I never served in the military, I knew I had a huge hole in my knowledge that needed to be filled with information. I really never saw any sense in the daily drills and protocols, not being a person who enjoyed, or even adhered to, discipline. The police academy was the closest I ever came to actual daily routines. But, I did know at least one person who knew this stuff—almost like a pro, having sat on her father's knee while he went over his maps and photos. Lauren was a good jumping off point. And, if worse came to worse, I knew I could always call on Bill Dawson to help me if the spy stuff became relevant.

As to the criminal stuff, Cindy would be my best source of information. I needed both girls, and I needed them right away. Our plan had to go into effect right away.

Afraid to explain too much to anyone while I was at the station, I called the girls again and asked them to meet me back at the house. When I told them why I needed their help, they readily agreed to meet me at the house in about a half-hour.

The girls were pulling into the driveway just as I pulled up to the house. The yellow tape from the previous night's escapade was down, again, and the seal on the front door was removed. It told me that the crime scene guys were done and, with the lack of security so far, evidently someone above my pay grade had decided to release the scene, again. I found myself shaking my head in frustration. I obviously was not the detective in charge.

Damn!

Oh, well, I thought, *I would have just broken into the house and resealed it had it not been released.* So, I put away my annoyance at the disregard for my place as senior detective and decided to concentrate on the project at hand.

I greeted both girls warmly. Cindy was bouncy and happy. She looked refreshed and rested. Lauren, though, looked pale and tired. I stole a look at her otherwise shapely legs and saw the telltale sign of swelling. I had been around enough women friends to know that swelling of the ankles was not a good sign in pregnant women. So I hustled the two inside and put Lauren in the large easy chair and pushed the ottoman over to elevate her legs. She gave me a grateful sigh.

While Cindy busied herself in the kitchen making tea for her sister, I sat with Lauren.

"Lauren, I know we already went through your father's files," I said, "but I really, really, really need the criminal file on Ito, as well as your dad's notes."

Lauren sighed, and shrugged. "Cindy, do you know where else Dad would have kept his files?"

Cindy joined us, setting the cup of tea next to her sister. "Okay, we've gone through the files in the garage, and we've gone through his file cabinet, so there's not a lot of other places Dad would have kept files," she said.

Lauren sipped her tea and closed her eyes, resting her head on the back of the chair. Her breathing slowed. I thought she was asleep, when suddenly her eyes popped open. "The secret safe," she cried, bolting upright, splashing her tea across her ample belly.

"Of course," Cindy said, rushing into the guest bedroom.

Lauren struggled to get to her feet, with me helping to pull her the rest of the way out of the chair. We followed her sister into the second-ary bedroom.

Cindy was already at the closet with its door open, and she was pulling at the carpet. The carpet gave a distinct scratching sound as it pulled loose from the Velcro strips securing it to the floor. With the carpet rolled back, Cindy removed a plywood piece from the floor and exposed the floor safe.

"What the heck?" I asked, surprised to find a safe in an unlocked bedroom after seeing the extreme security measures taken in the judge's office.

The girls looked at me, then Cindy gave a hearty laugh. Lauren folded herself onto the bed, curling up into a tight ball, while merriment twinkled in her eyes.

"Daddy's little secret," Lauren said.

"Daddy was paranoid about some things," Cindy said. "He believed in multiple layers of security."

"Yeah, with a locked office, locked files, and a safe in the master bedroom closet for Mom's jewelry, somehow this safe seemed to be invisible to anyone snooping," Lauren said, closing her eyes.

Cindy started working the knob on the combination lock and, a few twists later, it popped open.

"What?" I said with my surprise elevated to a new level at the two girls and their working knowledge of their father and his secrets.

"Don't ask," Lauren mumbled. "Cindy knew almost all of Daddy's secrets."

"This is where he kept his very secret stuff," Cindy said. "I found it by accident one day when our cat was a kitten and got locked in this closet. I found her here, but she had pulled at the corners of the carpet, and I found the Velcro. I thought it was strange and just kept snooping until I found the loose board, then the safe."

"And the combination?" I asked.

A smile played on the corners of the older sister's mouth. When she brushed back her dark hair over her ears, she looked like a radiant minx, ready to do mischief. Her beauty in that moment was undeniable, and almost irresistible. I had to give myself a hard shake to snap myself back to the job at hand.

"In plain sight," Cindy said. "Daddy had a code, and kept things in plain sight, buried within the code. If you knew where to look, and knew the code, all the combinations were easy to figure out."

"Did he know you knew?" I asked.

Cindy just shrugged. Lauren rolled over onto her back and took a deep breath as she struggled to sit upright. "I doubt it," she said, holding her belly. "Daddy loved us, but sometimes he was, like, you know, vacant."

"Vacant?" I asked.

"You know, even when he was home he didn't see us," Cindy said, anger tingeing her voice.

Lauren sighed and lay back down. "Yeah, he could get really wrapped up in everything else and sometimes forgot to see us. We could be invisible, but I know he loved us."

Cindy didn't answer; she was busy pulling a brown file folder from the safe. Also, she pulled an envelope from the safe with a return address from the Department of the Navy. She handed me the file and quickly opened the envelope. Inside was an official-looking document addressed to Commander Mark Henning.

"Hey, Lauren," Cindy said, extending the envelope out toward her sister. "These look like orders. What do you think?"

I handed the envelope to Lauren, who read through the paper quickly. Tears sprang to her eyes as she finished, then handed the letter back to me.

"Yes," she whispered, "they are orders. Daddy was reactivated, and was being shipped out to the Far East. Looks like Japan."

"No," Cindy said. "I don't believe you. Daddy wouldn't have left Mom right now. Not now."

Both girls looked stricken, and I felt a funny tingle in the small of my back. I didn't want to believe what my detective instincts were telling me. Instead, I turned the girls' attention back to the file.

The file was a multi-sectioned brown folder entitled *United States v. Ado Ito*. I had expected a much larger file, but the front section held an envelope with about eight CDs in it. Cindy, apparently putting her pain behind her, explained how the case was so complicated that the government gave the defense the CDs on which all the documents had been copied. It was standard practice to do that since it made it easier for both sides to set up systems to identify the all the documents, investigative reports and grand jury transcripts that made up the "discovery" aspect of the case by using computerized filing codes. She also told me that her father and his documents control person probably had created notebooks of the documents they used at trial, but they would be stored somewhere else because it would be too bulky to keep with the main litigation file.

She was speaking so quickly and with so much assurance I quickly formed the impression that maybe she had wanted to be a lawyer. She disabused me of that idea, telling me that she had worked in her father's office since she was fourteen—and loved almost every moment of it. But, in her mind, she wasn't aggressive enough to consider going to law school. She was sure she couldn't do what her father did every day. In the end, Cindy decided what she really wanted was to be like her mom: stay home, cook for her husband and kids, and contribute to society through her charity work.

"So, Cindy," I said, picking up the brown folder, "what should I expect to see in this file. How is it arranged?"

She took the file from me and flipped it open to its first section. "In this first section you will find correspondence on the right side of the folder, and my father's notes on the left side. The second section has the motions. Right hand is from the defense, left from the prosecutor. The last section is what they used in trial. In a case like this, it would be the indices of the exhibits, and maybe some other stuff. By the end of any trial, my dad's files were always a mess unless he had the paralegal go back through and reorganize."

As Cindy had suspected, the file was somewhat disorganized, but I did find beneath the envelope of CDs numerous letters from Ado Ito to Henning and some from Henning to Ito. More importantly, Henning's notes to the file indicated numerous trips to see Ito after the trial. I wanted to match the notes with the letters and see why Ito was so insistent about Henning coming to see him. As much as my logic didn't want to believe there was a connection, something in my inner core felt there was.

Okay, okay, a gut instinct is not something that can be used at trial, but my gut was rumbling, and it wasn't hunger for food. It was hunger for the truth.

While Cindy and I went through the file, Lauren got up from the bed and returned to the overstuffed chair in the great room. She was so quiet that Cindy and I finally went to check on her. She was sound asleep, and her face was pale.

"You know, Detective Swanson, my sister doesn't look too well," Cindy said. "I think I should get her back to the hotel. Maybe even take her to a doctor. What do you think?"

Why would I know that? I thought. *I'm a man, and a man who's never had a kid. I know some stuff, but nothing about birthin' no babies.* Then it dawned on me. Ahhh, Sally would know. She'd know what to do. A quick phone call to her, and she arrived about fifteen minutes later.

Sally arrived in her light blue Maserati convertible, looking like her usual ravishing self. Her blonde hair was pulled back tightly into a chignon, and she was dressed in a short black cocktail dress.

"Hey, Jakey," she said, giving me a brief kiss on the lips. "I was on my way to the club. I have a large party there tonight and should make an appearance. But, what do you have?"

By this time Lauren was awake. She was ghostly pale, and her breathing was heavy. Cindy was looking at me and looking at her sister with a look of concern.

"Jake," she whispered, "I think something may be wrong."

Sally bent down and looked at Lauren who barely acknowledged her presence.

"Okay, Jake," she said. "You were right to call me. Let me call my doctors and have them meet me at Hoag Hospital. Help me get her to my car."

"Should we call an ambulance?" Cindy asked.

"My car is faster," Sally said. "By the time the boys get here, I can have your sister to the hospital."

Cindy looked at me, and I added, "Sally knows everyone in this town. If she says she'll have someone waiting for your sister when she arrives, they'll be there."

The three of us got the nearly unconscious woman into the car, and Cindy said she'd follow in the rental car. Seconds later, Sally was chirping her tires as she pulled out of the driveway while Cindy followed closely behind.

This left me alone in the house, which was fine with me. My need to snoop was overwhelming me. I just knew there had to be more here than what the crews and daughters had found. The safe in the guest bedroom was cool, but the file I held in my hand did not have what I was looking for. I know that the careful lawyer would have taken notes at his meeting with the Feds and Ito. Yet, even with a cursory look through the file, I knew those notes were missing. They had to be somewhere. But where?

I wandered back to the open office door and stood in the center of the room, shutting my eyes. I let my mind go blank and just stood there. What kept flashing in my head was a movie I had seen where the spy had kept a floor safe beneath his desk under the carpet. It was the only thought that kept reverberating in my head.

Opening my eyes, I fastened my sight on the heavy oak desk in the middle of the room. There was a large black executive chair pushed out of the leg well, but under the desk was a plastic floor mat. It hadn't been disturbed in the search as the carpet beneath it was heavily mashed.

Oh, what the hell, I thought. I pulled up the floor mat and set it aside. Then I got down on my knees and ran my hands over the carpet. The carpet was thick, and it stood up immediately when I fluffed it with my hands. I played around the edges of the flattened area, but it wasn't until I went directly to the center of the leg well area that I found the patch.

The carpet was very well patched and held in place with Velcro just like in the guest closet. I pulled it up and, son of a gun, there in the floor, just like in the movie, was another floor safe — one that I had no idea how to open without letting someone know I was still searching around in the house.

"Damn!" I said to myself. I looked at the Rolodex on the desk, but quickly realized that even if I knew what I was looking for, I never would figure out the code for the safe.

But my urge was strong. More than ever I wanted to crack into that safe. I finally thought of an old mope I had arrested years before for drugs. He had eventually worn himself out doing drugs and going to jail. As part of his rehabilitation he had become a locksmith. I could call him, or I could get one of the crime scene guys out with a certified locksmith. But, if I called my squad, then that NCIS clown may take whatever I found in the safe.

A few seconds later I was on the phone with Jacobo, the old mope. I promised him cash and that was all he needed to get out of the house and come to me. He said it would take him about a half-hour to get from Costa Mesa to Newport Beach, but he'd leave right away.

With Jacobo on the way, I took a seat on the floor after carefully replacing the carpet and floor mat. I had time to go through the *Ito* file and see what it meant, if anything.

I was most interested in Henning's notes to file. He had made copious notations and it was clear that Ito had information that Henning thought was important. Henning went to see Ito almost every week. He had continued putting the sentencing of the defendant out for more than year. That in itself was strange. I thought I remembered lawyers saying the Feds moved the criminal cases through the system with lightning speed. For a defendant to be left in the local detention center that long after trial and before sentencing was unusual.

Also, there was mention of meetings with Homeland Security Officers and with FBI officers. All of them were called out by name, and I found their cards in an envelope attached to the very back of the corresponded section. From what I could ascertain, Ito was trying desperately to give the government information, but for whatever reason, the Feds weren't biting.

I looked up when I heard what sounded like a truck coming up the street. The last thing I wanted was for Jacobo to park his truck in the driveway, especially if it had printing on the outside.

As feared, the truck was an old panel van with faded beige paint, but it also had loud red and brown paint announcing that the truck belonged to a locksmith. I hurried from the house to have him park on the street.

As I bent in to greet Jacobo, I realized why he would want to make sure everyone knew he was in the neighborhood for legitimate business. Though rumor had it he was no longer on street drugs, his face, hair, and mouth was a visible reminder of his past life. His hair, what he had left of it, was long and dirty blonde, sparse on top, and still had the straw texture of someone who routinely used meth. His face was heavily lined, and he was missing several teeth. But his eyes were bright with intelligence, and the hand he extended to me didn't shake.

I quickly explained to him that I was on a "stealth mission" and didn't want to announce his arrival at the house. Shaking his head, he parked the truck on the street several doors down from the judge's house.

Jacobo grumbled all the way up the street when he had to carry his box of equipment. He grumbled even louder when he had to climb the steep driveway. But when he saw the safe, he grinned broadly and got to work.

"Wow, Jake," he said, "I haven't seen one of these models since I left school. Old as the hills, but tough to break. Good luck for you, the tools I bought are secondhand, and I think I have a drill that'll take out this lock."

"Can't you just break in without damaging the lock?" I asked.

"Man, Jake, I was a druggie, not a safe cracker," Jacobo said. "You gotta know that, or parole woulda' never let me near a locksmith school."

"Well, I could hope," I said. "I want what's in this safe without anyone knowing it was broken into."

"Ah, Jake, still up to your usual tricks, I see: spitting in the eye of authority. Fine. Let me try," he said. "Sometimes, if you're really careful, you can feel the pins drop as you move the dial. That's why the companies moved away from this type of lock-and-pin device. The steel is better, but the locking mechanisms are for shit."

Jacobo did a few arm stretches, twiddled his fingers, and gave me a grin, "Saw them do it like this on TV," he said.

I rolled my eyes at him and he began. We were so quiet that I heard the first pin definitely drop. Jacobo told me to write down the number fourteen. Then he turned the dial back very slowly, and the pin dropped again at fifty-three. The last number didn't come easily. He had to twist the dial back and forth to different directions. I was glad we at least had saved the first two numbers. After what seemed like forever, and we weren't really sure what the number was, we heard a distinctive 'thunk' and the lever moved freely in Jacobo's hand.

"Well, there you go, Jake," he said. "I guess I can now call myself a 'safe cracker' thanks to a homicide detective."

"Listen, Jacobo," I said, pleasantly, "You tell anyone about tonight, and you'll have another dope charge on you so fast you'll get whiplash from the streets to prison."

He just smiled at me, but his eyes told me he got the message. His smile got wider when I peeled off a couple of hundred-dollar bills and gave them to him.

After he was gone, I lifted the door to the safe. Inside was a small brown envelope and inside that were numerous yellow sheets of paper from a legal pad.

I started to unfold them when I heard a car in the driveway. I quickly closed the safe, recovered it with the carpet and slid the floor mat back over it. I had just enough time to stuff the envelope between my holster and my back and pull my shirt back down before Andre Robinson came into the office.

"You burning the midnight oil, Swanson?" he said, a smile playing around his lips. "Or are you sneaking around behind my back?'

"You're back?" I asked, trying to keep my voice innocent. "I was just following up with a criminal file to check for possible links to Henning and one of his old clients."

For a flash, the NICS officer's eyes narrowed, but he quickly recovered. "There must be hundreds of suspects if you're going in that direction," he said, again smiling. "Enough to keep you busy till midnight for years."

"Years and years," I said.

"So, why are you here?" he asked.

"I told you, the daughters and I came here just to check on the criminal files he saved," I said. "Didn't you see them stacked up in the garage?"

"All I saw was the light on in an office I thought was off limits," Robinson said.

"It's cold in the garage, and I came in here after Lauren left for the hospital," I said, trying to misdirect him.

He said nothing, but stared at the file in my hand. "What file are you going through?" he asked.

"Nothing. Just an old criminal file from when he was still a defense lawyer," I said. I didn't show him the file.

"So, you think he's a suspect?" the guy said, moving closer to me and the file.

"Not likely. He's still in the pen."

"Yet, you're holding onto it like it's important," Robinson said.

"Not important, just interesting," I said.

He finally bent down and took the file from me. I was going to resist, but I decided it would only bring more attention to me and the file.

"*United States v. Ado Ito*?" he said, reading it aloud.

"Yeah, some guy got on the wrong side of the SEC and Henning represented him," I said.

"So why do you find this interesting?" he asked.

I just shrugged and said, "I guess I find human nature fascinating when they still whine about how badly they were treated by the justice system. Here this guy was a CEO and supposedly smart, yet he's still whining to Henning years later, trying to get out. Obviously, the info he gave Henning and the Feds didn't interest them or he'd be out."

"Yeah, pretty stupid," he said. He leafed through the file and read a few of the pleadings. Then he looked at some of the correspondence. Finally, he handed the file back to me.

"Well, have a good night, Swanson. Don't ya stay up too late, ya hear?"

It creeped me out to hear him fall back into that phony Texas drawl. He was up to something, and I had no idea what it was. The hairs on the back of my neck stood on end again, and I looked at the file in my hand.

Too much coincidence for this detective, I decided.

I worried about the encounter with Andre Robinson all the way back to my apartment over the garage. Every hair on my arm was quivering and I kept checking my rearview mirror to see if I was being followed. I even stopped at the Starbucks to see if I was followed. I couldn't tell, and I cursed myself for my inability to play spy.

As I was pulling into the garage, I saw that, again, my space was taken by one of the girls' cars. *Damn!* I thought, *of all nights I wanted to put Intrepid safely away in the garage.*

Then I asked myself why I had even thought that. But I finally found a place two blocks down and on a side street. On the walk back to the house, I kept looking over my shoulder, finally deciding I was paranoid. There was nothing behind me I could see or hear.

Just as I was about to open the gate to the side yard leading to the patio between the house and garage, Sally called me.

"Hi, Jake," she said, her voice silky and smooth. "I just wanted you to know that my doctors wanted to keep Lauren overnight. They're a little concerned about her blood pressure and her swollen ankles. She's in Room 206, if you want to give her a call tomorrow. Her sister is going to stay with her a while. I have to get to my party. You want to come to the club for a drink or two?"

I had to smile. There was nothing I wanted more than to spend some time with Sally, but I wasn't dressed for her kind of party and I had work to do. Besides, I had to drive to Lompoc the next morning and I was tired.

"Ahh, my beautiful Sally," I answered. "I'm not dressed and I'm working. Can we make it some other time, just the two of us?"

"Jake?" she said, her voice questioning, "Are you getting all romantic on me?"

I gulped. Where had that come from? Sally was my best friend. Romance was not possible between us. She was much too classy for me, and I was too crazy to settle down.

She laughed at me when I didn't answer. "Jake, I was teasing," she said. "I figured you are working, but you also looked like you could use a good meal. How long has it been since you ate?"

I had to think. When had I eaten last? Having no idea when I had last eaten or what I had last eaten, my stomach answered for me with a huge growl.

"I don't have the faintest idea," I answered. "But I still can't come to your party, as much as I would love to. I'm really too tired and have too much to do. Rain check, for reals?"

"Of course, Jake," she laughed. "For reals."

Smiling to myself as I opened the gate, I completely missed the shadow that silently withdrew.

CHAPTER SEVENTEEN

The next morning was another glorious morning on the Balboa Peninsula. The in-line skaters were up early, and it was their laughter and the sound of their skates that awakened me. I had missed both my dog and my cat the night before when I got home. Neither was waiting at the gate for me, so I figured they must have mooched dinner and a cozy place to sleep from the ladies in the front house. Not that I blamed them: the ladies always fed the animals better than I did and, even as old as I felt, the thought crossed my mind that I wouldn't mind sleeping on Scat's lap. I could only hope Cisco did it for me.

For me, dinner was a frozen Marie Calendar dinner of fried chicken, mashed potatoes, and mixed vegetables. It was enough to silence my growling stomach and ease my hunger headache.

I still regretted not going to Sally's party. But, deep down, although the food and the drinks would have been great, I knew that where I had once traveled with ease when I was my mother's son was now becoming only a memory. Because I was a cop, I was no longer really in their league, though my good looks still counted for something with the wealthy cougars. Still, I didn't feel like being the hunted, so it was much better I skipped that party.

I shook off my feelings of regret, and busied myself with getting ready for the day's activities. I had things to do and people to see. Ado Ito was the first person on my list. If I got back soon enough, I might squeeze in Cheney.

Oh, damn, I thought. *Cheney probably would have been at the party.* That was the kind of party Sally always threw — heavy on wealth and the need for the wealthy to see and be seen. I gave myself a mental slap for my stupidity in letting a chance to meet him pass by me. Couldn't do anything about it now, I thought.

I quickly zipped through my shower and morning chores, minus feeding my animals. Once again I had to go on the hunt for my car, which slightly irritated me. But then I thought of how the ladies took such good, loving care of Mandy and Cisco. I forgave them for taking my parking spot.

The trip to Lompoc Federal Prison took me a little over three hours. My appointment was for one p.m., but I got there a little early. As I drove down the main boulevard to the prison, much to my surprise, I recognized a car going the opposite direction. It was Navy issue gray, with government plates. A tall blonde man sat behind the wheel.

Andre Robinson! Damn, what was he doing here?

I all but turned around to follow him, but thought better of it when he didn't seem to see my car or me. It was probably better that he not know that I had figured out the connection of Ado Ito to Henning or why I was interested.

Once I passed through security and escorted to the attorney room to speak with Ito, I had a few moments to collect my thoughts. I jotted a few notes to myself and waited.

About a half-hour later a thin, pale man of Japanese descent came to sit in front of me. He was dressed in a white jumpsuit and it had "Medical" stamped across the back. I stood to shake his hand, and he tucked both hands under his arms. He took his seat without speaking.

"I'm Detective Jake Swanson," I said. "I'm here to talk to you about Mark Henning."

The man said nothing; he just shifted a little in his seat.

"I don't know if you know this, but he was killed the other night, along with his wife," I said.

The man shifted in his seat, but still said nothing.

"It's kinda sad," I said, "he was well respected as a judge and man."

Ito looked at me, held my gaze for a few seconds, then looked down.

"I understand his wife was also well loved, not only by her family, but she also did a lot of good work in the community," I said. "A good woman died—it looks like because she walked out of the house to greet her husband coming home from work. Really sad. . ."

Again, Ito looked at me. His eyes were sad, and he shrugged his shoulders.

I tried a different tack. "From what I have read," I said, "you were trying to get some information to the government. Probably important information. Stuff that would have helped with a possible Rule 35 release."

The man sighed. He finally took a breath and spoke. "I was told you may come," he said. "I was also told not to talk to you."

"Really?" I asked.

"I was also told you couldn't help me because you're just a cop from Newport. I was also told that only the federal government can help me," he said.

"Hmmm, whoever told you that, they're probably right," I said. "You may have nothing that can help me. I'm not even sure that Judge Henning's death has anything to do with you."

The man again sat silent.

"It's just that I saw the letter you sent to Henning," I said. "I also read his notes from his interviews with you. I think you're important, even if the Feds want to make sure you never see the light of day again."

"You saw my letters?" the man asked.

"That's why I'm here," I said. "Looks like you may have something that is vital to our national security, and you wanted Henning to know it."

"Now he's dead," the man said.

"Yes, now he's dead."

We sat, not saying anything for about ten minutes. Usually, I can out-wait a suspect by not talking. They can't stand the silence, and they begin to fill the empty air with words. A lot of times that leads to a confession. This time, though, it was me who broke first.

"Listen, Mr. Ito," I said. "I don't know why I'm here. I just know that there's a Naval Intelligence guy stepping all over my investigation. I don't know why he's involved, but it pisses me off. I figure you're the only link I can find from something federal and Henning's death. So, tag, you're it."

"You think I had anything to do with his death?" Ito said, surprise written all over his face.

I looked hard at him, then asked, "Well, did you?"

The man jumped out of his seat, warranting a warning over the loudspeaker from the custody officer to take his seat, which he did quickly. Sitting back in his seat he clasped and unclasped his hands and bounced his knees. Finally, he spoke.

"Detective, right?" he asked, and I nodded to signify yes. "Mark Henning was the best lawyer a man could have. He warned me from the very beginning to not go to trial. He did everything he could to make me see how the law worked, but I was too arrogant at the time. I would not see his wisdom. Had I taken the deal that was offered to me, and then given the government my information, maybe then they would have listened to me. But, back then—well, back then it was too far-fetched for anyone to believe the information I was giving them. And since I was not only a convicted felon, but a felon convicted of fraud, my word meant nothing to them. As Mark said, 'If you are convicted of fraud, which you will be, you will be considered a convicted liar and everything you say will be suspect.' He was right, of course. Everything I told them wasn't believed."

"Well, what did you tell them?" I asked.

"That I can't tell you," Ito said.

"Why?" I asked.

"These walls have ears," he said. "If I tell you what I told Mark Henning, it will get back to the person who told me not to speak to you. In fact, not only will my life be in danger, but yours could be, too."

"Right," I said, letting my disbelief color my voice.

"Yes, 'right,'" he said. "You don't know what you're dealing with."

"So, why don't you tell me before your information gets buried again," I said.

"How did you know about that?" he asked.

"Look," I said, "I read Mark Henning's notes and letter to the U. S. Attorney. He also met with the FBI and Homeland Security, yet here you sit. Make any sense to you?"

"What makes sense to me," Ito said, "is that Mark Henning got reactivated *after* he last spoke to me. You tell me what *that* means, okay? You tell me if no one is believing me now, okay?"

"I'm sorry, what?" I said. "How did you know Mark Henning was reactivated into the Navy? He's a sitting judge and has cases."

"He told me himself," Ito said. "He came to see me about two weeks ago, and told me something should be happening with my case. He also told me that he was going to be away for a while and didn't know when he'd be back. And, that he was sure I'd have a hearing soon for possible resentencing."

"Really? He told you he was being reactivated?"

"Well, not in so many words," Ito said. "He told me that he was going to Japan, and maybe to China. Did I want him to give my brother a message? I figured it out. I know he used to be in the Navy and went to the Far East all the time. I know he wouldn't leave a judgeship unless someone made him. I think his wife is sick, too. I remember him being very much in love with her. She was in the office quite a bit when he was working as a defense lawyer."

"She *was* sick," I said. "She's dead now, too."

The man in front of me put his head down before looking back up at me.

"Yes, you told me that, didn't you? But I am even surer there is something more to his death, and you're right to believe it has to do with the information I gave to him."

"So will you tell me what you told Henning and the Feds?"

This only agitated the man, causing him to again bolt from his seat to begin to pace. Again he was warned, and again he sat down, bouncing his knees off the toes of his feet. His stress was clearly radiating throughout the room.

I pressed again, "Well. . .?"

"I can't," he said. "I want to live, and I know this information can get me killed."

I sat for a few minutes trying to make the pieces fit. I really needed Ito to talk to me. Finally, I hit on a strategy.

"Listen, our federal government has a way of not keeping their word," I said. "You know that. Anyone who's read our history knows our government, especially the Feds, lie all the time. What if nothing happens with your case? Don't you want someone to *know* your story now that Mark Henning is dead? Don't you want someone other than the Feds to work with your attorney and make sure you get your hearing? Don't you want the judge to know what you gave them? Do you really trust the guy who was just here?"

Ito sat and considered my words for a few minutes. Then he moved forward in his seat. Sweat peppered his brow, but he was ready to talk.

Taking a deep breath, and lowering his voice, he began. "My father and my brother work in the nuclear plants in Japan," he said. "After the earthquake and the meltdown, they had nowhere to go. The tsunami destroyed their city and their homes, and took most of their family. My mother is missing, my sister-in-law and two of her small children are dead — killed by the wave. And my father is ill from radiation poisoning. Everything my brother had is dead or gone. He sees what this government did to me, and he says he hates the United States. He blames the U. S. for everything. Worse yet, I know that Iran needs scientists. I knew that four years ago when I tried to tell the government that I knew how Iran was getting the enriched uranium and parts to build nuclear weapons. I tried to tell them then."

A stab of fear went through me. Maybe my worst fears were being realized. Maybe I was living a Ludlum spy novel. But I need the information whether it scared the holy shit out of me or not.

"So, tell me," I said, "what did you tell the government?"

"I told them that the Russian mob had made an alliance with a Chinese tong to ship the parts through China and down to Hong Kong and over to Iran."

"How did you know that?" I asked.

The man looked very sad, and said, "I was a very stupid and very anxious entrepreneur. I wanted to build my company too fast. I used the wrong money to get it going. I didn't want to wait for an IPO through the stock exchange. I just issued stock to some characters who needed to launder their money. Unfortunately for me, the SEC caught up with my bookkeeping practices... and here I sit."

"But how does that relate to the weapons and China and the Russians and Hong Kong?" I asked, not following him.

Again Ito began to furiously bounce his knees. The sweat ran off his face in a stream before he used his sleeve to wipe it off his chin. Then he moved even closer to me, looked over his shoulder to see where the guard was, and lowered his voice to a whisper.

"The men who came to me were affiliated with both the Russians and the Tong. I was the 'escrow' for the account," he said. "Neither side trusted the other, so they used me: an innocuous but reliable Japanese."

"And when the SEC caught up with you?" I asked.

"When they caught up with me I was smart enough to shift the money offshore, but my books became a liability. The Feds served their search warrant a day too early. My investors were not happy," he said.

"Is this how they got to your brother?" I asked. "Like you said, the Iranians need scientists to put it all together."

"Hmmm, you put the parts together quickly," Ito said. "Maybe too fast. But, yes, you are right. Iran needs reliable nuclear scientists to finish what the Russians gave them. The military sold the parts, but not the *How to Build a Bomb* book."

"And your brother?" I asked.

"My father is dying and has nothing left to keep him in his old age. My family is dead, and my brother has nothing but his hatred. The men who believe I owe them went to him to 'help' him out. My brother wrote to me that he was looking for work in Iran and was leaving Japan. I put the pieces together and met with Mark. My brother is brilliant, and I know he will find a way to build their bomb."

"Wow," I said. "That's heavy shit. And you told the government all this?"

"I only told them about the shipments through Hong Kong. As for my brother, I only told Mark Henning, and the next thing I know, he's being sent to the Far East."

"So, do you think he was chasing the bombs?" I asked, afraid of what Ito might say.

"No, he was chasing the people that would make the bombs."

There were times when I really wished I wasn't a cop. I wondered what it would be like to live in a world where evil didn't lurk behind every bush. I wanted to be innocent and not know. The information Ado Ito gave me chilled me to the bone. I didn't want to know it, but yet, I now wondered if it really did have something to do with Mark Henning's death. Not Judge Henning, but Commander Henning.

Holy shit. I needed to get back to my station.

I quickly said my good-byes to Ito and promised him I would make sure his information got into the right hands. He thanked me profusely and he bowed his way out of my life.

CHAPTER EIGHTEEN

I got home from Lompoc just in time for dinner. Again, I had forgotten to eat, and by the time I entered the patio between the house and my apartment, I could have eaten a horse. Immediately, I smelled barbecue coming from the deck overlooking the bay. I followed my nose and found Scat, Teresa, Raeline, Mandy, and Cisco all gathered out on the deck. There was a tri-tip roast on the grill, and Scat was bathing it in some kind of wonderful sauce. Cisco sat on the outdoor bar watching her work, and Teresa was tossing a salad.

As soon as Mandy saw me she wagged over to greet me. Scat gave me a hug and immediately went inside to get an extra plate. Raeline went to the bar and started a martini for me. She grabbed the Grey Goose and ice, sloshed some lemon into the shaker and shook it hard, then poured the icy mixture into a frozen glass for me. Handing it to me, she toasted me with her red wine, and I gratefully found my cushioned chair. With Mandy curled at my feet, I finally felt the scare I received in Lompoc begin to recede.

"You look tired, Jake," Scat said, handing me a small plate with chips and freshly made guacamole. "Tough day?"

"Tough if you mean driving to Lompoc and back and learning the end of the world is near," I said, taking another deep drink of my martini.

"Oh, Jake, you're so silly," Teresa said, giving my shoulder a brief brush with her hand. Her perfume was intoxicating, but again I reminded myself she could be my daughter if I had started young. I just sighed and continued to drink the Goose. Ah, yes, the Goose and me. The Goose and me and the bay. Better still, the Goose, me, my dog, my cat, and my girls. Life was again good.

The dinner was just what the doctor ordered for this very tired and very hungry detective. Scat grilled the tri-tip to a perfect medium rare and shared her baked potato with me. The dressing Teresa made for the tossed salad had a raspberry and champagne flavor that coupled perfectly with the berries and baby lettuce. With Mandy at my feet and Cisco scarfing whatever he could steal from our plates, the meal couldn't have been more perfect.

Slumped in my lounge chair, I enjoyed the sound of the soft music the girls had playing in the background and the murmur of their voices as they cleaned the patio from our dinner. I was just about asleep when one of the other girls of the house came out to sit down on the arm of the chair next to me. It was Ronnie, the same girl who had been on the arm of the presiding judge the night of the murder.

"Jake, are you asleep?' she asked softly.

I opened one eye and looked at her. She saw the eye and smiled.

"I think I need to talk to you," she said.

I sat up straighter in my chair and opened both eyes to look at her. She took that as her cue and began to speak.

"I was at Sally Deming's party last night," she said. I nodded and she continued. "I was there with the man you saw me with the other night at the police station."

"Okay," I said.

"Well," she said, pausing, "I think I may have overheard some stuff that I'm not sure I can or should tell you."

"Why's that?" I asked.

"Well, I'm not supposed to tell anyone about what my dates say when I'm on a date," she said. "Sally expects me to be very discrete, and . . ."

"Is it something your date said?" I said, wondering what the presiding judge could have said that she thought I should know.

"Not exactly," she said, heaving her shoulder with the big breath she took.

"Was it something said to him?" I asked.

"Kinda," she answered.

The poor girl looked so troubled and so anxious, I felt I needed to give her permission to speak. If necessary, I would confess my sins to Sally if it became something that was explosive.

"Why don't you tell me what happened and, if it's really bad, then I'll take care of it without anyone knowing you told me," I said.

Ronnie thought about it for a more seconds, then sighed again. She finally took a deep breath and told me something I definitely wanted and needed to hear.

"Well, Jake, I was with my date when Mr. Cheney came over and started talking to him and a couple other men. Usually, my date excuses me when he is talking business, but I guess he forgot I was still standing near him. Cheney was saying things like, 'Well, with Henning gone, it looks like you won't have to worry about that stupid. . .' something. I'm not sure what he said." She said, her face clouding.

"Was it the contempt hearing?" I asked.

"Oh, yes, he definitely talked about the contempt hearing. That I understood, because I learned about that in school. But the other word was like 'reuseable' or something like that," she said.

"Recusal?" I asked, thinking of the minutes I had read.

"Yes, that's it," Ronnie said. "Mr. Cheney was celebrating and saying stuff like he could see his daughter any damn time he wanted and now that Henning was out of his hair, he could get on with his life."

"Did your date say anything?" I asked.

"I think he was angry," she said. "I think he thought Cheney was too happy about Judge Henning's death."

"Anything else?" I asked.

"Well, the part that scared me was the way Mr. Cheney kept saying, 'Woulda liked to have killed him myself' and 'Now my little girl can get on with her life.' The one that scared me the most was when I saw him talking to a young woman. He said to her, 'Money well spent.'"

"Money well spent?" I said. "What did you think it meant? Why did it upset you?"

The serious young woman took a deep breath and answered, "After all I saw that night, I really got scared Mr. Cheney paid someone to kill Judge Henning. He just seemed so obsessed by the judge's death, and he was so happy that the man was dead. Mostly, I spoke with the young woman he was talking to and I found out it was his daughter."

"How did you find that out?" I asked.

"When she saw me standing close when Mr. Cheney said, 'Money well spent,' she started to cry. Then he walked away and she came over to me. I sat with her out on the terrace and she said she was afraid her father had done something stupid."

"And, of course, you asked her what it was?" I asked.

"Yes. By that time she and I were becoming friends, especially when she found out I came with the judge," Ronnie said.

"Hmm, why do you think that?" I asked.

"Because she wanted me to tell my date that she knew Judge Henning was her friend and that he understood how much she loved her husband. She really wanted my date to make sure her father left her alone so she could get back with her husband and their daughter to be a family again."

Ronnie was almost in tears by then. "Jake, can a father really make a woman leave her husband, even if she really, really loves him and wants to be with him?"

"Ah, Ronnie," I said, pulling her onto my lap and holding her head on my shoulder. "No, a father shouldn't be able to keep a daughter from her husband if she really, really loves him."

"Jake," she said, sighing, "Can you help my friend? Can you help Bridget get back with her husband? She really, really loves him."

"Do you think your friend is afraid of her father?" I asked Ronnie.

"I don't know for sure," Ronnie said. "But I think she really would like to talk to you. Can you do it? She gave me her phone number, and everything."

"Of course I can, Ronnie," I said, taking the proffered cocktail napkin from the distraught young woman. "I'll do it just for you, okay?"

"Thank you, Jake," she said, sighing into my shoulder.

The two of us sat like that for what seemed like forever. It wasn't until my forty-two-year-old legs went to sleep that I finally made her move. She drifted off to the main house and I whistled to Mandy to go upstairs. Cisco trotted along behind Mandy and me as we went off to bed.

Troubled dreams of nuclear holocaust and fathers pulling their daughters away from their crying husbands disturbed my sleep that night. It was not a good night to be a detective in a town with so many powerful people. No, it was not a good night at all.

CHAPTER NINETEEN

T he next day I immediately went to the station to check on my partner and at least let the lieutenant know I was still alive. I also wanted to talk with Melissa about what I had learned and what she thought. I had come to depend on her ability to sometimes see things I missed. And, besides that, she was great with the paperwork.

When I went to the break room to get some coffee, I found her chatting with that blonde-haired nemesis, Andre Robinson. The two of them were standing with their heads bent close together, speaking softly. Something stirred in me — an unidentifiable emotion, something I dismissed immediately

"Hey, you two," I said, trying to be jovial. "You two conspiring or something?"

Melissa immediately blushed and looked guilty. Andre merely smiled that broad, irritating smile of his.

"Ya'll got a guilty conscious, or something, Swanson?" he asked.

"Naw, cowboy," I said. "It's just my partner sometimes gets a little distracted is all."   The look Melissa shot at me would have melted chrome off the bumper of a 1958 Buick. She looked so pissed. She didn't even do the hair toss thing when she stomped out of the room.

"Ya'll been missing in action, I hear," Andre said to me.

"If you'd taken the time to notice the shore break, you'da known where to find me," I said. "Gotta catch the waves when I can. The dead will still be dead tomorrow, I always say."

"Swanson!" Lieutenant Graber said, just over my shoulder. "I need you in my office, NOW!"

Damn. Robinson had set me up. I turned around to skulk into the lieutenant's office.

"Please tell me you weren't really off surfing yesterday," Graber said.

I was hurt! How could the lieutenant think such a thing? Okay, okay, in the distant past I had been known to do such things, but this was the present, and I had a killer to catch.

"Lieutenant," I said, "I was up at Lompoc. Didn't your secretary tell you?"

"No, why would she?" he asked. "She's not your keeper. Unfortunately, I am. The Chief is asking for updates, and I have nothing to tell him."

I took a seat and quickly filled Graber in on what I had been doing and what I had learned from Ito, as well as Ronnie, being careful not to disclose her as my source. But I also cautioned him that I really didn't want it made public yet. There were too many loose ends and too much I didn't understand. When I finished with my full report, Graber sat back in his chair and looked out his window.

"You really think the Iranians will get their nukes?' he asked. "Don't you think the Mid-East is unstable enough as it is? Christ, our stupid Congress for fighting the accord to limit their nuclear stuff."

"Naw, LT, this goes around the suggested treaty agreement," I said. "This allows the enriched stuff to come into country all ready to make the bombs. If Ito is correct, his brother is the missing piece."

"And this fits into our murder here?" Graber asked, scrubbing his face with his hands.

"Listen, LT," I said, "I don't know how all this fits into a murder here in Newport Beach. It's way too crazy to believe some internation-al-dude-type killer came here and offed the judge and his wife. But, is it any more reasonable to believe a very wealthy, very powerful man paid someone to kill a judge just to get him off the case?"

As I said that out loud, both the lieutenant and I started to laugh. Of course a very powerful and very wealthy man would think to pay someone to kill a judge. We had seen the stupid things egomaniacs did. Our city's history was rife with scandals having to do with the uber-wealthy trying to buy themselves in or out of something. Why not believe a man would pay someone to kill a judge who got in his way?

When we finished laughing, I told my lieutenant not to really talk to the chief about what I had said. I didn't want Cheney to know that I was headed off to see his daughter. I wanted to speak with her without her father knowing I had been around.

Leaving the lieutenant's office, I pulled Bridget Cheney McAllister's phone number from my pocket. It was on the paper napkin from the party at the supper club.

The receptionist answering the phone identified the number as belonging to one of Cheney's land developing companies. I was a little surprised that Bridget used that number to give, and that surprise heightened into concern when I asked the receptionist for Bridget, and she put me through only after making sure she knew who I was.

The voice on the other end of the line was soft and well-modulated, though she sounded very young. When I told her that Ronnie had asked me to meet with her, she started to cry. She then insisted we meet at a discrete restaurant in Tustin, away from Newport Beach and the well-known places there.

Pushing away from my desk, I stood to gather my things to go meet Bridget Cheney McAllister. Andre Robinson was nowhere to be seen, but my partner was at her desk. I tried to speak with her, but she studiously avoided me.

"Damn it, Sanchez," I finally said, raising my voice to the point the other detectives stuck their heads out from their cubicles. "You are my partner and, damn it, you will get your shit together and come with me. I have a witness I need to interview, damn it!"

A couple of the other detectives clapped and Melissa just steamed. She grabbed her satchel-like purse and followed me out the door.

"What the hell, Sanchez?" I said as we left the back door and headed toward the Intrepid. "What have I done now, or are you just being PMS-y?"

"You didn't let me know where you were at all yesterday," she said with a pout. "You say I'm your partner, but you disappear for hours… or like yesterday, all day. What am I supposed to think?"

We got in the car without saying anything else. I wondered how I could tell her I didn't trust her with the information I had to get yesterday. Instead, I just told her about Cheney and what I had gotten from the 'Shark.' I told her about Bridget Cheney McAllister and my belief that she wanted to be back with her husband. And I told her that Bridget is afraid her father paid someone to kill Henning.

The little coffee shop where we were supposed to meet Bridget was located on a three-sided corner on Tustin Avenue. It had been many different establishments over the years, with one of its lives as a great barbecue place. I had loved the ribs and beans, and especially the pretty bartender who made my drinks extra strong. But now, it was just a little coffee shop with its windows covered in bamboo, making it the perfect place to hide.

When Melissa and I arrived I didn't immediately see Bridget. But after my eyes adjusted to the light, I saw a petite blonde sitting in the back corner booth. Her hair was shiny and long, her clothing demure. When she looked up, I was struck by how sad she looked. It wasn't that her eyes were red, just that there were lines in her face that no surgeon could ever remove. They were the type of lines that come from carrying the weight of the world without any hope of relief.

Melissa took one look at her and immediately did the thing I hoped she'd do. She slid in next to Bridget and took her in her arms and put the young woman's head on her shoulder. Bridget began to cry, and the two women sat like that for at least five minutes. I had the good sense not to interrupt them while they sat and bonded.

When Melissa finally looked up, I got up and joined them.

"I am Detective Swanson," I said. "You've already met my partner, Melissa."

Bridget extended a trembling hand to me and asked me to take a seat. I pulled a chair up from the next table and sat down. I wanted to make sure I could look Bridget in the face, and I didn't want to crowd the women.

"Thank you for coming," Bridget said. "I really appreciate you coming. I don't know what to do now that Judge Henning is dead. He was the only one who seemed strong enough to stand up to my father. Now, with him gone, I don't know if I'll ever be able to go back to John."

She started crying again, and I just let her sob. A few pats from Melissa and she finally turned to me to talk.

"I'm so scared," she said. "I'm afraid of what my father may have done. He was so angry with Judge Henning when he ordered him to stay away from me until after the next hearing. When I moved into the apartment in Irvine I thought my dad would have a stroke. I know he had me watched. Then, my dad and his lawyers did this massive huddle and they told him that the judge made an order that he couldn't enforce. Something about my father not being a part of my divorce, though he's the one who started it and it's all his fault. Then, when my father came to see me anyway and kept bugging me about moving back in with him with my daughter, Chloe, I told the judge."

"Did your lawyer tell the judge?" I asked.

"No, no, she said it would be better if I just wrote a letter to him all by myself," Bridget said. "Ms. Delgado thought the judge would be more persuaded by it if I also sent a copy of it to John. I did all that, and John immediately called me. I can't believe he still loves me! He even said he'd sign whatever papers my father wants him to sign so my father knows John doesn't want my money."

"So then what happened?" I asked.

"That's when Judge Henning had my father served with the contempt of court papers, and my father just about blew a gasket. He raged all over the place and said he would see the judge dead before he let a blue-collar nobody come between him and his little girl." Bridget started to cry again, and Melissa kept handing her tissues from somewhere deep inside that satchel purse of hers.

"Do you think your father meant it?" I asked.

"You don't know my father," Bridget said. "I've seen him destroy people over stupid contracts. He would deliberately do things to financially wreck their companies and drive them into bankruptcy. You don't know my father!"

"So, tell me exactly what you heard him say," I said, moving a tape recorder onto the table. "And, by the way, do you mind if I record this?"

"Please do," Bridget said. "I think my father is just crazy enough right now that he would kill me if he thought I was thinking of going back to John. And, if anything happens to me or to John, I want someone to know how scared I am."

I had already flipped on the recorder before pulling it out, so I was able to capture everything Bridget said. What she said next almost put a few nails in Old Man Cheney's coffin.

"I was at the office with my father just after John and I had an argument about my spending too much on a pair of shoes I wanted. I was pregnant, and I was all screwed up on hormones. I was also mad at John because he had to work an overtime shift instead of staying with me to finish our argument. He said he had to work the shift to pay for the shoes I just bought and didn't really have a choice. I was a stupid, stupid, stupid little girl. I believed the world revolved around me and my father could fix everything. So I told Daddy that John was neglecting me and he didn't want our baby. I told him we had argued and John got really mad at me. Next thing I know, my father had me moved back into his house and Ms. Delgado filed paperwork saying John abused me and was trying to make me have an abortion."

"Was it true?"

"Of course it wasn't true!" Bridget answered, her eyes snapping in indignation.

"Then why didn't you stop your father, and the proceedings?" Melissa asked.

Bridget turned her attention to my partner and gave a helpless shrug of her shoulders.

"You don't know my father," she said. "I was young and had never stood up to him."

"But this was your life," Melissa answered. "And what about the baby? Didn't you care about the baby not having a father?"

Bridget gave another helpless shrug and lowered her head, burying her face behind her blonde hair.

Melissa looked over at me, giving me that questioning stare she sometimes uses on me when she seems to be lost in the culture differences between Santa Ana and Newport Beach.

"Meliss," I said, trying to answer her unasked question, "You know what it's like in your neighborhood. You know girls who can't get around their fathers. . ."

Melissa just shrugged her shoulders and bent back to Bridget. "But, John. Did you love him?"

"That's the point," Bridget answered. "I had never lived on my own. I didn't know how to cook, how to clean a house, how to do laundry and, suddenly, I had to know all of it. I was so stupid. I just didn't think."

"But where did that leave your husband in all of this?" Melissa asked again.

Bridget started to cry again, and I felt my shoulders start to do the hunchy-crunchy turtle roll upward. I hated seeing women cry, and when the tears got to be too much, it was my habit to pull inward, just like the turtle I was beginning to imitate.

Melissa knew I was retreating; she gave me that stare that is meant to level the strongest man. I just turned away from her. I had come to depend on her to step into those situations where most men feared to go. She didn't let me down.

"Bridget, you asked for help," Melissa said, her voice getting firm. "Jake has come here and pulled me along with him, even though we are in the middle of a murder investigation. We don't have time for your tears or self-pity. Either tell us something that we can use to help you, or we are leaving."

Bridget sniffled a few more times, then turned to Melissa and told her story.

"I met John at a Fun Run 5K to raise money for charity. He was so cute in his running shorts, and really nice. He wasn't like the other guys that are all up in your face, macho and trying to impress me with their stuff. He was all shy and sweet; he was helping me after the race and didn't even ask for my number or anything."

"So, how did the two of you get together," Melissa asked.

Bridget lowered her head, then did that look up underneath her eyelash thingy women do when they're getting all coy and flirty. She smiled, then answered, "I made up an excuse to find out what station he was working out of and then took some cold cuts and rolls over with the excuse of using it as a 'thank you' for all of his help. When his lieutenant called him in from the field, John was all embarrassed and funny about the fuss. That's when I knew I liked him a lot, so I asked him if he would like to run in another charity fundraiser, but for my daddy's company instead."

"And, of course, he said 'yes,'" Melissa said.

"Sorta," Bridget answered. "His lieutenant heard me ask, so he rounded up a bunch of guys to form a team, and they all ran. Daddy was really impressed. He was all proud and had a bunch of pictures taken with all of them because they raised so much money. After it was all over, I asked John and his crew if they wanted to come to the house for a party so we could show our appreciation."

I was sitting back listening to all of this, just taking it in. I had been part of relay teams for the Newport Beach Police team for several years and the after-parties were the special part of the fun. In my case, our team got kinda crazy and someone always ended up in the pool. I asked, "So, who ended up in the pool at the party?"

Bridget blushed a deep red and shyly answered, "One of the guys hoisted me up and heaved me into the pool. I was so surprised I screamed. Next thing I know, John is in right next to me pulling me out. That's when I kissed him."

"You kissed him?" I asked, "In front of his crew?"

"You bet I did," Bridget answered. "I just called him 'my hero' and kissed him for pulling me out. All the guys were hooting and hollering, and that's when my daddy's then latest girlfriend got all up in the fun and started kissing all the guys. Next thing I know, everyone's in the pool, kissing her and trying to kiss me. I saw Daddy in the background, and he was all turning red and getting pissed. John must have seen it too, because he wrapped me up in a towel and took me away from the group. That's when I confessed to him I set all of it up so I could see him again."

"Hmmm, and what did your father think of that?" Melissa asked.

"Oh, he didn't even know at first, because he was all upset about his girlfriend and the guys in the pool," Bridget said. "I mean, these guys were hot! I don't blame her; she was like all of twenty-something, like my age, and here were all these hot guys all over her. Daddy was PISSED! So, like, I just faded from view with John."

"So, you started dating?" Melissa asked.

"Hmmm, yeah," Bridget answered, getting a dreamy look on her face. "It was like, you know, so different. John wasn't always telling me how great he was, or how much money he made, or how much money his father made, or what schools he went to, or what law firm he was joining. All he seemed to care about was making me happy."

"Like, how?" Melissa asked.

"You know, like we would do all that stupid romantic stuff, like walk on the beach and have bonfires and roast marshmallows. Stupid stuff like that," Bridget said. "We would window shop in Laguna, he took me up to his favorite place in the mountains, and we hiked up a stream to a waterfall. He even packed a picnic lunch for us. It was perfect."

"Hmmm, sounds dreamy," Melissa said, smiling.

"It was," Bridget answered. "I mean, he was always a perfect gentleman; I was the one all over him. And, you know, he was even perfect when I told him I missed my period."

"Oh?" Melissa said.

Bridget blushed again. "You know, my father always says Chloe was 'premature,' but she really wasn't. When I told John, he was all sweet and said he 'wanted to do the right thing by me.' So, we just went up the coast and got married. We didn't tell anyone, we just did it."

"So, how did your dad feel about that?" I finally asked, joining the conversation in earnest, thinking back to what Delgado had told me about Old Man Cheney being devastated at not only his daughter getting married, but not being present at the ceremony.

"Oh, my God," Bridget said, "he was furious! He pounded the table, and almost threw John out of the house when we got home and told him what we did. I think he was more angry about me not doing one of those prenup things that he was always talking about with his friends. I mean, really: I know why Daddy and his friends all have them, because they are going with all these gold-digger types who are getting all *Housewives of Orange County* on these guys, but they deserve it. I mean, who wants to have a wife that is the same age as their kids? Who are they kidding? Like, you know, these girls are marrying them for, what—love? Pffsstt!"

"And John loved you?" Melissa asked.

That is when Bridget started to cry again, her tears streaming down her face in bluish-black river, taking all of her mascara with them. She started sobbing hard enough the waitress came to the table to check on us. I flashed my badge at her, and she backed off, but continued to stare at our table.

I was again getting impatient when Melissa stepped in, bringing some semblance of order to the table and all of Bridget's tears.

"Bridget, this still doesn't give us anything of importance. I mean, what? Why are you afraid of your father? I guess John must have loved you, considering how hard he has worked to get you back," Melissa said. "Or was it just that he wanted to make sure he got his gun back?"

Bridget flared at Melissa, showing some her privileged upbringing by rising up to her full height in the booth and leveled a stare at my partner that would have shriveled a lesser human. Instead it was two alpha dogs staring at each other.

Bridget finally broke the stare. She turned away from Melissa and began to talk to me.

"Unlike some people believed," Bridget said, "John never lost his gun. The orders were never issued, despite what my daddy and his attorney wrote."

"Really?" I asked. I already knew that, but I didn't want her or my partner to know I had that knowledge.

"No, after the first judge issued the first orders, Judge Henning undid them right away. That's why Daddy got so pissed," Bridget said.

"But during the first orders?" Melissa asked.

Bridget did not answer her question, but instead kept talking to me. "John took leave time to try to get me back. When I left our apartment he was so devastated he came to Newport to get me. Daddy had the gooney squad remove John, and that's when Ms. Delgado started the paperwork."

"His 'gooney squad'?" I asked.

"You know, all the guys he has around him and their only job is to make sure Daddy's safe… and stuff," Bridget answered with a shrug. "They are always around; you just usually don't see them because they are always dressed like part of the crowd. But, if you look closely, there's always one or two around him."

"They're loyal to him?" I asked, getting a funny feeling, like I had heard this before, and it was just breaking through my consciousness.

"All of my dad's friends have them," Bridget answered. "It's like they started making sure they had them when they started getting all paranoid about the Mexicans and the cartels and the kidnappings, and even the Russian stuff."

"Russian stuff?" I asked.

"You know, some of my Daddy's stupid friends got some investment money from some Russians, and in the downturn some if it was lost—you know, like all investments, some of it went bad. So, like the Russians started getting all weird for their money, and my dad's circle started hiring guys that were Army rangers or something like that."

"Mercenaries as bodyguards?" I asked.

"Yeah, whatever," Bridget said. "But, like, you know, after I got over being mad at John, I was afraid for him because he would try to see me, and these gooney guys would be all over him. I think they even beat him up once."

"Really?" I asked. "And you didn't tell your attorney?"

"Pffsstt. Like Ms. Delgado ever really listened to me," Bridget said.

Melissa was shaking her head and hunching her shoulders as if she were taking body blows. Finally, she just erupted.

"Bridget, I just don't understand you," she said. "I mean, do you really think your father would kill to keep John away from you? And, why would *you* let your father hurt the father of your child? Why didn't you just go back to him? I mean, if you loved him, and he was the father of your child, why not just leave and be done with all of this craziness? I don't care if your father is the king of the world, why didn't you just do what you did before and just leave?"

Bridget looked momentarily startled, as if Melissa had said something blasphemous and she expected the heavens to open up and strike all of us dead.

"Go against Daddy?" she asked. "You just don't understand. He has the money to do anything."

"Again, does your father have enough money to hire someone to kill a judge?" Melissa asked.

"Of course he does," Bridget answered. "That's why I am so afraid. That's why I want someone to know about what I heard last night— that Daddy was so sure the 'problem' was taken care of. I don't want to think he'd do something like that, but. . ."

She left the rest of the sentence hanging.

Melissa pressed on, "You went against your father when you married John, so why not just go back to him and tell your father to take a hike?"

Bridget blinked a few times at Melissa, then looked at me. "Really? Like, you know, just take Chloe and leave?" she asked me. "Can I do that? Even with all the court papers and stuff? But, do you think Dad would send his gooney squad after John? And like everything that has happened in court. What about that?"

I shook my head at her. How could she be so privileged, and yet so naïve? I would have thought that she knew she could leave. She was not a prisoner, I didn't think. Even with his "gooney squad," it seemed improbable that her father would send them after her, and John was protected by the blue wall of other cops. Any hint of real trouble for John, especially if they were out of Orange County, and his buddies would be all over it. But, then again, the real question was whether Bridget was a prisoner of money and great wealth. It was hard to give up.

"Can you live on what John makes?" I asked. "I mean, he's just a cop, and he doesn't make a lot of money, I would think."

"No, he doesn't," Bridget said. "I mean he was saving up to buy a house, but used all his money to pay his attorney, then had to fire him because John ran out of money. So, I guess he doesn't have any."

"But, can you live on that?" I asked, again.

Bridget shrugged again, "I guess I can. I mean after I had Chloe, I stopped caring about shoes and stuff. Everything is about her, and that's great. I like it that way."

"Can you give up the lunches with your friends and stuff?" I asked again.

"Pffsstt! They're gone. As soon as I married John, and everyone found out I was pregnant, they just went 'poof.' Like, you know, I know they wouldn't even speak to me except their fathers have business with my father, and they have to. So, yes, I know I can give that up. Besides, all the officers who work with John have wives and they all get together and do barbecues and stuff. It could be fun!"

"If what you say is true, then choose John," I said. "Choose him and let Chloe have her father back."

As I was saying that, my phone rang. It was Cindy calling me to ask if I was coming by the hospital. We had left everything up in the air when Lauren was rushed away.

My answers were noncommittal, not wanting to let Melissa know too much. It was getting weirder and weirder to have a partner; I did not really want her in on what I was doing. But, some habits were hard to break. I had spent too many years doing my "own thing," and it looked like I was headed down that path again.

Disconnecting from the call, I told Melissa we needed to get back to the station. She nodded and said her good-byes to Bridget, cold as they were. Obviously, Melissa had taken the earlier slight, and was testy with the wealthy little wife. There would be no more sympathy for Bridget from my partner.

CHAPTER TWENTY

I left Melissa at the station, asking her to log in Bridget's statement and get it transcribed. Also, I thought we were getting close to seeing if we could get a warrant for Cheney's financials given what Bridget had said at the coffee shop. Though with the number of limited partnerships and limited liability corporations, as well as his main corporation, I had no idea where he would have buried the money to pay for hit men. It would be like looking for a needle in a haystack. It was something our forensic accountants would have to hunt. Even then it would take weeks, if not months, to figure it out. It was the perfect task to give my partner to keep her away from me.

I lucked out; Cindy was at the hospital with Lauren when I arrived. Lauren was looking a little pale, but at least she was sitting up. I had remembered to stop at my favorite florist and picked up a small bouquet of flowers in a small bunny vase. I looked like the perfect thing to give a pregnant woman.

"Hey, ladies," I said, setting the vase of flowers on her nightstand.

"I'm glad I caught both of you together. How are you doing, Lauren?"

"I'm doing better," Lauren said. "Thanks for the flowers; they're really cute."

"Have you heard anything from Tim?" I asked.

"Of course," she said. "He's even conferred with my doctors, who by the way are great! Can you thank Sally for me? She's been by a couple of times, and I really like her."

"Sally said that if Lauren needs to see Tim," Cindy said, "she'll see what she can do about having him sent home for an emergency visit."

"Really?" I said. I should have known Sally would know someone who knew someone who could get things done. "So, is Tim coming home?"

"No," Lauren sighed. "I don't want to interfere with his posting onboard the ship. It could ruin his standing, and I can't let that happen. He's worked way too hard for me to be selfish."

"But are you sure?" I asked.

"Yes, I think I'm just tired and the stress of Mom and Dad's death just was too much," Lauren said. "I'll be fine, and the doctors are watching out for me."

"If you're feeling okay, then can I ask you guys some questions about your dad?'

"Of course, silly," Cindy said. "That's why we're here."

"Yeah, that and you just want to be away from your kids," Lauren said.

Cindy looked momentarily guilty, but then smiled and said, "I feel great. I had no idea how much energy they sucked out of me until I was away from them—enough energy to help Swanson solve Mom and Daddy's murder."

I pulled my chair a little closer and spoke softly to the girls, telling them what I had learned from Ado Ito. When I was finished, both girls just sat quietly, not saying anything.

A tear began to run down Lauren's face as she spoke. "You know, Daddy was an expert about the Far East. He always said that the best nuclear scientists were Japanese. But he also said their sense of honor would never let them assist the Iranians in building a weapon. He said that the fear of a nuclear holocaust was embedded in their DNA. They had too much fear to ever assist in weapons building."

"But with the destabilization of Japan because of the earthquake and tsunami?" I asked.

Both girls thought about it. Finally, Lauren said, "It could happen. Especially with the nuclear plants being destroyed and people dying from fallout. Some could blame us for that industry. The Japanese have a strong belief that fate is a strand of interlocking lives. If we hadn't bombed them in 1945, then they wouldn't have the nuclear plants. And, if they didn't have the nuclear plants, their families wouldn't have been in that village that was devastated. So, therefore, we Americans are at fault."

"Wow!" I said. "That's an awful long line to get to it being our fault."

"Yes, but it is an ancient civilization," Lauren said. "According to

Daddy, they can measure their history in millennia rather than de-cades. Sixty or seventy years is nothing."

"If that's true," Cindy said, "then we need to get busy with our plan, right now!"

"But how can you do it without me?" Lauren asked. "You need me to help with the maps and photos!"

"Maps and photos of what?" a familiar and unwanted voice said, coming into the room.

Robinson! Damn, what was he doing here?

Andre Robinson entered the room carrying a small arrangement very similar to the one I had gotten for Lauren.

"Maps and photos of Russian and China," Cindy said before I could hush her.

"Oh?" Robinson said, looking at me. "Why would you be looking at those?"

Lauren slammed her lips shut, and narrowed her eyes at the NCIS guy, but Cindy was ebullient and had obviously forgotten my warning to her from the other night.

"Daddy may have been following some nukes from Russia to Chi-na!" Cindy said.

Lauren grabbed her hand and squeezed. I wanted to grab her throat and squeeze.

"Is that right?" Robinson said, again staring at me. "And why would you think that?"

The silence in the room was deafening. Andre crossed the room and looked at Cindy. "Why would you think your father was follow-ing nukes from Russia?"

Looking stricken, Cindy turned her eyes toward me.

Robinson turned his back on the women and stared hard at me with narrowed eyes. I shrugged and said, "It's just a crazy theory that floated in from left field."

With cold narrowed eyes, Robinson looked at me, seemingly try-ing to pierce my shield of resistance. Then, suddenly, he changed.

He turned back to the girls and put on that large, toothy smile and broad Texas accent. "Well ya'll know if ya'll think your daddy was killed for something he knew as a military man, I'm going to have to take over this case. And, ya'll know, the military and the federal gov-ernment is much better equipped to handle this case than some small town cop, right?"

No! Not right! I wanted to shout. But I held my tongue instead, watching the girls.

Lauren was the first to speak. "Detective Swanson was telling us something crazy about an old client and the Russians and nuclear de-vices. I told him the client was crazy and would say anything to get out of prison. Lauren turned on Cindy and finished with, "Of course, Cindy here is ready to believe anything bad about Daddy and the mil-itary. So that's why we were talking about maps and stuff."

Andre Robinson, NCIS officer, stood stock still, sniffing the wind like a hound dog. Lauren picked at the sheets on the bed and Cindy wrung her hands. I just stood there, saying nothing, waiting for Robinson to make the next move.

He looked at me and motioned me to follow him outside.

"Why are you upsetting these pretty young women with your crazy theories?" he asked me. Gone was the drawl; in its place there was threat.

"Yeah, pretty crazy," I said.

Robinson looked at me, and his eyes again turned cold. "Listen, Swanson, you think you're some golden boy hotshot around here. You've got the lieutenant fooled, but not me... or your chief. You are stepping into areas you don't belong. You keep going there, and I'll have to do something about you, you hear me?"

"That a threat?" I asked, my voice just as cold. I was tired of dancing with this jerk and my temper was getting short.

"That's what I figured, Swanson," Robinson said. "You're not a fool, so don't miss my meaning when I tell you... back off the Russians and the Iranians."

"Funny, Robinson," I said, "we never said anything about Iran. You telling me something I need to know?"

"You, you don't need to know anything about Russia or Iran or China or Japan to solve this murder," he hissed. "Leave it alone."

"Leave it alone, or what, Robinson?" I taunted.

"This is serious stuff, Swanson," he hissed again. "People who stick their noses where they don't belong... sometimes they lose those noses, get it?"

I just laughed, and continued laughing as Robinson stormed

down the hall to the elevator.

"Ladies," I said, going back into the room. 'Operation Sneak' is back on the table. Lauren, Cindy, and I will see you later tonight. Cindy, you remember the plan?"

"Roger that, Captain," she said giving me a thumbs up.

"Roger that; over and out," I said to the two of them as I left the room.

I would see them later that night. But first, I had work to do.

CHAPTER TWENTY-ONE

I was headed back to the station when my phone rang. The voice on the other end was not one I recognized, but whoever he was, he was mad, not just angry/mad, but spittle-spewing, raging mad.

"Listen, you son of a bitch," the voice raged. "I will have your sorry ass fired, do you hear me?"

"Hello?" I said. "This is Detective Jake Swanson, and who are you?"

"I know who you are, you son of a bitch!" he said. "This is Jack Cheney, and I want to see you, RIGHT NOW!"

I took a deep breath. My first reaction was to give him a smart response, but I held my tongue. Actually, I couldn't believe my luck. I needed to interview Old Man Cheney, but never in a million years would I have thought I would get through his phalanx of lawyers to get to him. But there he was, inviting me into his den.

"Sir, where did you want to meet?" I asked, hoping it wasn't his office.

"My office," he said.

I winced, and tried a tack I hoped would work. "Sir, do you really want a place where we have secretaries, lawyers, and others to hear our conversation or see me speaking with you?"

"I have nothing to say to you that cannot be heard by others," he roared.

"Hmmm, maybe so," I said, "but, then again, secretaries do talk about what they hear."

There was a long pause interrupted only by the sound of heavy breathing. Again, I waited, letting him fill the gap in the conversation.

"Fine, meet me at the house," he snapped, and gave me an address on the bluffs on the Newport Coast in the upscale, gated community of Pelican Point. It was located just south of Corona del Mar on the Pacific Coast Highway and was also referred to as the Pacific Rivera.

I agreed to meet him in forty minutes, and hoped it would give me enough time to stop by the station for another micro digital recorder. Also, I decided it was important to tell the lieutenant where I was headed and why.

A quick swing through the station and I was soon sitting in front of Graber telling him everything—and I do mean everything. I let him know about my meeting with the judge's daughters; the unannounced visit by Robinson to Lauren's hospital room; the meeting with Bridget; and, lastly, my upcoming meeting with Cheney.

"Don't you want to take your partner with you?" he asked.

"At this point, no," I said. "Cheney is angry, and I think he is vulnerable because of that anger. If I show up with my partner tagging along, he might consider her to be my reinforcement and play it cool. No, sir, I want him hot, and I want him angry. And, most of all, I don't want my partner anywhere near us."

The large man swung back and forth in his chair. He kept his finger on his temple, leaving a small pale indentation. "It's a dangerous game you're playing, Swanson," he said.

"I know, sir," I said, appreciating his concern. "But think about it. I am meeting him in his home, at his request, and we haven't focused our investigation on him as a viable suspect. No Miranda is needed. No interrogation and no police coercion. It's a great plan."

"You know you're going into the lion's den," he said.

"Yeah, but I'll be fine," I said, not wanting to tell him about the "gooney squad."

The trip down the coast to took me about fifteen minutes. I was stopped at the guard house, and gave the guard my name. With a quick check to see that I was on the list, he opened the gate for me.

I followed a faux cobblestone street that wound around through a maze of multi-multi-multi-million-dollar mansions — each seemingly striving to outdo the other with massive amounts of imported stone masonry, corbels, imposing porte-cocheres, and impressive drives up to the manses. At the end of the street where it swirled into a dead end, almost at the Pacific Ocean, I found the house belonging to the man I was about to confront. I felt a slight shiver, then a smile spread across my face. I knew the type, having grown up around them all my life.

The house was a monumental testament to his ego — the kind of ego I could exploit.

The house was designed and built for the grand effect in the style of recent homes along the Newport Coast. In other words, it was a faux Italian villa of about eight thousand square feet, with most of it facing the Pacific Ocean. The stone driveway led into a six-car garage, which sat below the main portion of the house. There were two parallel curving stairways leading from the porte-cochere to a double door entry covered by a stone portico. The windows of the lower floors all had leaded glass windows facing the Pacific Coast Highway, with the upper floors sufficiently recessed into dormer-like cupolas — I was unable to see their actual structure. The house, at least from where I was entering, was magnificent, reeking of money and ego.

Before ringing the doorbell, I reached into my pocket and started the recorder. A dark-haired woman in a black uniform opened the door immediately. She silently led me through a short hallway to a room paneled with heavy, darkly stained mahogany. Floor-to-ceiling French doors, which lead out to a balcony overlooking the deep blue of the ocean, framed a stone fireplace. Two red leather couches faced each other, with an antique table centered between them. At the end of the room a large carved desk faced into the room, with ceiling-height bookcases behind it. Cheney was sitting at the desk, and two well-muscled men with military haircuts flanked him. The men at his side were dressed in what must have been the uniform de rigueur: pale yellow golf shirts with the Cheney logo, khaki Dockers, and Top

Sider loafers. Each of the men was at least six feet and multiple inches, probably outweighing me by at least thirty pounds. I was sure none of the extra weight was fat—probably steroid-induced muscles. I almost laughed at the lunacy of needing guards in a man's own house on the Newport Coast, but decided that was too obvious a choice of reaction. Laconic was probably not the best choice.

When the maid and I entered the room, Cheney came out from behind the desk. When he stood I realized he was extremely short in stature, maybe five feet, five inches. He too was dressed in a golf shirt, but his trousers appeared to be finely woven wool. He too wore Top Sider shoes, but his feet were without socks. His head was balding, with what looked like the remnants of prior hair plugs. Unfortunately for him, the plugs had not stopped the slide of his hair from the top of his head to just over his ears. The balding palate was well tanned, with flakes of prior sunburn. But it was his eyes that held me captive. Even from across the room they telegraphed a piercing intelligence and coldness in their icy blue color. It made me take a mental step back. Old Man Cheney would not be an easy foe.

The maid and I stood at the top of the two stairs that led down to the study, each of us waiting for direction from Cheney. He told her to bring him coffee service for two and she silently withdrew; I stepped down into the room. I raised my eyebrow at the two goons flanking the old man. He made a quick gesture with his hand, and then they left. With only the two of us in the room, I felt a quick adrenaline rush at the thought of the upcoming confrontation. Cheney gestured to the couches for us to take a seat facing each other. His face was clouded. I hoped mine was impassive.

"So, you're Detective Swanson," he said, not offering his hand to me.

"Yes, sir, I am Detective Jake Swanson with the Newport Police Department," I said, so my voice would be identified on the recording. "I'm not sure why you called me here to your home, sir." That should show it was a meeting called by Cheney and, therefore, voluntary. I took my seat on one of the red couches and Cheney sat across from me. We said nothing, waiting. A few minutes later the maid again appeared, this time carrying a silver tray with a coffee service. She poured for both of us, then withdrew.

"I presumed you'd want coffee," the man said. "You are on duty, correct?"

"Coffee is great, sir," and it was terrific—a freshly brewed exotic blend of some sort, dark with a smooth finish. It put to shame the sludge at the station.

After taking a few long draughts of the coffee, I put down my cup and said, "I assume you didn't call me to your home on this beautiful fall day just to sip coffee and admire the view."

"You are interfering in things you don't understand," he said, leveling the icy stare at me.

"What things?" I asked, trying to sound innocent.

"My daughter and granddaughter," he said.

"I'm not sure what you are saying," I said.

"Did you not tell my daughter she was free to leave me?" he said.

"Again, I'm not sure what you are implying," I said. "I never told your daughter to leave you. She is over eighteen, and an adult. There was no statement telling her to leave you. It was only a question posed to her as to why she let you run her life."

"I *do* run her life!" he said, coldness dripping from every word.

"Last I heard," I said, nonchalantly, "children are not possessions. When they reach their age of majority they are free to make their own way."

"Not my daughter," he said.

"Seems pretty unreasonable to me," I said. "She's married, has a daughter by a man, who, from all accounts, loves her. I would think she should be free to do as she pleases."

"Not my daughter. Not when I have plans for her. Not when her future cannot be diminished by a blue-collar nothing," he said, snapping his fingers.

"Again," I said, "it's the twenty-first century, and bondage and slavery have been abolished; Bridget is free to do as she thinks is best for her and her daughter."

I could have sworn I heard something pop. The controlled, icy demeanor of the man in front of me changed dramatically. In seconds he went from a man who could lord over a boardroom full of powerful people to a raging imitation of Mr. Hyde. It sort of reminded me of the Hulk, only Cheney didn't turn green; he turned purple.

"You damn son of a bitch," he said. "How DARE you interfere with me and my daughter's life... and the plans I have for her!"

"Pardon me?" I asked.

"Don't play coy with me, Swanson," he said. "Your chief said you were a slippery one and that entire stupid-blonde act is just that, an act."

"I'm still not sure I understand what you're talking about, sir," I said.

"I am talking about you telling Bridget to just run away and go back to her HUSBAND!" he raged, the veins on his neck bulging. "I am talking about her being married to man who could never run this company I have built from the ground up! Just after I had her safely away from that man, you told her just to leave and go back to that, that... cop!"

"Sir, that's not exactly what was said, sir," I said, knowing I had him off-kilter. "The question was asked why she didn't go back to John if she wanted to. It wasn't a suggestion or even a statement, sir."

"I don't give a diddly god damn if it was a question or a statement; the effect was still the same. She left!" he raged. "She just packed up her's and Chloe's things, and she's GONE! Gone back to that nothing, son of a bitch, blue-collared, uneducated, overly buffed buffoon!"

"Well, sir," I said, "she *is* free to go. She is a married woman, and it is acceptable for her to live with her husband and child."

"She's NOT a married woman!" Cheney yelled. "Her damn divorce would have been finalized had that stupid-assed judge not carried it on and on and on!"

At his outburst, one of the previously dismissed men appeared at the door, flexing his muscles as he entered.

"Sir," I said, trying to keep my voice low and non-threatening, "do you really want anyone else in on this conversation?"

Cheney looked up to see his goon, and waved him away again. The man silently withdrew, but not before leveling a silent threat at me. The look told me in no uncertain terms he would snap my neck in half a second if asked. I answered his threat with my own silent threat, except mine was just as urgent, and real. *I'm a cop. Mess with me, and see the inside of a prison.* He just smiled and shrugged.

The encounter told me that the conversation was not really private and was being monitored by some unseen force.

When the guard with the overgrown biceps was gone, I turned back to the angry father. "Yes, and now that 'stupid-assed judge' is dead," I said, keeping my voice low.

"Damn straight he's dead," Cheney said. "None too soon, either. Not soon enough for my little girl, though."

"I don't catch your drift," I said.

"Listen, you son of a bitch," he snarled. "I paid over five hundred thousand dollars to get my little girl away from that blue-collar PRICK, and back where she belongs. I'd pay whatever it took to see him gone."

"Seems pretty steep, even for Shark Delgado," I said mildly. "Are you sure you got your money's worth?'

"Lawyers, pfffssst!" he said snapping his finger at me. "SCUM— they all are. They're as worthless as tits on a boar. Two years we dicked around with that worthless piece of shit of a judge. TWO YEARS! Two years of my little girl's life she wasted waiting for that divorce to be final. What a waste. Lawyers, pfffsssst, sometimes you just gotta take matters into your own hands! But then you come along and ruin everything I've done to protect my little girl. EVERYTHING!"

"I don't understand, Cheney. What do you mean, 'take matters into your own hands'?"

"I mean that when the courts go too slowly, you just got to kick the lawyers out of the way and do it your own damn self.

God, I was hoping I got that all on my digital recorder. That sounded like an admission to me. But I would need evidence to back it up. I needed proof, not the ravings of a grief-stricken father. Maybe he was just trying to play hero.

"Like killing a judge?" I asked.

He narrowed his eyes at me and reached for his cup. Looking hard at me he shrugged and smiled.

That, I couldn't get on tape. Damn. If ever there was something that was incriminating, that smile was it. Double damn. I needed to push a little harder.

"So, Bridget is gone with little Chloe?" I said. "A waste of a dead judge."

"Not a waste," Cheney said. "I can buy and sell every asshole in this county. Henning was the only one who thought he was above everyone else! Damn fucker. Just wouldn't listen to reason."

"Maybe it was you who wouldn't listen to reason,' I said. "Maybe you just didn't want to understand that your little girl found someone else to love and live with. Maybe she was tired of being your 'little girl' and wanted to be a grown-up wife and mother."

"Listen, you fucker," Cheney snarled. "You keep those ideas out of my little girl's head. Your hear me?"

"I'm just telling you what I observed," I said. "She seems to love her husband, and you're interfering with their marriage. Maybe Judge Henning was right when he ordered you away from her and Chloe."

"Damn you, FUCKER," Cheney yelled, spittle flying from his mouth. "I told you: stay away from my little girl. You stop putting ideas into her head. Do you HEAR ME?"

"It's not that I don't hear you," I said, watching the man begin to disintegrate in front of me. "It's just that I think Bridget deserves to be with her husband, and Chloe deserves to be with a father who loves her."

In a flash, the man who was at least twenty years my senior was across the small antique table separating us. He had me by the throat and was beginning to squeeze, while spewing spit into my face. "I told you, you knuckle-dragging piece of blue-collared SHIT! STAY AWAY FROM MY DAUGHTER!"

I did a quick turn to my left, using the man's own body weight against him. He and the table crashed to the floor as he lost his grip on my throat. I scrambled to my feet, while the older man splayed across the broken table and floor.

"Listen, Cheney," I said, putting my foot on him to keep him down.

"I'm on your trail. I won't let go till I find out who killed Nancy Henning and Mark Henning. If it was you, which I'm beginning to think it may have been, you're going away. Do you hear me? AWAY!"

"And you hear me, Swanson: you're dead. Do you hear me? Dead."

"Yeah, right, old man," I said. "Words are cheap. Thanks for the coffee, and I'll show myself out."

But, before I could turn around, two sets of very strong hands were securing my arms to my body, and my feet were lifted from the floor. I was literally carried to the front door, and thrown out of it.

Even with the hard landing I had to smile. If nothing else, I had the goons for assault on a peace officer and Cheney for terrorist threats. It was something to keep in my back pocket to use later if necessary. However, in the meantime, maybe I should have taken his threat a little more seriously. But who believes an old man's threats when he's rolling around on the floor like a beach ball? And what cop really believes his life can be in danger from a respected, tax-paying citizen?

Silly me.

CHAPTER TWENTY-TWO

L eaving the gated community of Pelican Point, I lowered the windows in the Intrepid, letting the sea air wash over me as I drove back north to the check in at the station. With the days getting shorter, with fall evolving, it was almost dark when I got back to the barn.

My partner was gone, but she had left for me a stack of interviews from the patrol officers on the night of shooting. With all the reports neatly tabulated and indexed, she was obviously already compiling the murder book of reports and lists of evidence we prepared for the prosecutor.

Unfortunately for us, we had no real suspects—other than Old Man Cheney—and I still wasn't sure about him. If he had been anyone else other than a high-powered, politically connected person, I would have brought him in just to rattle his cage for terrorist threats he leveled at me.

But who would ever believe a man his age and size posed a real threat to me. After all, I was at least twenty years younger and towered over him by at least seven inches. No one I knew would consider him a threat. But the gooney squad: that was different. Those guys I had cold. The marks from their fingers lingered on my arms from where they grabbed me to so rudely and physically escorted me from the premises. Rubbing my arms, and feeling the incipient bruises, I stopped by the front desk to see if anyone was around to take pictures, but everyone was gone after the change of shift. I hadn't realized I had been that long.

Even with the station cleared of detectives and clerks, Graber was still in his office. I wandered on in and sat the recorder in front of him. After we listened to it, I asked him if it was enough for a search warrant for his financials and his office.

Graber rubbed his face a few times, swiveled in his chair, and finally looked me in the eye when he spoke. "You know, Jake, the Chief and Cheney play golf in the same foursome almost every week."

"Yeah, I know," I said. "So?"

"Well, think of it as Cheney's insurance policy," Graber said. "Chief has already been riding my case about you even looking at the Cheney daughter's divorce case."

"It wasn't my idea," I said. "It was the clerk and the presiding judge who gave it to me."

"No," Graber said. "It wasn't the presiding judge. He, too, has called the Chief to ask him if the divorce case had any relevance to this murder investigation. Mind you, he wasn't putting pressure on me, just inquiring."

"At this point, given what Bridget said, and given what Cheney did, I can't rule him out,"

I said.

"Did you at least ask for an alibi?" the lieutenant asked.

"No, I didn't think to do that," I answered. "It never crossed my mind that he did the shooting. It was too professional—too closely spaced. But I did meet some of the guys Bridget refers to as the 'gooney squad.' They're all former military: probably sharpshooters and familiar with military weaponry. I would also say they're familiar with hand-to-hand combat, given they made sure I left Cheney's place without my feet ever touching the floor."

That brought a slight smile to Graber's face. "So, you were eighty-sixed?" he asked.

I just nodded, and showed him my arm with the slight redness where their fingers had left their mark.

The lieutenant again rubbed his face and swiveled some more in his chair. "Okay, Swanson, you need to be careful. I have to let you run this as you see fit. But, remember, you're dealing with this city's elite and the Chief's social class. He loves rubbing elbows with the rich and powerful. If we take down one of the boys from that clique, the Chief may lose his golfing partners, and we may lose our jobs, even if the guy is guilty."

I understood the warning Graber was giving me, and why he gave it to me. I also knew he was right. In Newport Beach, California, it wasn't the arrests an officer didn't make; sometimes it was the people he did arrest that got him into trouble.

He and I sat a few more minutes, not really talking. Then he said to me, "Swanson, I know you try really hard to be a laconic surfer boy, but you really are rubbing the Chief the wrong way. He's looking for a reason to get rid of you."

I didn't know what to say. My life was always somewhat unstructured. First I had gotten by on my looks and my mother's social connections, then the former chief's protection, but now? Hmm, somehow I thought the fact I cleared most of my cases and I got the job done should be enough. Evidently, that Stanford grad, former FBI prick didn't agree with my assessment. I started to cloud with anger.

"See?" Graber said, "Look at you right now: you're starting to get angry at the thought of reining yourself in a little. I'm trying to protect you, but you've got two powerful forces working against you. You've got that NICS guy, Robinson, who is just waiting for you to mess up or for the case to be related to the judge's service in the military, and you've got one of the richest men in the county now yelling in the Chief's ear. For God's sake, watch yourself. Now, get out of here. I want to go home."

We stood and shook hands. I could see the worry etched on the man's face. He was probably as close to a father, a real father, as I would ever get, though he was maybe only a decade older than me.

I tried to take the lieutenant's words to heart, I really did. But I had a murder to solve, and I had things I had to do whether it stepped on toes or not. This meant waiting until I was sure that I had the station to myself. With the swing shift out on patrol, and the patrol sergeants not really caring about a detective who didn't belong to them, it meant I was usually safe to do whatever snooping I needed to do. While I waited, I read through the statements in Melissa's binders — most were interesting.

One neighbor observed:

"I was outside watering that dry spot on my lawn and I saw this dark car keep circling the block. I didn't recognize the car as belonging to the neighborhood. It didn't circle continuously, only every ten minutes or so. No, I didn't get a look at the driver. There may have been even more than one driver. I don't really know. All I saw was the car. I guess it was black, and the windows were tinted."

Another neighbor said:

"Over the last couple of weeks, I saw this grey car in the neighborhood. I could have sworn it was a Navy car. It had government plates on it, and it looked like the kind of cars the Navy issued to its officers. I saw it parked in front of the Henning house several nights and one Saturday morning. I think it may have been driven by a youngish blonde man. But I'm not really sure of his hair color because he always wore a baseball cap. It wasn't a uniform 'cover,' like the hats the guys in the military wear—more like a black cap with writing on it."

Hmm, I thought, that sounds like ole' Andre Robinson may have been meeting with the good judge in the weeks leading up to his death. I made an extra copy of that report to tuck into my zipped folder where I was keeping my important notes.

The next report gave me pause. The officer who took the statement from the original reporting witness must have recorded his statement and then transcribed it in its entirety rather than paraphrasing it. The statement was long, but it gave me quite a good background. It said:

"There is always a lot of traffic noise on MacArthur Boulevard on Friday nights. This night was no exception. I had my back slider open, and it faces MacArthur and over one street. I still get the noise, but not as bad. Still, it would have been hard to hear anything. But my dog kept barking and, in this neighborhood, we don't like barking dogs. I kept trying to hush her, but she kept going to the front door. I finally took my dog outside in the front to see what all the fuss was about. She's a Rottweiler and very sweet, but something was bothering her. I could hear some of the other dogs in the neighborhood also barking, and my dog was on alert. I opened the door and she ran right out, not even waiting for me to let her out. She ran across the street and I was afraid she'd get hit. She was sighting on some bushes—and, you have to understand, when Rottweilers are sighting on something they are not sure of, they don't bark, they just look. It had to have been something she didn't like because she didn't bark; she just stood with her head up and sniffing the wind. Then she started circling the bushes next door to the Henning's house, and then she ran along the wall. I had to call

her several times before she came back. I went across the street and looked, but couldn't see anything.

"No, the Henning's garage door wasn't open then. I didn't see any cars that seemed out of the ordinary in the neighborhood.

"I took my dog back inside and just after dark I heard the distinctive sound of Mark's Porsche come up the street. He has a tendency to chirp his tires when he downshifts to go up the driveway. We always tease him about it because he has to come out every month or so and use 'Goo Be Gone' to clean the tire marks off the street and sidewalk. We keep asking him when he's going to learn how to take that driveway without leaving skid marks. He always says, 'Probably never.' And we always laugh.

"I heard that chirp, knew it was Mark, but then my dog went crazy! She was barking and sniffing at the door and just being nuts. I looked out the door and saw Mark's light on in the car, and the garage door open, but nothing else. So I just closed the door and tried to hush my dog. But she kept circling the front door. Finally, she howled and howled, and I made her go to her bed and be quiet. A little while later, maybe a half-hour later, I went to the front door to check, and the garage door was still open; I still could see the light in Mark's car on. That's when I reported it to the police as an "open garage door' and asked them to do a safety check."

I read and re-read the statement. It seemed to give the best timeline of the event. More importantly, it was the foundation for a "Laying in

Wait" special circumstance murder allegation that could lead to the death penalty. Whoever shot Mark and Nancy Henning waited to find him and shoot him.

There were more reports about people seeing cars in the neighborhood and they were always gray or dark sedans. The dark sedan had tinted windows, making it too dark to see the interior, and a man wearing a black baseball cap was driving the gray sedan.

The silence in the station was complete. I could hear the slow tick as the wall clock in the bullpen ticked the minutes by. I looked up, and it was almost eight p.m.

Time to meet Cindy.

Exactly at eight I heard a soft knock at the back door. I opened it up to my coconspirator. She was excited and barely able to contain herself as we snuck down the hall to the locked storeroom conference room.

I jiggled the lock and put pressure on the door and the flimsy lock gave way. I pulled her quickly in with me and shut the door, relocking it. I turned on the lights, but closed the worn curtains that were at the window. Cindy stuffed her sweatshirt at the crack in the door to keep the light from leaking out. Once the room was secure, she pulled out her small notebook computer and turned it on. A few seconds later, we could see Lauren propped up in her hospital bed. She was smiling and, for the first time in days, there was some color in her face.

We tested the sound of our receiving computer and turned it down so we could barely hear it. I didn't want any stray sounds leaving the room. When we were set and ready to go, from the water bottle

I brought with me I poured water into the coffee pot and turned it on. Soon steaming water was pouring into the pot. It only took a few minutes to loosen the seals, and peel them back from the boxes. Cindy was giggling and had to clamp her hands over her mouth to keep from laughing out loud.

"What are you doing?" I asked her.

"I can't help it," she said. "I can't tell if I'm scared or excited. If Charles knew what I was doing, he'd have a fit! Do you think this is a federal crime? I mean, can I go to jail for this? Wouldn't that just tie Charles into a tight little ball to have a felon wife." She giggled again, rolling her eyes; she finally coughed softly a few times and spoke into the screen of the computer.

"Lauren, you ready?" she asked her sister.

"Ready when you are," Lauren answered.

"Okay, Lauren, what are we looking for?" I asked.

"You're looking for satellite photos in a file marked "Noodle Factory,'" she said. "You're also looking for photos in a file marked 'Waste Dump.' Then, if you can find Daddy's map, I might be able to reconstruct the pinholes to tell you what he was working on.

Cindy and I shuffled through the boxes and found the files with the photos. I had no idea what we were looking at. But, as we held them to the screen, Lauren gave a description of each photo. She suggested we keep a log of the numbers and the title she gave them so we'd know what they were if it was important. I started the handwritten log while Cindy held the photos to the screen for Lauren.

We worked fairly quickly. But, as Lauren identified the photos, I began to feel the skin on my neck crawl and all the hairs were sticking up on my arm. We were putting together a situation that terrified me. I looked over at Cindy, and I could see tears gathering in her eyes. "This is scary," she said to no one in particular.

Lauren just stared into her screen; some of the color had left her face. But her eyes held a fire in them. "Damn," she said. "Tim needs to know about this. He needs to know just how close they are to having missile and nuke capabilities."

Suddenly, from somewhere beyond her screen camera, a voice came across the connection. "Who has missile and nuke capabilities?"

Suddenly, Lauren's screen went dark. She had obviously slammed her screen shut, cutting off the connection.

Cindy and I looked at each other. Fear rippled in the room between us.

"Oh, my God," Cindy said. "Was that the NICS guy?"

I didn't bother to respond. I just grabbed the files we were working on and stuffed them into my zippered folder. Working quickly, I tried to seal the boxes as cleanly as I could.

I grabbed Cindy by the arm and pulled her out the door of the conference room. We ran down the hall and out to the parking lot.

"Cindy," I said, "I'm going to the hospital. You've got to go to somewhere safe, and I don't think it's the hotel or the hospital."

"But my sister! What about my sister?" Cindy cried.

"I'm going to the hospital to get to your sister," I said. "You just go to a restaurant in the mall and wait for me there. Go to Flemings'. It stays open late, and there is always a crowd at the bar. Wait at the bar for me. Got it?"

"Go to Flemings' and wait for you there in the bar?"   Cindy responded.

I waved my hand over my shoulder as I sprinted for the Intrepid. I fired her up, squealing my tires as I put her in gear. I gave Cindy the thumbs up and flew out of the parking lot. Racing as hard as I could, I flew down PCH and over to the on-ramp to Newport Boulevard. I tore up the on-ramp and slammed into the first left turn lane to get me up to Hoag Hospital on the hill. I didn't bother to find a parking space, but rather just left the Intrepid in a red zone, flipping down my visor with the special police ID.

Jamming my finger on the elevator button, I cursed it as it slowly opened its doors. The ride was interminable, and again the doors opened slowly. I ran down the hall to Lauren's room. It was empty!

Oh, shit! What had I done! How could I have been so stupid getting the daughters involved in this stupid curiosity of mine?

As I leaned against the door to her room I heard a toilet flush and Laruen waddled out of the bathroom. She looked at my stricken face and began to laugh.

"Oh, Detective Swanson. I'm so sorry," she said. "Did I scare you?"

I clutched at my chest where my thumping heart was doing a tattoo against my rib cage. My head began to swim and I felt faint.

Lauren grabbed my arm and led me to the guest chair by her bed.

She took some ice from her water pitcher and put some of the cubes against the back of my neck. I put my head between my legs. Finally, the room stopped swimming.

"We've got to call your sister and tell her you're okay," I mumbled from between my legs. "She's scared to death something happened to you."

Lauren laughed so hard, she had to excuse herself back to the bathroom. By the time she reemerged, I was again steady enough to sit up straight. Lauren called her sister to tell her she was fine.

"I saw him sort of sneak in out of the corner of my eye," she told Cindy. "I shut my computer but didn't do it fast enough. He must have heard part of our conversation."

My heart again plummeted to my feet, as I started to again gasp for air. The stupidity of my putting the girls in danger again overwhelmed me.

Lauren must have seen my stricken face because she quickly added, "No, no, Detective, I don't think he saw anything because he didn't say anything to me. He just left. I think he said something like 'Swanson' as he left, but nothing to me." I told Lauren to tell her sister it was okay to come back to the hospital.

While we waited for Cindy, Lauren and I talked about the implications of what we had found. I told her about the neighbors seeing a gray Navy car around the neighborhood in the two weeks before her father's death. She agreed with me it was probably Robinson.

"So, now what do we do, Detective Swanson?" she said.

"Lauren," I said. "This shit is way over my pay grade. I'm not a good spy; I'm way to flakey for that. So, how come you know all this stuff?"

Lauren again laughed and patted my arm, calming me. *She'll make a good mother*, I thought.

"Like I said, Dad wanted me to go to the Academy," she said. "He thought I was smart enough, but I was too busy being popular. That didn't stop him from teaching me stuff. The rest I just picked up from Tim and my dad when they'd talk. I guess my dad wasn't afraid of me spilling any secrets."

"What do you think this all means?" I asked.

"I think you're right: my dad knew the Russians were shipping stuff through China to Iran. The Noodle Factory is the rail lines through China, and the Waste Dump is the suspected factory in Iran."

"But the photos just look like a real dump," I said.

"Of course. The facility is underground, under the dump," she said. "Perfect hiding place: hide it in plain sight."

"Lauren, usually I'm the one who puts the pieces together," I said, "but my mind just can't wrap itself around the idea that some foreign agent came sneaking into this country to kill your father. It's just too preposterous."

The girl lay back on her pillows and shut her eyes. After a few minutes she opened them and said, "I agree, it is ridiculous to think someone would come here to kill my father. It just doesn't make sense."

"Well, whether we think it or not, I'm going to call my partner to come sit with you two until I can arrange around-the-clock protection," I said.

I gave Melissa a call, and she agreed to sit with the girls until I could arrange security. She didn't ask why, but I figured I'd get hell later. That was just the way she worked. She'd address the task, then make me pay later for my indiscretions.

Cindy arrived just as I was hanging up the phone. She told me she was relieved that my partner was coming to sit with them while I arranged protection. But, it was becoming obvious that them staying in Newport was becoming too dangerous for them, and for my investigation. A quick call to Santa Barbara, and Charles said he would arrange for a limousine to pick up the sisters and take them back to Cindy's house once Lauren was released. It was also decided that, if necessary, they would have Lauren admitted to Cottage Hospital in Santa Barbara.

With arrangements made, we chatted while waiting for Sanchez to arrive. For the next half-hour we regaled each other with stories about our lives growing up in Newport Beach. We found our lives weren't that much different. Across the generations there were kids with too much money and no supervision, drugs, beach parties with alcohol, and teachers who knew better than to fail the rich kids. It was the typical Newport Beach story. The only difference with Cindy and Lauren is they were lucky enough to have a mother who was not only a stay-at-home mom, but she actually cared about how her two girls were raised.

When Sanchez arrived she looked like her usual put-together self. She was dressed in jeans, short riding boots, a white shirt, and a camel hair jacket. I told her I would go back to the station and try to get a patrol officer over to the hospital as soon as they could get there. She just nodded and I left, but not before kissing each of the sisters on the cheek.

CHAPTER TWENTY-THREE

I hurried back to the station and found the watch commander, explaining to him that there were unidentified unsavory characters lurking around the daughters. He arranged for a uniformed officer to sit with the daughters at the hospital, after agreeing with me that it wouldn't do the city's image any good to have the daughters of the murdered judge killed, especially since one of them was pregnant. We knew our decision risked the chief's ire about the overtime for the security, but we both decided it was necessary to keep the daughters safe.

I was leaving the station to go back to the Intrepid when a tall blonde man emerged from the shadows next to my car.

"Swanson," Andre Robinson said. "Swanson, I thought I told you to leave that stuff alone."

"I don't know what you're talking about," I said, too tired to be snide.

"You and the daughters have been snooping where you don't belong," he said.

"Leave me alone, Robinson," I said, opening my car door. "If you want this case, just take it. It's a pain in my ass and, quite frankly, I don't want it."

"Too tough for you, small-time detective," he said. "Ya'll just over your head?"

"Robinson," I said, "I don't know why you're here. You keep snooping around, and yet, you don't add anything to the equation. You're just a pain in my ass. If I didn't know better, I'd think you're the killer, and you're just here to keep me from finding out."

The glare from the NCIS man was intense. Yep, the chrome on my '58 Buick ego's bumper was getting thin from all the glares.

"Swanson," he snarled, "you're full of shit, you know that?"

"So I've been told," I answered.

"You put any of these crazy ideas in your reports?" he asked.

I just shrugged.

"I'm telling you now, if you did, you remove them, now," he threatened. "I won't have you sullying my Navy with your shit."

"Or you'll do what?" I taunted. "Your Navy? I'm a civilian, at least the last I checked. There's nothing you can do to me."

"You're wrong, Swanson," he said. "There's a lot I can do to you. Federal government versus city police. Think about it, boy, ya hear?"

I'd had enough. I slid into the seat of my car and started the engine of my trusty Intrepid. I was done for the night. D-O-N-E! Done!

I waved to him as I pulled out of the station parking lot and headed for home. My thoughts were too obsessed with my disdain for the blonde-haired Navy prick that I didn't pay any attention to the black vehicle that pulled in behind me.

CHAPTER TWENTY-FOUR

The next morning I awoke to find my dog curled up tightly against me and my cat asleep on my pillow. The blinds at my open window were rattling against the window pane from the wind blowing through it. Sometime in the night the Santa Ana winds blew in from the high desert. The beach was in for a hot, dry, and very windy day. But until the sun got to its zenith, the wind blowing across the bay was cold.

I struggled out of bed to close my windows. Mandy just snuggled closer into the blankets, and Cisco moved over to my vacated warm spot. Neither of them appeared interested in helping me shower or shave, so I left them to take care of myself.

I quickly shaved, drank a cup of coffee, and finally whistled up the dog for her breakfast. She reluctantly got off the warm bed and wagged her way out to the kitchen. With his best friend gone from the bed, Cisco came out to join us for coffee and breakfast.

When we had all finished with our respective meals, I called for them to leave with me. I grabbed up my waist holster and the manila folder with the photos I had taken the night before from the secret files at the station. It was my intent to go to the local Kinkos to make my own copies of the photos and the notes I made the night before. Then I hoped to slip everything back into the boxes before anyone knew they were gone.

Not being a spy specialist, and having not paid attention in geography class, none of the photos made sense, even with the notes I took from what Lauren told me. It was my intent to meet with Bill Dawson and see if he could help me decipher exactly what I had.

I was in a good mood despite the fact the night before I had played another round of parking roulette. The girls had made a good point about the fact that sometimes it was dangerous for them to park on the street and walk back to the house alone after dark. I bought their argument, and left the parking issue alone. After all, I had parked on the street for years when Red was my landlord. What was the safety of the girls versus a nightly walk for me?

Several blocks up the street from the Pavilion, I found the Intrepid. It was parked in the spaces on the median where Balboa Avenue splits with an island in the middle of the street to give more parking to a parking-starved community. Since it was street sweeping day, all the spaces were empty except for my lonely Intrepid. I removed the parking ticket from my windshield and walked across the street to throw it away in the trash receptacle.

As I turned around and started back across the street, I hit the remote keyless entry on the car. No sooner had I stepped off the curb toward the Intrepid when a shockwave knocked me to the ground and a ball of flames soared over my head, filling the daytime sky.

I lay on my back, not hearing a thing — just floating with the clouds. I saw a sea gull soaring overhead; but I couldn't hear its call, so I closed my eyes. Darkness engulfed me. I remembered nothing more until I felt hands gently shaking me.

I looked up and a man in a grey-blue uniform was shaking me by the arm. I blinked at him. I noticed that his lips were moving, but I couldn't hear what he was saying. I tried to move my head, but I felt hands on my head, holding it in place. My body felt like lead. I wasn't sure if I still had arms or legs, so I decided not to try to move them. I found it totally comforting to just float and watch the man's lips move. Closing my eyes, I floated away again.

Suddenly, I felt something sharp in my arm and I came back to earth with a thud. All the sounds of the Peninsula again came rushing back, only this time I could hear voices around me and sirens in the background getting closer and closer.

Lieutenant Graber's concerned face loomed over me. "Swanson, what the hell?" he said.

I smiled up at him. Anyway, I think I smiled at him. I felt like smiling at him as someone lifted me onto what felt like a stretcher. Then, everything went black again.

I awoke with a blinding headache. It felt like my skull was trying to pop off the top of my head. I felt a scream start in my throat and I let loose, but all that came out was a croak. Suddenly, a dimple-faced blonde woman bent over me.

"So, you're awake," she smiled at me, her symmetrical dimples deepening. "Detective Swanson, do you know where you are?"

I closed my eyes and tried to think. I didn't exactly know where I was, but figured it wasn't heaven. So, I opened my eyes and looked around. Ahh, it was the emergency room at Hoag Hospital—a place with which I was becoming much too familiar.

"The honeymoon suite at Caesar's Palace?" I croaked at her.

She laughed and turned away from me. "He's awake and oriented," she said.

A doctor of Indian descent came into view and said, "Are you sure he is oriented? I distinctly heard him say he was in the honeymoon suite. That is not correct."

There was another laugh from a different voice outside of my field of vision. "Yes, he's oriented. He's aware enough to be joking," she said, with a laugh in her voice.

A beautiful brunette bent over me and listened to my chest with a stethoscope. "How you doing, Jake?" she said.

"Hey, Valerie," I said, recognizing her from my previous visit. "It's been a while."

"Can you feel your toes?" she asked.

"Don't know," I said. "I think I can feel my arm, but I'm not sure I have toes. Valerie, do something for me, okay? My head hurts like crazy bad."

I heard voices somewhere out of sight and suddenly dimples appeared again with a hypodermic needle and put something in the valve of my IV. My head stopped hurting almost immediately.

"Okay, Jake," Valerie said. "Can you sit up?"

"Don't know," I answered, beginning again to float on the cloud.

"All right, let's try something easier," she said. "I'm going to touch you all over your body, but not tell you where. If you feel something, I need you to tell me."

She methodically, and I thought cruelly, poked me with a needle all over my body. When she was done using me as a pincushion she bent back over me, a twinkle in her eye.

"Well, your nervous system seems to be intact," she said. "If you've got feeling in your extremities, your lying around is just because you're lazy. So, let's sit up, good-looking. I need to check your other injuries."

She and Dimples sat me up with me groaning the whole time. The doctor, who I learned later was just an intern, watched off to one side. For a brief moment I felt bile rise in my throat. Dimples was there with an emesis basin and caught the little bit of yellow spittle and some leftover coffee. I coughed a few more times, then asked to lie down again.

I lay there for what felt like forever, and finally Valerie opened the curtain to let a very worried Lieutenant Graber and Melissa come to my bedside.

Melissa looked scared and the lieutenant's face was crisscrossed with deep lines, making him look a decade older than his given age.

"Black vehicle, maybe a sedan, maybe a SUV, but something

black," was all I could think to say to them. "I think I saw a black vehicle following me."

I don't know where that thought came from, but somehow it made sense to me. I could have sworn I saw a black sedan or maybe a black SUV somewhere in the night—I think it followed me—but I wasn't sure.

"Melissa," I said, motioning her to come close. "Get the reports you collated for me. There's something about a black sedan."

"I'm on it, Jake," she said, stepping away from my view.

The lieutenant pulled his chair up to my bedside. "Jake, this is serious," he said. "A judge, and now you. What were you doing last night?"

I raised myself up on my elbow to look at him. My head swam for a few seconds, then it cleared.

"Lieutenant," I whispered. "I saw that NCIS guy at the back of the station last night. I don't like him. I think he's connected to all of this somehow. The neighbors all saw him meeting with the judge before the murder. He met with him several times. I just think he's tied in more than he's letting on."

The lieutenant chewed on that for a few minutes.

Suddenly, I thought of something. *The maps and photos. Where were the maps and photos?* I had them in my hand when my precious Intrepid blew up.

"My papers? Where are my papers?" I asked the lieutenant.

"There were photos and sheets of paper everywhere when I got to the scene," Graber said. "I don't know if anyone picked them up or not."

"Get them," I said. "Send someone out to get them. They may be the key."

"To what, Swanson?" he asked.

"I'm not sure," I said. "But every time I get near those satellite photos, Andre Robinson shows up."

"Maybe it's because you're not supposed to be anywhere near those photos," the lieutenant countered.

"No, it's more than that," I said. "I don't like him."

Lieutenant Graber pushed back from me a little and looked me in the eye. He studied me for a moment, then laughed. "Swanson, you don't like him because he is the buttoned-down and younger you. He's what you would have been had you tried a little harder."

"Why would I want to have been him?" I asked, hurt by his observations.

"Maybe because Melissa Sanchez, your partner, is completely smitten by him, and not you."

I snorted. That was preposterous. Melissa was my annoying partner. She was ten years my junior, and other than gorgeously beautiful, and incredibly smart, she so wasn't my type. Besides, she was like my sister I never had. No, no, I disliked Robinson for some other, more sinister reason.

The lieutenant's observation didn't warrant a comment so I didn't even try. Besides, I couldn't find the words. Pretty soon, just trying to talk to him became too hard, so I drifted off to sleep.

I vaguely remember being moved out of the emergency room as I was wheeled by an orderly up the elevator and into a private room. Another nurse came with another needle full of something delightful and I drifted off to Never Never Land.

It was very dark, I remember that. In fact, the room seemed very, very dark, like my nightlight had been turned off and the lights from the hallway had been extinguished. I felt hands on me, and they weren't friendly. Maybe it was the pillow that was thrust over my mouth and nose, or the feel of someone's knees on my chest, but I knew whoever was in my room was not there to make me feel better or minister to my medical needs. I needed to fight. With all my might I fought back.

It probably was the years of surfing and building up my shoulders and arms; or even the swimming that strengthened my legs; or maybe it was just my sheer will to live that gave me the strength to fight my way out of the drug-induced fog. But I bucked and tucked my chin to my chest and grasped the arms that tried to put the pillow over my face. Somehow I managed to roll onto my knees and throw the person off me. I yanked the emergency cord on the wall above my bed and, suddenly, alarms started sounding all up and down the hall. The hands holding the pillow threw it back at me. I saw my door open and a darkened figure run out of my room.

Nurses and a doctor surrounded me in no time. They were dragging a crash cart just like they have on the hospital TV shows. When they came into my room and saw me kneeling on my bed, they stopped dead.

A nurse bustled over to the alarm switch and turned it off, while someone went to the light switch and toggled it up and down a few times. Neither the overhead lights nor the light above my bed came on. It wasn't until someone tried the switch in the bathroom that some light came into the room.

"Did you see them?" I asked. "Did you see the guy who came out of my room?"

All the medical personnel looked at me like I had lost my mind, which maybe I had.

"All we saw was the orderly who turned on the alarm," one of the nurses said. "He's the one who called 'Code Blue.'"

"That wasn't an orderly," I said, getting off my knees. "Not unless you hire homicidal maniacs. He tried to kill me!"

I got a couple of pats on the shoulder and a few empathetic shrugs, but soon the crew left the room. I was left alone with my scare and my determination not to get killed.

Pulling the IV out of my arm, I looked around for a bag with my clothes. I found a bag, but all it had in it was my cell phone and a pair of shoes. I was going to have to make my escape without clothes.

I mulled it over a few minutes and decided a sheet to cover my backside and my shoes was enough. I was sure someone would be more than happy to help me make my escape, even if I didn't have clothes.

About ten minutes later I emerged from the bushes when Sally's blue Maserati pulled up to the emergency stairwell's exit. I slunk into her car and hung my head.

Sally said nothing as she safely navigated the parking lot and headed down Newport Boulevard. A couple of quick turns and she pulled into her condo building's parking structure. It wasn't until we emerged from her private elevator to her penthouse suite that she finally said something.

"So, Jake, do you want clothes, or are you just going to lounge around here in your hospital gown?" she asked, not really laughing and not really smiling.

"Clothes, please," I said.

A couple of minutes later she emerged holding a sweatshirt and a pair of sweat pants. "Here," she said, "these should fit you."

I excused myself and went to change. When I joined her back in her living room, she was sitting on her couch. Her feet were tucked under her, and she had a worried look on her face.

"Jake, what happened?"

All I could do I hang my head. With everything so out of control, I didn't know where else to turn. So, I spent the rest of the night telling my very best friend in the world everything I had witnessed, everything that had happened, and every impression I had. I did not finish until the dawn was turning the sky behind the bluffs red. When I was done, she led me into a bedroom and tucked me into bed.

This time I slept like I was dead, not just dying.

CHAPTER TWENTY-FIVE

It was the soft touch on my shoulder that roused me from my deep slumber. I looked up to meet the deep blue eyes of Sally Deming. Her face still carried the worried lines from the previous night, and her mouth was slashed into a firm line. It was only after she knew I was awake that her lips softened into a slight smile.

"So, you're awake?" she said, taking a seat next to me. She set a steaming mug of coffee on the nightstand next to me. "Here, I know what really gets you going in the morning."

I squirmed into an upright position, only to have my head explode with a light show of fireworks behind my eyes. In a flash, Sally's cool hand was on my forehead, soothing it slightly with her gentle touch.

"Here," she said, extending her hand to me, which held two green liquid gel Advils. "This might help."

"Nothing stronger?" I asked.

"Hmmm, not when you check yourself out AMA," she said.

"I didn't leave against medical advice," I said, feeling a pout coming on. "I left to stay alive."

"Even so, Jake," she said, "you left without doctor's orders; therefore, there is nothing stronger, so don't even ask."

I gulped the two pills with a swallow of the deeply rich coffee. The burning at the back of my throat still didn't hurt as much as my head. I groaned and tried to slink back down into the deep coverlet of the bed, but Sally's hand stopped me before I could get too comfortable.

"Don't," she said, handing me my cell phone. "It's been burning up all morning. Lots of people are trying to find you."

"You didn't tell them where I was, did you?" I asked, afraid of dragging another woman into my mess.

Sally laughed her merry chortle, the one she uses on me when she finds me exceptionally amusing — the one she did not use the previous night. Shaking her head, she told me the only people she spoke with were Scat over at the house and Lieutenant Graber. Scat was bringing some clothes by, and had made sure the dog and cat were fed. The lieutenant was expected shortly.

"So, you better get up and get a shower," Sally said. "There is a razor and men's products in the lower right cupboard of the guest bath. Fresh towels are by the shower."

She turned away from me and started to leave the room, but was stopped short when I gave an involuntary groan as I started to get out of the bed. The act of sitting upright again brought on another round of nausea, and pain shot through every part of my body.

"Oh, Jake," she said as she came back to the bed to help me.

"Don't!" I said, as the covers fell away from me, exposing the fact I had slipped into bed the night after taking off the sweat pants. "I'm naked!"

Bless Sally; she didn't even laugh at my attempt at modesty. She just smiled that all-knowing smile of hers, and pulled the sheet from the bed to cover me.

"You came with only a sheet, so I guess it's okay for you to keep wearing one," she said, the laughter bubbling around her voice, but not quite exploding outward. Her merriment was contained to happy squint lines around her eyes as she helped me to the bathroom.

I had to lean heavily against her as we walked the few steps to the bathroom. I wasn't sure what I would do once I got there. Everything hurt—my eyes, my head, my body—everything! I moaned at every step, willing myself to put one foot in front of the other.

Once inside the bathroom, with Sally safely on the other side of the door, I slid gratefully to the floor. The tile was cool, but not cold on my exposed buttocks, and I quickly fell over on my side. How had I managed to escape last night? How could I have sneaked down three flights of stairs and made it out to the car when I could barely walk the several steps to the bathroom? All I wanted to do was curl into a ball and not move.

I don't know how long I lay on the floor, but there was suddenly a strong knock at the door. Before I knew it, the door was pushed open and the large frame of the lieutenant loomed in the doorway.

"Swanson, what the hell?" he thundered.

I squinted a smile at him and tried to roll into an upright position. Though the will was strong, the body was weak, so I just closed my eyes, and lay back on the floor.

A few moments later I heard the shower start and the room began to fill with warming steam. Strong hands lifted me from the floor and perp-walked me to the shower. I kept my eyes closed, afraid if I opened them I would start spewing coffee and bile. As I leaned against the shower wall, strong hands soaped me, then used the spray handle to rinse me. More hands toweled me dry, and wrapped me in a towel blanket. I was soon lying back on the bed, but this time I was clean.

After a while the room stopped swirling, and I dared to open my eye. I could see both Scat and the lieutenant standing off to the side, speaking softly to each other.

"Where's Sally?" I asked, not really wanting to know who actually showered me and toweled me dry — afraid of what the answer would be.

"She's calling a doctor," Scat said, coming to stand next to me, her hands on her hips, legs spread slightly apart. It was the stance of a warrior princess, or a really pissed off mom. In any case, I knew she meant business. "You're a mess, and you need a doctor!" was all she said as she towered over me.

Graber came to stand next to her and his look softened as he bent close to speak to me. "Swanson, what the hell do you mean checking yourself out of the hospital last night? Look at you. You should be under a doctor's care."

"Didn't Sally tell you?" I asked, beginning to feel slightly better as the Advil began to kick into my system.

"Tell me what?" Graber asked.

"About the guy who tried to kill me last night!" I said.

The lieutenant looked quizzically at me, then shrugged his shoulders. "Not really," he answered. "She just called me and told me you were here. She didn't go into details."

"There was some maniac at the hospital last night who tried to smother me with my pillow," I said, starting to get angry. "Everyone seemed oblivious to my problem and so I left. By the way, where are the judge's daughters?"

The lieutenant looked aggrieved as he answered, "After your car exploded, and after it was discovered you had security attached to them, it was decided they should leave for Santa Barbara. They left yesterday."

"Good," I said.

"Not so good," Graber said with a sigh. "A very pissed off Charles McDermott came through the station on his way to pick up his wife and her sister. He was accusing us of putting his wife and sister-in-law in danger. He had a limousine waiting to take them home. The last I saw, he was leaving the Chief's office trailing threats of lawsuits behind him. You want to tell me about that, too? Is it connected to the bomb and the destroyed car?"

"I don't know," I answered. Then, thinking about my beloved car, I asked, "Intrepid is destroyed?"

Graber rolled his eyes at me, and nodded. "Yep, a burned-out, twisted mess of metal. If you'd been in it, you'd been a crispy critter… or at least what would have been left of you."

I cringed and slunk lower into the bed.

Graber chewed on the inside of his cheek, then asked, "So, why did you arrange for protection? Why did you have swing's watch commander put a uniform at their door?"

"Look, Lieutenant," I said, "I told you yesterday, with all the stuff that's been going on with that weird stuff from China and Iran, and then the stuff with Cheney, I'm not sure about anything anymore."

"Hmm, seems pretty far-fetched," he said.

I tried to nod my agreement, but the light show of pain started with the movement of my head. I moaned, and added, "I just know that the Andre Robinson creature keeps showing up. And, whenever he shows up, I get the willies."

"Yeah, you keep saying that," Graber answered, finally lowering his towering frame into an overstuffed side chair. "You usually have good instincts, but I'm just not sure why you have such a hard-on for this guy."

"Hmmm, because I don't like him," I answered. "He's the connection to the maps and the satellite photos. . ."

"The ones you're not supposed to have," the lieutenant countered.

"Okay, the ones I wasn't supposed to have," I agreed. "But, nonetheless, he is way too interested in them. Just ask yourself why?"

"Because he needs to know why the judge was killed," Graber answered. "Because if it was connected to his service commitment, then the judge's death belongs to the government, not us."

"Then why not just assert jurisdiction over it and take it?" I asked.

The lieutenant just sat still, not answering my question.

As the two of us sat in silence, Scat reappeared with a mug of coffee for Graber, and a hanging suit bag of clothing for me. Dangling from the hook of the suit bag was a smaller satchel, hopefully with underwear and socks. Although, given my current state, I wasn't sure how I felt about putting on clothing.

Scat again took the warrior princess stance after hanging the suit bag on the doorframe. "So, Jake, what's this all about? What is this I heard about your car exploding? You weren't in it, were you?"

"Why?" I asked. "Did you want me to be?"

All of a sudden the self-possessed Ph.D. candidate, knower of all things ancient, dissolved into tears. Warrior princess was replaced by worried and scared friend. "No, of course not," she said. "I mean, what would happen to Cisco and Mandy if you were killed?"

I patted the bed next to me, and she came and sat next to me, squeezing my thigh. The tenderness was as unexpected as was the intimate gesture. I felt a blush start to creep up my neck, with an unwelcome reaction from the hinter regions of my groin.

Graber lifted an eyebrow at me, and gave me his secret smile. Seeing that smile I felt the blush deepen.

The interlude was broken when Sally joined us with a woman in her mid- to late forties. The woman's jet black hair was pulled back into a tight chignon, and her black eyes bored holes into me. I saw an earpiece of a stethoscope trying to make its escape from a pocket in her jacket.

Ahhh, she was the doctor Sally must have summoned.

"So, you are the one who left the hospital last night, causing quite a stir, are you not?" she said more than asked.

"Maybe," I countered.

"Of course he is," Graber interrupted. "But, then, if your hospital had kept him safe, he wouldn't need to be here, would he?"

The doctor turned on the lieutenant who was by then standing, towering over her by at least a foot and a half. She eyed him up and down, then turned back to me, evidently deciding to ignore his hulking frame.

"So, what is your problem today such that my good friend Sally calls me out of an important hospital meeting to come tend to you?" she asked.

"Everything is my problem," I answered.

"I do not care about psychological problems," she retorted, "only physical ones. The others, you must tend to on someone else's time."

I looked over at Sally, wondering why she would have called a she-devil to take care of me. Sally saw my look and smiled, giving me a shrug.

"Dr. Hadhi, Anita," Sally said, "he's harmless. He thinks he's charming. Just let it go. I am worried about him. Is that enough?"

The good doctor turned back to Sally and shrugged. "Of course, my friend," she answered. "I will determine for myself his ills."

With that she removed her stethoscope from her pocket, along with a small flashlight. She flashed the light in my eyes, then had me try to follow the light as she moved it back and forth, then up and down. The light hurt my eyes and I had to squint just to follow the path she traced.

After blinding me with the flashlight, she bent over and took my head in her hands, moving it back and forth and up and down, much like she had the flashlight. When she was done with torturous head twisting, she brought out the stethoscope and listened to my chest. After palpating my back, and several spots on my body, she stood up.

"Does your head hurt?" she asked, using the deadpan physician voice—caring, but not concerned.

"Yes, as in I find myself praying for death," I answered.

"Hmmm, not likely, unless you find yourself in another explosion," she answered. "How about the rest of your body. Does it hurt?"

"Also, yes," I answered. "Same feeling—praying for death."

"Hmmm, again, not likely," she answered, this time a slight smile played on her lips.

Dr. Hadhi turned back to Sally and said, "Is he eating or taking fluids?"

"Last night he had tea, but the coffee this morning made him nauseous," Sally answered, her lips pursed.

"Hmmm, he is slightly dehydrated, and definitely has a concussion," the doctor said. "If he were in the hospital, he would have fluids."

All four sets of eyes bored into me: the lieutenant's, Scat's, Sally's, and the doctor's. I shrank away from their accusatory looks.

"Someone tried to kill me," I croaked.

"Death by dehydration is much slower and much more painful," the doctor responded.

I wasn't sure if she was joking or what. My head was exploding in pain, and my sense of humor was deserting me.

Turning back to Sally, Dr. Hadhi said, "I can start him on IV fluids, if you can keep him confined… and quiet. I can also administer intravenous pain medications just once. However, the script I give you must be filled, and it, too, will be for pain. But he must rest. Moving about can cause lasting debilitation to his brain. He definitely has a concussion."

Again, four sets of eyes bored into me. I turned my head away from the looks, only to have my head explode in pain. An involuntary gasp escaped from deep inside of me. I shrank lower into the bed, trying not to whimper out loud.

Sally whirled around, pulling the sheet low enough so she could see my face. I tried to smile as I looked back into her deep blue eyes, but I received no returning smile.

"He will stay here, of course, Anita," Sally said. "I will bring in reinforcements if necessary to keep him quiet."

"But the investigation?" I said.

I was cut off from further protestations by a glare from the lieutenant. "Swanson, under the snowballing considerations in this matter, I have to agree with Ms. Deming. You will stay here until cleared by the doctor."

"Snowballing considerations?" I asked, not sure what he meant, and not sure whether to blame my blinding headache or something else.

The lieutenant sighed that sigh I have heard him use too many times when thinking of the chief of police and me. He rolled his eyes, hunched his shoulders, then pulled a chair to my bedside and took a seat. He sighed again and, for a moment, I thought he was going to pat my hand. I buried my hand under the covers just to make sure he didn't.

"Swanson, besides the obvious fact someone has now tried to kill you—apparently twice—and the fact you are seriously injured, others who have an interest in the investigation are making noises at the Chief, and he isn't pleased. Also, let's not forget you had police property destroyed."

"I didn't 'destroy' police property!" I protested. "Someone else did!"

"Be that as it may, the Chief still holds you responsible for the destruction of the Intrepid. And, he's not pleased about having his golfing foursome in an uproar due to you questioning Cheney. He wants you off the case. Your injury is the perfect excuse for him, as well as political cover. You're benched for now."

I found myself wanting to protest, but the words died on my lips. How could I expect the chief to sympathize with my plight when he would measure me against the rich and famous who had much more political pull than a mere detective? It was not his style nor his inclination to protect me. I was an anathema to everything he held dear: power, money from power and, most of all, political connections. He considered me a "hold over" from a previous administration that, unfortunately for him, was vested and not easily removed. For the chief, a surfer dude who knew the underbelly of his city, as well as many of the wealthy families, was not an asset, only a miserable debt from a former chief to his mistress. I was the gift that kept on giving misery. Best to be done with me.

Graber knew this, and knew I knew it, too. It was a discussion we had held too many times in the past. Yet, even with all of the lieutenant's warnings I could not—no, would not—change. I knew how to surf through my town, how to get the information I needed, and how to kick over the right rocks to find the information I needed. The only unfortunate thing for me was I had yet to find a weakness in the chief. There was nothing I could exploit or hold like the hidden ace up my sleeve. He was the Stanford grad, top in his class, former FBI agent, and the best-looking man in the department. All of his qualifications, including the physical, kept him safe as long as he kept the department away from the top echelons of our city and county. Just as importantly, his dazzling smile always held the promise of something the council-women held tight in their secret desires.

No, I thought, *the chief is untouchable, and I am expendable.* Yet, the feeling I had about the judge's killer kept niggling at the back of my spine. I needed to convince the lieutenant to let me continue with the case.

"Hey, please, LT, don't bench me," I pleaded.

His response was a harsh laugh and a shake of his head.

Sally stepped between the lieutenant and me, apparently seeing my distress, putting a hand on my forehead as she spoke to Graber. "Stop," she said. "Just let it rest for now. He's injured and needs his rest. We can handle the rest when he is stronger."

I didn't protest. She was right, of course. I couldn't handle anything right now but the pain behind my eyes. It only deepened when I heard Graber sigh again. But, when I looked up, Scat was leading him from the room and he was not protesting.

Dr. Hadhi and Sally conferred briefly, and the doctor withdrew. Sally sat on my bed and continued to stroke by brow. The unexpected tenderness surprised me, but also comforted me.

"Well, Jake," she smiled at me, "it looks like you are my prisoner for at least a short while, if you don't mind too much."

"As if," I smiled back at her.

"No, Jake, no charm today," she said, suddenly serious. "Doctor

Hadhi says you have a concussion, and deep contusions not only on your body, but also your face and head. You need to rest so your brain doesn't swell. Leaving the hospital last night was stupid."

"Not stupid," I said. "It saved my life!"

"Okay, no arguments," Sally said, again taking on her soothing voice. "But you are staying here."

As she said that, the doctor returned, carrying a small bag of instruments and an IV bag. She quickly took my arm, slapped it a few times, then tied a rubber tourniquet around it. When she found a vein she quickly slid a needle into it, and I immediately felt warmth spread throughout my body.

When I felt my eyes begin to droop, she took my hand and slipped another needle into a vein in my hand. But this needle had tubing and an IV attached to it. With the IV started she bandaged my hand with more tape than I have ever seen.

"There," she said. "I dare you to get this needle out of your hand this time."

"Don't dare him," Sally said. "He'll take it as a challenge."

I started to protest, but then everything floated away. I remember nothing more of that morning.

CHAPTER TWENTY-SIX

I really don't know how long I slept. When I awoke, Scat was sitting in a chair near me reading a book. She looked up when she heard me stir.

"So, you're awake?" she said more than asked.

"What time is it?" I asked.

"You mean, what day is it?" she answered.

"Hmmm. Okay, what day is it?"

"Thursday," she said smiling.

I groaned by way of response and turned to roll over to reclose my eyes. However, Scat had other ideas.

"Oh, no you don't," she said. "You've been out of it for more than two days, and I am tired of tending you like a sick child. You need to get up, get showered, and eat."

I suddenly had a horrible thought: if I had been unconscious for more than two days, what about... what about, you know, that stuff?

I slid back the covers and my worst fears were realized: I had a tube sprouting from my most private area. And I was on something I had seen at the hospitals; it was like a diaper, but not actually on me, just under me.

I groaned. "Oh, God," I said to no one in particular. I shut my eyes tightly trying not to think of who had been caring for me, and what that actually meant. When I tried to dive back under the covers, Scat pulled them off. She wasn't smiling.

"Oh, hell no!" she said. "You can't hide from me and this. You need to get up!"

"But, the… you know… the stuff," I said, blushing.

"Well, yeah, the 'stuff' will be removed," she said. "There is a nurse coming in about ten minutes and she'll take care of that. In the meantime, I am supposed to keep you company and make sure you are oriented to time and space—whatever that means."

"You said it is Thursday morning, and I suppose it is the same year, so, yes, I am oriented," I answered.

"Good. Let me go get you some coffee," Scat said. "How's the head?"

I squinted my eyes a few times and only a brief pain floated out, so I figured the worst was over. "My head is fine," I answered.

Without another word Scat left the room. Shortly thereafter Sally came in, and she was smiling. She looked her usual stunning self, with her hair caught up in the signature French roll, and dressed in a business suit.

"Good, Jake," she said taking a seat on my bed. "There are people who need to speak with you, and the doctor said it is really time you rejoin the living."

I didn't reply, but only groaned when I remembered why I was here and why people probably needed to speak with me. The murders: how could I forget?

Suddenly, the room was bustling with activity. A man came in wearing scrubs, with a plastic bag and some other thing that didn't look familiar held in his hand. He shooed Sally from the room as he quickly gloved his hands and removed the sheet from my naked body. I would have blushed, but he was too professional for me to protest.

With the tubing removed he helped me sit up. When I was steadied, we walked to the bathroom where he started the shower. With his help I showered and dressed in the underwear, slacks, and shirt Scat had brought those eons ago.

I walked a little unsteadily to the dining room table where Scat had a steaming mug of black coffee for me and a plate of scrambled eggs. Smelling the eggs I suddenly realized I was starving! Falling on the eggs, toast, and coffee like the starving man I was, I finally felt that I was going to live.

Scat joined me as I pushed the plate away. She sat looking at me, and her eyes were troubled.

"Jake," she said, "you were almost killed. Why?"

"I really don't know, Scat," I answered. "I am hoping to find out soon. By the way, has anyone from the Force been looking for me or wanting to see me?"

"Melissa has called a few times, and the lieutenant has been by to see you," she said. "Also, there is a guy who says he's from the Los Angeles Police Department who keeps leaving messages for you at the station. Melissa thinks it's important. So I took his name and number. Do you want them?"

I tried to think of whom I knew at the LAPD, but no one immediately came to mind. I shrugged and held out my hand. Scat handed me several pink messages. As soon as I looked at them I recognized the name, and it all came back: John McAllister. Of course, he was Bridget Cheney McAllister's husband.

I took the proffered phone and quickly dialed the number on the message note. The voice that answered was resonant, business like, and with a typical California flatness.

"McAllister," said he said.

"Detective Swanson, Newport P.D," I responded. "You called?"

"Swanson! My God, man. What happened to you?" the voice said, changing from professional cop to concerned human being.

"Someone took offense to me driving a Dodge Intrepid on the Newport Peninsula," I answered. "They decided to blow it up."

"That's what I heard!" he said. "It was all over the news! Are you okay?"

I groaned inwardly. This was not the kind of publicity the chief liked to have for his fair city. No wonder the lieutenant was concerned earlier. Once again I had dishonored the city.

"Hey, I'm going to be just fine," I answered. "By the way, you're the one person I wanted to speak with about the judge's death. You do know about that, right?"

"Yes, of course. Besides it being all over the news, I have a personal reason for wanting to speak to you," he said.

"You going to confess, or give up the killer?" I asked, trying to be smart. But I only caused my head to hurt.

"No, sir," he said quickly. "I want to thank you for sending my wife and daughter home to me."

"I'm sorry, what?" I asked wondering if my confusion was head oriented, or something else.

"Bridget, my wife: she came home to me," he said. "She told me told me you were the one to tell her just to come home if that was what she wanted, and she did. I owe you big time, sir. But that's why I am worried."

"Worried, why?" I asked.

"You know who Bridget's father is, don't you?" he asked.

"Of course," I said. "Met up with a few days ago."

"Then you know he's got to be fit to be tied that Bridget is home with me," McAllister said.

"Yeah, I would say that," I said. "But, listen, I still need to speak with you and get your statement. You okay about talking to me with- out a lawyer?"

There was only a slight pause before he told me he had nothing to hide and nothing to fear. We agreed to meet at my favorite haunt back in Sunset Beach since it was halfway between his station and Sally's.

Hearing my end of the conversation I was met with a frown from Scat. "Are you sure you should be leaving?" she asked.

"Need to," I answered. "Work to do, and it won't get done with me sitting here."

"Sunset Beach. Isn't that up the coast?" Scat asked.

"Yeah. So?" I asked.

"How're you going to get there?" she asked.

"Ahh, shit!" I said. "I don't have a car! You're right!"

I squinted at my predicament. I wasn't really back on duty yet. I didn't even know what my status was since I was injured. Was I suspended because of the car, or was I out on leave? The lieutenant hadn't been really clear before Sally cut him off those many mornings ago. I hesitated from calling him to clarify my situation. Better to do what I thought needed to be done, and deal with the consequences later.

Scat watched my face, and understood immediately my concern. "Do you need a ride?" she asked. "I guess you shouldn't drive and all."

"Probably," I said. I tried to decide if I should call Melissa just to see if she and I were still partners, but a niggling voice inside of me caused me to pause.

Running through the possibilities in my head, I realized it was either Scat or Melissa. Scat it was!

Twenty minutes later we were running up the coast in her Volkswagen convertible. She had the top down and the sea breeze was bracing. She didn't ask me what I was doing; she just keep humming along with the songs on the radio. Her voice was pleasant, and the otherwise quiet company was peaceful.

We arrived at the friendly bar just as the lunch crowd was starting to gather, making it difficult to decide who McAllister was in the crowd. It was he who approached me, his hand extended.

"Swanson?" he asked.

His handshake was strong but not overpowering. He was about five feet, eleven inches, with light brown hair, gray eyes, and even, white teeth. Dressed in 'civies,' he still had a 'cop' demeanor about him in that he stood with his legs slightly apart and arms just wide enough to spread over the gun belt he wasn't wearing. John McAllister was definitely a street cop. But his eyes were soft, and he radiated concern and gratitude. I immediately liked him.

We took a table outside while Scat took a seat at the bar.

We stared at each other for a few minutes, then John took the lead.

"Like I said, I want to thank you for getting my wife home to me. She and my daughter are the love of my life. I couldn't believe this has happened to us. I lost almost a year and a half of my daughter's life. She barely knows me!"

"I wish I could say it was me," I said. "It was just my partner who couldn't understand why, if Bridget loved you, she just didn't go home."

"Yeah, that sounds like Bridget. She wouldn't know how to go against her father. Someone had to put the idea in her head," John said.

"I thought you two were in therapy? Didn't the therapist tell her to go home?"

McAllister snorted, "A therapist? You've got to be kidding. They don't tell anyone to do anything. They just listen and suggest, but never tell."

"And Bridget didn't get the hint?" I asked, somewhat incredulously.

"Again, a therapist isn't someone who could stand up to her father. It had to be someone who Bridget considered to be as strong as the goonies her father has around him. So, no, it never crossed her mind to leave and come home."

"Funny, she used exactly that same expression the other day when we spoke with her. 'Goonies, or goon squad,'" I said.

"Yeah," McAllister said with a smile, "the Goon Squad. A bunch of guys who haven't given up playing war. They went to war and couldn't get enough of it, so they came home and decided to do 'protection.'"

"Yeah, I got to meet two of them firsthand," I said, rubbing my arms where they had left their marks. "I understand they provide protection for big-bucks clients. So why would your father-in-law need protection?"

"You know who Cheney is, don't you?" McAllister asked.

"Sure, the biggest developer in Orange County short of Donald Bren," I answered. "But, still, this is Orange County, not some crazy Third World country."

"Well, Cheney still thinks this is the Wild, Wild West," McAllister snorted. "He takes what he wants. And, if anyone gets in his way, he runs over them, figuratively — and now, maybe literally."

"You mean me?" I asked.

"It could have been you, given how shortly after Bridget's homecoming it was," McAllister said. He paused a minute, then played with the fork on the table, rolling it from side to side. When he finally set the fork down, he looked me straight in the eye and answered. "Listen, Swanson, Cheney has explosive experts on staff, and all kinds of weapons guys, but I am not sure it would have been enough time for them to set up. They are very careful. There wasn't much time for them to have reconnoitered you and then set the charges. Also, if one of his crew wanted you dead, you'd be dead. It wouldn't have just taken you out of commission."

It was my turn to play with the fork at the table. I found myself mimicking him, rolling it from side to side, not really paying attention to what I was doing; I was just thinking about how close I really came to dying. If I hadn't gone across the street to throw away that ticket, and if I hadn't clicked the opener before stepping off the curb, I would have been next to the car, and probably would be dead. It wasn't a co-incidence or fate that I wasn't dead, only an accident that I lived. But I didn't tell McAllister all that. I just sat, rolling the fork back and forth.

"You going to ask me if I killed the judge," McAllister said, filling up the blank space of our conversation.

"Sure," I said. "Did you kill Judge Henning? How about his wife; did you plug her twice in the heart? Did you kill the woman who was dying of cancer and only had another week or two to live?" I asked, my voice getting hard.

"Whoa!" McAllister said, reacting to my hardened tone. "First, let me flat out deny I killed the judge. He was the best friend I had during this whole process. He didn't issue those restraining orders when any other judge would have, and I would more than likely have lost my job. Not a lot of calls for a patrol officer who doesn't have a gun and can't patrol. Secondly, I knew nothing about Judge Henning's personal life. He was just a very competent guy in a black robe. Nicer than most, but still just a guy in black."

I'd like to think it wasn't because McAllister was a cop. I'd like to think I believed him because I had great cop instincts, and my instincts said he didn't do it. But I had to ask one more question, just to make sure.

"So, how do you do on the range?" I asked.

"The range? You mean the shooting range?" McAllister asked.

"Yeah, the shooting range."

"Christ, man, almost lost my qualifications," he said.

"Why was that?" I asked, knowing I already believed him, but curious.

"I don't know. There's something with my eyes and my sighting. I just can't seem to get my sighting correct. I think I've sighted on the target, but I'm always just off. Worse, I can't get close enough to do what I need to hit. I think I'd do better if I threw my gun at a perp rather than try to shoot them."

I knew the shots to Mark Henning were up close from behind. Even a novice could do that if given the chance at stealth and a good opportunity. But the shots to the wife were from a distance and they were definitely the shots of a marksman. While my instincts had told me McAllister did not have the ability to do the shootings, especially the wife, I made a mental note to get his range reports to confirm what he said.

"Cheney do it?" I asked, deliberately taking a different direction.

"It's Bridget's biggest fear that he did."

"And you?"

"I wouldn't put it past him, but I'm don't think so," he answered.

"Why?"

"He had too much ego to do something like that," he answered. "Cheney believed he absolutely controlled his daughter. There would be no need for him to go to extremes like that. If it had happened after Bridget came home, then, yeah, I'd say he'd do it."

"Hmmm," I said. "So why all the black sedans going by the judge's house leading up to his killing?"

"Sedans?"

"Yeah, a whole parade of sedans going up and down the judge's street leading up to the murder."

"Naw, Cheney's Gooney Squad uses SUVs, just like the Feds. He's too egotistical to use sedans. Do you know the make?"

"Not really," I said. "The witnesses weren't clear, and the patrol officer taking the statement didn't think to ask. Why?"

"In LA the make of the car usually gives us a good jumping off point," he answered.

"Really?"

"Yeah. I was at a recent in-house seminar given by the gang squad guys and they were talking about how the different gangs lean toward different auto makers," he said, the cop in him getting excited. "Like for instance, crazy as it is, the black street gangs gravitate toward Nissan models: the Crips toward Maximas, and the Bloods tend toward the upscale Nissans, the Infinities. And, of course, the black drug runners show their style by loving their Cadillac Escalades. Asian gangs, if it is the punk-assed kids, go for the Lexus IS types. For the Latin gangs it is Hondas. Go figure. No one wants American unless they're a drug runner!"

"What about plain ole' American black sedans?" I asked.

"Sounds like military," he laughed. "Yeah, like military would be cruising a judge's house. Ha, ha!"

It caused me a moment's pause. In fact, I knew that military *had* been cruising the judge's house, and they had actually been spending time in the judge's house. So, now what?

"Well, you know, in fact the judge was military. He was recently reactivated and was being sent overseas," I said.

"Judge Henning?" McAllister asked.

"Yeah, the judge was military, as well as a former criminal defense lawyer," I said.

"Whew, a lot of people would or could want him dead from just being a criminal defense lawyer," he said.

"Yeah, never mind being a judge in family law," I answered.

We both laughed, and the ice was completely broken.

Evidently, Scat saw us laughing and joined us at our outside table, taking in the boats and the yachts moored on the docks just beyond where we were seated.

I introduced Scat to John McAllister, and we chatted for a while. A personable waiter everyone called "Papa" took our order.

A delicious meal of high carbohydrates and fat followed. The restaurant's garlic fries and crab cakes were damn good. If I had kept eating that way, I was afraid a heart attack would end any speculation about my eminent demise. But I decided not to think about it. Instead I focused on the beautiful woman at my side, and the charming man sitting across from us. He kept Scat amused with his stories of the streets of LA, and I focused on the boats.

I needed to know what kind of sedans were cruising up and down the street in the weeks before the judge's death, and maybe one of my former suspects could help me understand what it meant. I considered it sufficiently helpful to the department and to my case that I picked up the tab, kept the receipt, and decided to charge it to the department.

With warm good-byes and wishes for my speedy recovery, the three of us left the bar feeling full and relaxed.

Maybe I shouldn't have been so relaxed. I completely missed the black sedan that pulled in behind us as we turned south onto the Pacific Coast Highway.

CHAPTER TWENTY-SEVEN

After I dropped Scat back at the house, I retrieved the keys to the British racing green Porsche 914-6 parked in the garage. I rarely used it except when out on the town for pleasure. I never took it to the station. But given that my dear Intrepid was a smoldering heap of twisted metal, I had no other choice.

At the station I hunted down my partner, curious to see what she had been doing in my absence. After all, we still had a murder to solve. It wouldn't have been good for her to be sitting around doing nothing while I was out.

I found her at her cubicle, surrounded by what looked like bank records and financials.

"Hey, Homes, what ya doin'?" I asked.

"Told you not to call me that," she said, not looking up.

"So, okay... Little Beaver, what ya doin'?" I asked again.

"Looking at some of Bridget's husband's bank records," she answered.

"Why?" I asked, suddenly feeling guilty for having lunch with the guy while my partner went blind looking at numbers.

"I really want to see who he really is. You know, see if he is as broke as he told the judge."

"And?"

"Yep, he's as broke as a dog without a bone," she said.

I was startled at the phrase and the slight drawl she used in her answer to me. Where in the hell did that come from? I found my eyes slanting at her. I knew that drawl, and that phrase definitely came from somewhere in Texas, and belonged to someone who thought he was too smart by half.

"So, you been spending time with that Navy douche, Andre?" I asked.

Sanchez whirled on me so fast I thought she'd hit me with her chair.

"Don't call him that!" she said, starting to rise from her chair, her hand curled into a fist.

"Whoa! Slow it up there, partner," I said, seeing the fist. "I'll ask again, nicely. So, what have you and Andre Robinson been up to while I was away? Are you two rats—I mean mice—playing while the cat was away?"

"You just can't leave it alone, can you, Swanson?" she snarled at me.

"Leave what?" I asked.

"Never mind," she said, again taking her seat.

About that time Lieutenant Graber came out of his office and made a beeline for me.

"Swanson," he barked, "what are you doing here? I thought you were on leave?"

"Sorry, sir," I answered. "I really don't know what my status is. I've been out of it for a while and we still have a murder to solve. I was just trying to get an update from my partner."

Again the lieutenant sighed and gestured for me to follow him. We went into his office and he closed the door. Immediately, I felt my armpits get wet. It was never a good thing when the lieutenant called me into his office *and* closed the door.

He took his seat and gestured for me to take one of the guest chairs. I was now positive whatever he wanted was not going to be good news. Usually, we conversed with me slumped against his doorjamb or me slouched in a chair. But something told me to sit in the chair and not slouch.

The lieutenant fiddled with the pens on his desk, took a couple of deep breaths, then said, "I thought I told you the Chief has reassigned the case. More importantly, I distinctly told you it was best for you to stay away."

"You did? Why?" I said. I was hurt, but I understood the work had to go on, even while I slept away the days. "Was it before or after the good doctor gave me something that kept me dead asleep for these last several days?"

Again the lieutenant grimaced and played with his pens. "You want the official?" Graber finally asked.

"My injury, yadda, yadda, yadda," I said.

"Close."

"Okay, what then? Not the car thing again?" I asked. Then I added, "By the way, who'd he give the case to?"

"He's decided to give it to Detective Sanchez to work with NCIS Agent Robinson."

I was too stunned to even respond. I just looked at the lieutenant like someone who had lost his mind. We both knew who it was: it wasn't me and it wasn't the lieutenant.

"She's barely had her shield for six months," I countered.

"I know."

"And he's slime," I said, more forcefully. "And, somehow, I think he's into all of this."

"No he isn't, other than to work solving the murder," the lieutenant said. "After we went through the boxes, it was decided that this was military related."

"You went through the boxes?" I demanded.

"Funny, too, the seals just lifted right up. Funnier still, Agent Robinson agreed that we should all open them together rather than wait. All of this happened after your little incident."

"My little incident almost got me killed," I said, getting angrier and angrier. "By the way, did anyone collect the papers that blew to hell during my little 'incident'?"

Graber smiled a half smile, and pulled an envelope from his desk.

"You mean these?" he asked.

I reached for them, but he kept them from me, putting them back in his desk. "Keep out of my desk, Swanson," he said. "I know your tricks."

"So, why not give them to Robinson and Sanchez?" I asked.

Graber slanted his eyes, then turned his chair away from me to stare out his window. The blue Pacific shone brightly as a thin line on the horizon. He stared for a long time, then turned back to me. "You may have been almost killed because of these," he said. "Let's just say I don't want to put any more of my troops in danger."

"But that's why I need to solve this case," I said. "That's why I need to be on it."

"That's why you're off the case," Graber said more firmly.

I started to protest again, but he waved me off. He then spent the next fifteen minutes explaining to me how and why he agreed with the chief to remove me from the case. All of his reasons made semi-sense, but all of it hurt my pride, and all of it proved to me what an asshole the chief really was.

It seemed that Cheney had finally made such a fuss about my abusing him at his house, and the fact that Bridget had gone back to her husband, and numerous other indignities, the chief decided to remove me. The presiding judge had finally agreed that something had to be done, if nothing else to keep harmony in their golfing foursome. Evidently, I was the goat that needed to be slaughtered.

When Graber was done telling me all that had transpired, I again realized how little status I really had. I was just a lowly detective and the son of a socialite, but nothing else. I had no money of my own, I didn't play golf with that crowd—couldn't afford it anyway—and I didn't have any brass on my shoulders. I was nothing! Nothing but expendable.

I sulked out of the office and took my seat at my cubicle. Sitting in my chair, looking at my almost clear desk, I saw my copy of the murder book sitting off to one side. At least they had not thought to take that from me.

Pulling it to me I leafed through the pages until I found the witness statement describing the sedans that had been cruising the street before the shooting. All he said was that they were black. But, at least I knew who the witness was. Maybe if I spoke to him myself I could get more information.

I gave him a call, and got his home outgoing message. I left a brief message and hung up the phone. I decided that I could go by his house later that evening and talk to him. In the meantime, I was on leave.

"So, yer off the case, huh?" a voice smarmed behind me.

I slammed the notebook closed and put my arm over it in an attempt to keep what I was reading away from the snooping jerk.

"Good news travels fast around here," I answered.

"Good news?" Robinson asked. "I thought you were the hotshot detective who solved all the murders around here. I thought you'd have your feelings hurt being upstarted by your new partner, and all."

"By all, you mean you, don't you?" I said, sliding the binder down between my legs.

Robinson just laughed and sauntered away.

I gathered up my book and slouched out of the station, trying to act as a usual carefree dude while hiding the book.

Once in the car, I sighed in relief, and started up the engine of the Porsche. But, just when I was ready to make my getaway, there was a knock on the plastic roof of the car. I looked up to see the smiling face of Robinson.

Damn, he just couldn't leave me alone, I thought, getting into a murderous mood.

"Pretty snazzy ride for a dee-tec-tive," he said, running his hands over the front fender of the collector's grade 1970 Porsche 914-6.

I wanted to yell at him not to leave his snail-trail handprints all over my car; instead, I rolled down my window and smiled back at him.

"A gift," I said.

"Gift?" he said, rolling the word around in his mouth, then smiling. "Nice collector car like this? Must be some generous benefactor."

His smile told me he thought the 'gift' was from a woman, but actually it had come from the grateful manager of Newport Fine Imports and Muscle Cars. I had kept him out of prison after a huge drug bust, and this car was in my possession having been lent to me by the owner of the agency. When the Feds roared in and confiscated all the cars on the car-carrier, this one was not among the inventory. It also could never go back to the agency for complicated legal reasons, so I just kept it. With a few swipes of his pen, Jaime had made the car mine.

"So, what do you want?" I said.

"Just want to make sure you leave safely," Robinson said.

"Just as safe as can be," I answered, throwing the car into reverse.

"Well, okay. Drive safe, ya hear?"

I squealed the tires as I threw the car in first and roared out of the parking lot. Juvenile, I know, but I was tired of that man always in my business, and always around for no particular reason. There was just too much I didn't understand, and it was getting under my skin. I needed answers, and sitting around the station feeling sorry for myself was not going to get them for me.

CHAPTER TWENTY-EIGHT

Twenty minutes later I pulled into the garage at the house on the Peninsula. As much as I loved being at Sally's, enough was enough. I needed to see my dog, and I needed to be in my own space.

Waiting for me at the wrought-iron gate that separated the patio from the breezeway were Mandy and Cisco. Mandy's affection for me was clear by the ecstatic wagging and twirling she did at the sight of me. Cisco's was only evident by the casual way he wrapped himself around my legs as I climbed the stairs to my apartment.

Once safely inside, I felt something I wasn't used to: a sudden surge of apprehension. Was it only four days ago that I had almost been blown to smithereens? It seemed like a lifetime ago. But now I had two cases to solve. I was going to find the killer who murdered the judge and his wife, and I was definitely going to find who killed my precious Intrepid.

Solving this murder case was beginning to feel a lot like surfing:

waiting and waiting for the big wave to come, then when it does, it's scary as hell, until the surging power of the wave courses through the board up to my body. Conquering that wave was a feeling that's hard to describe. Conquering my fear was just like conquering that wave. I was going to catch those murderers, and I was going to make it right.

I traversed my apartment. After deciding it was clear, I carefully placed the murder book on the coffee table.

But, the run-in with Robinson while I was in the flashy British racing green Porsche 914-6 unnerved me. I needed another car — one that wasn't so visible or obvious.

The first call I made was to my 'good friend' Jaime, the manager at Newport's Fine Imports and Muscle Cars. With the owner of the agency doing sixty months on a federal sentence for conspiracy and money laundering, and Jaime walking free, it seemed to me that he owed me. After all, Jaime had known of the laundering, but he was first in line to jump to the Feds, giving them the info they needed for the convictions of the Venezuelan doctor and others — thus earning himself not only a reduced sentence, but also a nice bonus while working with the Feds. None of this would have happened for him had I not interceded. In my mind he owed me. And I needed a car.

"Hey, Jaime," I said when he answered his phone, "I need a car."

A brief moan escaped from Jaime at the sound of my voice and at my request.

"Ah, Jake, why do you only call when you need something?" he said by way of response.

"And why do you walk around a free man today?" I countered.

"Ah, Jake, it's not the same. Red is gone, and technically his daughter owns the place now. I only manage. It is difficult for me to let a car just disappear, especially given your need to see cars blown up."

Ouch! The reminder of the car's explosion hurt, but it only strengthened my resolve.

"Jaime, I need a sedan, preferably dark and not too flashy," I said.

Again a soft moan escaped from his lips, then a sigh and an answer. "Okay, Jake, come by and I'll see what I have. One of the salesmen may have a trade-in that could work for you."

I quickly said my good-byes to my animals, and took off to find Scat to drive me to the dealership. There was no way I was leaving the Porsche with Jaime. It may remind him where it came from originally.

Scat wasn't home, but Teresa was more than happy to lend me a hand.

At the dealership Jaime was sitting upstairs in his glass-walled office working the phones. From his aerie he could see not only the sales floor, but he also had a view of the repair stations as well. Red had designed the office area; he made sure he could keep an eye on all that happened in his kingdom. Maybe even then he was nervous about his criminal activity.

Seeing me, Jaime waved for me to come up to his office. He was still on the phone when I entered his office, but I took a seat, lounging with one leg over the arm of the chair. It was my intent to make him understand this was a casual, expected courtesy he was extending to me. This was not a 'favor.'

Hanging up the phone, Jaime turned to me. His expression was not friendly; rather, it was more panic stricken.

"I thought our business was over," he said.

"You testify yet?" I asked.

"Only at the Grand Jury," he answered. "There is still the murder case of Dr. Anchado hanging out there."

"Then our business is not over," I answered.

"I didn't think I would 'owe' you cars for the rest of my life," he said in a plaintive voice.

"No, just your freedom, and maybe the fact you have a life," I answered. "But, for now, I just want a car. Nothing fancy. Not one of your collector cars or muscle cars… just a sedan."

Jaime winced, then said, "Okay, okay, Jake. It turns out I have just the car for you. We got a guy from Des Moines, or something like that. The guy decided his Buick wasn't good enough for Newport. He just traded it for a three-year-old Mercedes. I really don't have no use for the Buick. I'd just send it to auction, so I guess it don't matter if it goes this week or next."

He grabbed a set of keys and I followed him out to the back lot. An almost new Buick Lucerne was sitting all alone among a fleet of Mercedes, Lexus, and muscle cars. It was dark blue in color and huge. But the interior was clean, and it really didn't need a wash. Whoever owned it previously had taken good care of it, and I thought it was perfect for what I needed: not flashy, dark in color, and American made. Perfect.

Jaime started to attach some dealer plates to the car, but I stayed his hand, suggesting the Iowa plates were better for me. He straightened up, gave an involuntary shudder, then flipped the keys to me.

With a wave good-bye, I put my foot on the accelerator and was surprised when the V-6 engine gave me enough power to leave the dealership with a flourish.

I was down the block and headed up Newport Boulevard before I realized where I was headed. It seemed Lompoc was calling me, and the need to see Ado Ito flooded through me.

Unlocking my phone, I was grateful that my prior call to the federal prison had been from my cell phone, making it a number listed on my previous calls. I tapped the number on my screen, and I made the appointment to see Ito in the late afternoon.

My drive back up the coast was pleasant enough. The Buick had a sunroof that slid open and let the late fall weather flow into the cabin of the car. The sound system, while not great, was still better than that of the Porsche, and the previous owner had an active XM satellite radio system that had not yet been discontinued. With my favorite blues streaming through the cabin and the wind blowing my hair, I felt calm for the first time in too long.

Ado Ito was the key to the judge's murder. I felt in my bones. Better, still, I might even get a bead on the NCIS agent. Just thinking about that made me smile. Yep, the trip was definitely the salve to my injured ego.

CHAPTER TWENTY-NINE

Three and a half hours later I pulled up to the guard shack at the prison. I was on the visitor's list, but the surprise waiting for me at check-in almost knocked me to my knees. In the less than three hours since making the appointment, Ado Ito was shanked and was in critical condition. He was not expected to live, and all visits were cancelled.

I asked to see warden who invited me into his office. He was not pleased to see me, and it wasn't because Ito had been stabbed.

"Detective Swanson," he said, steepling his fingers and blowing out his breath at me. "Or should I say, Mr. Swanson. What are you doing here, and why did you misrepresent yourself to my secretary?"

"Misrepresent myself," I said, not understanding either the hostility or the question.

"It has come to my attention that you are not active. That you have been suspended," he answered.

"I'm not suspended!" I answered, camming full-throttle into anger. "I am an active detective with the Newport Beach Police Department. I am investigating a murder of a judge that happened to be the criminal defense lawyer of Ado Ito, a man I would like to point out to you was under your care and custody."

"You are not investigating a murder at this point having been removed from the case," he replied, not responding to my anger. "You are also on leave, which means suspended in my book."

I slanted my eyes at him. The only way he could have gotten this information was from my most unfavorite NCIS agent, Andre Robinson.

"You heard that from my lieutenant?" I asked.

"It doesn't matter from where I received the information; it only matters whether or not it is true. You are on leave, correct?"

"I am on medical leave," I answered, having learned a long while ago not to lie to federal officials. They tended to get really testy and a prison sentence could result.

"Hmmm, medical leave?" he asked.

"Hmmm, yes," I answered, then backed off my Southern California beach snotty, and tried to win him over with my predicament. "My car was blown to smithereens a few days ago. I was lucky I wasn't blown with it. My medical leave comes from a concussion and bruising, but none of it is more important that finding a judge's murderer. Did Andre Robinson also tell you that the judge's wife was also killed at the same time as the judge?"

Now it was time for the warden to act surprised. He steepled his fingers again, and leveled a hardened stare at me. I suppose it worked on inmates and guards, but I was used to stares like this from Chief Bitterman. This was nothing compared to what I got at the station.

The warden broke off the stare when he realized it was not working with me. Finally he relented and said, "Why is Ado Ito so important to you and to this NCIS agent?"

I thought for a moment, and then decided a possible ally was more important than keeping this secret. Besides, this secret was weighing way too heavily on my psyche for me to keep much longer.

"He told the judge that he had information that put this country in danger," I finally said.

"Sounds like typical inmate talk," he answered.

"That's what I thought until I found evidence that corroborated his statements. Now it is imperative that I talk to him again."

"You can't," the warden said. "He's in the hospital ward and, at this point, there is no telling if he will live."

"That's why it's critical I speak with him," I said, almost pleading.

The warden thought for a moment, then seemed to relent. He picked up his phone and placed a call to what I surmised to be the hospital ward. He asked whoever answered the phone about the status of Ito, but frowned at the response. When he placed the phone's receiver back in its cradle he looked solemn.

"I was just told he passed away not five minutes ago," the warden said, lowering his voice. "I hate losing an inmate, especially when it is violent like this. He was due to get out in a year or so. What a shame."

Now I was scared. It was too coincidental that Ito was killed when I needed to speak with him. It was also too coincidental that Robinson had already informed the prison that I was on leave. All of this pointed back at Andre Robinson again, and I didn't like the look of it.

In desperation I asked the warden if they had a suspect in his stabbing. The warden informed me that it was too soon to tell. It had happened as the prisoners were lining up for chow call for lunch. The prisoners tended to mill around, making it nearly impossible to tell who did the stabbing until all the tapes were processed and reviewed. That would take several days.

"Look, sir," I said, "All of this is somehow connected to things going on outside of here. I really need this information so I know how to proceed. I should be back on duty by the end of this week or beginning of the next. Until then, I still need to keep working. I still need to find the killer who took out an innocent woman just because she came out to greet her husband coming home from work. There are daughters who need to know who did this. This was a family, a good family. They deserve answers."

This was more than I usually said to strangers, especially authority figures. I was a little surprised at my behavior. But it worked. The warden's eyes misted over, and he told me he just lost his wife of many years to cancer. When I told him the wife who was shot was also only a few weeks out from passing with cancer that ravished her body, he lost it. With tears gathering in his eyes, he promised that as soon as he knew anything he'd give me a call.

I wrote my cell phone number on my card and gave it to him. With that, I took my leave.

On the way back down the coast, I remembered the phone call I wanted to make to the neighbor who saw the black sedans. All I needed was the possible make of car, and somehow I thought it might make a difference for me and for the investigation I was no longer heading.

I pulled into the rest stop just north of Gaviota State Park on the 101 and looked through the notebook for the name and phone number of the witness. I programmed his number into my phone and made the call.

He was home, and he was surprised at my question. A few seconds later I had the answer to my question: Mercedes Benz S550. This was definitely *not* a government car.

My next call was to John McAllister.

"Hey, McAllister. Swanson here," I said. "What if I told you the car that cruised the judge's house was a Mercedes S-Class 550?"

"Chinese Tong would be my guess," he said without hesitation.

"Chinese Tong?"

"Ancient Asian gangs from China, believed to have been started by monks from monasteries," he answered.

"Wow, that quick? You know this stuff?" I said.

"I told you I just did a gang interdiction seminar with all the branches of our gang units. The best guy at the podium was from our AGU," McAllister answered.

"AGU?"

"Asian Gang Unit," McAllister answered. "He's especially knowledgeable about the Chinese Tongs. He's seeing too much human trafficking and drugs associated with them. They're becoming very prominent not only in our China Town area, but also the nearby cities of Temple City, Arcadia, Hacienda Heights, and even down into some parts of South LA."

"So, do you think you could hook me up with this guy?" I asked. "I really have some questions for him, and I really need the help."

"So you off my father-in-law as a suspect for the murders?" McAllister asked.

"Don't know," I said truthfully. "It depends on what I learn about Tongas... or Congas... or whatever."

"Tongs," he said. "The word is Tongs, T-O-N-G-S."

"Yeah, okay, but can you set me up?"

McAllister promised to make a few phone calls and get back to me.

In less than ten minutes he called me back to tell me that David Chu would meet with me, and asked if I could come by the new station house.

I told him I was just passing through Santa Barbara, and it would take me about an hour and a half to reach them. We confirmed that he would be there with Chu.

It took me about an hour and forty-five minutes to reach the station, but it looked like I only beat Chu by minutes.

A handsome Asian man of about five feet, ten inches came through the door shortly after McAllister came to the lobby to escort me back to the conference room. John introduced us, and I found I immediately liked the AGU guy. There was an intensity about him that said, "all business." Yet, like John McAllister, there was also a kindness in the eyes. Looking at the two of them I realized that both, younger than me by more than a decade, were professionals who took their jobs serious-ly. It made me pause to realize that maybe I needed to reflect on how I presented myself to the public. But, as quickly as the thought formed, it flew away.

"So, Detective Swanson," Chu said, "what is so important that one of my best students from the seminar called me away from my night to play soccer?"

"I found out that the cars cruising by a murdered judge's house just before he was killed was a black Mercedes S-Class sedan."

"And?" he said.

"I understand that you are the best there is as far as knowledge about Chinese stuff and possibly gangs?" I answered.

He just shrugged and pointed to chairs. We all took a seat.

"Why would a black Mercedes Benz concern you that an Asian gang was behind the murder?" he asked.

It was a simple question, and one I would ask if another officer was asking me about my city. But, nonetheless, I was afraid to tell him why I needed to know the information. Yet, without his knowledge I was stuck. It left me no choice but to answer his question.

I took a deep breath and filled him in on all that I knew or suspect-ed. Leaving nothing out, I included the maps from the judge's house, the satellite photos, the girls' suspicions, and Ado Ito, who had just been killed that day.

"So, you're telling me that you believe the Russians are selling off nuclear waste or weapons to the Iranians and the Chinese are somehow brokering the deal, with Japanese scientist helping the Iranians put the weapons together? And because the judge knew this, or at least suspected it, some Chinese gang came and killed him. Right?" David Chu asked.

Having him repeat it back to me made it sound preposterous. What was I thinking? This was stupid at the very least and crazy. But all I could do was nod in the affirmative.

David Chu turned to John McAllister and said, "John, you need to leave. What I am going to discuss with this detective is classified."

John started to protest, but something in the eye of the other officer made him snap his mouth shut and back out of the conference room, shutting the door behind him.

Chu began to pace once the other officer left the room. He looked at me, then said, "This is dangerous stuff you are asking."

"Don't you think I don't know this?" I asked. "My car got blown up on the streets of Newport Beach, and I was almost killed in the explosion. If that wasn't enough, some guy tried to smother me in my hospital bed."

"Yet, here you are," he said. "Executioners from the Tongs are not usually that careless. You are either very lucky or this is not their work."

"But can you tell me what is going on?" I asked.

"The Tongs used to be a benevolent organization providing protection to merchants during a time when the aristocracy of China was capricious and demanding. And, although it has not been that way for a very long time, there was still a need for protection. Merchants fled the country as the literati were being rounded up and sent to "reprogramming camps," which were like concentration camps. People who could afford it moved their money and their families off mainland China onto Hong Kong or Taiwan, and then even to the United States. It was the Tongs who arranged much of that. It was imbedded in society that paying them for protection was just part of life. But, as with many criminal cultures as the young sought to gain influence and power, they realized that money was power, and power was everything. They turned to human trafficking of those who were not rich, and when they could not pay, they indentured them into sex slavery or worse."

"Worse than sex slavery?" I asked.

"Have you not heard of the mines in Nigeria, or the factories in Iran or Saudi Arabia?" he asked. "These are nothing but a new form of concentration camp. The poor Chinese actually sell themselves to the Tongs to get out of China to make money. Only it is a cruel joke. The workers do not keep their money; only the Tongs and managers keep the money. The workers are worse off than if they never left China!"

"But nukes to Iran?" I asked.

"Of course the Tongs would sell the nukes to Iran," David said.

"The Russians cannot directly sell their waste or weapons to Iran, so they use intermediaries. The Tongs are perfect for this."

"But why kill the judge?" I said. "I understand the Ludlum spy stuff for Tongs and Chinese and Russians, but why an American judge in America?"

"It may not have been the Tongs," Chu said again.

"Then who?" I asked, realizing I sounded frightened and confused. "I'm sorry, Detective Chu," I said. "With everything that is happening around me, I'm not my usual self. Maybe I need alcohol... or drugs."

The gang detective laughed out loud. He slapped me on the back and said that I probably did need drugs and alcohol.

"Have I helped you at all?" he asked.

"So are there nukes coming from Russia through China to Iran?" I asked.

"Did China invent noodles?" he said by way of response.

Suddenly a chill went up and down my spine. Of course, the Noodle Factory! Chu was part of the military underground tracking this stuff.

When Chu saw that I made the connection he sat back in his chair and nodded.

"Navy?" I asked.

"Navy," he answered.

"So you would possibly know Commander Mark Henning?" I asked.

The detective looked closely at me, then shrugged. "A good man.

An expert in all things Far East."

I sat back in my chair. A chill ran up my spine, and my head began to throb with pain. For a brief moment I thought I would spew anything left in my stomach all over the detective sitting across from me.

Swallowing hard, I asked the next most obvious questions. "I guess NCIS would be looking into the judge's death, then?"

David Chu looked hard at me, then answered. "NCIS is strictly internal investigation into Navy matters. It is not the popular NCIS as depicted on TV, but rather more institutionalized in nature. It is a branch that investigates matters that are of concern to the Navy and its structure or secrets, but criminal only when they may impact the Navy's reputation. It was reformed to be civilian in nature as a result of the Tail Hook problems from the early 1990's. Why?"

"Would Mark Henning be investigated by an internal branch of the Navy?" I asked.

The detective, cum Naval officer, again stared hard at me. Finally, he asked, "Why?"

In a rush, I answered, "Because there's this puke who keeps showing up waving a NCIS badge at my chief and making my life miserable. I think he was meeting with the judge just prior to his death, and now he's got his nose all up in my investigation."

I've always heard that the Asians are inscrutable—a silly bigoted belief. However, the detective who was sitting in front of me became the epitome of *inscrutable.* I could not read him, and he did not answer me.

Finally, after a minute of silence that felt like years, I rose to shake his hand. "Well, okay, then," I said. "I guess I will be leaving. I know I need alcohol now. If I'm lucky I'll even find some leftover pain meds from the bombing. I need to get out of here."

David Chu walked me out to the exit where we nodded our good-byes. Then I spent fifteen minutes looking for a black Intrepid instead of a dark blue Buick.

CHAPTER THIRTY

As I was traversing down the 405 Freeway toward home, my phone rang. A quick look at the screen told me it was my partner, or supposed partner, Melissa Sanchez. I almost ignored the call, but when she hung up and called again, I decided to put my Bluetooth back in my ear and answer.

"You called, Homes?" I asked.

I could almost hear her gritting her teeth. "Don't call me that," she said.

"Or what, Little Beaver... you'll have me removed from the case so you and your new boyfriend can work together?" I retorted.

"Stop it, Jake," Melissa said, "I didn't do that!"

"Right," I said.

"Jake, please stop," she said. And this time I heard something in her voice that sounded almost desperate.

"What's up?" I finally said, relenting, softening my voice.

"I got a call from the lab, and my friend was so upset he called me down to the lab to tell me in person," she said. "There's something weird going on around here, and it is scaring me."

"Why?" I asked. "What could possibly have my Little Beaver so upset that you're calling me now, especially now?"

Her voice was shaky as she responded, "Jake, the analysis just came back on your car bombing," she said. "The stuff was C-4 explosives."

"So?" I responded.

"Jake, the stuff is military grade, and only available through specialized channels. It is not an open market thing," she said. "Jake, what are we going to do? Not only was the explosive military grade, but the primary was also military. The stuff they used on your car: it was military shit all the way. Someone with military connections was trying to kill you. What are we going to do?"

"Whoa there, kid," I said. "First off, I'm not sure what you're saying. What is a *primary*, and what do you mean... military? Everyone talks about C-3 and plastique explosives; is this what you're talking about?"

Melissa responded with another shaky sigh. "Jake, this is the sort of stuff I learned about in the Marines. I'm not even sure how whoever bombed your car got the stuff they used. I don't know what we're going to do!"

"You keep saying 'we,' Little Beaver," I said. "We stopped being a 'we' when you got a new partner and I was removed from the case."

"Please stop," Melissa said. "I really need to talk to you... about everything."

Again there was something in her voice that caused me to pause. With my softest voice I continued, "It's okay, *we* can talk. Where are you now? I hope you aren't at the station for this call?"

"God, no, Jake. I'm in the car, heading back from the lab," she said. "I had to call you right away. I'm so afraid for you. This is serious stuff they used on you."

"Can you start at the beginning?" I asked.

With a final gulp of air, my partner laid out the situation and type of explosives used on my car in someone's attempt to kill me.

"The C-4 explosives were a plastique explosive similar to the C-3, but designed to burn hotter, and definitely more deadly," she said. "They are, I think, if I have this right, from the RDX family, which means 'royal demolition explosive,' with an additive binder that makes them easy to mold into shapes, but less sensitive to shock and heat than the other stuff. The chemical markers are designed to make them traceable, and this stuff definitely was for the security forces of our military."

"The lab guy could tell you all this?" I asked.

"Not only that," she said, "but he could trace the batch back to its manufacturer, and the final end user. It was definitely sent to our special op forces in Afghanistan. Worse yet, it came from a batch that went missing about the same time some of our guys left. Nothing was ever proven, but still. . ."

As her voice trailed off, it was apparent that finally, now that it was almost too late, my partner was finally feeling the same things I had been experiencing ever since this case started.

"Meliss," I said, "you know I am supposed to be on 'leave.'"

"Yeah, I know," she answered. "But, I really need to talk to you."

Again, I was taken aback by the desperation in her voice.

"Okay, meet me at my place and we can talk there," I said.

"Jake, are you sure?" she asked. "I mean they—whoever 'they' are—knew enough to find your car where you live and try to blow you up. Do you really want to be there?"

It's funny. I hadn't really thought too much about that. I mean, for the last few days I was oblivious. Before that I didn't know someone was trying to kill me. And before that it was just a murder. And, well, before that I was sitting on the deck with three beautiful women, my dog, my cat, and a chilled martini. Everything that was safe and familiar was somehow now out of whack. But ghosts can find you anywhere, so I decided that I would rather face them at a place I knew rather than somewhere I didn't.

"Yes, Sanchez," I answered, "meet me at my place in about an hour. I am coming down the 405 now and I'm about an hour out with traffic."

An hour and twenty minutes later Detective Melissa Sanchez was on my couch, her boots kicked off at the door, her feet tucked up under her, and she had two ice cubes making swirls on her temples. I was fixing her a Diet Coke and rum—a Stoli on the rocks for me. With our drinks fixed, I handed one to her, and took the recliner chair under the window facing the street.

"Bad day?" I asked.

Melissa opened one of her gorgeous brown eyes and fastened a deep stare on me. "What gave you that idea?" she asked.

"I don't know," I said. "Maybe the fact I've rarely seen you drink alcohol, much less beg for it, or the fact you are curled on my couch like an ingénue, or that you look beat to shit. Your choice, take your pick."

She smiled that dazzling smile of hers, then winced, and rubbed the ice on her temples again before plopping them into her drink.

"Jake, I'm such a dope," she said.

There were too many retorts I could have used, but I left them unsaid.

When I said nothing, she continued, "Look, Jake, the lab guys were almost too afraid to put this in print. He did his analysis of not only the explosives used to demolish your car, but also the primary, or preliminary blasting cap used to ignite the C-4."

"Huh?" I asked.

"The primary," she said, removing two cubes from her drink and again rubbing them on her temples. She looked up and must have seen the puzzled look on my face, so she continued her explanation. "The C-4 is used because it is inert without something to set it off. That's why it's so popular. In order for the C-4 to explode it needs a first explosion to set it off. That's called a primary. The military uses varying amounts of different primers as detonators to give the C-4 enough heat to explode. There are several different types, and each is favored by a different branch of the military. In this case, the detonator and the primary can be traced back to the Navy. It was a lead azide."

"You know all this?" I asked. "How did you learn all this?"

Melissa slanted one eye at me, then closed both her eyes.

When I didn't get an answer, I formed my own conclusions.

"Hmm, military-grade C-4 from a batch sent to Afghanistan, traceable to the Navy, probably special ops, which means SEALs, and — let me guess — Robinson is, or was a SEAL?" I asked, watching my partner closely.

She shook her head, then buried her face into the pillow she clutched on her lap.

I pressed a little harder. "Melissa, tell me, was Robinson a SEAL? Did he serve in Afghanistan?"

Finally, she looked up at me and answered, "I thought that because Agent Robinson was attached to the Naval Investigative Services, and military and all, he was a good guy. But, I was such a dope."

"Hmm, why do you say that, Little Beaver?" I asked.

She told me that during their time together they began to tell each other war stories of serving in the military. Of course they had both done their stints overseas, but she had never actually gone to a 'hot zone' in the Middle East. Robinson had done multiple tours, first in Iraq, then in Afghanistan. But he was probably intelligence. He never was a SEAL.

"So why do you think it was Robinson who tried to do me in?" I asked.

"Jake, he has an agenda," she said. "He wanted you off the case when he realized you were really good at what you do. He thought he could go around you, but… well, let's just say I helped. I'm so sorry, Jake. I'm just a dope."

I chewed on that a minute while I watched my partner stir her Diet Coke and rum with her finger, then take a large gulp. Finally, I asked her to explain.

She told me that she gave him some information, thinking it would remain confidential, but he immediately took it to the chief to get me off the case. Melissa knew I had gone through the boxes in the conference room when she saw the colored water in the pot and figured out that I had steamed the seals of the boxes open, especially when she was able to easily lift them off of the boxes. She knew I was adept at breaching the conference room door, even when locked, and it wasn't a leap to infer I had been in the room and gone through the boxes.

Worse yet, she thought she was doing the right thing when she told Robinson about it. But the next thing she knew, he was in the chief's office and insisting that the boxes be examined for tampering. When, of course it was clear that the boxes had in fact been tampered, it didn't take long for the chief to put the blame on me. The only thing that saved me from immediate discipline was the fact that I was almost killed. Also, the lieutenant literally threw himself on that grenade of the chief's anger and kept him away from me while I slept. Sally of course kept me comatose to also keep me away from the chief until things settled down.

I listened to all that had swirled around me in the last few days, and thanked my lucky stars that I had friends like Sally, and even a boss like the lieutenant. They both protected me when I couldn't take care of myself. Now my partner was making a choice that could get her demoted or fired.

"Are you sure you want to cast your lot in with me?" I asked her. "I thought you detested me, or at the very least barely tolerated me."

For whatever reason this caused her to smile. Her smile was dazzling until she winced again in pain.

"Arrggh!" she coughed. She took a deep draught of her drink, coughed, and took a smaller sip. She smiled again and began to speak.

"Jake, I had heard such stuff about you I didn't know what to think. When I was brought in from the streets and the drug task force, I was ecstatic until I realized I was going to be working with you. Damn, I was afraid of you. You are so good-looking, and so easy to talk to, and everyone but the chief loves you. And then, working with you on the murder of the blondes... you just put everything together without seeming to even work. Everyone warned me that it wouldn't be long before I was in love with you. It scared me. How could I ever live up to what you are and what you do? How could I ever resist your charm and still be me? Then, I just realized you'd teach me — teach me in your own way. I'd become great if I learned from you. Also, you *never* made a pass at me, and you were kind when you weren't kicking my butt, and that made me mad. Then... then this new murder, and

Andre Robinson came and he was everything I thought I admired. He was military, organized, disciplined, and looked like the better half of you. I couldn't help myself. I'm sorry."

I sat stunned at her words. I didn't realize all this was going on in the head of my partner. She was like my kid sister, the kid sister I never had and always wished I had. I didn't know what to say. Buried in all she said were compliments and confessions and things I wasn't sure what to do with. After all, I wanted not to be the man she first thought I was.

I remember that day we met so clearly. I was nearly accused of killing a young girl—or worse, raping her and then killing her. Again the lieutenant came to my rescue and assigned Melissa to me to "keep me straight," when what he was really doing was giving me cover. Melissa had hated me on sight, or so I thought, and now here we were.

My partner had committed the greatest sin a partner can commit against another: she had ratted me out. Worse yet, it wasn't even to save me. It was to get close to another man.

All I could do was sit and stare at her. Finally, I took a gulp of my Stoli and asked her what she wanted from me.

"I want you to forgive me," she said. "And I want to know why you never made a pass at me. Am I not good enough?"

Tears sprang to her eyes as she took another sip of her drink. Mandy was sufficiently concerned; she wagged over to Melissa and put her face in her lap. Cisco jumped up on the back of the couch and licked her hair. The scene made me laugh. I couldn't help myself.

I got the look I wanted. Melissa's mouth slashed into a grim red line, and she glinted her eyes at me. "You're a fuck!" she said.

I set my drink aside and stood up. I lifted her up and gave her a brotherly hug. "Listen, Little Beaver," I said. "First of all, every detective, every officer, and every guy I know in this county is envious of me because I have you as a partner. You are my partner; you're like family. I can't make a pass at you; it would be like making a pass at my little sister."

"Eeww!" she said as she buried her face in my chest.

"Right, eewww," I mimicked. "Just in case you care, you are more than good enough for me — too good, actually. And, I will kill any man who hurts you… just a like a big brother," I said.

For the first time I saw her cry. She sobbed real tears and she was wobbly in my arms. I led her back to the couch, and the only thing I could think to say was, "But, Little Beaver, if you ever, ever, ever snitch me out again, I will leave you in a heartbeat. I want you to think of who is left to partner with, then decide if you ever want to do that again. By the way, I hope you got some good information for all your troubles."

Melissa sighed and shook her head in the negative. "That's the problem, Jake," she said. "That's when I realized that what was happening. I was giving all the information, and he was taking it and giving nothing back. I learned some unimportant stuff, but nothing substantial. And, now to think… he may have been the one who tried to kill you!"

I laughed again, and led her back to the couch.

"Listen, Homey," I said. "I can't stand Robinson, but there are other people around who are just as likely to want me dead, and may be more likely to have the stuff you're talking about than a straight-laced current military guy. If the stuff was 'lifted' as suspected, and it was recent, think of the time line. Was it really a guy who is now in Investigative Services, or someone who was more recently overseas?"

Melissa just stared at me, then scrunched her face in concentration.

"You're right, Jake," she said. "Robison's last deployment was several years ago; it wasn't him, unless he's hooked up with some underground illegal pipeline."

"So, okay, it may not have been him, but," I said, staring hard at her, "I hope you have learned again an important lesson. The Feds are the Feds. It doesn't matter whom they work for. They are all about taking and not giving back," I said. "I hope you learned your lesson; never sell us out again... ever!"

She stood up from the couch and slapped my arm, but at least she stopped crying.

With all of the drama out of the way, we got down to the business of what was scaring the hell out of both of us.

I told her about the nukes from Russia and the Chinese Tongs and the Japanese scientists and, most of all, that I was really afraid that the judge's murder was tied to all of it. I told her that I was certain that he knew about the nukes and could prove it, and somehow his being reactivated had to do with going to the Far East to stop it. I just wasn't sure if he was stopping the scientists from Japan or the nukes from Russia, or all of it. It was just too crazy to contemplate. But, I also told her about having met the Gooney Squad, and it was more likely that one of them had the access to the military-grade C-4 that was used on my car.

Sanchez chewed on this for a while, then took the murder notebook with all the reports and leafed through it.

"So, the gray car is military, right?" she said. "Andre?"

"I don't think so," I said.

"Why?" she asked.

"Wrong branch within the Navy. He's Investigative Services, while whoever was here was intelligence," I answered.

Melissa lifted an eyebrow at me. "Where did you learn that?" she asked.

"My sources," I answered. I still wasn't sure I trusted Melissa, despite her tears. I learned long ago that tears from women can be turned on and off depending on the need. I wanted her as my partner, but once again I also needed to keep her at a distance, but not too far away.

"Hmm," she said. "And the black car?"

"It was a Mercedes Benz S-Class 550," I answered.

"Sources?" she asked.

"Yeah, the witness in the report. I called and asked him if he knew the make and model of the black sedan," I answered.

"Hmm, detecting I see," she said. "Did it belong to Cheney's crew?"

"Not likely," I answered. "Cheney's Gooney Squad drives SUVs, and they're paramilitary types."

"Sources?" she asked again, smiling.

"John McAllister," I answered. "He also told me that gangs have 'types' of vehicles they prefer. Like the black gangs like Nissan products, and Latin gangs like—"

"They like Hondas," she answered.

"Yep, and Chinese gangs like—are you ready for this?—Mercedes or Lexus."

"Hmmm," she said.

She jumped off the couch and grabbed a sheet of paper from my printer. Then she started drawing circles and writing words, and connecting everything with lines. When she was done, she took another sheet of paper and began a list. She handed it to me and I helped her add and delete items on the list. We worked together, pooling our information. It was after midnight when we decided that we had a road map of where the investigation was heading.

"Jake," she said when she was done, "I think we've got the pattern, but I don't know how we'll prove it."

When I looked at her chart I found I agreed with her. It was time to call in the big guns and get the lieutenant involved. But, given the time, we decided to wait until morning.

CHAPTER THIRTY-ONE

The next morning, Melissa and I stormed the back door of the station together. We were again a team, and we were on the hunt. Even though I was a little worse for wear having slept on my couch—my partner slept off her rum and Coke in my bed—I was ready to do battle.

The air in the station felt like it was charged with a weird energy when we rolled into the detectives' bullpen. Several of the detectives were at their desks, but when they saw us, they immediately put their heads down and did not meet our eyes. I was almost used to it, but Melissa didn't even notice. She was determined to get to her computer and begin working her sources and her information to see what she could confirm from last night's hypothesis.

I, of course, having known the guys in the bullpen much longer, immediately felt the shift in their energy. While I was used to some of them avoiding me when the chief was on a rampage, this time it felt as if the entire squad were ignoring me.

Shrugging it off, I went to grab a cup of coffee; hard stares from the two secretaries met me. One was Jenny, the lieutenant's secretary. She was not happy and definitely frowned at me when I entered. The other grabbed her mug and quickly left the room.

"You dick," Jenny hissed at me. "You don't have the sense God gave a rock. At least when God puts a rock down it has sense enough not to get up or move."

I shook my head at her. "What?" I asked.

"Swanson, you're a dick," she said again.

"Yeah, yeah, you said that, but why?" I asked.

"The chief is in the lieutenant's office, and they've been shouting for the past half-hour," she said. "And, it's your name that keeps coming up."

"I'm supposed to be on leave," I said.

"That's the point," she said. "Evidently you've been snooping around, using your badge and getting into all kinds of trouble when you're supposed to be on sick leave."

"I'm not 'sick,'" I said, falling back on the juvenile response of misdirection.

"Fine. Medical leave, then," Jenny retorted. "Never mind. You're still the cause of whatever is going on in there."

I wandered on down the hall and heard the voices coming from the lieutenant's office. Even through the closed door it was clear the two men were arguing. Jenny was correct: my name was used over and over. Whatever was going on was not good. It appeared that the lieutenant was not calming the chief.

After all the times that Graber had taken the hits for me, I couldn't let him take another. This was just too crazy, especially since the judge's murder was nearly solved — if not yet provable. More importantly, I needed his help to get to the stuff I needed. With a deep breath, I knocked on the door, entering without invitation.

"Hey, LT," I said, acting as if I had not heard the argument. "I've got some great shit for you. I think I may have gotten a handle on the judge's murder..."

I didn't get a chance to finish the sentence. Chief Bitterman was on me like a rabid dog, and the lieutenant's shout to get out could not drown out the chief's order to remain.

"Swanson, don't you move!" the chief yelled. "I want you in my office NOW!"

My initial reaction was to smarm back at him about the inconsistent order, but the stricken look on Graber's face froze me in place, and silenced my lips. I knew I was being judged, and I did not like the way the judgment was going. It was not looking good for me.

"Chief, Swanson," Graber said, using a voice that was commanding yet respectful, "let's just stay here. Let's just all take a seat and sort this out in a nonjudgmental way."

I immediately took a seat, but Bitterman paced back and forth a few times before he, too, took his seat, but not before turning the chair so it faced me, rather than the lieutenant.

With Bitterman and me seated, Graber lowered his six-foot, six-inch, former pro linebacker frame into his oversized chair.

"Swanson," the chief growled, "this time you've really gone too far. You've deliberately tampered with evidence, maybe making it unusable. You've interfered with a government investigation, and you've put this department at risk of a civil suit from the murder victim's family. You put the victim's daughters in mortal danger, and one of the husbands is threatening a lawsuit. What do you have to say for yourself?"

"Chief," Graber said, interrupting him, "Swanson has the right to have his rep or an attorney present before he answers that question."

Bitterman whirled on Graber and told him to keep out of it, or he, too, would be facing charges.

That was enough for Graber to once again stand and tower over the chief. The chief responded by also rising to his feet. I thought for sure they were going to engage in hand-to-hand combat.

"Wait!" I yelled at both of them. "Stop! Just stop. Let's take this one at a time. I'll answer your questions, Chief, but I need to understand what is going on. I'm out of the loop, so can you catch me up?"

Graber was shaking his head as I was saying this. I could tell that this was something serious, but I needed to get some things out in the open so I could get everyone back on track to solve the judge's murder.

"What do you want me to answer first?" I asked.

"Why aren't you out on medical leave?" the chief asked.

"I thought I was," I answered.

"Then what were you doing up at Lompoc yesterday?" he asked.

"I was feeling better and I was bored. Then I had a hunch, so I went up there to follow up on a hunch," I said. "But, how did you know?"

"The warden called to say they have copies of the tape and are following up on stabbing of an inmate named Ado Ito. They think it may be gang related," Graber said before the chief could stop him.

"Asian gang, right?" I said.

"Presumably," he answered.

"Fits," I said.

The chief was standing and holding his hand up like a stop sign, but by then Graber and I were ignoring him.

"Why do you say that?" Graber asked.

"Because it fits with everything I have learned since this whole thing began," I answered.

"What fits?" Bitterman asked, finally intrigued enough to stop holding his stop sign.

"Do you mind if we sit, and I can explain to both of you?" I asked. "I am going to need some heavy hitters here, and I know it's not me."

Graber turned to Bitterman, who nodded, and we all sat down in our seats. Once we were seated, I filled them in on all the scary stuff I had learned, and all the stuff Melissa and I put together the night before. When I was finished, both men's faces were drawn with concern—Graber's most of all.

"You mean military-grade explosives were used on your car and almost killed you? And you think we had foreign nationals come here, to our city, kill one of most respected judges and his wife, then disappear? *And* you think that maybe one of this county's most prominent citizens may have paid someone to kill you?" Bitterman asked, concern being replaced with incredulity.

"Sir," I said respectfully, "crazy as it sounds, yes, I think all of the above is possible. But all of it needs more investigation. The more I work on this, the more likely it looks like the work of Chinese Tongs. They had too much to lose if the judge was fully activated and working in the Far East."

"I don't believe you, Swanson," Bitterman said. "It is too preposterous. And, besides, we have NCIS working with us now; they say it's not related to the judge's military standing."

"And just how did he come to that conclusion?" I asked.

"That is confidential," the chief answered.

"Right, and where are the boxes I am supposed to have tampered with?" I asked.

"Who told you that?" Bitterman asked.

I shook my head in the negative and closed my mouth tightly. My partner may have ratted me out, but two wrongs never made a right. I would never answer that question.

Seeing my refusal, Bitterman said, "Never mind. I know you won't answer. But they are gone. I released them to the Feds."

"You released them?" I asked, startled at the implications, but immediately understood that without the boxes, the tampering could not stand as a negative on my record. I had the right to have my own representative look at the boxes and, if they were gone, so was any discipline against me. I stopped my protest in midstream.

"Yes, Swanson," the chief said. "I released them to Agent Robinson on his request. Lieutenant Graber and Detective Sanchez agreed with the decision, not that they actually had any say in the matter."

Lieutenant Graber's face remained placid; not a muscle moved. Having already understood the implications of the missing boxes, I did not say much other than, "Is he taking over the case, then?"

"I already told you," Bitterman said, "Agent Robinson's assessment is that it was a local matter, not federally related to the judge's military duties."

"But," I said, "I don't think we have any other leads."

"I told you, the Feds think it is local, even if it may be gang related. Right? Aren't you looking local? Don't we have Asian gangs in Westminster? And what about criminals from Henning's past, or even his family law case load?" Bitterman asked.

"You mean Cheney and his crew?" I asked, expecting him to flare. He did not disappoint me.

"You idiot!" Bitterman said. "It's not Cheney. He is a respected member of our society, and never would he involve himself in something like that."

"Right, like money, power, and ego have never led to murder before," I said.

Bitterman's face reddened and he rose to his feet. Pointing his finger at Graber, he said, "I told you before, and I'll say it again, rein him in or it's you who is gone!"

With that he slammed out of Graber's office.

I winced at what I had once again managed to create. Even with good intentions and a determination to do what was right, I messed it up. All I could do was slink down in my chair. Graber said nothing and just stared off into space.

When the silence finally got too heavy, I broke it. "Sir," I said, "I really think there is a skunk in the henhouse, and I really believe there is a foreign influence at work here."

Graber didn't answer immediately. He just continued to stare out his window that overlooked the Newport Coast.

"Sir?" I said again.

"Yes, Jake," he said, "I heard you."

"Then we really need to do something," I said.

"Are you medically cleared?" he asked.

"Why?"

"You need to be medically cleared before you can come back to work."

"Speaking of that," I said, "who's working on that?"

"Rogan and Macy, picked up the case," he said.

"You know that the explosives were C-4?" I asked.

The lieutenant snapped back to attention, staring hard into my face. "How do you know that?" he asked.

"Sanchez got the info from the lab last night," I said. "I don't think there's a written report yet, though."

The lieutenant smiled for the first time that day. All of a sudden he started to laugh. He laughed until tears formed in his eyes.

"You want to let me in on the joke?" I asked.

Wiping the tears from his eyes, he said, "Damn, she's taking after you more and more. She'll make a great detective."

I wasn't sure what the joke was, but at least he was back in good humor. I decided to see if he was also receptive.

"Can we tell you what we figured out last night?" I asked.

"Get her in here, and let's get to work," he said.

An hour later, and my head spinning from Graber's questions, Melissa and I finally left his office and got to work.

CHAPTER THIRTY-TWO

I'm going through all the tapes collected from security cameras from the surrounding area," Melissa said after we left the lieutenant's office.

"Yeah, and we need the tapes from the preceding two to three weeks, if they still have them," I answered. "You know what you're looking for?"

"Yes, boss," she answered. "I am looking for license plate numbers for all black Mercedes S-Class sedans. Not like there are many of those in Newport Beach," she added ironically.

"Right, we need to know who those cars belonged to and why they were in the area," I said.

"Duh," she said as she hurried off.

I needed to go see Sally and get my medical clearance. But first, I had a call to make.

Carmen Delgado answered on the second ring. "You called for a follow-up to our lovely lunch, Jake?" she purred.

"Sure, why not?" I asked.

"Really?" she squealed.

"Carmen, be serious," I said. "You know I was almost killed the other day."

"Jakey, I heard," she said. "Let me take you to lunch."

Having faced real death the other day, her invitation no longer scared me. And what I needed from her would probably be more forthcoming in a casual setting. My decision could not be delivered too quickly, or she would be suspicious.

"Carmen, can't we just talk on the phone?" I asked.

"But, Jakey, I so love your company," she pouted.

"You know that Bridget is back with John McAllister," I said.

Carmen sighed, and said she'd heard.

"Kinda cuts into your retainer and fees," I said.

"It was going to happen sometime," she said. "It might as well have been sooner rather than later. A baby needs its father."

Surprised at her response, I finally said, "Okay Carmen, as long as there are no hard feelings, maybe lunch, but not a long one."

"Thanks, Jake," she said, more subdued than I expected.

We agreed to meet for lunch at the Village Inn on Balboa, taking us closer to her office and mine, but not where we would expect the Newport Beach power crowd to meet for lunch.

An hour and a half later I was seated next to Carmen in a secluded booth. Again she came dressed to conceal her figure, but a she had made a surprising change: her hair was heavily streaked with dark brown, blending in the blonde, but softening her looks and making her skin glow. It went beautifully with the navy blue pants suit and pale grey blouse.

"Carmen, you look beautiful," I said, kissing her on the cheek.

Blushing, Carmen stammered out a "thank you" and kissed me back.

"Why the change?" I asked.

"Oh, hell, Jake," she said. "When I saw how natural you look with your tan and almost white blonde hair and the endless blue eyes, I realized that my attempt to fit in with the blonde crowd only made me look silly. I am who I am: the daughter of field workers. But I am proud, and should be proud of what I've done."

"Pretty drastic change," I said.

"No, Jake, just something a long time coming," she said. "Shall we order or talk about why you called me?"

"Order first, then talk," I said.

She ordered an ice tea and the steamed clams with garlic bread. I followed her lead, and in no time we were slurping down the best steamed clams anywhere on the coast.

Eating clams didn't leave much time for talking, but when we finished eating, Carmen turned to me and said what I was now beginning to expect from her: an insightful question. She asked me if I was there because I thought Cheney had bombed my car.

"Actually, Carmen," I said, "I am hoping he didn't. But, the evidence is beginning to pile up that it may have been someone from his

Gooney Squad."

"Hmm, why do you say that?" she asked, not looking at me.

I hesitated. The lab report wasn't even written and, despite the pun, the contents of the report were explosive. I decided to evade.

"Let's just say I hope, for my sake, it wasn't Cheney."

"That's a change from you, darling," Carmen said. "Earlier you were sure it was Cheney who killed the judge, and I am sure you want him for the bombing, too. What has changed your mind?"

"John McAllister," I said.

"Oh?"

"He thinks Bridget would be devastated if her father really did any of those things," I said. "He really does love his wife, and doesn't want to see her hurt."

"Well, Jake," Carmen said, "he or his guys may have done the bombing. I really don't think he did the killing, but the bombing… maybe."

I was shocked at her statement. Could Cheney's pet shark really be changing that much in just a few days that she'd give up her main source of income? It seemed unbelievable that she'd go that far.

Being the great attorney that she is, she read my expression and responded. "Jake, Cheney was furious after your meeting with him at his house. You violated him in ways he has never experienced. You were not intimidated by him or his wealth. You do know he is using, or trying to use, his power to get you fired?"

"Yeah, I got a taste of that earlier today," I said.

"Hmm, that was quick," she said. "He just asked me yesterday how I could draft a complaint to scare the Chief of Police into firing you."

"Tell him not to bother, unless you want the fees," I said.

"Why's that?" she asked.

"The husband of one of the victim's daughter is already threatening a lawsuit," I said. "He's convinced I put his wife and sister-in-law in danger, which, of course, I probably did."

"Oh, Jake, remorse?" she asked.

"Some," I said, thinking of pregnant Lauren and the eager Cindy. I knew they were only trying to help me. But, after I was almost killed, it struck me that I also put them into danger. That was all part of the reason I wanted to speak with Carmen; shark though she was, she was still smart — attorney smart.

"Listen, Carmen, not that I want to take your boss out of the line of fire, but let me run a few things by you," I said. "I respect your ability to put pieces together."

Carmen merely nodded, and bent her head to hear me as I lowered my voice.

"First, although I know Cheney's Gooney Squad are all prior military, the stuff that blew up my car was C-4 plastique, military grade, lifted from a compound in Afghanistan. It could only have come from recent military stock. From my encounter with his 'squad' the other day, at least two of them look like recent grads from military life. So you may want to be careful about asking if they have an illegal supply

train that gives them that stuff. If they do, well, you can guess the rest.
. ."

Again she only nodded.

Secondly, there's a guy hanging around that has the chief's ear, but I don't trust him," I said.

"But your partner?" Carmen asked.

"Absolutely infatuated up until about twenty-four hours ago, but still don't trust her," I answered.

"What can I do?" Carmen asked.

"Given all the grief I've taken from Cheney and all the stuff he's done to his daughter, maybe he can find some karmic harmony by you doing me a favor?" I asked.

This made the attorney snort through her nose; spraying the ice tea out before she could recover with her napkin. She choked a few times, then smiled and nodded.

I outlined a plan for her to use her investigator to run some security checks on Andre Robinson. I knew I'd never get the permission at the station, and I needed only what Carmen could get through her unregulated sources. Since I never expected to use the information in court, I figured she would be the best source for me.

After hearing my plan and my reasoning, she readily agreed. And, when I offered to pay the bill, she finally stopped being agreeable, and returned to type as a high-priced lawyer for a powerful man.

"Oh, Jakey," she purred, "how could I ever let you pay when I so love your company? And, after all, this was just a friendly lunch... between friends...

right?"

"Which is I why I should pay," I said.

"Oh, no," she said. "I would love to let you, but I do know you, Jake, and you'd expense this lunch slicker than snot, and then my boss would know. I can't let you do that. No, no, let me pay. I may dislike Cheney, but until I rebuild my practice, I still have to dance to his tune."

"Rebuild your practice?" I asked.

"Of course," she said, then lowered her voice and added. "You made me so ashamed the other day when we discussed what I did to Bridget, John McAllister, and the baby, I just couldn't look at myself."

"Really?" I asked. "Isn't that a little dramatic?"

"You mean more than my hair color and my desire to get back to my heritage?" she asked.

"Hmm, yeah, well, this is Newport, land of the Newport Bitch Blondes," I said.

"Yeah, the BBs," she said.

"And?" I asked, giving her a chance to explain.

"I don't know, Jake," she said. "I've gotten used to the money, but I'm not sure I want to sell my soul for it anymore. I can only pray I do escape. Working for a man that can damage his daughter's life the way Cheney did, and working for the others like him, I finally realized all the money couldn't wash away my guilt. You just put a period on thoughts that have been clouding me for quite a while. I need out—out of this life, and out of selling my soul. Pray for me, okay?"

I kissed the palm of her hand again, and agreed that I would offer my pitiful prayers for her.

We spent the rest of the afternoon in companionable conversation. Once she stopped eyeing me as prey, I realized that I actually liked the woman. She was funny and witty, and her stories of her client's foibles kept me in laughing a real laugh.

It was late afternoon when we finally left the Village Inn. The air tasted like fall. The fog that was gathering, dragging the salt from the sea, mixing it into brine that tickled the nose, and rested on the tongue. The air was getting heavier, and the temperature was dropping. I felt the chill, and missed having my silk blazer jacket that I always kept in the trunk of the Intrepid.

Just thinking of my car made me sad, but also reminded me of the work I had yet to do that night. The dark blue Buick was perfect cover, and I definitely needed it.

A half-hour later I was parked outside of the Embassy Suites in Irvine. It seemed like eons ago that I had met the girls and we had conspired. I hoped they were doing well, and found I missed their conspiratorial help.

I sauntered into the lobby and asked for Andre Robinson. The clerk at the desk was not one of the usually dim and beautiful women hired to work front desks of businesses in the area. Instead, she had a soft Midwestern accent and perky attitude—willing to help, but not break the rules. Worse yet, she was immune to my charms. She would not give me his room number, but did agree to direct me to a house phone where she would connect me to his room to speak with him.

A few minutes later, with no answer in his room, but knowing he was still registered, I took advantage of the dark Buick and took up surveillance outside to wait.

Not long afterward, I was rewarded when a black sedan pulled into the parking lot. The sedan was not a Mercedes, but it was a new Ford Taurus, a favorite of Navy types. Following the black Taurus was another Taurus, grey in color. Andre Robinson emerged from the black sedan, as expected, but an unknown figure exited the other car.

Hmmm, I thought.

I watched as the two men shook hands and went inside. I couldn't really follow them inside. I was, as they say, too obvious. Damn my six foot, two inches of height and blonde hair. If the two men were in the lobby bar they'd see me immediately.

Damn.

I needed to snoop. But I couldn't snoop until the sun finished setting over the western horizon, or until the men emerged. I was stuck.

I sat in the front seat of the oversized American car, tapping my fingers on the steering wheel, listening to a XM station called *Coffee House*. It was playing a soft collection of acoustical music from mostly unknown artists, making it the perfect accompaniment to my mood. Soothing my nerves, the music washed over me, taking me back to a time when my life seemed charmed and good. Now it was *crap*.

Lost in self-pity reverie, the bell tone of my cell phone jangled me into attention. The caller ID told me it was Carmen Delgado.

"That's quick," I said by way of answering the phone.

Her chuckle made me smile. "Had to get back to my honey as quick as I could," she said. "Besides, you need this news to keep from getting yourself seriously injured, if not killed," she added.

"Really?"

"Yeah, really," she said. "My investigator is tops, former military himself. Knows everyone he needs to know. Reminds me of you."

"Is that good," I asked.

"The best parts of you," she answered. "Anyway, Robinson is definitely military, and still attached. He's not really NCIS, but sort of a separate branch, if you will. He carries NCIS identification, but he's more of a *cleaner*."

"A what?" I asked.

"*Cleaner*," she said.

When I didn't say anything, she continued. "Didn't you ever watch programs like the *Sopranos*? They're the ones that go in and clean up the messes made by other people to keep the authorities from getting too close to the operations."

"*Cleaner*?" I asked again. "You mean he was cleaning up a mess? What mess?"

"That is something my guy couldn't get. All he could get was his classification and he knew about the rest. More than that, my investigator couldn't, or wouldn't, tell me. You have to do the rest," she said, her voice somewhere between concerned and sad.

"Am I the mess?" I asked her.

"Jake," Carmen said very urgently, "I don't know how to answer that, other than to tell you to be extremely careful. I wish I could tell you more, but I can't get it out of my guy. He sealed his lips tight when he gave me Robinson's classification."

"Carmen," I said, "listen, you've been a great friend. What you've given me just confirms some of my suspicions. But, please, keep this between us, okay?"

She sighed her promise and we disconnected the call.

Letting out a deep sigh, I realized I had been holding my breath. All the feelings I had harbored over the last week were crystalizing. More than ever I needed to get into Robinson's Taurus. But how?

I mulled over the possibilities, but nothing seemed viable. But, while I was lost in thought, nature stepped in for me. The fog that had been rolling in from the sea made its way seven miles inland and filled in the parking lot and surrounding area. Even with the lights that came on with the gathering gloom, I still had cover.

I slipped out of the Buick and ambled over to the grey car. It had military plates and was stenciled with United States Navy on the front doors. On the front seat lay a notebook and folio-type briefcase. I wanted both. But I also wanted whatever was in the black Taurus.

Robinson's car was parked several stalls over from the gray car. I walked over to it and found both seats empty. Robinson was obviously much more careful than his Navy companion. But the trunk beckoned.

I knew that most newer models of American cars had computer chips in the keys that made it next to impossible to start the car without the proper key. I also knew that the later model cars all had alarm systems. But this was also Southern California where car alarms go off constantly. Their blaring horns were so routine, hardly anyone ever even paid attention. And, even if they did, who would respond?

Robinson? At the very worst he was in the lobby bar. It would take him at least ninety seconds or more to get to the parking lot, even if he heard it.

Security? I was a cop with a badge; I could get around that.

Security cameras? Yeah, likely. But that would take several days if anyone suspected that anything was truly amiss.

I assessed the risk again, rolling it around in my mind.

The trunk beckoned again, its siren call too tempting to ignore. It was my chance, and I finally decided I had to act or never forgive myself.

I rummaged in the trunk of the Buick for a tire iron, and was glad to see it was one of the few cars that still had a spare tire. I grabbed the iron and crossed quickly to the black Taurus. A quick stab and wrench and the trunk was open. Of course the blaring of the alarm quickly followed. But I had the trunk open.

I really expected to see an empty trunk. Robinson struck me as being way too careful to leave anything incriminating around where a snoop like me could find it. But I was wrong.

Tucked in the wheel well under what looked like a carelessly thrown jacket was a small gray packet wrapped in clear wrapping. It was no more than three inches by three inches, but I knew I recognized it.

I scooped it up, slammed the trunk lid, and walked quickly back to my car. I made it inside just before a security guard came out the door and looked around. He saw the Taurus's blinking headlights and blaring horn. It was enough for him to amble over to the car and look inside. When he saw nothing, he shrugged and walked away.

After he was gone I started up the Buick and quickly left the parking lot.

Driving back over to the 55 Freeway I called Melissa's cell phone. She answered on the first ring. When I told her what I suspected I had in my possession, she said nothing—not even questioning where I got it.

I asked her if she would call her friend at the lab to do an analysis for me. She quickly agreed and told me she would meet me at the sheriff's crime lab in Santa Ana.

The lab was dark when I arrived, but parked in the parking lot was the pathetic white Dodge Stratus. With its tinted windows it was difficult to see who was inside, but when the lights flashed on and off a few times, I surmised it was my partner.

Smiling to myself, I sauntered over to her car, package in hand.

"Doing a little spy stuff, are we, Little Beaver?" I asked.

"What?" she asked.

"The lights," I said, motioning to the switch for her headlamps.

"Oh, that; I wasn't sure it was you," she said. "Where did you get this car?" A Buick? My father would kill for a car like this."

That did make me laugh out loud. Jaime at Newport Exotic and Muscle Cars considered this a "throw away" car, while someone from Santa Ana would love to have it.

"Just for your info, Little Beaver, I almost did kill for it," I said. "But, for now, it's my only ride."

"So, you got the stuff?" she asked.

I handed her the package and started to open her door for her. But she declined, explaining that it was best for me not go inside with her. Her work needn't have me as a witness.

This, too, made me smile. In so many ways my partner was just like me—always knowing whom she could work to get what she needed.

With a firm good-bye from my partner, I got back in the Buick and headed for home. Only a slight headache behind my eyes reminded me why I was driving Big Blue, the Buick, instead of Intrepid.

I started to sigh, but it turned into a brief prayer—for my partner, for Carmen, and for all those whose lives I touched. I prayed that no one else would get hurt.

CHAPTER THIRTY-THREE

The next morning I arrived at the station eager to let the lieutenant know what information I had gathered the night before. But he was not in his office when I arrived. His door was closed, and he was nowhere to be found.

When I wandered back to my cubicle there was a note on my desk that the chief wanted to see me. I immediately felt my shirt get damp, but I took a deep breath and wandered on down to his office.

Seated in the chief's office with a small smirk playing on his lips was Agent Andre Robinson. The chief was also seated, as was Lieutenant Graber. Graber's mouth was slashed into a deep frown, his forehead furrowed with deep 'elevens' between his brows.

"Swanson," the chief said, his voice neutral, "Agent Robinson is here to report a crime."

"Oh?" I said.

"It seems his car was broken into last night and highly classified documents were stolen from the trunk," the chief said.

I saw the trap immediately. Robinson was setting me up to take a hit for something federal, like stealing classified documents, not just breaking into his trunk and taking military-grade C-4 explosives, which he probably never should have possessed off a military base.

My reaction was critical. I saw from the lieutenant's face, neutral as he appeared to be keeping it, the sheen of sweat breaking out on his lip.

"I'm sorry to hear that," I said, also trying to keep my voice neutral.

"He seems to think you should handle the case," the chief said.

"I don't do car burgs," I said. "And, besides, I'm on medical, remember?"

"Yet, here you are, again," the chief said mildly.

"Can't seem to stay away," I said, hoping my voice carried a nonchalance that I didn't feel.

I saw the lieutenant's shoulders relax slightly. Evidently, I was playing true to form, which was what he must have needed.

"Swanson, this break-in happened here in Newport Beach, down near the Peninsula," the chief said. "No one knows the characters better than you."

"But, Chief," I protested, "I don't do car burgs." The 'break-in' did not happen in Newport Beach, but rather on the Costa Mesa/Santa Ana boundary. Another trap.

"Well, since Agent Robinson has done some further investigation, he has come to the conclusion that the judge's murder is federal. He will be leading a task force of federal agents to handle this case. This leaves you plenty of time to work a car burglary in your neighborhood," he said.

I tried desperately not to let my face show my shock. I had been working under the assumption that the case was going to be under my partner's control and we would solve it together, keeping Robinson out of the loop.

I started to protest, but the chief dismissed me. I turned on my heel and left his office. As I stomped back to my cubicle I saw Melissa swing her purse onto her desk and start to take her seat. Grabbing her by the arm, I dragged her outside the station's back door.

"We're off the case," I said.

"What?" she said, disbelief written all over her face.

"We're off the case, and Robinson is bringing in a team of Feds," I said.

Melissa rocked back on her heels and glared at the back door. She started to reach for the door, but I grabbed her again and steered her clear.

"Don't," I said. "Robinson is in with the chief, and so's Graber. It looks grim in there. If you go in, it may get worse. Deniability, remember?"

"Deniability?" she snarled. "Deniability? The stuff you gave me is the exact chemical makeup of the stuff used to torch your car. You want 'deniability' for Robinson? He's part of this!"

I wish I could say I was surprised, but I wasn't. Not after the information I had gotten from Carmen Delgado's investigator. But more than anything, I needed to protect Melissa from me and my stupidity. I had snooped where I didn't belong and, for whatever reason, I was supposed to pay the price. Someone or something very big wanted— no needed—me off the case. The die had been cast. It was time to let it go.

"Melissa, you need to let it go," I said. "This mess is way beyond us, and we can't interfere. Think of your career. . ."

"My career?" she cried. "What about the case? It will never get solved. Those grieving daughters will never know who killed their father."

Now it was my turn to rock back on my heels at her intensity.

"Why would you say that?" I asked, hoping she didn't know as much as I did.

"Jake, wait here," she said, as she turned on her heel, not answering my question.

She disappeared back inside the station. When she returned, she had a banker's box of tapes and other evidence, as well as her copy of the notebook of reports we called the murder book.

"You got a car?" she asked.

I pointed at the Buick and we took off together. Once inside the car she made a call to the station. She told them she had just gotten an emergency call and needed to take some personal days. With a nod of her head, she told me to take us to my place.

Hours later, after watching innumerable security tapes, we knew two things for certain. First, there was indeed a black Mercedes S-Class going in and out of the neighborhood. We even got a clear picture of its license plate. The second thing we knew, a black Taurus was also going in and out of the judge's neighborhood.

We also learned a third thing. It made me angry, and it made Melissa, my imperturbable partner, cry. We reviewed the security tape from the Bristol Farm Market's security camera the late afternoon of the judge's murder. This market was located across McArthur Boulevard and at the intersection of the Pacific Coast Highway, making it just a short walk from the parking lot to the judge's house. Captured on the tape was a black Taurus car pulling into the lot on the Friday afternoon of the judge's murder. The same car was parked in the parking lot until long after the judge was killed, and well into that night. More importantly, a tall blonde-haired man was seen getting in and out of the car. In his hand he held a Bristol Farms recyclable grocery bag when he exited the car. But, when he returned to the car, the bag was gone.

"Jake, what are we going to do?" my partner asked, once she composed herself.

"It's still not conclusive," I said, not sure if I wanted it to be what we both feared. "We still need to run license plates, and finish our work before we accuse anyone. This is what real detectives do. We set the snare, catch the rabbit, then wring its goddamned neck! But, first the snare."

My partner looked at me like I had lost my mind. "Set snares?" she asked.

"Yes, we are going to tie this thing up in such a tight ball that our little bunny cannot escape," I said.

"Quit with the bunny thing," Melissa said. "I had a bunny and one day we ate if for dinner and I never forgave my father."

"Okay, Little Beaver," I said. "You get your buddy over at the Sheriff's station to run these plates. Once you do that, I'll call my guy who knows about all this spy stuff. You up for that?" When she nodded, I continued, "Until then, keep quiet. No one can know. I've already lost a car; I don't want to lose a partner."

Sanchez started working the phones while I put a call into Bill Dawson. I reached him on his cell phone and asked him if he wanted to meet the most beautiful woman in Southern California. Of course he couldn't resist, and agreed to meet me later that evening.

By the time the evening fog enveloped the beach, Sanchez and I were ready to head up the coast. In her notebook she had all the license plate numbers of all the black sedans that were captured on the security cameras in the preceding three weeks before the murder, including the license plate of the black Taurus.

Walking into the Pelican Isle, my partner was dressed in her usual black jeans, white blouse, and camel hair blazer. Her long dark hair was swept up into a ponytail. Her presence elicited more than a few stares. We took the two empty stools next to the end of the bar. Bill Dawson, baseball cap firmly pulled down to his eyebrows, raised it up just enough to get a good look at my partner. He smiled and took one more draught of his Coors Lite.

"You weren't kidding when you asked me if I wanted to meet the most beautiful woman in Southern California," he said. "But you were lying; she's the most beautiful in the world."

He put out his hand to my blushing partner and introduced himself.

"Detective Melissa Sanchez," she said.

"Your partner?" he asked.

"Yep," I answered.

"Lucky mutt."

"Yep."

I ordered a rum and Diet Coke for Melissa and a Stoli on the rocks with a twist for myself. We each took a few gulps of our drinks before I began to speak.

"Dawson, you have a CD player on your boat?" I asked.

"Small one," he said.

"You got gas?"

"Always."

"Sanchez and I would love to go for a nighttime boat ride," I said.

Dawson looked at my partner, took another slug of his beer, and gave me a hard stare. Nodding, he finished his beer and gathered his cell phone, wallet, and keys.

We hurried out onto the docks to his boat. When we reached his Sea Ray, he motioned for Melissa to step onto the dive step of the boat, but asked her to remove her boots. She also slipped out of her socks and threw both the socks and her boots onto the stern of the boat. With his help she lightly transitioned from dock to dive step to deck of the boat. I stayed ashore to untie the lines.

When we were under way, Dawson asked how far we needed to go. I suggested we just tour the Huntington Harbor area and let Melissa ogle the million-dollar mansions while he reviewed a CD we had.

The tour took about an hour but, with the houses shrouded in fog, it wasn't much of a tour. It was, however, enough for Melissa to still get a flavor of the money that flowed in places other than Newport Beach. It was also enough time for Dawson to view all the pertinent comings and goings of a black Taurus, a blonde man, and of course a black Mercedes S-Class.

When he was done, I pulled back the throttles, putting the boat into idle. Bill disappeared below deck and came up with three cold beers. All of us twisted off the caps and took deep drinks of the alcohol. The silence deepened until Bill finally broke it.

"I take it the black Taurus is military," he said.

"Yep," I said. "Purports to be NCIS—Navy."

"Hmm, and the black Mercedes?"

"Registered to a rental agency in Beverly Hills that specializes in renting high-end cars," Sanchez said.

"Do we know who rented the car during that time?" he asked.

"No yet," Melissa said, "but working on it. We may need a warrant. The owner is not cooperating, but he sounds Oriental. Maybe Chinese, but I am not really good with accents other than Vietnamese."

"And you brought me out here on this foggy night because... why?" he asked.

"Because the NCIS guy is face first into this investigation, and he's pulling the plug on our involvement. The time that you saw the car parked at the Bristol Farms parking lot was concurrent timing to the death of the judge. Other than that, I don't know why I would want you around."

"She's not cleared," Bill said.

"I've got military security," Melissa said. "Marines. MAGTF. Marine Military Police, Logistics Combat Element, sir."

Dawson smiled at her, giving her the "HOO-RRAAH" and a thumbs up.

"So what do we do about the civilian among us," Dawson said to Sanchez.

"Answer his questions then shoot him, sir," Sanchez said, smiling.

That brought another broad smile. But I had to bring the party to a close and get back to business. I felt a terrible threat coming and knew we were under some sort of time limit.

"Dawson, why would a NCIS guy and a Chinese Tong being cruising the judge's house? Especially when the NCIS guy is not intelligence and the judge is?" I asked.

"Goes back to the nukes and Russians, probably," Dawson said.

"I figured that," I said, "but who would be more likely to kill the judge?"

"Chinese hit man," answered Dawson.

"That's what I thought," I said.

I pushed the throttles forward and the boat moved slowly back to the dock area. My partner and Dawson spent the rest of the cruise talking about the Marines and their time in the service. By the time we docked, I was sure the crusty old guy was deeply in love with my partner.

CHAPTER THIRTY-FOUR

Back on the road again, I made one last call. It was to David Chu of the Asian Gang Unit. I had one question for him.

"David, this is Jake Swanson," I said. "I've got a question for you. Could or would the Chinese Tong be able to compromise one of our military personnel to kill someone who was a heavy in our government?"

"Certainly," David said. "Why?"

"I'm afraid that our judge here in Orange County was killed by one of our own military personnel. I was just wondering if it was possible that they had that much influence."

"Money is power, and power is influence. You do the math," David answered.

"Okay, thanks."

I hung up the phone and Melissa stared hard at me. When she saw my look she knew it wasn't good.

"We're going to get help," I said to her.

"Who?"

"The only one who has ever consistently believed in me since I made detective," I answered.

A quick call, and it was agreed we would all meet back at my apartment, though it was closing in on midnight. It wasn't long before the six-foot, six-inch frame of the lieutenant loomed in the doorway of my apartment.

We showed him what we had, and it took a long time for him to say anything. When he did, it was only "Son of a bitch."

"You sure?" he asked.

"Sure enough for a sit down with him," I said.

"And the car rental?" Graber asked.

"Owner is uncooperative, sir," Melissa answered.

"Without it there's wiggle room," he said.

"I know," I said.

Graber sat on my couch ruffling the ears of the dog he helped me save. She stood patiently letting him use her strength until he finally made a decision.

"Swanson," he said standing, "you are slippery—never where you're supposed be, drink when you're supposed to be working, working when you're not supposed to be working. Blowing up cars because you piss off the wrong people and, generally, you're the best detective I have, or ever had. The only good thing is you're teaching your partner all of your best traits."

"Thank you, sir," I said.

"Not 'thank you,'" he said, "you'd better be right. And I hope you are, because my career rests on what I am going to do next."

As he started out the door, he turned to me and said under his breath, "Get rid of this box. Take if from your partner. Don't tell her where you put it; just get it some place safe. And I don't mean the station."

He left, leaving me to figure out how to get the box of evidence out of my partner's possession without her knowing it. But, as luck would have it, she suddenly ran after the lieutenant and asked him to walk her to her car.

It was the last time I saw Lieutenant Graber for a very long time.

CHAPTER THIRTY-FIVE

The next morning I circled by the Greyhound Bus depot in Santa Ana. It was one of the few places that still had the old fashioned lockers. Several dollars of coins later, the box with the videos, and my murder book, were safely stored in a locker. I attached the key to my house key ring and left for the police station.

I was headed down the Bristol Boulevard with the intent of cutting across to seventeenth when I got the call. A sobbing woman was on the other end of the line, and I could barely make out her voice through her tears.

"Dolores?" I asked, recognizing the voice. "Dolores, is that you?"

"Jake Swanson, you son of a bitch! You took everything from him. I hope you die. In fact, I wish you had died!" the sobbing voice of Dolores Graber said over the phone.

"Dolores, what is going on?" I asked, more alarmed at her hysterical tone than the words she used.

"It's my husband, you son of a bitch! He was fired! You did this to him!" she cried.

"What?" I said. "No, it can't be. The chief can't fire him, not without a hearing and all sorts of evidence."

"It's as good as fired," she said. "He was given the choice of retiring or facing an inquiry! You know what he chose! He's done… fired!"

As she was saying this, my phone alerted me that someone was beeping through. It was Sally.

"Dolores, I need to speak with him, but I've got another call," I said.

"No, don't you come near us," she said. "I don't want you anywhere near us!"

I didn't need to disconnect, because she did it for me. I answered Sally's call.

"Jake, I need you to come to my office before you go to the station," Sally quickly said after my greeting. "I have an attorney for you. And, before you argue, let me tell you, you need one."

"Sally, this is crazy," I said. "I just heard that Graber was forced off the department."

"That's why I need you to come by here first," she said. "I think I can head off disaster for you, but I need you to cooperate with me for once in your life."

When I arrived at Sally's office high in the Fashion Island Towers, she was flanked by several attorneys, and strangely enough, Bill Dawson. Also with her was Andre Robinson. Instinctively, I curled my hands into a fist.

"What is this?" I asked. "You didn't tell me you were throwing a party. You especially didn't tell me you invited a murderer to this soiree."

"Jake, for just once, take all of this seriously," Sally said, grabbing my arm and steering me away from the blonde man standing just out of my reach.

Robinson shrugged but, for the first time, his face was grim. His usual smirk was absent, and his eyes were sad. Bill Dawson's face was also grim, as he took the younger man's arm to follow Sally and me.

With Sally's firm grip on my arm, I closed my mouth and followed her into the large back office area. It was her inner sanctum, a place very few people were ever allowed, yet she invited us in and made us comfortable.

The office was decorated in shades of ivory and vibrant tones of blue and yellow, furnished with a large antique desk, and several love seats covered in striped damask. She had a stunning view of the Pacific, but I couldn't enjoy the view that day. There were too many grim faces staring at me.

"Jake, I think you know Bill Dawson?" Sally said.

Yes, I knew Bill Dawson from the Pelican Isle, but this Bill Dawson was not someone I had ever seen. He was dressed in a pale gray suit, white shirt, with a grey and blue paisley tie. The baseball cap was missing, and his white hair was slicked over the bald spot on his head. More importantly, I could see his eyes were a clear blue, without a hint of red.

"Hey, Bill, you clean up real good," I said.

"Swanson, you need to take a seat, shut up for a while, and listen to me. This is serious, and I am here to make you listen to me," he said.

Startled at his tone, I hesitated. But when I saw his harsh stare, I backed away, shut my mouth, and sat on one of the loveseats while the rest of the party found seats in the chairs. Sally poured coffee for each of us from a silver tea service then took a seat behind her desk. She stared off at the Pacific and refused to look at me.

Robinson remained standing while he studiously ignored me. The two other men in suits did not introduce themselves. From their stern expressions, white shirts, conservative ties, and dark suits, I figured they were lawyers.

"You called me here," I said, "it must be critical based on the looks on your faces."

Bill took a sip of his coffee, shuffled his feet, then began to speak. "Swanson, this whole case is a mess right now, and you are making it worse."

I started to protest, but Sally swiveled around her chair and held up her hand in the universal sign to stop. Seeing my friend's hand, I snapped my mouth shut.

"You and your partner got the tapes that should never have seen the light of day. Somehow our guys didn't think to inventory the boxes released to them to see if you did, in fact, have the surveillance from the surrounding businesses. I can't believe their incompetence but, then again, they didn't expect you to be that far ahead of them, either.

"I'm sorry, but that's Investigation 101," I retorted. "We routinely collect these tapes, as would any competent police agency when trying to solve a case. It's an elementary step. But, then again, who says I have any tapes?"

Sally slanted her eyes at me, so again I shut my mouth with a snap.

"Maybe you don't," Bill conceded, "and who's to say you do? But, at this point, the tapes are missing, and the businesses all say it was Newport P.D. that collected them. Nonetheless, it was missed when we collected your stuff from the conference room, and it was so elementary they didn't even think to ask if there were any security tapes from surrounding businesses or intersections."

Bill looked over at Robinson, who continued to stare out the window, not meeting anyone's eyes.

"What we do know, is that there were probably persons, shall we say, who need to remain 'unknown' on those tapes. Again, those tapes were never meant to see the light of day."

I was seething inside. I knew who was on those tapes. The man in the black Taurus was Andre Robinson: mystery man from the deep. He was there; he was the one who killed the judge and his wife. I was sure of it.

Yet, even as I was fermenting this thought into a thick, poisonous brew, ready to spew it all over the room, Andre Robinson turned away from the view of the ocean and turned to face me.

"Swanson," he said, his face hard, "I know you think I killed Mark Henning, and his wife, Nancy, but let me tell you I did not."

"Right," I said. "You just parked your car across the street, took a bag from your trunk and disappeared from the Bristol Farms parking lot for a period of time that directly coincides with the time frame the judge was shot. . ."

"Damn it, Jake," Sally exploded at me. "Just shut up."

"Well, we at least know who has the tapes," Bill said.

The two men in the dark grey suits put down their coffee cups in unison and took a breath to speak.

Sally again put up her hand as a stop sign. We all stopped talking except Andre Robinson.

"Swanson," he said, "this is government business. I am sorry you dragged your partner into all of this. Melissa knows all of this, I presume?"

"Melissa?" I said, whirling around on him. "Not Sanchez? Not Detective? It's like that is it?" I said, seizing onto the one thing that maybe I shouldn't have. "You compromise my partner, then dare to call her 'Melissa'? What kind of dick are you? She's young and impressionable."

"Yes, and she's also smart, beautiful, and too good a detective to be partnered with someone like you," he answered.

That was it! I was on my feet, with fists balled tightly. Robinson also swung around to fully face me. Again it was Sally who stopped us.

"Boys, stop it," she said mildly, using her soothing voice. "Just put your testosterone back in your pockets and sit down."

When Robinson remained standing, she leveled a look at him that made him move away from the window to sit next to Dawson on one of the loveseats.

"Okay, we need to find a solution to all of this," Dawson said. "We need the tapes, we need silence, and we need all of this to go away. The tapes are not the issue in this case. They may give a wrong impression."

"Pffsstt, is that all?" I asked. "Make the murder of a judge and an innocent woman just 'go away'?"

Bill turned full front to face me. "Yes, Jake, that is exactly what we need." He then proceeded to explain why.

It was never expected that I would figure out about the nuclear devices being sent from Russia to Iran. It was also not expected that I would find Ado Ito or understand his connection to what the Russians and the Chinese Tong were doing

When Dawson finished telling me this, I had too many questions, but the one burning in my brain was only why. Why let a good man die?

"Jake, this is crazy; I've already told you more than you should know. Understand, I can't tell you all of it," Dawson said. "But, do you really think we would let the Iranians get nukes?"

"It sounds like it," I said.

"Jake, do you remember during the first part of the last century when Japan and China were at war?"

I racked my brain, but nothing came to me.

"Okay, during that war the Chinese and the Japanese ended up hating each other. Over the centuries there have been battles and slaves, and counter battles and slaves. They have memories that last millennia, not just years or decades. The Chinese, even a criminal organization, would never use the Japanese for any of their endeavors, nor would the Japanese allow themselves to be used. The scientists were plants put in place to aid Iran by volunteering to help do away with 'American imperialism and nihilism.' The scientists were going to be used to make sure the Iranians never perfected their devices that they got from Russian and the Tongs."

"But Ito told me his father and brother hated the Americans and were going to Iran to spite us," I said.

"We know," Dawson said. "That's how we got to Ito's father and brother in the first place. It was the information he gave to Henning that allowed us to put into place the counter move. They were going to Iran, but only to ensure failure."

"But, I thought we had an agreement with Iran that they would not develop nuclear bomb capabilities?" I said. "Why all this subterfuge and spy stuff?"

Dawson rolled his eyes, took a deep breath, and leveled a stare at me as he answered.

"That 'agreement' was worthless," he said. "Our Congress is still dawdling with it, and the wording in the agreement said that the Iranians would not *enrich* plutonium or uranium. It didn't say anything about reconfiguring bombs that were already made. Stupid fucks."

"But the inspections?" I countered.

"Inspect — what?" he answered. "Inspect nuclear power plants and centrifuges for uranium to drive power plants for electricity? Again, stupid fucks. The Iranians understand contracts, and wording in contracts. They also have spent a millennium learning how to step around wording in contracts. Cheating is an art form for them; getting caught is the only sin."

I shook my head, not sure what Dawson was saying. Robinson must have sensed my confusion because he stepped in to answer.

"Swanson, the Iranians were not just importing enriched uranium from the Chinese Tongs, they were bringing in fully functional bombs detached from Russian missiles. Admittedly the generals disabled the bombs before selling them, but that's where the scientists came in. It was their job to reset the bombs and mount them on delivery apparatus.

"But the inspectors?" I said again.

"Inspectors weren't looking for a 'Waste Dump'," Robinson said.

A chill went up my back as I made the connection — hiding in plain sight. The girls were correct; the Iranians were hiding their cache of weapons in plain sight beneath a waste dump. My world felt suddenly much less secure.

As I mulled this new revelation around in my mind, a thought bubbled to the surface.

"But if Mark Henning was activated as part of military intelligence—he was intelligence, wasn't he?" I asked.

Dawson nodded in the affirmative.

"Okay, so if Henning was military, and Andre Robinson *is* military, why didn't they know each other, and why let Henning die? Why not just 'deactivate' him, and let him stay home with his dying wife? Why didn't he know about all this?"

"First, we didn't know his wife was dying," Dawson said. "If we had, maybe things would have been different. But he never let on to his handlers. Mark Henning was a very private person when it came to his family. Secondly, Robinson's mission was much different than was Henning's"

"But, the Navy car coming in and out of the neighborhood?" I asked. "What or who was that?"

Robinson just shook his head, and Dawson answered.

"That was, in fact, Henning's handler," Dawson said. "He was briefing Henning on what he would expect to find in Hong Kong, and how to handle any information he may have discovered."

"And my ole friend here, Andre?" I said, sarcastically, why was he touring the neighborhood?"

"Security," Dawson answered.

"Security?" I said, dumbfounded. "What security? Henning died in his driveway, and his wife died in her garage. That doesn't sound like security to me."

Dawson just shrugged and left the conversation hanging. I looked around the room, and the lawyers, including Robinson, all had serious faces. Sally was again staring out her window, refusing to look at me. It made me angry that they all appeared to know something — something they weren't telling me. Especially Sally: she was my best friend in the world. What did she know that I didn't, and why was she keeping it from me?

"Dawson, you're not answering my question," I said. "Why didn't Henning know about the counter thingy, the *plan*, or whatever you guys are calling it? Why deliberately send him into harm's way?"

Silence again hung heavy in the air. No one looked at each other, and especially no one looked at me.

Deep inside of my need to solve homicides, ideas began to rush up from my gut to my throat. It was like magma in a volcano, and just like that magma it erupted in a fiery storm.

I looked from face to face, feeling the heat rising from my throat and radiating from my whole body.

"Fuck you ALL!" I said. "He was expendable! You couldn't control him, is that it? He thought it was too dangerous to let Iran have the bombs, so he would have stopped it. His allegiance was to the country, not to some silly spy stuff, right? So, now a very decent man is dead and growing cold in our morgue, and you all sit here pompous as hell while he and his beloved wife lay unburied. For what? A childish prank?"

"Jake," Sally said, swinging her chair around to look at me, "let it go."

I couldn't believe what she just said to me. "Let it GO?" I asked. "Let it go... go where, Sally? What and where am I supposed to let it go?"

"You're supposed to let go that you are a homicide detective solving a case," Robinson said. "That is all. Simple, really."

"Really? Simple?" I retorted.

"Yes, the case has been removed from you. You let it go to the Feds, and they will handle it."

"But you know who killed him, don't you?" I said, rather than asked.

"Actually, no," Robinson said. "We are working on the belief it was a hit from the Tong, but we don't know who the shooter was. Probably dropped in, then flew out."

"But, you were there... there when it happened," I said. "Why were you there? And why did you let it happen? Don't tell me it was 'better to let the Tong do it' when it was crazy not to stop them? What if they hadn't done it? You would? Oh, yea, that's right, Henning was expendable. You knew it, and you guys let him die for not playing ball with you."

For the first time, Robinson looked stricken. Vestiges of what may have passed for a conscience seemed to be written on his face. He exchanged looks with Dawson. The two men looked at Sally, and she finally looked at me.

"Jake, you can't know; you can't understand," she said, her voice gentle but firm.

"Why not? And who are these goons?" I asked no one in particular. "Are they *my* gooney squad? What... they disappear if I—what—refuse to cooperate?"

One of the men in the dark suits stood and introduced himself as Rory Callahan from Callahan, Drury, and Strong.

"Mr. Swanson," he said in that typical attorney voice that is meant to be soothing and confident—I find it annoying and condescending. "We are here at Sally's and Mr. Dawson's request. We are here to protect you and work out a deal so you can remain with the department. If you are reasonable with your actions in the next few days, and probably weeks, we can bring this to a resolution that benefits you and your department."

That did it. I remembered the hysterical call from Dolores Graber. Callahan's words just took me over the edge.

"My department?" I asked no one in particular. "The same department that fired a decent man and never bothered to investigate my car bombing. The same department headed by a man who'd rather play golf with the elite of Newport Beach and Orange County than take care of his men? The same department that is 'letting this go'? Why would I care about the department? And what about my partner? What about her? Again, why all this?"

"Because I care about you," Sally said. "And because Newport Beach needs you to protect them. But now, I need to protect you. If I can take care of you, we can work something out for Melissa."

Her voice was reasonable, but I was still angry and beyond hurt. This *letting it go* went against everything I stood for, everything on which I based what little identity I still had left. But, in the end, it was Sally's expression of concern that made me finally take my seat.

"I *need* to know," I said. "I still know where the security tapes and evidence are, and I won't give them up unless I know."

"You could go to federal prison for treason or, at the very least, obstruction," countered Callahan.

"Don't care," I said, then added smugly, "but I still hold all the cards, as it were. I still have the evidence and the tapes. What are you going to do… Guantanamo me?"

It was at that point that Dawson laughed, and the temperature in the room changed.

"Fuck you, Swanson," he said. "I told them that hardball tactics would never work with you. Damn, your surfer boy attitude hides a work ethic that we could use in our section."

"Your section?" I said, catching the word, almost afraid of what it meant.

Dawson smiled again. It was the smile that clicked everything into place.

"Just like the movies and Ludlum novels?" I asked.

Dawson just smiled again.

"Can I at least know why?" I asked.

There were looks all around the room, the attorneys sat stone-faced, and Sally exchanged looks with Dawson. I saw her almost imperceptible nod to Dawson. He took a deep breath and finished the story.

"When Henning came to the U. S. Attorney with a proffer of proof for a downward departure from the Federal Rules of Sentencing under Rule 35, the U. S. Attorney was incredulous and disbelieving. But part of his duties is always to pass on the information to his boss who passes it on. The FBI was not interested, but we were. We sent some of our people in with badges to get the information from Ito, but we also had to corroborate it. Once we did, we formed the plan to sabotage the sale, but we couldn't figure out how to do it. All of this took time."

"Is that why Ito was left hanging onto hope for all those years?" I asked.

"It wasn't years, only about eighteen months," Dawson said. "But it was when we got word about the tsunami and Ito's brother and father that the plan finally clicked."

"But why not let Henning know, or even Ado Ito?" I asked.

"Mark Henning most likely would have let Ito know, even if unintentionally," Dawson said. "Ito was a criminal, remember? He did illegal things. In fact, he was in because of his associations, and the deals he made for them. He was in with members of the Chinese Tong that we now know were associated with the initial sale of weapons from Russia to Iran. We were able to interrupt that sale by freezing assets and not allowing money to be moved around. But, as you know, criminals will always find a way around whatever safeguards we set up. We knew we had to freeze the program in Iran, but not through the sale. Israel was getting itchy, and we were afraid that bombs were going to start raining down on Iran. We couldn't have that.

Despite what much of the public thinks, there are more moderates in Iran than radicals. You can see that with the new president they elected. But, don't misunderstand, radicals still run the country, even it is it is more behind the scenes now. We're hopeful that will change, but nothing is for certain in that part of the world. More importantly, we couldn't let a war start between Israel and Iran. Both are too powerful, and despite the Arab Spring, if those two countries destabilized, there is fear the entire world would destabilize. Oil is power. And, if there is no oil, there are too many countries, powerful countries, that would go to war to get that oil. The only country that might profit is Russia because they have their own reserves."

"So, you made a deal, with who... Israel?" I asked.

Again Dawson smiled, turning to Sally he said, "You were right; he does catch on quickly. Thank goodness I believed you from what I know of him." Turning to me he asked if he could continue.

I nodded, and he continued.

"Yes, a deal was made that if Israel gave us six months, and accepted the 'international agreement', we would set into play a way to ensure that the Iran's nuclear program would be seriously interrupted. We began, of course, with the brilliant work of a few hackers working off their federal sentences. I am sure you've read about the virus infecting Iranian scientists' computers?"

I nodded again, and he picked up where he left off.

"This gave us enough credibility to buy us the time we needed to put Ito's brother and father into play. They are in Iran now, just waiting for the delivery."

"You mean you are *letting nuclear stuff go to Iran*?" I said, alarmed at the implications.

Dawson only smiled. It sent chills up my back. Nuclear material in the hands of crazy radicals that would use it to make bombs — it scared the *shit* out of me!

"It may have had a little modification along the passage aboard ship," Dawson said. "But, yes, it will be unloaded shortly, and we will have what we need."

"Okay, but Henning worked for our *government*," I said. "Why was he left out of the loop?"

"He is, rather was, military. Military and State don't always agree."

"You mean the State Department is in on this?" I asked.

"Only the few that need to know," Dawson said.

"But his death? Why, because he was expendable?" I asked.

"No, Jake, not really. We knew there was a compromise somewhere in our link. We weren't sure who or how, hence Robinson. He needed access to the judge's — or should I say Commander Henning's — files. That's why he was sent in. Also, he needed to keep you away. It was meant to be just an "unsolved,' but you were too far ahead of us. Always too far ahead of us," Dawson said, shaking his head. "I knew it when you approached me the first time."

427

"Why didn't you just play dumb?" I asked.

"I, we, needed to know how much you knew. We made the mistake of underestimating you. So then we had to get you off the case."

"My car!" I said, with sudden insight. "I *loved* that car!"

"Sorry about that," Robinson said. "Also, sorry about the charge. It was a little more than we expected. But we also needed to take you out, at least temporarily."

"So, you *did* do that?" I asked, again feeling the heat rise up in my chest.

"Again, what can I say," Robinson said. "You just kept showing up, and showing up, and definitely getting in the way. We needed you out... out of commission."

"But, my Intrepid!" I said. "Why did you have to kill my car?"

Everyone in the room looked at me like I had lost my mind. Maybe I had. All of this was too much for me to understand. It hit a core level that scared the holy shit out of me. My government did this to someone as respectable and highly placed as a judge; what could they do to a nobody like me?

It definitely made me pause. Then it hit me—"And the guy at the hospital?" I asked.

"Hmm, that wasn't us," Dawson said. "That was someone else. Crazy how that worked out, though. It drove you right to where we needed you."

"Sally, you were in on this?" I asked. When she refused to look at me, I gasped. "Sally, just who are you?"

Dawson again redirected me back to the story and away from my friend, whose mouth was slashed into a grim frown.

"But then you came back! Damn, can't you just stay down?"

"I had a murder to solve, and a car bombing that was kinda keeping me occupied," I said. "Oh, my God! My partner! Again, what about Melissa Sanchez? She knows just about everything!"

"No, she doesn't," Dawson said. "She just thinks she does. You are going to 'fill her in' on this meeting, but you will have a script and you *will* use it. It is for her protection that you tell her that Robinson did not kill the judge — which by the way, he didn't. The Chinese really did get to him before Robinson could cross the street in time. He made the mistake of hiding in the neighbor's yard, not Henning's. The hit man must have been in place earlier than Robinson. It happened too fast. But I guess, in the long run, it all worked out. Henning was not the kind of man to go along with our plan. It wasn't his style. He was determined to go to the Far East and disrupt the shipment. It was the military way of thinking that they could use force to stop what we considered to be inevitable. Russia still has hungry generals and their own criminal enterprises that will always find other criminals ready to do business. The only way we can stop it is at the end user. But Mark and his Navy intelligence buddies would not agree."

I sat in stunned silence, my mind turning over all that had just been said. It was too fantastical for me. It really was one of my worst nightmares: a government gone crazy with power and subterfuge.

Through the mist of all that was said, a sudden thought bubbled up from the depths regarding my own employment.

"Hey, I understand there may be a pending lawsuit—Charles Mc-Dermott may be filing suit? Is that true?" I asked, wondering if that was part of Graber's sudden retirement.

My supposed lawyer, Callahan, spoke up. "Yes, Mr. Swanson, that is also part of the deal. His family and the Hill family will receive compensation from the government. It is all worked out. In exchange—since you are pushing this, and we need your cooperation—in exchange, if you cooperate, they will drop their suit against Newport Beach Police Department."

"So, it's true?" I asked

"Mr. McDermott believed you put his wife and his sister-in-law in grave danger with your little scheme," Callahan replied. "It caused him grave distress to see his sister-in-law so ill from the danger in which you put her. And, his wife—he feels you played very fast and loose with the mother of his children by putting them in such danger. He also feels you exposed them to possible federal criminal indictment, and he was very concerned about how it would affect his status in that small community in Santa Barbara."

"And did he ever ask his wife, Cindy, for her comment about that?" I asked. "And the girls: did they agree to his suit and this 'agreement'?" I asked, not believing for a second my coconspirators would agree.

"He said he was acting in their best interest when he made the preliminary claim against the city and your police force. He believed they would come around, because he knew that the Hills needed the money."

"That slimy bastard," I said, again standing up.

"Jake, sit down," Sally said in a very stern voice that I rarely heard her use. "This gets you nowhere. We have it handled. Leave it."

I wanted to turn on her, but her face looked distressed. Her composure was cracking. Maybe the others in the room would not see it, but I could. The lines between her eyes were deepening, and her smile had not appeared once during our entire meeting. I sat because Sally was my friend and because I saw her distress.

"Let me continue, since we are on the subject," Callahan said. "The McDermotts will rescind their claim against the City and the Police Department. You will not lose your rank, and this will not appear on your record. Lieutenant Graber agreed to retire, taking the blame for any misdeeds that may have occurred on his watch. His retirement, given his years of service, and his accumulated vacation is quite substantial. I also believe we may get him a new assignment in a pleasant place if he desires to go back to work. All you need to do is make sure you and your partner do not create any blowback from this."

"Blowback?" I asked.

"You keep your mouth and your partner's mouth shut. This is an unsolved murder. The Chief understands there are so many leads that this case needs to go to the Feds, and it will fade from your department's case load. Periodically, there will be a news release that the government is still following leads. But in the end, it will remain unsolved."

I slunk back in my seat on the small couch and said nothing. My head swirled with everything I had heard. Conspiracy theories were never something I much bought into, yet here I was right in the middle of one: a conspiracy perpetrated by my own government. It was too much.

We all sat, none of us saying anything. It was Sally who finally broke the silence.

"Gentlemen, if you will excuse me, I need my office back for a while. I will have someone from my staff take you to the conference room for some refreshments."

She lifted her phone and said a few words. A beautifully built brunette appeared at the doorway. All the men rose to their feet and started to follow her out, but I stayed.

"Sally...?" I asked, not finishing my question.

"No, Jake, you stay," Sally said.

The men left and I stayed. I stayed with my friend. We had too much to talk about, and I felt our friendship was at a critical crossroads. More than anything, I didn't want the price of my employment to be the death of our relationship.

CHAPTER THIRTY-SIX

With the lawyers and other men out of the room, it was time for me to find out who my friend really was.

Sally motioned for me to take a seat on the couch, and she sat across from me. Taking my hand in hers, she fastened her dark blue eyes on mine as she began to speak, "Jake, I can only imagine how much this is to process," she said, stroking my hand. "I need you to listen to your attorney. I need you to do as they ask. Most of all, I need you to not be you, for just a little while. You are truly a great detective, better than the service gave you credit for. But now you need to let this rest."

"Sally you knew, didn't you?" I asked. "In fact, you've always known... right?"

At first she shrugged, but when I pulled my hand away from hers, she leaned back into me and again looked deeply into my eyes.

"Yes, Jake, I probably have known for a long time," she said, her voice sad.

"Known what? And, just who are you?" I asked.

Tears gathered in my friend's eyes, and she looked down at my hand.

"Your hands are so strong, Jake," Sally said, caressing it. "Is it strong enough to hold me — not judge — just let it be?"

"Let what 'be'?" I asked.

"All of it," she answered.

"All of what?" I said, getting irritated at her non-answer.

"All of me — all of who I am," she said.

"Sally, that's just the point. I *don't know* who you are," I said, judgment bubbling up inside of me. "You ask me not to judge, yet I can't help it. Here the government acted as prosecutor, judge, and jury, and their judgment was *death*. They killed — or, should I say, let a good man *be* killed. And now I find out you knew? *Knew what?* You ask me not to judge, but I don't even know where to begin. Is everything we are a lie? Am I also as judgmental as the government? Should my judgment be death — death of our friendship? I just don't know where to begin."

This woman, this beautiful woman whom I came close to loving, but about whom I never really allowed myself to think such thoughts, stared hard at me. Her eyes again filled to overflowing with tears. She finally broke my stare and lowered her head.

"Jake, think about it: how can I stay in business? Why since that one time you raided me I have kept my business going? Why do I even exist?"

Her words twisted me and I put everything together. "You are part of *them*," I finally said.

"Yes," she whispered. "I am part of them. I never intended to be part of that world but, like you, I made a decision to survive, and the price was to cooperate, just like you need to do now. If I had not, my judgment would have been death of my business and prison—if I were lucky. So, yes, I am a part of them."

"But how?" I asked.

Then, with complete disregard for the men waiting outside her office, my dear friend told me her story. She spoke without interruption until her life was laid bare for me to see all of it. Her only prayer was for me not to be too judgmental when all of it was told.

Sally Deming, mistress of the high-end escort service, came to California from Minnesota, never intending to start the business from which she became rich. No, like so many other beautiful, talented women, she came seeking fame and fortune in Hollywood, only to realize there were too many beautiful women attempting to take the same career path.

It was not enough that she came with a degree in fine arts from Gustavus Adolphus, a small Lutheran liberal arts college just south of Minneapolis. It also was not enough that she sang as part of their internationally known choir that toured Europe her junior year, or that she sang two solos as part of their touring program. Nor was it enough that she had done several commercials for her local TV station, and had a revolving spot on that station's morning show. When she arrived in Los Angeles she was just another petite young woman too short to model and too sweet to find her job on the casting couch.

But Sally Deming was smart and had business savvy. She was also observant, and what she saw were too many men who were lonely and too afraid of commitment to find a long-term relationship, though they longed for the comfort of one. Also, during the period of time she reached Los Angeles, there were also too many men who did not want the world to know they preferred the company of their own sex, and were unwilling to be seen in public without a woman on their arm. Sally also knew too many women just like her — well educated, smart, and needing work, but unwilling to compromise their morals and find work on their backs.

With this knowledge, and an angel of a business man who understood the same things Sally saw, it didn't take long for them to start a business which made Sally, and other women like her, available for "dates" with men. All of the dates were always with the understanding that it was for appearances only. There was never physical intimacy, just company and a willing ear to listen to them, and a gorgeously well-groomed woman to complement them for the evening.

But it was a dangerous time in Hollywood and L.A. Too many times the dates demanded more; it was even expected at the end of the dates. It was then that Sally's angel developed a screening system that kept those men away from her and the other women. Her angel kept his book of clients for her. When he passed away from complications of AIDS, he bequeathed his book to her.

Keeping the "book" was not all he did for her. He invested her money for her, and taught her to live frugally — though, with her strict Midwest upbringing, the lesson was not too difficult. In time, her wealth grew, as did her fame as a hostess. It was her parties that drew her clients to her, and her parties that kept her clients in the know about who was a rising star in the *industry*, and who was on the rise as a captain of wealth and power.

It was only when she moved her headquarters to Newport Beach that she lost some of her protection. Though the former chief of police knew her from her introduction to him by the chief from Los Angeles, it was never relayed to his lieutenant in vice. That was where I came in; I was the one who led the raid on her business. That was when Sally and I became best friends. Yet, even with the intimacy of that friendship, I never really understood how or why her business was allowed to survive. I just assumed it was her power or knowledge that kept her alive and unscathed.

In a way, I was right; it was her power and her knowledge that kept her business running. She called one of her clients, a congressman with a position on the intelligence committee, and he put in a word with the then chief of police and the elected district attorney, who left the matter to the federal government. Then, like me, she faced the same query: "Are you going to work for us, or are we going to make your life miserable until you shut your doors?"

She went to work for the government. Too many times people with very loose lips attended her parties and let slip important information that was relevant to the government. Also, her most reliable "girls" were assigned to the dates most likely to produce information the government could use.

Sally's stock in trade was information, which became her power base. Because, just as her clients were sometimes too loose with information, so too were some of her handlers. Her book was dangerous, and her book was her mind, and maybe more. But she never let on just exactly what she knew, or what she kept stashed away in a secret vault. In exchange, she was allowed to flourish unmolested.

But, with the new arrangement, Sally was much more careful to keep much of her wealth portable—hence the diamonds, sapphires, and gold she took as "gifts" from clients. Also, her real estate was transferred into a corporation that no longer used her name.

The secrets poured from her—secrets she had hidden from everyone for a very long time. It drained from her, taking with it her pride. When she was finished, she was just a very tired businesswoman, no longer a mystery—just an exhausted woman who had made a deal with the devil. It was the same devil with whom she now wanted me to lay down.

"Really, Sally?" I asked. "After all this, you want me to cooperate?"

She didn't need to answer. I already knew. Her future, and mine, rested on my answer. When she made me promise to follow instructions, I finally agreed.

But, judgment was passed; in my mind, I was left wanting. I wanted answers that would never come, and salvation for my part in it all. That was the worst of all, murder most judgmental: a detective complicit in one that would never be solved, and a friendship that would never be the same.

I lay down that day. I lay down with the devil. I promised to not allow the secrets to leave my mouth, and I promised to not sacrifice my partner on the cross of my obsession to solve a crime.

When I made that deal with the devil, I prayed that somewhere in my judgment of all that had passed I would come to realize that Sally Deming had made the same deal to save me.

CHAPTER THIRTY-SEVEN

The funeral for Judge Mark Henning and his wife was beautiful with full military pomp and circumstance. Not only were the Hennings given a funeral with full military honors but, since he was a respected judge in the county, all the police agencies and deputies from the sheriff's department were present, along with judges and court staff from all over Southern California.

The new Catholic cathedral, formerly known as the Crystal Cathedral, was filled to capacity with people from all walks of life coming to show their respect for the fallen judge and his wife. Police and sheriffs from throughout the state were present. The church was filled with the deep blue of police uniforms, the khaki of the sheriff's and highway patrol's uniforms, and the various full honor military uniforms. Even my partner and I showed up in our dress blues.

Since the cathedral was soon to be rechristened as the Orange County Catholic Diocese's cathedral, the cardinal and the monsignor oversaw the ceremony.

A boys' choir from a local Episcopal church sang, their voices rising in soaring harmonies that surely moved the angels. Tears flowed—even mine. Bagpipes filled the cathedral with their mournful cries as the caskets were wheeled from the altar.

The procession from the cathedral to the hillside cemetery snaked for miles. Clearly a thousand vehicles moved in slow cadence from Anaheim to Newport Beach. The streets were blocked and traffic stopped for more than two hours. News helicopters were ordered to keep above a level that their sounds could not be heard.

Mark Henning and his wife, Nancy, were buried on a hill in Newport Beach overlooking the deep blue Pacific Ocean. As requested, they were laid side by side, not separated even in death. Mark Henning had never wanted to be separated from his wife; therefore, he chose not to be buried in a national cemetery—although he certainly deserved it.

Lauren and her husband, Timothy, were present. He was flown back from the Middle East to be with his wife, and he added the perfect touch in his dress blue uniform. Cindy, her children, and her husband were also present. Tears again flowed when the bagpipes began to play *Amazing Grace,* followed by the twenty-one-gun salute. A squad of Navy jets flew over the cemetery with one jet breaking away to symbolize the missing pilot.

Finally, a solo trumpet played *Taps*, which left most of us with tears—some shed down cheeks, others wiped away surreptitiously with white gloves and tissues.

When it was over, an American flag was given to each of the daughters. Cindy received the flag that had draped her mother's coffin, Lauren her father's. It was only when the ceremony was over, and the crowd began to disperse that Lauren bent over, crying out in pain.

Straightening up, she started to walk, only to bend over again in pain. It was clear she was in labor, and the limousine in which she and Timothy had traveled to the cemetery was blocked in, and she couldn't get out.

A brief radio call and a Black Hawk helicopter swooped in to pick up Lauren, Timothy, Cindy—and, surprisingly, Melissa and me per Lauren's request.

Her labor and delivery were quick. Within minutes, the ecstatic father held his beautiful baby daughter, with the joyful aunt looking on.

It was too perfect—the circle of life repeating itself. A death, a life; a family torn apart, then put back together.

Hours later, Melissa and I left the hospital holding our secret close. The murder of Lauren's and their parents would never be solved, but a life was given by God to salve the hurt.

Judgments, decisions over life and death, carried out in the coldness of small rooms, made by only a handful of people, will never win approval from me. Call me judgmental, but murder is still murder, no matter who makes the call.

CPSIA information can be obtained
at www.ICGtesting.com
Printed in the USA
BVHW040612310523
665078BV00016B/675/J

9 781467 539029